To Barbara, **with love**, appreciation,
and thanks
for your **warmth**, caring,
and companionship

**And in memory of Uncle Ken,
Aunt Gladys, and their children,**
Judy and Jed

SUMMER
OF '69

SUMMER OF '69

Todd Strasser

CANDLEWICK PRESS

Copyright © 2019 by Todd Strasser

First edition 2019

Library of Congress Catalog Card Number 2018961332
ISBN 978-0-7636-9526-2

LSC 24 23 22 21 20 19
10 9 8 7 6 5 4 3 2 1

Printed in Crawfordsville, IN, U.S.A.

This book was typeset in Adobe Caslon Pro and Typeka.

Candlewick Press
99 Dover Street
Somerville, Massachusetts 02144

visit us at www.candlewick.com

MUCH OF WHAT HAPPENS in this book is based on events in my life during that momentous time of revolution and reform. However, for the sake of the narrative, the locations and dates of some events have been modified.

THURSDAY, JUNE 26

Just east of Worcester, the greenish paisley clouds morph into the faces of Washington, Lincoln, and a couple of their pals.

Every sound SOUNDS LOUDER: The wind whistling in through Odysseus's vent windows. The hum of tires on the Mass Pike. The Hammond organ of Procol Harum splashing through the speakers.

Next to me, Robin draws her knees up under her chin and hugs them. Strands of her long hair vine away in the breeze. Robin is Botticelli's Venus on a passenger seat, only with dark-brown hair and eyes. She is Juliet to my Romeo, Olive Oyl to my Popeye, Lady to my Tramp, the lady I love.

Alas, my heart is as heavy as an anvil. Tomorrow she will depart for the Canadian wilderness, vanishing from my life for two full months. Dreading the thought of this summer without her, I reach over, take her slim hand in mine, and squeeze.

Don't go north, my love. There's still time to change your mind. Surely you must feel the same?

But with businesslike deftness, Robin guides my hand back to Odysseus's steering wheel and says, "Are you sure you can drive, Lucas?"

The question does not come unexpectedly out of yonder filigreed blue. An hour ago, back in Cambridge, we were loitering beside a brick wall on which was scrawled "Make Love Not War" and "Bring the Troops Home." A barefoot, glassy-eyed freak with Jesus hair and beard wandered by. After clocking Odysseus, Robin, and me, he dug into his pocket and produced a wrinkled baggie filled with tiny orange barrel-shaped tabs. He then uttered those most magical of inducements: "Free, man."

From the shape and color of the tabs I swiftly deduced that the offering was Orange Sunshine. Fabled West Coast acid, said to rival Owsley as the purest ever produced for mass consumption. Without a second thought, I plucked a barrel out of the baggie and swallowed.

Now, on the Mass Pike, as we poke along at Odysseus's maximum velocity of fifty-eight mph, the industrial rhythm of the tires has a symphonic quality. In the cockpit, sonic tides ebb and flow—faint, louder, LOUD, less loud, faint. Out in the distance, the greenish cloud-faces of President Washington & Co. grin down from the heavens. Mount *Rush*more, indeed!

In the meantime, I am tasked with reassuring my ladylove that even in my thoroughly dosed state I am capable of maintaining both altitude and a steady flight path. (I always meant to teach her to drive a stick, but like so many of my intentions, it was left unrealized.) "Have no fear, my daffodil, I am in complete control of the sit—" This would be the very moment a humongous eighteen-wheeler barrels past, intent on blowing us off the road. With a panicked gasp, Robin grabs my thigh and squeezes while I wrestle my boxy German tin can back into the lane.

> **The back of the 18-wheeler,**
> **An elephant's square gray rump,**
> **Leaves us in**
> **The New England dust.**

Tock, tick. Robin hasn't uttered a word in . . . five minutes? Ten? As Captain Lucas attempts to navigate his flimsy vessel homeward, stewed synapses sputter inside his skull, then spark with tiny twinkles of light. He imagines that if he'd taken the time to have a second thought back in Cambridge before dropping the Orange Sunshine, it might've gone something like this: *It's going to be a long enough drive home to Long Island without dramatically increasing the risk of taking an imaginary exit into the vast unknown.*

Or into a ditch.

How long will the drive be? Hard to say. Acid time is spongy—not that Captain Lucas is complaining. The irreversibly toxic tick-tock from present to future is the enemy. In less than twenty-four hours, the love of his life decamps for the frozen tundra.

• • •

Odysseus oozes to a standstill. The thing that from a distance resembled a garden trellis stretching across the highway and draped with green vines and shimmering pink flowers is in reality a row of tollbooths.

Ah! Sweet relief! The trippy nervousness that usually accompanies any interaction with a Straight Person of Authority mellows when the toll collector appears to be not much older than me. Bushy sideburns. Dirty-blond hair creeping out from under his cap and down over the collar of his green uniform. Face made of pink doll plastic.

Our eyes meet, and the toll guy grins knowingly—as only someone intimately acquainted with Lucy in the Sky with Diamonds would. "Outta sight, man. Wish I could be where you are right now."

"Wish you could, too." I offer him a handful of viscous coinage that has puddled together in my palm like lumpy silver mercury.

My plastic-faced comrade chuckles and plucks out what's owed. "Peace, brother."

"Hang loose, man."

And away we—

"For God's sake, Lucas! What if he was a cop?" Robin wigs out. Taken by surprise, I unintentionally wrench the wheel, making the microbus swerve violently. Tires screech as Odysseus rocks like a boat tossed on stormy seas.

I've just regained control of my trusty rusty ship when a voice from behind us mumbles, "Huh? Cop?" It's Milton. I've forgotten that he's sleeping on the mattress in the back. On our way home from a brief but torturous visit to Maine, we stopped in Cambridge to pick him up.

"It's nothing, man. Go back to sleep," I tell him. Meanwhile, Robin's twisted around in her seat, hands locked into fists, peering out the back window as if expecting the entire Massachusetts Turnpike Tollbooth Cavalry to be thundering up behind us. In the past, my ladylove has, on occasion, been known to err on the acute side of uptight, but given my currently blitzed sensibilities, am I truly in a position to cast judgment?

"A tollbooth collector cop?" I whisper so as not to alarm Milton. "Is that *really* possible?"

"What do *you* think, Lucas?" Robin answers harshly. She swivels to face forward but angles the rearview mirror so she can continue to scrutinize the traffic behind us.

What do I think? I think butterflies were originally called flutterbys until someone with dyslexia got involved. But what if she's right? Said toll collector's skin *did* look plastic. Is he, at this very moment, issuing an all-points bulletin? *Attention, units! Be on lookout for suspected dope fiend. Glassy-eyed. Straight brown hair past shoulders. Last seen headed west on Mass Pike in brightly painted psychedelic microbus!*

We'd be hard to miss.

Arms crossed tightly, Robin peers into the rearview mirror for a convoy of flashing cherry tops. This is bad. What if I've done something that will jeopardize her future? *Idiot. Idiot. IDIOT!* Unlike me, her life has direction, purpose, a goal. She starts at Middlebury in the fall, plans to major in environmental studies and international relations. I've never heard of either, but they sound important.

> **If you look at your surroundings,**
> **Is that environmental studies?**
> **If you have cousins in France,**
> **Are they international relations?**

"See anything?" I ask.

No answer. My queen is royally ticked.

Moron. Moron. MORON! You only have a few hours left with her, and look what you've done. What if she's right and we get pulled over? What if they ask me to walk in a straight line? Even worse, what if they ask me to *think* in a straight line?

Time to engage in emergency fence mending: "I . . . I love you so much. And I know I'm not always right about things, but . . . he really didn't strike me as a cop, babe."

Robin's eyes leave the rearview mirror. Her face softens. She sighs with exasperation. "Oh, Lucas, like you could really tell *anything* right now."

Out in the distance, the famous presidents have given way to pulsating purplish jellyfish clouds with long gray and blue tendrils. So far, no sirens have wailed, nor lights flashed, in pursuit of Captain Lucas and crew. No plastic-faced toll-booth narcotroopers have parachuted out of Lockheed C-130s overhead. In the back, Milton's snores sound like a turboprop struggling to gain altitude. When they picked him up back in Cambridge, he said he'd been awake for the past thirty-six hours writing a paper on the impact of microprocessor chipsets on the future of space travel. (Say *what*?) In the seat beside Captain Lucas, Robin tilts her head back and gazes upward, where, next to the dome light, is taped an R. Crumb cartoon of Mr. Natural saying, "The whole universe is completely insane."

"Lucas, can I ask you a question?" she asks.

Uh-oh, sounds like trouble. "I'm an open book."

"A stranger comes out of nowhere and offers you LSD and you just take it?"

"You saw that freak. He was cool."

"How did you know it was really LSD?"

How does Lucas the Impulsive know that the acid he took an hour ago was acid? Could it have something to do with the hundreds of tiny silverfish currently wriggling around inside Odysseus's one-eighth-inch-thick windshield?

And yet Robin's concern, though unlikely, is not without merit. Creative chemists the world over have been known to lace their product with a little something "extra" to boost the rush. Feeling motormouthy and having two thousand thoughts per second? Your acid, *mon ami*, is mixed with speed. Muscles tight and yearning to stretch? A pinch of strychnine has been added. (Know what's *truly* freaky? Strychnine is rat poison. But it's like the cyanide in apple seeds. In microscopic amounts, it won't hurt you.)

But Professor Lucas digresses. Back to Robin's inquiry. "You mean, you think someone would go to all the trouble of making little orange barrels that looked exactly like Orange Sunshine, but weren't? Why would anyone do that?"

"I don't know, Lucas. I'm just saying, is this what you're going to be like next year if you get into Goddard?"

It's not immediately clear how they went from the authenticity of the Orange Sunshine to his expected enrollment at Goddard College, but El Capitán finds it reassuring that Robin's thinking about their future. He reaches over and strokes her shoulder. "Listen, everything's groovy. I promise I'll be cool with the next toll collector. I'll get us back to Long Island in one piece. I'll do whatever I need to do next year."

Is it his bugging imagination or does the smile Robin returns appear a bit brittle? She gazes out the passenger window. Odysseus sails onward, toward Long I Land.

> How could it be
> That someone so smart and pretty
> Could be into me?

At age thirteen, Lucas is a medium-size, slightly chubby, Dumbo-eared, poorly coordinated, and somewhat befuddled young suburban individual. The father expects progeny who will become prosperous businessmen tennis players. The mother asks merely for academic brilliance. It appears that Lucas is destined to achieve neither. At school, he is adequate at best. The popular kids ignore him while they communicate in their secret indecipherable language. Baffled, he adapts by becoming invisible, creeping around corners, blending into the background.

But then begins the Semi-Miraculous Transformation. In the span of eighteen months, he grows eight inches. His shoulders broaden, voice deepens, waist narrows, cheekbones appear. He passes an afternoon in the hospital having the *auris elephantus* pinned back. It is now freshman year of high school, and girls who never knew he existed do double takes. Guys who'd never let him play punchball with them at recess suddenly have an open seat at their lunch table.

This transformation is as mystifying to the transformed as it is to everyone else. Inside Lucas, nothing has changed. He is still muddled and befuddled. Still lacking the athletic and intellectual makeup the progenitors had hoped for. But they have bestowed upon him a genetic blessing, a letter of transit through the tempestuous ninth-grade social scene — a chassis that gives Lucas a facade of poise.

Robin, on the other hand, is hatched of the choicest Grade A, 100 percent excellent hereditary material. As far back as kindergarten, she has been universally liked and admired, and not in that unapproachable, cliquey, I'm-not-sharing-my-blocks-with-you kind of way. Someday people will say she has an aura — strong and determined while soft and caring.

In elementary and junior high schools, she and her friends are the serious, studious ones. Together they are tracked into smart-kid classes. They dominate such extracurricular activities as yearbook, literary magazine, student government, and model railroad club.

Robin will scrape elbow and knee in field hockey and volleyball. She will also become very pretty. (Who ever said life was fair?)

Spring ahead to a warm and sunny 1968 senior-year October day. Robin sits under a tree studded with red and gold leaves in the courtyard, reading *The Stranger*. Lucas passes on his way to chemistry class. On impulse, he abruptly doubles back. After all, they are seniors now. Grown up, mature, risen above (or so they pretend) childish concerns about popularity—equals soon to be dispersed to institutions of higher learning hither and yon. It has been not quite a year and a half since the hippies flocked to Haight-Ashbury for the Summer of Love, sixteen months since Jimi doused his guitar with lighter fluid and set it ablaze and Janis's plaintive wails first gave people shivers at Monterey. Freaks in bell-bottoms and hippie beads have begun to sprout like weeds among the well-trimmed populace. Lucas is a weed with a chassis.

Until this moment, he has never said more than three words to Robin. His heart thumps nervously, the imprinted low social expectations from his awkward Dumbo-eared formative years leading him to prepare to be shooed away (but because she is Robin, he can at least hope for a gentle shooing). He nods at the book in her hands. "What do you think?"

(If nothing else, he has now succeeded in saying a total of seven words to her.)

The sun shines down from over his shoulder. Robin squints up in the brightness and says that she prefers to see meaning and purpose in life. "And you?" she asks.

Him? Having spoken on impulse and thus failed to arm himself with a reply to her reply, he mumbles something about meandering through meaninglessness and leaning toward existentialism.

Then hastily adds that he is open to other interpretations.

And thus he is invited to join her on the grass. They sit side by side, chatting and watching the squirrels busy themselves with acorns. Meanwhile, somewhere within the brick walls surrounding the courtyard, a chemistry class begins and ends. Lucas and Robin are still sitting on the lawn when the next period bell rings. Robin gathers her books, saying she must get to gym. They stand. For the first time since Lucas joined her, their eyes meet without the sun in hers. She blinks, and recognition creeps onto her face: "You're Lucas Baker."

He bows. "At your service, madame."

She smiles. "Call me tonight?"

He does.

Amber sunlight slants through Odysseus's windows. It's late afternoon on Long Island and I've descended from the peak acid plateau to that mutable base camp where one can act straight if circumstances (i.e., encounters with parents) demand it. After we drop Milton at his house, it's a short hop to Robin's. In her driveway, she quickly gathers her things. Her adieu is hasty, her desire for a long, hot shower paramount. She says that she'll be busy this evening packing for Camp Juliette in Ontario, so I will not see her again until the dreaded morn, when we will say our final farewells for the summer. In the setting sunlight, she has to squirm out of my arms. Otherwise I might try to hold on to her until the dawn.

A little while later, I'm sitting on the mattress on the floor of my room, surrounded by scattered clothes, records, *Ski* magazines, and books. The walls are plastered with posters of Dylan and Hendrix, and Brando from *The Wild One*. My heroes: rebels one and all. But I am feeling far from heroic. Sadness throbs like an open wound.

Earlier this spring, when Robin first told me she was going to be a counselor for the summer, I beseeched her to reconsider. That was back in March, when we were greenhorns in the divine realm of love. The prospect of months apart felt—continues to feel—unbearable. But Robin had attended Camp Juliette for half a dozen years as a camper and had always planned to cap her experience in a counselor role. If what we had together was real, she said, it would still be there when she returned.

(I didn't tell her how badly those words shook me. It never occurred to me that what we had might not be real.)

Our trip to Maine was meant to be a few last precious and uninterrupted moments together; instead it was a bummer of epic proportions. Beyond the quasi-liberal boundaries of the New York suburbs, people openly stared at us. NO SHIRT, NO SHOES, NO SERVICE signs—and the anti-counterculture sentiment they signified—were ubiquitous. At a clam bar in Bar Harbor, a white-haired old salt wearing red suspenders and a plaid shirt grumbled loudly about us "long-haired degenerates." At the L.L. Bean store in Freeport, a kid excitedly pointed and blurted, "Look, Mom, hippies!" as if we were some rarely glimpsed breed of exotic biped. When strangers flashed the peace sign, it was usually in a taunting manner.

But it was the Maine fuzz who were most responsible for turning our excursion into a ginormously bad trip, constantly harassing us with obscure regulations designed to keep us disconcerted: laws against cooking with a camping stove in a parking lot, rules against parking at the beach without a permit. At least once a night, we'd been jarred awake by banging on Odysseus's door, followed by the blinding glare of a flashlight as yet another "peace" officer informed us that we were loitering and ordered us to depart immediately.

To much of the Maine populace, we are symbols of all that is wrong with this country. Me with my long hair, bell-bottoms, and Frye boots. And Robin, whose much longer brown hair falls to the middle of her back, and who on the trip wore a headband and a peace pendant on a strand of leather around her neck. And then there's Odysseus. Covered with brightly painted flowers, paisley designs, rainbows, and peace signs, my microbus is a highly visible rolling advertisement for what Down Easters must assume is a deviant/promiscuous, pansy peace-loving threat to society. Robin and I would have preferred a quiet, uneventful vacation, but we'd be damned if that meant hiding our freak flags and pretending to support a government that sees nothing wrong with the wholesale slaughter of Vietnamese civilians.

• • •

Now, in my room, with the effects of the Orange Sunshine worn thin, there are things I should probably do. Wash my clothes. Straighten the mess. Figure out what to do with my life. But all I want to do is write to my ladylove.

6/26/69

Dear Robin,

I hope you're taking the longest, hottest shower ever as I write this. I'm sorry you didn't have a chance to take one during the trip. It wasn't something I thought about. But I want you to know that I do think about you, all the time. You haven't even left for Canada yet and I'm already missing you. I hope this letter will keep you company on the trip to Ontario. I hope you'll read it over and over. I hope it makes you miss me so bad that when you get to Lake Juliette you'll decide to turn around and come straight back home. (Not really. Well . . . yes, maybe really.) I love you. I'll miss you this summer. I'm already looking forward to seeing you in a month when I drive up there.

Love, love, love,

Lucas

When I go to my desk for an envelope, I notice that lying on the blotter is an article neatly clipped from the newspaper. This is my mother's way of informing me that a government entity called the Federal Trade Commission wants to force tobacco companies to put warning labels on packs of cigarettes.

Mom has underlined in red a sentence stating that smoking might lead to cancer, heart disease, and emphysema.

But it is the *might* that foils her argument. Cigarettes might lead to those ailments. Smoking grass might lead to reefer madness. Taking acid might lead to chromosomal damage and attempts at unaided human flight from sixth-floor windows. But according to whom? A government that insists that drugs are bad and war is good.

Bullshit.

Into the garbage goes the newspaper article. But lying under it are two additional items. One is a yellow post office change-of-address form. My name and a new address in Bay Shore have been entered in the paterfamilias's tiny handwriting. This is puzzling. Am I being evicted? Did my parents find a new and improved replacement offspring while Robin and I were in Maine? I don't have time to wonder long about this, because the other item is a letter from Goddard College.

I pick up the envelope and feel its thinness between my fingertips. In my chest, my heart deflates as fast as an unknotted balloon. My skeleton dissolves, leaving a puddle of protoplasm on the floor. *Crap. Crap. CRAP!* Blasting through the residual mind-alteredness fomented by lysergic acid diethylamide comes the stark, undeniable, very real, and very HEAVY FACT that yours truly, Lucas Baker, recent high-school graduate, future human question mark . . .

Is completely, totally, and royally screwed.

15

FRIDAY, JUNE 27

Days Until My Trip to See Robin at Camp Juliette: 28

> I'm in the death queue now.
> I'm not behind the plow.
> If I can't get out,
> I'll be worm dirt no doubt.
> I'm in the death queue now.

Cousin Barry stands at his front door bare-chested, wearing a pair of tight hip-hugger bell-bottoms. An unfiltered Camel is squeezed between his nicotine-yellowed fingers. His dark sideburns are long and thick. His full, wavy hair falls to his shoulders.

"How was it?" he asks when I hand him the camp stove I borrowed for Maine.

"Bummer. They're really straight up there."

Barry takes a pensive drag. "They hassle you?"

"Hell, yeah."

We share a moment of wordless commiseration over the sucky state of straight over-thirty America, Maine rednecks, and the deadly and immoral conflict against the North Vietnamese that we've been told is necessary to avoid communism taking over the world. A conflict that, until yesterday, I had expected to avoid dying in. But that thin envelope from Goddard College has changed everything.

I'm in the death queue now.

Dear Mr. Baker,

The Goddard College Admissions Committee has completed its evaluation of this year's candidates, and I write with sincere regret to say that we are not able to offer you a place in the Class of 1973.

 I realize that this decision may come as a real disappointment...

When I read those terrible words last night, I briefly considered calling Robin, then changed my mind. She said she'd be busy packing, and I didn't want to bum her out with such bad news on her last evening at home. Besides, I'd expected to see her this morning for our final pre–Camp Juliette farewell. Then on the phone a few hours ago, she said she didn't think there'd be time to say goodbye in person. She hadn't finished packing, and it already looked like she might be late for the camp bus.

I managed to dash to her house just as she and her father were pulling out of the driveway. Robin looked startled when she saw me. It was an awkward moment, with her father in the seat beside her. She rolled down the window, and I gave her the letter I wrote last night for her to read on the bus. I wanted to kiss her, but we never displayed physical affection in front of our parents. Still, I leaned into the window, pecked her cheek, and whispered that I loved her. She didn't reply, but maybe I couldn't expect that in front of her father. Her eyes began to fill with tears, and so did mine. Her father said they were late and really had to go. Then they were headed away down the street, Robin rolling up her window, tears rolling down my cheeks.

I follow Cousin Barry upstairs. He's barefoot; the tattered, stringy hems of his bell-bottoms drag on the steps. It's not like he needed the camp stove right away. I've come here because I don't know what else to do now that Robin's gone. I'm usually pretty good by myself, but not today. Today I'm a lost, empty glove that needs a hand.

Barry's bedroom smells of cigarettes and turpentine. A mattress occupies a corner of the floor. Some colorful plastic kites are piled in another corner. The rest of the room is awash with clothing, art books, record albums, and music magazines. Nearly every flat surface higher than the floor is covered with half-squeezed tubes of paint, brushes, palettes, and cans of turpentine and paint thinner. Nearly every inch of wall space is hidden by canvases, posters of rock bands, or scribbles. Barry jots his thoughts on the walls, where they are less likely to get lost in the clutter.

Taped to one wall is an ad for the Woodstock Music and Art Fair. It's billed as "An Aquarian Exposition" in Wallkill,

New York: Three Days of Peace and Music, with an art show, a crafts bazaar, workshops, and "hundreds of acres to roam on." More important, it will feature a gargantuan lineup of top music acts like nothing anyone's ever seen gathered in one place before.

"You going?" Barry asks when he sees me studying the ad.

"Definitely. It's gonna be incredible. Thousands of people, man." A month ago, Milton, our mutual friend Arno Exley, and I decided to send away for tickets. What better way to celebrate our last gasp of summer together before Arno starts his freshman year at Bucknell, Milton goes back to MIT, and I—as of yesterday, fill in the blank: ____.

I'll be worm dirt no doubt. . . .

Upon hearing that I'm planning to go to the Aquarian Exposition (whatever that means), Barry purses his lips and furrows his brow. It's an expression I know well. Cousin rivalry. He's a year older than me, and for most of our formative years, it was no contest. He was top dog, looking down on me literally *and* figuratively. Then the Semi-Miraculous Transformation took place, and now he must train his gaze upward. But the competitive streak is alive and well, at least until my corpse is flown back from Nam in a flag-shrouded coffin.

"Yeah, I'm pretty sure I'm gonna go, too," Barry announces.

"For real?" I blurt out, then instantly feel bad for reacting with surprise instead of encouragement. For three of the past four years, Barry hardly left his parents' house. Then, starting roughly a year ago, he began to venture out locally, but rarely farther than a long walk or short drive.

19

Trying to cover up my gaffe, I wave an arm around the cluttered room. "You've been busy, man." Barry's canvases are colorful and hard-edged in the style of Frank Stella's Protractor series. I have no critical basis for judging them, and anyway, it doesn't matter. After years in a morose housebound purgatory of cigarettes, music, drugs, and black moods punctuated by stays in the loony bin, my cousin has begun to paint at a frenetic pace. Along with this astonishing creative outpouring has come a pronounced lifting of his spirits.

From the hall comes the sound of the toilet flushing. A moment later, a vision strolls into the room. She is petite and waif-like in a diaphanous peasant blouse and tight hip-hugger bell-bottoms, with long straight blond hair and flawless, soft-looking skin. Through the stink of turpentine and cigarettes comes the heady scent of patchouli oil.

"Lucas, Tinsley." With a cheesy grin Cousin Barry performs the introductions. He's met Robin a few times, so I suspect he's proud to prove that he can attract a pretty girl, too.

"Hello, Lucas. Barry's told me about you." Tinsley's hazel eyes stay unwaveringly on mine. Her voice is soft, sultry. I swallow back a twinge of anxiousness. It wasn't that long ago that someone so attractive and alluring would have prompted me to nervously blurt out something dumb and self-deprecating. But that was before the God of Genes bestowed this new chassis upon me. Now I channel James Bond, though in these antiestablishment times, it's not his perfectly groomed, suave, debonair-with-a-license-to-kill vibe that I emulate, but rather his quietly bemused air of self-assurance. It's an act, to be sure.

But I've learned something about acts: if you stay consistent, they can be pretty convincing.

I offer my hand, hearing Sean Connery's Scottish accent in my mind: "Nice to meet you, Tinsley."

"And you." She takes my hand firmly in hers and we shake.

"Tinsley's a photographer," Barry says. "She's making slides of my paintings."

Tinsley picks up a black-and-silver camera and aims it at a canvas propped against the wall. When she kneels, the ends of her straight blond hair nearly touch the floor and her hip-huggers slide low, revealing a possible absence of intimate apparel.

Barry gives me a nudge. "Got any weed?"

"Are bears Catholic?"

"Wanna smoke?" he asks Tinsley.

"I'm cool, thanks." She presses her eye against the eyepiece, and the camera's shutter snaps.

As I follow Barry out of the room, I can't resist looking back. Tinsley must feel my gaze. Or maybe she expects it. Either way, still kneeling, she glances up from beneath lowered eyelids and smiles coyly.

On the back patio with Barry, I tap a joint out of my pack of Marlboros. Robin's departure this morning (by now the camp bus should be passing Albany) and the suddenly distinct possibility that in the very near future they'll shave my head, shove a rifle in my hands, and ship my sorry ass to a jungle halfway around the world are foremost in my mind. But the look Tinsley just gave me has muscled its way in. Was that not a come-on? But we don't know each other, and it appears that she's with Barry. It doesn't make sense. I must be reading too much into it. Maybe it has something to do with the lonely ache I'm feeling for Robin. Or perhaps it's a result of certain personal chemical proclivities. Do enough drugs, and reality becomes a moving target.

I light the J with my Zippo, toke, and pass it to Barry. The patio is just large enough for two rusty metal chairs and a small filmy-glass table. In a yellow plastic ashtray, a dozen unfiltered cigarette butts float in a brownish broth.

Barry takes a hit. "We met at the library. They had a show for local artists. You were allowed to enter two pieces."

"She's an artist, too?"

"No, man, photography." He hands the joint back.

"There's something about her." I'm being disingenuous. After the look she gave me upstairs, I'm curious about their relationship.

"Dig it—she's got that vibe, right? Black-magic strange-brew voodoo chile." Barry sings the next sentence: *"She put a spell on you."*

I take another hit. Tinsley's not the only one practicing sorcery. So's this weed, thanks to my best friend and dealer, Arno. "You guys been together long?"

Barry shakes his head. "Not her thing, man. She does what she pleases with whomever pleases her."

Ah, the sweet melody of free love. Earmark of the hippies, conceived and nurtured in the crash pads of Haight-Ashbury. But that's out in California, where, it's been said, all the nuts rolled when they tilted up the northeast corner of the map. In my experience, there's been scant evidence of sexual revolution washing up along the beaches of the South Shore.

"You okay with that?" I ask my cousin.

Barry shrugs, but with a devilish glint in his eye. "Cuts both ways, right?" (If this new jauntiness is Tinsley's influence, more power to her.)

Joint smoked, we head for the kitchen, where Barry jabs a V-shaped hole with a can opener into a quart of Hi-C fruit punch. He offers me a glass of sweet red liquid, pours one for himself, and lights a Camel. Barry does a French inhale, releasing a mouthful of smoke and drawing it up through his nose. Then he blows one smoke ring through another.

Wicked cool.

Then again, he's had four years of self-imposed solitary confinement to practice.

Lucas the Spellbound follows Cousin Barry back upstairs, where Tinsley is sitting lotus-style on the floor, thumbing through a shoe box of black-and white photographs. She holds up one from a day camp Barry and Lucas attended when they were single-digits. Observe Barry sporting a spit curl and cocky smile, beginning to look muscular. But who's that awkward-looking humanoid next to him, crew-cut, chimpanzee-eared, baby-fat-faced, clearly still being groomed by Momma?

Tinsley points at the photograph. "That's you?"

While it's easy to recognize the younger version of Barry, the boy beside him looks nothing like what Lucas has become.

At six feet two inches, he is the tallest in their nuclear family. More than once, Lucas has been told that he looks like a long-haired Montgomery Clift. (Thank you, daft croupier who oversees the capricious roll of the chromosomal dice.)

Cousin Barry reaches up and noogies the top of Lucas Clift's head a little harder than necessary. "Yeah, look at the little twerp now."

Barry can't resist reminding Lucas of the nerdy kid he used to be. Always, Lucas senses, with a dose of resentment: *Why did it have to be him? Why couldn't it have happened to someone who deserved it?*

When Barry turns away to stub out his cigarette in an ashtray, Tinsley raises an eyebrow and tilts her face provocatively. Goose bumps run down Lucas the Perplexed's arms. Unless he's completely off his rocker, he's almost certain he's been offered an invitation.

The question is, to what?

Back home later, in the den of the house of dashed dreams, my fourteen-year-old brother, Alan, sits cross-legged on the white shag carpet in front of the TV, watching Bozo the Clown. As usual, he's sitting too close. I give him the sign, and he scooches back without taking his eyes from the screen. Alan is chomping on strands of uncooked spaghetti. The pink bite plate with his false front teeth lies half-hidden in the fibers of shag beside him.

The high from Barry's may have diminished, but I've still got the munchies. "Lemme try?"

24

Alan extends the blue box of Ronzoni. I pull out a few strands and crunch down. Yuck. Tasteless and nearly impossible to chew. Alan must be starving if he's willing to eat this. "Mom around?" I ask.

He shakes his head.

"How about I make us something?"

Alan nods. His eyes stay on the boob tube.

In the kitchen, I ponder what to prepare, my culinary skills being limited to scrambled eggs and tuna fish sandwiches. In the refrigerator, "normal" fare takes a back seat to the paterfamilias's "health" food: A jar of "natural" peanut butter containing a layer of yellowish oil over a foundation of brown paste with the consistency of nearly set concrete. Wheat germ, "beef juice," carrot juice, bottles of vitamins, and Protein from the Sea (the label proclaims that it "Builds strength and muscle fast!"). Musclini—Arno gave the paterfamilias that nickname, after Benito Mussolini, the fascist leader of Italy who sided with Hitler during World War II—consumes this mishmash in conjunction with his tennis games and three-times-a-week weight-lifting routines in his attic gym.

In the freezer is a box of mini-pizzas. Each one is the size of a dessert plate. Left to his own devices, Alan would eat them frozen. I turn on the oven and slide four of them in on a cookie sheet.

By the time Alan was four, my parents knew something was wrong. He wouldn't listen. He went outside without any clothes on. He ran across the street without looking. You couldn't let

25

him out of your sight for a second. Other kids teased him. This killed me. Not only because I was still young enough to think it implied that our whole family was somehow defective, but also because I could see that the teasing left my brother hurt and bewildered. Alan was aware of what they were doing, but he couldn't understand why. None of the specialists and doctors who've tested him have come up with a precise diagnosis. He's "slow"—to learn, to think, to comprehend—and stubborn. Can't catch a ball. Not even one tossed gently from close by. Has a speech defect that makes his *th*'s sound like *f*'s. Kids used to tease him mercilessly for that; now he hardly speaks.

The thing is, it's not just me who's going to be affected now that Goddard (and the other colleges Mom applied me to) has turned its collegiate back on me. It's Alan, too. In this country, if you are a physically and mentally fit antiwar male of draft age who's not going to college, you have two choices: move to Canada or go to prison for draft evasion. Either option would mean leaving home and Alan for a long time (in the case of Canada, forever) without a chance of visiting. I know he's not going to starve (not as long as there's raw spaghetti and frozen pizzas in the house), and except for going to an amusement park now and then, it's not like I do that much with him. But I also know that having me around is a comfort. Together, we're soldiers on the home front. Not all war zones are on the other side of the globe.

Speaking of which, the pizzas still have a few minutes to go when the door from the garage opens and Musclini enters, dressed in his tennis clothes. He's lean, ropy-muscled, tanned, and about four inches shorter than me (which I sometimes suspect compounds his need to be the intimidating patriarch). His white alligator shirt is darkened with patches of sweat, and a white towel hangs around his neck. His face is still flushed from playing, but his short wavy brown hair is combed back to near perfection. Combing his hair is always the first thing he does after a match.

There isn't much eye contact between us. Maybe someday I'll ask him why, if I can figure out how to do it without eye contact. Silently, he leaves his tennis bag by the door and proceeds deeper into the house. On many evenings, I don't see him at all (which is fine with me). If he isn't off somewhere "working late," he's at the club playing tennis.

In the oven, the mini-pizza crusts have, as they say on TV, turned golden brown. It strikes me that, except for chocolate, brown is not a good color when it comes to food. Whoever came up with the "golden" bit was a genius. I call into the den and Alan appears. He used to be a scrawny kid, but now he's chubby and round-shouldered from sitting on the floor in front of the TV all the time. I put two mini-pizzas on his yellow Superman food tray, pour him a glass of milk (soda and sweet fruit drinks are banned substances in the house of dashed dreams), and back to the den he goes. There used to be a rule that we weren't supposed to eat in the den, but that was before the war at home went from covert to overt.

I've just settled at the kitchen table with the other two mini-pizzas when the squeak of tennis sneakers on linoleum trumpets the return of Musclini. He's carrying the yellow post office change-of-address form. (Within these walls there is no privacy. My parents go into my room whenever they want. I keep my weed and condoms in a sock at the back of a drawer, where they are meant to be discovered. Hopefully that will discourage further investigation. One has to unscrew the bottom of my record player to find the pills and acid.)

"I want you to sign this." The paterfamilias places the yellow card in front of me.

The childish instinct to obey quickly flits past, followed by the young man's urge to resist. "I don't get it. Am I moving to Bay Shore?"

"No."

I await further explanation, but none follows.

"How will I get my mail?" I doubt Robin's even gotten to Camp Juliette yet, but I'm already yearning for sacks of love letters from her. Also, the tickets to the Woodstock music and art festival should be winging this way soon.

The paterfamilias is steely quiet, as if incensed that I have the temerity to question his authority. Or maybe it hasn't occurred to him that I actually get mail? "I'll arrange for that," he says.

"Can I get it myself?" Bay Shore is probably a two-hour round trip, but if that's what it will take to retrieve a letter from my ladylove, I'll gladly make the journey.

The paterfamilias rears up to maximum possible height, as he always does when challenged. The next words are clipped, almost a growl: "I said I'll arrange it."

In the house of dashed dreams,
The paterfamilias makes the rules,
The paterfamilias breaks the rules.
What are we who are ruled to do?

The paterfamilias has gone to take a shower. I bite into the golden-brown crust of a mini-pizza. The yellow post office form lies unsigned on the kitchen table. Now that it's understood that I'm not being exiled to some Siberian existence in Bay Shore, I'm pretty sure I know what this is about. It's another one of his business scams. I've been an unwilling participant in the paterfamilias's hustles since I was old enough to ride a bike and sign my name. After he got the chain of Laundromats—I was around twelve at the time—he added an additional chore to my role as indentured family servant and child laborer: two or three times a week, I had to get on my one-speed balloon-tire Schwinn after school and pedal to banks, where I would convert a couple of natural peanut butter jars' worth of coins into bills. For every one hundred dollars of nickels, dimes, and quarters, my father took ninety-five and gave me five. He mapped out a dozen banks that I could bike to, each one visited roughly once a month so as not to raise suspicions. The farthest ones took nearly forty minutes to reach and required that I pedal along the curb of the Long Island Expressway service road, where cars barreled past at more than fifty miles an hour.

If someone at a bank asked where I'd gotten so much change, I was supposed to say that I babysat and walked dogs, cut lawns and shoveled driveways, raked leaves and washed cars.

Strangely, no one ever asked why I only brought in change and never bills. And my father never explained why I had to pretend I'd earned the money myself. But you'd have to be a major doofus not to think it was part of some scheme to get around a corporate regulation or avoid paying taxes.

Actually, I don't mind helping the paterfamilias avoid paying taxes to a government that uses the money to invade small countries and incinerate their citizens. So, mini-pizzas finished, I sign the change-of-address form and add my own chicken scratch to the bottom of his note: "Expecting mail soon!"

SATURDAY, JUNE 28

Days Until Trip to Camp Juliette: 27

"When was the last time anyone was down there?" Arno asks while I clear old toys and games from the floor of the playroom closet, then heave open the square red trapdoor made of quarter-inch iron plating.

"Don't know." In the early sixties, around the time of the Cuban Missile Crisis, my parents added two bedrooms, an attic, and a playroom to the house. Under the playroom, the paterfamilias had a fallout shelter built in case of World War III.

For years it has lain unused and nearly forgotten . . . until this hot, humid summer day, when it has occurred to Arno that the poorly ventilated subterranean surroundings might be the perfect place to get high.

The damp odor of mildew wafts up. Milton squints into the dark below and wrinkles his nose. He's finally begun to let his hair grow. It's getting wavy and curls up at the sides and in back. He's also started to cultivate something over his upper lip that could be construed as a mustache. Before he left for MIT last fall, Arno and I tried to get him to give up his leather sandals with the black soles made from car tires. He wouldn't budge on that, but he did agree not to wear socks with them. All in all, these are positive steps toward his indoctrination into the cultural revolution.

"Why can't we smoke in the backyard?" he asks.

"Afraid of the dark?" Arno needles.

"Half-wit," Milton shoots back.

I climb down the cold metal rungs that jut from the cinder-block wall of the shelter. Arno follows. When we reach the bottom, the scrape of our shoes on the bare concrete floor echoes off the walls. It's almost chilly in here. Milton stares down from above. The shelter is the size of a walk-in closet. He doesn't like tight, dark spaces.

"Don't be a pussy," Mr. Sensitivity calls up to him.

"Genital wart," Milton mutters, and climbs down. We sit side by side on a bunk under a bare lightbulb. The cans of food on the shelves are darkly spotted with mold. The cinder-block walls are stained brownish with moisture.

Milton groans. "Wonderful ambiance."

"We won't be here long," I assure him.

Arno lights up. The hypothesis is that a suitable degree of wreckage can be achieved by doing one joint and then rebreathing the smoky air.

"Guaranteed bad trip," Milton continues to complain.

"Quit bellyaching," Arno snaps. "And wash your face. You've got dirt over your lip."

Milton self-consciously touches his fledgling mustache. Arno passes the J to me. "Your festival tickets come?"

"Not yet." I remind myself to call the post office and find out how long it takes for a change of address to kick in.

"Mine just came," Arno says. "Yours'll probably be here in a day or two."

"Where're we gonna stay?" Milton asks.

"Who knows? We'll bring sleeping bags."

"And a tent?" Milton asks.

"Sure, a tent." Arno turns to me. "So how was Maine?"

The mention of tents must have reminded him. I tell them it sucked.

"Robin leave for camp?" Milton asks.

I nod. She's been gone roughly thirty hours, and I've already written two letters. Three, if you count the one I handed her through the car window yesterday morning.

"Heard from Goddard?" Arno asks.

I hadn't planned to tell anyone about the thin envelope. Not until I come up with a strategy to keep from getting a one-way ticket to Southeast Asia, since that is bound to be the next question everyone will ask. But Arno knows what my hesitation means.

"God . . . damn idiot." He draws out the words, then switches to his Lucas imitation: "'Man, with my SATs, Goddard's gotta take me.'"

Oh, the inescapable agony of regret! Robin's first choice was Middlebury, and with her grades, SATs, and extracurriculars, it had been a near certainty. Goddard is about half an hour away from Middlebury, and I thought I fit their applicant profile perfectly: alienated, antiwar, underachieving, and perpetually stoned (institution of *higher* learning, indeed). Perhaps my grades weren't what they could have been, and my extracurricular activities were limited to reading, skiing, writing poetry, getting wasted, and sexual intercourse. But my SAT scores were (surprisingly) good, and I thought the epic poem I composed in iambic pentameter as my essay (in a single night with the help of a couple of Arno's mom's diet pills) was so unique and groundbreaking that the admissions people at Goddard would instantly recognize the boundless creative potential inside me crying out to be unleashed.

My mother, being more circumspect, had filled out applications for four additional colleges, even going so far as to write the essays for me. All I'd had to do was sign my name. I'd been rejected by all of them and wait-listed by Goddard, which asked to see my final-semester grades before making a decision. That meant that while everyone else got to enjoy senior slump, I was supposed to study hard and apply myself. I'd intended to. . . . I really had, but mostly I'd applied my tongue to rolling papers.

"Told your parents?" Arno asks, and again mimics me before I can answer: "'No way, man. They're the *last* people I'd tell.'"

"Can it, zitface," Milton cautions, then leans toward me, his voice solemn: "Great Neck's probably the toughest draft board in the country."

"How're they gonna know I wasn't accepted?" I ask.

"You're supposed to inform them within ten days if your status changes." Milton knows the selective service laws because of his brother, Rudy, who recently fled to Canada to avoid the draft.

"Man, talk about the last people I'd tell," I answer ruefully.

Milton shrugs. "Just saying."

The joint has burned down to the roach. Pinching it gingerly between thumb and forefinger, I take one last toke and, of course, get the roach burn I deserve. "Damn!" I drop the roach on the floor and touch my tongue to the raw dark spot on the tip of my index finger.

"Maybe there's still time," Arno says. "There's gotta be a college that'll take you."

"I don't know," Milton says. "It's almost July. Kind of late. If I were you, I'd talk to a draft counselor fast. The American Friends have an office in a church on Jericho Turnpike. I'll get the address. It's the place Rudy used."

Arno snorts. "Lot of good it did him."

"They'll lay out his options, douchebag," Milton says.

My life has come down to options. None of them good. I continue to have a hard time believing this is actually happening. A little more than a week ago, I was a high-school student and my biggest problems were scoring good dope and finding places where my girlfriend and I could have undisturbed sex. Suddenly I'm in very real danger of perishing in a war I am wholeheartedly opposed to.

How did I let this happen?

I wouldn't say that Arno's one-joint hypothesis has worked. I'm feeling a negligible buzz. Maybe it's because the air in the fallout shelter is a mixture of mildew and skunky smoke, with the heaviness of a damp log thrown on a fire. Maybe it's due to these suddenly pressing concerns about the future. Maybe it's Milton's obvious discomfort. Confinement in this murky gloom eventually proves too much for him. "I'm out of here. Great idea, Arno. Maybe next time we'll find a mausoleum and get high with the stiffs."

We're about to climb out of the shelter when the unmistakable tap of footsteps comes from somewhere above. It can't be Mom, because she took Alan to Adventureland in Farmingdale and won't get home until dinner. So it's got to be the paterfamilias.

"Let's wait a minute," I whisper. "He probably came home to change into his tennis clothes."

"But he's gonna know you're here," Arno whispers. "My car's parked out front."

"Doesn't mean we couldn't have walked somewhere."

Arno and I sit down on the bunk again. Milton remains standing, his arms tightly crossed, a tooth pinching his lower lip. He's the latecomer to our troika. Arno and I have been friends since kindergarten. We live only a few houses from each other. Milton lives down the block. He's more than a year younger, so he was barely on our radar until he got kicked up to seventh grade.

When he skipped sixth and joined us in junior high, no one wanted anything to do with him. Young and nerdy, he reminded us of the dorky preteens we were so relieved to no longer be. But Arno and I took pity on him — exiled to the back of every classroom, wandering alone through the junior high wing, getting accidentally bodychecked into lockers by crowds of larger

36

bodies—and decided it would be fun to have a pet genius. (Plus Milton could always be counted on to do our homework.)

From the fallout shelter, we hear a faucet run overhead. Milton cocks his head as water gurgles through the pipes. He takes a deep breath and starts to tap his foot. Maybe we should go up. It's not like my parents don't know I smoke grass. The paterfamilias has decreed that there shall be no smoking (of any kind) in the house. But we didn't actually smoke *in* the house. We smoked under it.

Milton shoves his hands into his pockets and starts to pace.

"Relax," Arno says.

Milton keeps pacing.

"So, how was MIT?" I ask. This is the first time I've seen him since the drive home from Cambridge, when he was busy sleeping and I was busy tripping.

Milton recently finished his freshman year. He got skipped again in ninth grade and graduated a year ahead of us, at age fifteen. Class valedictorian. Sixteen hundred on his SATs. Only applied to one college: MIT.

"A lot of really smart people and really stupid intro courses." Milton's answer is terse, anxious.

"Was it hard to make friends?" Arno asks. For all his bluster, he is deeply insecure about making new friends when he gets to Bucknell in two months.

"Everyone's new. They're all in the same boat." Milton looks up at the ceiling again, then at me. "Sorry, man. I gotta get out of here."

• • •

"Cherry Jag, man," Arno says. A polished red two-seat convertible is parked at the curb behind Arno's black GTO. Ten minutes ago, after climbing out of the fallout shelter, we waited silently in the playroom until the doorbell rang and the front door opened and shut. After that the house was soundless again.

The paterfamilias is gone and so is whoever owns this Jaguar. The car is long, curvy, and aerodynamic, with a tan leather interior. Affixed to the chrome grille are several round metal badges: Jaguar, Coventry, England; Bay Shore Sports Car Club; Veterans' Car Club of Great Britain.

I glance back up the driveway. The garage door is open. The paterfamilias's own classic two-seat convertible sports car, an MG TF 1500, is gone.

"Dig this, guys." Arno pops the trunk of the GTO, a big, out-of-fashion muscle car that he clings to in the misguided belief that it projects an aura of powerful coolness.

In the trunk is a green caddie vest from Piping Rock, a nearby golf club. Also, a pair of grass-stained golf shoes and some tees and golf balls. Arno keeps this stuff so his parents will think that his money comes from caddying. But that isn't why he's opened the trunk. From a cardboard box, he pulls a metal contraption with a funnel and a hand crank. "Take a guess." (He's never outgrown the thrill of show-and-tell.)

Milton leans close, points at the funnel, and begins to think out loud. "The raw material goes in here. Probably like a wet . . . No, it has to be a powder or dry mix. Then you turn this crank. . . . But why would you . . . ? Oh, I get it. You're

38

compressing it. Right. . . . So, what comes out here . . . Uh, okay. The result is something small that's been highly compressed."

This takes about three seconds. The guy is scary smart. He chews the corner of his lip. "Hamster pellets?"

"For human hamsters." Arno puts the thing back in the cardboard box and slams the trunk. "It's a pill press. There's gonna be something like ten thousand hippies at that music and art festival."

"You're . . . going to make pills?" Milton asks uncertainly.

"Aaa . . . cid." Arno stretches the word. "Ows . . . ley. Two . . . thou . . . sand . . . hits. Three days of peace and music for a bunch of stupid hippies . . . and *six thousand dollars* . . . for Arno Exley Junior."

Arno offers Milton a ride home, but he says he'd rather walk. As soon as the GTO roars off, Milton turns to me. "Monday night after dinner. We'll go to the American Friends office together, okay?"

Not that he has any reason to see a draft counselor. Like all college students, he's exempt from military service thanks to the vaunted 2-S student deferment. He's just worried I'll put it off.

"How's Rudy doing?" I ask, since fleeing to Canada has suddenly become a possibility in my life as well.

Milton scuffs a tire-tread sandal (still no socks, thank God) against the sidewalk. "Shitty. He's living with my uncle's family in Saskatchewan, the middle of nowhere. Doesn't know anyone. Doesn't have a piano. And guess where my uncle works? Dow. How's that for irony?"

Because the Dow Chemical Company produces napalm, it's the poster child for the American military-industrial complex currently reaping millions from the war in Vietnam. Napalm is a flammable jelly the military uses to torch vast swathes of Vietnamese jungle and people. Water boils at 212 degrees. Napalm burns at 2,000 degrees. Witnesses say watching it immolate jungle is like looking into a sea of fire. It sticks to human skin and melts flesh. Since it's dropped from bombers high above, the military has no way of knowing (and clearly doesn't give a crap) how many Vietnamese women and children it incinerates daily.

"So, see you Monday after dinner?" Milton may be young, completely lost as far as girls are concerned, and quirky about dark, claustrophobic spaces, but he is a solid dude.

"You don't have to," I tell him. "I said I'll go."

Milton looks dubious. "Promise?"

I promise.

Milton leaves. I stand in the driveway, gazing absently at the placid tree-lined suburban street. The tent caterpillar nests are still small, but there seem to be a lot of them this year. This is the street where Arno and I used to ride our bikes, throw footballs, and play fungo with a bat and a tennis ball. This is the driveway where Robin and I would park at night and make out for hours. It's a warm afternoon, but the military draft sends a shiver to my core. I can't completely process what's happened. It's like you graduate from high school and if you're not going to college, the party's over. Suddenly, dying and displacement apply *directly* to your own pitiful butt. I can't even ask why anyone didn't warn me. All the warning signs were there. The real question is, why didn't I take them more seriously?

From around the corner comes the downshifting burble of a well-tuned four-cylinder engine. A moment later, the paterfamilias pulls up in the MG. Riding shotgun is a heavyset balding man wearing a blue blazer, white shirt, and a red-and-blue-striped tie. He heaves himself out of the car.

"She's a beauty, just as you promised," the man says to the paterfamilias, who's also gotten out. (A few years ago, he had the MG painted a color called Rolls-Royce Willow Gold. With immense pride he will tell anyone willing to listen about the eleven coats of paint needed to achieve its deep, lustrous finish.)

"And hard to find. Probably less than three thousand in the entire country," the paterfamilias replies. He and the heavy man turn their gazes to me.

"This is my son Lucas," the paterfamilias says. "Lucas, this is Mr. Brown."

When I shake Mr. Brown's meaty hand, he doesn't release it right away. It feels like he's appraising me. Makes me uncomfortable. I gesture to the red sports car at the curb. "Nice Jag."

"Fifty-two XK One Twenty." Mr. Brown lets go of my hand. "Something, isn't she?"

"She sure is," I reply.

Introductions complete, the paterfamilias gives me a look that I interpret as an invitation to disappear.

With pleasure.

• • •

Last Friday, a few days before Robin and I left for Maine, I came home from her house to find the paterfamilias simonizing his prized possession. This labor-intensive process begins with a soapy hand-washing using only natural sea sponges, then a careful drying using special goatskin shammies, followed by polishing and buffing. I know the process intimately because for years it was my responsibility once every spring and fall. I hated it, just as I hated all the chores the paterfamilias foisted on me. As if I were conceived specifically for the role of household peon.

That afternoon, I paused to watch while he squatted beside one of the car's broad fenders, rubbing away the dried whitish simonizing compound with a soft cotton cloth. His tanned forehead was dotted with sweat, the slightly brownish trail on his temple evidence of the hair dye he's recently started using. I wondered if he was recalling the good old days when he'd been able to make me do all the work.

"Don't you usually do this in April?" I asked.

The paterfamilias wiped the sweat off his forehead with the back of his hand. "I'm going to a classic-car rally up in Newburgh."

That sounded odd. As far as I knew, he'd never gone to a classic-car rally before. Especially on a summer weekend, when his chief preoccupation was playing three or four hours of tennis each day.

A few hours later, he left.

Friday ended, Saturday passed, and on Sunday afternoon, Robin and I departed for our ill-fated Maine fling, heading east on the Long Island Expressway toward Orient Point, where we would catch the ferry to New London. We were near the Melville exit when something in the westbound lanes caught my eye. It was the gold MG with the top down. For a moment, it made no sense. The paterfamilias had said the classic-car rally was in Newburgh, which is in upstate New York, not out on Long Island.

But there he was in the driver's seat.

And next to him was a blonde.

SUNDAY, JUNE 29

Days Until Camp Juliette: 26

I would like to be
A famous writer.
But I am neither brilliant
Nor dead.

"I adored that book." Tinsley reaches over and touches the spine of my dog-eared copy of *Trout Fishing in America*.

"Yeah, pretty trippy."

She, Cousin Barry, and I are behind the junior high, on a blanket spread on the grass, keeping an eye out for school employees and police while we smoke a joint of hash and tobacco. It's rare that I see Barry more than once every few weeks, but Arno and Milton aren't around today, and I'm finding it difficult to adjust to the emptiness of life without Robin. Except for Easter vacation this year, we haven't been apart for more than a day since last fall.

The weather is overcast, warm, and breezy. Barry sits cross-legged, working a string connected to a red-and-black kite shaped like a ladybug fluttering a hundred feet above. He says the hash and tobacco mixture is popular in Europe.

Tinsley lies on her stomach, shooting photos of Barry's profile. I'm lying on my side reading the book, which is mostly not about trout fishing. Even more than usual, I'm finding it difficult to focus. Partly it's the hash, which is a lot more potent than the twig-and-seed-littered weed we often encounter. Partly it's the very dark and ominous cloud called Vietnam that now looms ever present in my thoughts. But at this moment much of my distraction is due to Tinsley.

According to *Time* magazine, we have entered the era of women's liberation. Females are throwing off their sexpot and housewife stereotypes and throwing *out* their bras, razors, and hair dryers. They call it going natural.

In Tinsley's case, it appears she's held on to the razor. Nor has she given up her eyeliner, mascara, and lipstick. The eyebrows she likes to raise tantalizingly are carefully sculpted, and her fingernails are glossy. But her peasant blouse has a loose, open neckline, and when she props herself on her elbows and holds the camera to her face, you can see her breasts all the way to the pink nipples. (I have to believe she's aware of this.)

Only it's more than bare skin. Her vibe is alluring, vulnerable and inviting, impossible to ignore. The way the small of her back curves. The way, when she lies on her stomach, her legs scissor at the knees, toes pointed upward.

Her presence makes me wonder if hanging out with Barry

today is a mistake. I shouldn't be entertaining these thoughts, even while high. My aching heart belongs to Robin. Plus there's the bitter memory of the blonde in the MG. It's not that I didn't know the paterfamilias cheats on Mom. He's been doing it for years. But it's one of those recollections that lies dormant in the distant reaches of some deep cave of the mind and only awakens when something like last Sunday jars it.

Thinking of Robin, I decide this is a good time to write another letter to her. I didn't bring any paper, but I can tear a blank page out of the back of this paperback. "Anyone have a pen?"

From her fringed leather bag, Tinsley produces a fountain pen with a gold nib. When she leans over to hand it to me, the neck of her blouse falls open, and my eyes suddenly have minds of their own. It's disconcerting. I've never encountered someone so overtly sexual before, someone who seems to harbor actual exhibitionistic tendencies. Barry's saying that she does as she pleases feels like something of an understatement.

"I love when he goes to the warehouse where they sell waterfalls," she says, not taking her eyes off mine.

"And you have to buy them in sections and put them together," I add. We share a smile, a connection, the intimacy that comes with being members of the subgroup of freakerati who subscribe to Richard Brautigan's off-kilter vision of the world. And today it's all amplified. The spacey hash high, the literary connection, and, yes, I'm forced to admit, the titillation of Tinsley's secretive exhibitionism.

"So, when're you gonna see your girlfriend?" Cousin Barry

asks without taking his eyes off the ladybug kite high above. Has he picked up on the vibe between Tinsley and me?

"Twenty-six days," I answer.

"Where is she?" Tinsley asks.

"A camp north of Ottawa."

Barry turns. "For real? Zach and Eva are crashing at a farm somewhere around there. He keeps saying I should make the scene."

"Avoiding the draft?" I ask.

"Naw, he's Four-F. Flat feet."

4-F for flat feet? That's a surprise. A borderline condition like that might exempt you from the army in places like Houston or Pittsburgh, where there is a plentiful supply of draft-aged grist for the military, but it's been my impression that at the army induction center in Brooklyn, they'd slap a pair of orthotics on your feet and ship your woeful behind straight to basic training.

And while I'd never begrudge Cousin Barry his mental problems, they do come with a silver lining. His stints in the loony bin have resulted in his receiving a 4-F classification as psychologically unfit for service.

Barry relights the hash joint. "Remember the first time I got you high?" he asks me in the tight, breathless voice of one who is trying to keep smoke from escaping his lungs.

Before I answer, I also take a hit. When Tinsley accepts the joint from me, her fingertips caress my hand in a way that doesn't feel accidental. "First time I smoked, I didn't feel a thing," she says. "Did you?"

47

"They told me to swallow the smoke," I recall. "An hour later, I burped and a puff came out."

"Zach and I were goofin' on you, man." Barry chuckles and tugs on the kite string.

Goofin' on Lucas was a regular pastime when I was in my prepubescence and Barry was my idol. Barry was edgy and daring. He had one of the first skateboards, wooden, pointed at the front like a miniature surfboard. There was a big chip in the nose where he said he'd crashed into a curb. At that age, being able to say you'd crashed into anything was a mark of distinction.

He was also athletic. You wouldn't believe how far he could throw a football at nine years old. He had a pull-up bar in the doorway of his room and could do a dozen pull-ups and chin-ups. He could ride a bike balancing on the back wheel, walk a few steps on his hands, clap between push-ups.

I idolized him; he did his best to ignore me. I was weak, physically timid, athletically unexceptional, prone to daydreaming. Hardly able to do a pull-up, and after five push-ups, I'd be as swaybacked as an old horse. I once watched, fascinated, while Barry—unaware of me—admired himself in a mirror. At that age, when I looked in the mirror, I failed to see anything worth admiring.

But even as a kid, there was a dark side to Barry. He could be pensive, moody, even morose. On those rare occasions when he submitted to my company—usually under duress at some family get-together—he might suddenly take a swing at me for no reason. Back then, I even found his unpredictable violence admirable. And to me, those brooding silences and sudden bursts of ferocity bespoke inner depth, although now I suspect that they were merely moments when his frustration at being stuck with his nerdy cousin boiled over.

No bra arouses
The imagination.
One can't help but wonder:
Panties?

Overhead, thick gray clouds have begun to gather. Lucas the Very Stoned can feel the dampness in the air. Maybe they should split, but that second round of tokes on the hash joint has left them all too zonked to consider movement without suitable cause.

Lucas turns on his side, props up his head, and tries to read a chapter entitled "Trout Fishing in America with the FBI," but the sentences don't begin with capital letters, and thanks to the hash, Brautigan's words have become difficult to string together into sentences.

Tinsley aims her camera at him. It says LEICA on it. A brand he's never heard of. The shutter clicks. Something stirs inside him. The hash has poked holes in the testosterone dam. Thoughts of cupping her breasts in his hands, the excited spark of her nipples against his palms. *But wait* . . . What happened to the letter he was going to write to Robin?

He's just torn a blank page out of the back of the paperback when the wind suddenly swirls, snatching the sheet and sending it across the field behind the junior high. His hair whipping across his face, Barry gets to his feet to control the kite. He and his friend Zach were among the first guys Lucas saw grow their hair long. One night a few weeks after they introduced Lucas to grass, Barry and Zach went to see the Young Rascals at the Westbury Music Fair. Neither of them was old enough to drive, so they took a bus. After the concert, they were waiting for the bus home when a bunch of guys jumped them.

These days, if you fly your freak flag, chances are that sooner or later someone's going to say something. But it's nothing like it was in 1965, when hardly anyone had long hair and the few guys who dared to were subject to daily harassment. Barry and Zach were badly beaten. Some of their hair was pulled out and much of the rest chopped off with scissors. (The police speculated that their attackers had come equipped for hippie hunting.) When Lucas saw Barry a few days later, his cousin's nose was bandaged, eyes blackened and swollen, lip split, a tooth chipped. No arrests were ever made — though Lucas the Cynic has doubts about how hard the cops looked for the guys who beat up a couple of long-haired dirty drug-taking peacenik faggot hippies.

What happened turned Barry into a basket case.

On the blanket behind the junior high, Tinsley inches closer on her elbows, her breasts in plain sight swaying inside the blouse. *This is crazy,* Lucas the Flustered thinks. He shouldn't look. She raises the camera, and he stares instead into the rainbow-reflective depths of the glistening lens. *Click.*

She lowers the camera, then reaches toward his face. Barry

is only a few yards away, his back to them as he works the kite string in the gusty breeze. Tinsley's fingers softly trace Lucas's cheekbones, nose, and lips. Her fingertips tickle and titillate. Her smile is beatific. Lucas feels off-kilter and weird. He also feels a growing tightness behind the zipper of his jeans.

> Robin, O Robin! **Wherefore** art **thou**
> **500 miles** away, in **the land** of
> Hockey, **maple syrup**, and **polar bears**?

Lucas the Aroused tries to redirect his eyes to his book. Tinsley's fingers trace the skin down his arm. Goose bumps sprout with abandon. Her hand closes over his wrist.

Now what?

She tugs and his hand follows, crossing a few inches of blanket and sliding into the blouse so that his fingers ever so slightly graze the tip of one breast.

What the . . . ? Should he pull his hand back? Robin's in another country, so she'll never know. And when you get right down to it, this is pretty harmless. But Barry's right here. *So what?* He's the one who told Lucas that Tinsley does what she pleases.

Tinsley lowers her body, trapping his hand between her breast and the blanket. She turns her face away and makes a soft purring sound. It could be a chapter from Brautigan's book. "Trout Fishing in America with Tinsley's Breast."

Lucas's hormone-and-hash-addled brain is blown.

MONDAY, JUNE 30

Days Until Camp Juliette: 25

"Let me take a wild guess, Mr. Baker: the Selective Service induction letter came and you're totally flipped out because you don't want to go to Vietnam."

The speaker is Charles. He is black, with an immense Afro and a Charles Mingus beard. His long legs are crossed at the ankles and propped on the corner of an old gray metal desk. His threads are jeans, cowboy boots, and a work shirt, a pack of Marlboros poking out of the left pocket.

His blatant antagonism has thrown me. I've come to this church basement office of the American Friends Service Committee for help, not ridicule. "I haven't gotten a letter, but if I don't do something, I probably will."

"Ahh." Charles nods with a knowing smile. "Planning ahead." It's close to eight p.m. When I got here around seven, there were two guys ahead of me in the waiting room. Both were what Barry would call plastic heads. Their hair longish but neatly trimmed and styled, their collared shirts pressed, and, perhaps most telling of all, their bell-bottoms carefully creased.

Charles scans the personal-information form I've filled out. "So, what's the problem, Lucas? You're from the North Shore. Just tell Daddy to pay for college and get your Two-S deferment."

I explain that I'm too late. This morning I spent several hours on the phone calling numerous institutions of higher learning to see if any were still accepting applications for the fall. The results were not encouraging. College applications last year hit an all-time high. A reflection, I've learned, of a strong economy (*see* military-industrial complex) and a heightened desire among young draft-age men to keep from having their nuts shot off in some Southeast Asian jungle.

Every day more and more people turn against the war. It's gotten to the point where even the veterans who fought in it are voicing their opposition at protest marches and on the news. Young men who might have voluntarily enlisted a few years ago are resisting. Those who can afford college are applying like never before. As a result, more borderline applicants than ever were wait-listed this year (*see* yours truly). From admissions office after admissions office, I heard the same thing: freshman classes are full. Yes, sometimes one or two accepted students don't show up in the fall, but the chances of getting one of those spots are slim to none, especially if I don't have some kind of pull.

Charles taps a Marlboro out of the pack and lights it. "So, tell me, Lucas, why don't you want to go to Vietnam?"

The answer is obvious. I don't understand why he's being such a dick. "Because I don't want to die."

He takes a drag and exhales smoke upward. "Riiiight. With the odds being one in five of getting killed or wounded, let some other sucka fight. Why risk your own neck?"

I'm here because Milton said this is the place to come for help dealing with the draft, and I guess I should appreciate this guy for volunteering his time, but his attitude completely blows. "No, I don't want anyone to fight for me. I don't want anyone to fight, period. I don't believe in war. It's wrong."

Charles flicks his cigarette ash onto the floor. "Oh, yeah? So you wouldn't have fought against Hitler?"

Again, the answer seems obvious. "You can't compare Vietnam to that. Hitler was a madman. He was killing millions of innocent people. Now we're the ones killing innocent people. And why? It's not like the United States is in any kind of danger."

Charles scratches the side of his nose thoughtfully. His eyes slide toward me. "Someone tell you to say that?"

What the hell? It's been a really weird couple of days. What happened behind the junior high yesterday nags at me. My hand didn't stay under Tinsley's breast for long. A few moments later it started to rain, so we left. Barry never knew. But my hand did. Why did it stay there even for those few moments? Why participate in whatever weird mind game she's into? It's not even like it was some kind of super-erotic moment. A breast squashed against your hand on the ground is about as exciting as one pressed against your back on a crowded school bus. No, I take that back. The school bus is more exciting. So all it amounted to was an act of betrayal to Robin. Ever since yesterday, I've felt guilty—and used. Even if I was seriously trashed on hash, why did I have to be so passive?

I shouldn't have taken *that* crap from Tinsley, and I'm starting to think I shouldn't take *this* crap from Charles. He can't be the only draft counselor around. I push my chair back, the legs scraping the floor. "Listen, man, sorry to waste your time. I'm looking for advice, not a hassle. Maybe this is the wrong place."

"Whoa." Charles slides his boots off the desk and sits up. "Don't go anywhere, Lucas. I'm here to help. Sit down. No one else is gonna be able to do anything I can't."

I lower myself back into the chair. Charles takes another drag and studies me. "Okay, you caught me at a bad moment. Those last two cats really messed with my head."

I cock my own head quizzically.

"I'm kind of new to this, dig?" Charles says. "I mean, don't get me wrong, I've done the training. I get the counseling thing. The problem is *who* I'm counseling." He plants his elbows on the desk and leans closer. "You *sure* no one told you to say that stuff about innocent Vietnamese dying?"

"Why would anyone have to tell me?"

Charles leans back. "Why? Because to be perfectly blunt, my friend, most of the rich white kids who come in here don't give a shit about Vietnam or the Vietnamese. Women and children dying? Not their problem. Working-class war? Mostly blacks and blue-collar kids getting killed over there? Too bad, suckas. Those last two guys weren't even sure where Vietnam is. 'Uh, somewhere in Asia?' As far as they're concerned, the war's for poor trash who can't afford college, not entitled brats who think they can enjoy the benefits this country offers without paying a price." Charles flicks ash on the floor again and stares at the red tip of his cigarette. "So, where's Vietnam, Lucas?"

"Southeast Asia. On the South China Sea, bordered by China, Cambodia, and Thailand." (I'm no geography whiz, but when I started dating Robin, it became clear that if I was going to have dinner with her antiwar parents, I had better know where Vietnam was.)

"Laos, not Thailand, but good enough." Charles studies the personal-information form again, thinks for a moment. "Okay, here's the deal. Your induction letter hasn't come, so we've got some wiggle room."

"Any chance it'll never come?" I ask. "Like they'll never find out I didn't get into college?"

Charles scoffs. "Believe in Santa Claus, man? You're in one of the toughest draft districts in the country. Your name is on that list, and naughty or nice, they'll check it twice and find your sweet ass. Catch the news tonight? Two hundred and twenty-three Americans died last week and another four hundred were wounded. Not to mention every month you've got nearly forty thousand deployments ending. That's a lot of bodies that need to be replaced, dig?"

They call the war a meat grinder, as in grinding up bodies. Back in May, there was a ten-day battle nicknamed Hamburger Hill for that very reason. Nearly 450 American soldiers were killed or wounded. They finally took the hill from the Vietcong, held it for a few weeks, then walked away. Within a month,

56

the North Vietnamese were back, as if the battle had never taken place. Nearly every day over there that scenario is being repeated—lives wasted for no reason.

Charles stretches his long arms and yawns. "Given that you have some time, Lucas, and based on your *sincere* belief that war is wrong, I think we should take a shot at filing for conscientious objector status. Believe in God?"

I shake my head.

"Well, you might want to reconsider. Know what they say? There are no atheists in foxholes." Charles dashes out his cigarette in an ashtray and slides a mimeographed sheet of paper toward me. "Here's a list of books. Familiarize yourself with Thomas Aquinas and just-war theory: *jus ad bellum* and *jus in bello*. In the meantime, I'll get the CO application in the mail to you."

I trudge out into the dark lot behind the church, feeling a weight on my shoulders, thinking about Chris. It might surprise Charles to learn that I have a friend over in Nam who fits the definition of blue-collar working class to a T. Chris actually enlisted. I tried to talk him out of it, but no dice. Now I'm racked by a jumble of disquieting emotions. Mainly guilt because I'm a "rich white kid" who hopes to find a way to stay out of the war—while many less fortunate white and minority guys have no choice but to go . . . and some will die.

I'm also feeling discomfort because growing up in my well-to-do, lily-white, middle-class suburb, I never thought of my family as rich. It wasn't until I began working at the pater-familias's bulk-mail company in Hempstead a few years ago that I realized how privileged my life really was, and how much I took for granted.

And then there's the angst of knowing that Charles is so right. Here I am, a middle-class white kid asking a black guy to help me stay out of a war that a lot of black kids have no way to avoid.

But here's what feels the most shameful of all: everything I've just thought won't stop me from accepting Charles's help.

Chris's most recent letter arrived the day before Robin and I left for Maine:

6/7/69

Dear Loogie,

It's a total shit show over here. No one believes we can win this war. Half the time we don't even know who to fight unless it's every gook we see. During the day the VC pretend to be farmers and village folk. The guy plowing behind a water buffalo. At night he puts on black pajamas and puts a bullet in your skull or a knife in your back.

Command says we'll win this war because we have a kill ratio of ten to one. That means 10 VC die for every American. But like everything else command tells us that's bullshit. Why? Because the VC don't care if they die. THE KILL RATIO COULD BE 30 TO 1 AND THEY

WOULDN'T CARE. This is their country and we're the invaders.

Loogs, what kills me ain't just what we're doing to the people. Burning their villages. ACCIDENTALLY killing babies. It's also what we're doing to their country. You never saw a more beautiful place. Beaches that make Jones Beach look like a crappy playground sandbox. Miles of green rice paddies. Mountains. Except we're bombing, burning, and defoliating it so fast, it looks the surface of the moon. Only with dead tree trunks.

In your last letter you wrote you couldn't believe the army censors didn't censor what I wrote. I got news for you, Loogs. Like everyone else, the censors don't give a shit. No one does. The other night our squad flat out refused to go on patrol. Everyone's sick of getting killed or booby-trapped in the dark. And if that ain't bad enough, it fucking rains leeches. I swear to God, Loogie, they fall out of the trees when they sense you under them. They get down your shirt collar, on your neck and back. You return from patrol and there are these big fat blood-filled worms all over your body.

Most of the time when we get sent on patrols, we sandbag it in a safe place in the jungle and wait till it's time to go back. You hear about guys fragging their hard-ass COs and NCOs. You believe it, Loogs? GIs *KILLING THEIR COMPANY COMMANDERS SO THEY DON'T HAVE TO FOLLOW THEIR STUPID ORDERS.* They call it fragging 'cause they use frag grenades to do the job. Don't have to worry about the guy getting away wounded.

There's a story going around about a company that raised $500 for anyone who would kill a CO who was ordering useless attacks. I believe it.

I'm counting the months weeks days hours minutes till I can get out of here. If I knew then what I know now I would have listened to you and *NEVER EVER SIGNED UP.* All I can say is you better keep your act together, man. *DON'T BE THE NEXT SUCKER THAT GETS SENT OVER HERE.*

Peace, brother
Chris

Obviously, the line *Don't be the next sucker that gets sent over here* has taken on a new urgency in my life. I fold Chris's thin white air-mail envelope with a red dragon printed on it and the word FREE scrawled where a stamp usually goes. (One of the rewards for needlessly facing death every day for your country is that the army doesn't make you pay for postage.) Each letter from him brings mixed feelings of outrage and relief. He's going through hell, but at least he's still alive—or he was three weeks ago when he sent it.

Anyway, it's time I penned a reply:

Dear Chris,

Great to get your letter. I'm blown away by the part about the military saying a kill ratio of ten to one is a success. Let me get this straight. They're completely fine with letting 10,000 American soldiers die if it means 100,000 Vietcong die as well? That's considered success? How could all that death ever be considered success? Would any of the military strategists who came up with that ratio ever volunteer to be one of the 10,000 soldiers they've agreed to let die?

I mean, seriously, this completely blows my mind. What altered state of reality are they living in? I thought I was the one living in an altered state (let's roll another one, my friend), but even wasted I know that life is sacred. You don't make deals with human lives as payment. I'll give you one of mine for ten of yours? There's one thing for sure about that level of insanity: whoever thinks it's acceptable for soldiers to die is making certain that no one they love and care about is part of that deal.

Anyway, despite all the madness, it's good to hear from you. It kills me to know what you're going through. I know for your family's sake you've got to do what you're doing, but I want you to know that a lot of guys who've come back from Nam are against the war. You're in good company.

In the meantime, I think you're totally justified in trying
to save your own ass. I can't help feeling guilty that you're
over there risking your life and I'm not. In high school I knew
that things could be unfair. That fat cats benefitted unduly
while workers suffered. But it was all kind of theoretical. It
feels a hell of a lot more personal now.

All I can say is, try to stay safe, my friend.

Lucas

A few summers ago, when I started working at the bulk-mail company, I was the owner's long-haired hippie freak son, on my feet eight hours a day running an envelope-insertion machine alongside the oppressed working class: high-school dropouts, minorities, even a few ex-cons.

No one spoke to me. I assumed they figured that if they hassled me it might get them fired. Most of them weren't only from a different socioeconomic class but from another generation. Even being three or four years older than me meant they'd grown up as hoods, greasers, or jocks, listening to Elvis, Roy Orbison, and the Everly Brothers instead of Dylan, the Beatles, the Stones, and acid rock.

There was one guy around my age. Pale, thin, and slightly built, he wore his dirty-blond hair in a greaser's combed-back pompadour and always had a cigarette parked above his right ear. He ran a machine a couple of rows over from me, but I rarely saw him anywhere else on the property.

It took about a month to realize that he was actively avoiding me. A sandwich truck swings by four times a day — breakfast, midmorning, lunchtime, midafternoon—to sell coffee, sand-wiches, and snacks. Those are the only times employees have a chance to mix. But if pompadour guy saw me near the food truck, he went in another direction. The same thing happened at the start and end of the day when we lined up to punch in/out at the time clock. One minute he'd be in line. The next minute, vanished.

Why was he avoiding me?

The answer came one afternoon during snack break. I caught a glimpse of him slipping out a door that led to the shed behind the building, where old insertion machines, spare parts, and mail bins are stored. I decided to follow. Out back, there was no sign of him, just the tall barbed-wire fence that surrounds the property. I stood there for a moment, puzzled, then heard cough-ing and saw a puff of smoke drift out from behind the shed.

I smelled it, too. Good old skunk weed.

Son of a gun.

When I came around the side of the shed, the guy let the joint fall to the ground and nonchalantly crushed it underfoot like someone might do with a cigarette. Only he crushed it extra hard and long so there was practically no trace left. With a quick nod, he started back toward the factory as if nothing had happened.

Was that why he'd been avoiding me? Because he assumed, perhaps correctly, that I was the only one around who could clock him for a head—and as the owner's son, I might rat him out?

The next morning, I got to work early and left an envelope

taped to his mail inserter. Inside was a joint from my stash of Acapulco Gold.

The day proceeded normally. As usual, he avoided me. But at the end of work the envelope was no longer taped to his inserter.

The next morning, I left another J for him.

It was a particularly hot and humid week, and even with the window fans running, the building was stifling. At the mid-morning break, I was sitting on the curb in the shade enjoying the first of two containers of orange juice when he sidled up to me. "That's some dynamite weed," he whispered. "How much you want for it?"

"Nothing, man."

He frowned. "Come on."

"It's cool, man. Enjoy."

He was wearing a T-shirt with a pack of cigarettes tucked into the sleeve. Only the cigarettes were Belair menthols. No real greaser would be caught dead smoking them.

He must have seen something in my face because he said, "Swipe 'em from my mother. She buys 'em by the carton."

I considered offering him a Marlboro, then rejected the idea. He might have taken it the wrong way. Like, *Of course the owner's son can afford Marlboros. Show-off!* Meanwhile, this guy had to steal his mother's crappy mentholated coffin nails.

He offered me a Belair and we lit up. The tobacco tasted like it had been dipped in mouthwash. Barf-o-rama.

"You're the owner's son, right?" he said.

"That's what they tell me."

64

He suddenly coughed hard enough that his body shook.

"You okay?"

"Yeah. Mild asthma. No biggie." His voice went raspy. "So, what's the deal? Since when does the owner's son have to work in his father's sweatshop?"

"That's what I keep wondering."

"But you get paid more, right?"

"Dollar ten an hour."

"For real?"

"Come Friday, I'll show you mine if you'll show me yours." Fridays are paydays.

He took a thoughtful drag. Hacked again. Spit. Wiped his lips with the back of his hand. "Everyone thinks you're a spy for your old man."

"Yeah, that's me, the Benedict Arnold of junk mail."

He scowled. I got the feeling he didn't know who Benedict Arnold was. But spy for my father? Not without feeling like a traitor to the cause.

There were five minutes left in the break. "Got that J?" I asked.

From that day on, Chris and I met at the shed every afternoon and got high. Like Cousin Barry, he'd dropped out of high school in tenth grade—not because he'd been severely beaten and had become a basket case, but because that's what everyone in Chris's family did. You went to school until you were sixteen and then got a job.

I miss those fifteen minutes with Chris each afternoon. He was funny, and real, and not caught up in typical middle-class striving for material success. A lot of well-educated, supposedly hip cats talk carpe diem, but Chris is the only person I know who really lives it.

But now he's over there, just another working-class "sucka" risking his life in a senseless war while most owners' sons like me don't have to. Damn straight I feel turmoil about that. You'd have to have a heart of stone not to be stricken by the unfairness of it.

TUESDAY, JULY 1

Days Until Camp Juliette: 24

When I get home from work, the mail is lying on the floor below the front-door mail slot. The mailman usually comes in the early afternoon, and now it's close to dinnertime. Those letters and magazines have been left ungathered for hours.

Did Mom leave her room today?

Even though Robin's only been gone for four days, I'm disappointed that there's no perfumed lavender envelope. According to the post office, it'll take about two weeks for the change of address to go into effect, so it's not like a letter from her would have gone to Bay Shore already.

On my desk is the reading list Charles gave me. I need to start on that because I'm going to have to write an essay for my conscientious objector application.

But I'd much rather write to Robin.

Dear Robin,

*How's life above the Arctic Circle? Do they have electricity
where you are? Have they heard of television? Here in the
US, they've developed something called a rocket and in a
couple of weeks some brave nutjobs are going to take off in one.
Guess where they think they're going? The moon! They know
what the moon is up there on the frozen tundra, don't they?
It's that big round thing that comes out at night in the sky.
If you're not sure what I'm talking about, look for the thing
Canadians howl at after dark. . . .*

By the time I finish the letter, it's the dinner hour and I'm
hungry. I leave my room and pass the den, where Alan's in his
usual spot. He's taken off his shoes and socks, and with his
eyes firmly fixed on the TV screen, he's bent his leg around so
that he can sniff his toes. I've learned to take his idiosyncrasies
in stride, but as a kid, I was often furious with him. Incensed
that he would pick his nose and eat it in public. That he would
scratch himself in private places and then sniff his fingers. That
he would wander into our baseball or touch football games with
no sense that he was interfering.

And that he wouldn't listen.

The paterfamilias gave him chores, but he'd lose interest
and then I'd have to do his chores as well as mine. The paterfamilias would punish him for not doing his chores by sending
him to his room, but unless someone stood guard, Alan would
wait a little while and then go back to the boob tube. When
the paterfamilias removed the round plastic channel dial, Alan

found some pliers and used them to turn the small metal post that changed the channels. When the paterfamilias took away the pliers, Alan searched until he found them. When the paterfamilias hid the pliers where Alan couldn't find them, my brother lay down on the kitchen floor and made us step over him.

When we were smaller, the paterfamilias would spank us both, but Alan got the worst of it. The paterfamilias would come home from work angry and wallop him for the merest transgression. As if spanking were a way for the paterfamilias to get out his frustrations with work and life, and Alan was the easiest target. The paterfamilias used to spank us with his hand until the day he hurt his wrist and couldn't play tennis for a few weeks. Then he started to use a yellow plastic Wiffle bat until I found it in his closet and threw it down the storm sewer. But it wasn't long before I wished I hadn't. Having lost the Wiffle bat, Dad turned next to a wooden racquetball paddle.

Ultimately, the spankings were meaningless. Alan would cry, and then stop crying and go back to the TV. Eventually he gave up lying on the kitchen floor. If he couldn't change the channel to the station he wanted, he'd watch whatever station was on.

The kitchen is filled with the scent of warming food in the oven. Two torn Swanson fried chicken TV dinner boxes lie on the counter, while Mom sits at the kitchen table in a housedress, reading a gardening book. Gardening is her chief hobby. Spring, summer, and fall, our house is surrounded by colorful, carefully curated flower beds. (Does she surround our house with beautiful gardens to mask the ugliness inside?) She looks up at me with a wan expression. No makeup, and her hair is flat and unbrushed.

"When were you going to tell me about Goddard?" she asks.

She must have seen the rejection letter on my desk. I'm surprised it took so long; it's been sitting there for nearly a week. I tell her not to worry because Charles the draft counselor is helping me apply for conscientious objector status.

Her eyebrows dip. "Didn't Milton's brother, Rudy, try to be a conscientious objector?"

I know what she's thinking: If super-smart piano prodigy Rudy tried the CO route and got turned down, what chance does nonprodigy Goddard College reject Lucas have?

"If conscientious objector doesn't work, Charles says we have time to explore other options."

"Such as?"

Prison, Canada . . . Nothing I want to lay on her until we see where the CO thing goes. "Mom, I'll figure it out. I promise."

When she squeezes her eyes closed, then lowers her face into her hands, I'm caught off guard. "What is it, Mom?"

A long moment passes. She lifts her head and has the look of someone who might have had tears in her eyes if they had any tears left. She shakes her head as if snapping herself out of something. "Nothing. It was just a thought."

"About?"

She focuses, looks directly at me. "That I can't lose you, too."

For an instant I assume she's referring to Dad. Then it hits me. Shit. *Shit!* From deep in the cave of forgetfulness comes a glimpse of what she must have been thinking. When I was around two and a half, a little brother named Brett was born. I wish I could remember him, but I can't. He died of pneumonia after six weeks. What I do remember, or think I remember, is the long period of gray stillness that followed at home. Alan was born a year and a half later.

And now Mom's facing the possibility of losing another son. The merest hint of which must be unbearable to her.

Way to go, numbnuts.

The tinny canned laughter coming from the TV in the den feels like it's aimed at me. I step closer. "Mom, I'm not going to Vietnam. I promise."

The oven pings. The TV dinners are done. Even though Mom is probably average weight or less, she wearily heaves herself up like someone who weighs a lot more. She puts a TV dinner on Alan's yellow Superman tray with a glass of milk, then gestures for me to take it to him.

In the den, Alan's no longer sniffing his toes. As usual, he's sitting too close to the TV screen, but this evening I don't have the will to tell him to move back. I put the tray on the floor beside him. He removes the false-teeth bite plate and picks up a drumstick.

Back in the kitchen, the other TV dinner rests on the kitchen table. Mom stands by the sliding glass doors, gazing out. Orange light bathes the backyard, illuminating the weeping willows, throwing shadows over the lawn and beds of orange lilies, white gardenias, and red and yellow marigolds that line the patio.

She grew up during the Depression, excelled academically, and was fortunate to get a college scholarship when there were few to go around. Graduated summa cum laude, got a job as an editorial assistant at *Time* magazine, hoping to someday be a journalist and writer. There she met the paterfamilias, who sold advertising space for the magazine. They married, had me, and moved to the suburbs. Mom gave up her career to be a mother and live the postwar American dream.

And now? She has a husband who cheats on her, one son she's buried, another who's not right in the head, and a third who, if the United States government has its way, could soon end up being just one more American casualty traded for the lives of ten Vietcong.

I seat myself at the kitchen table, feel the moist heat rise to my face from the warm TV dinner nestled in its compartmentalized tinfoil tray.

"How does the application for conscientious objector work?" Mom asks.

Between bites of chicken, mashed potatoes, and mixed vegetables, I explain that I have to write an essay justifying my antiwar beliefs. If the draft board accepts it, I'll then have to go in person for an interview.

"An essay?" Mom repeats with a grimace. The word is a charged one around here, and not only because I insisted on submitting my epic poem–college essay to Goddard without allowing anyone to read it. Mom and I had a deal regarding the other four colleges she wanted me to apply to: she'd fill in the applications; all I'd have to do was write the essays. But as the deadlines approached, the essays remained unwritten until she finally had no choice but to write them herself.

(If only I'd taken those applications more seriously. If only I had a college to go to now. Even a school hundreds of miles from Middlebury would have meant I could see Robin two or three times a month.)

Mom returns to the table and sits. "I wish you'd continued with Dr. Hill."

She's changed the subject to another highly charged topic. By junior year of high school, I was most definitely in *high* school.

> Stoned at school.
> Stoned at home.
> Stoned wherever the buffalo roam.

I'd get high at lunchtime or drop acid and trip through my afternoon classes. Sensing that something was amiss, Mom insisted that I start seeing Dr. Hill, a psychiatrist. At his office, the good doctor would ask how I felt about Alan. How I felt about my parents. About myself. (Didn't he understand that the whole purpose of taking drugs was not to feel?) I usually went into his office stoned.

"Mom, what's the point?"

"Didn't you feel it was helping?" she asks.

"Helping *you*, maybe."

She stiffens. "Why do you say that?"

"Seriously, Mom? Wasn't the point of sending me to a shrink to make you feel better? Like you were doing something instead of nothing?"

Mom's face scrunches and she takes a deep breath. I feel a rebuttal coming and wipe my lips with the napkin. "I'm not blaming you. You had your hands full with Alan. And it's not like you've gotten a lot of help from you-know-who."

"We're not talking about him," Mom says. "We're talking about you and Dr. Hill."

"You don't think it's all mixed together? Come on; we both know Dad has no interest in this family. We're nothing but a burden to him."

After a moment's stillness, Mom leans forward and speaks in a measured tone. "That is not true."

How can she defend him? Does she know about the blonde I saw in the MG a little more than a week ago? I'm certain she knows about some of the other women. *Why* would she defend him? I find it nearly incomprehensible. *Should I tell her about his latest dalliance?* Something holds me back. Is it that I can't imagine how telling her about this one would make a difference if the others didn't? Is it because this summer things between my parents already feel more strained than ever and I'm hesitant to make it worse?

Or is something else stopping me?

TUESDAY, JULY 8

Days Until Camp Juliette: 17

Work's over. In the parking lot, a pair of feet jut out from around the side of Odysseus. *Whoa.* I know I had a toke on the way to work this morning, but I think I would have noticed if I'd run over someone.

I round the microbus. It's Tinsley, sitting on the pavement in the shade cast by Odysseus. The bottoms of her bare feet are nearly black. Her legs spread wide under a long purple tie-dyed skirt gathered to her knees.

Uncertainty ripples through me. What's she doing here? Where's Barry? "Hi." I try to sound nonchalant while recollecting the awkward sensation of her naked breast squashed against my palm behind the junior high last week.

Tinsley doesn't respond. She's concentrating on three bronze coins that she's just tossed onto the asphalt. The coins have square holes at their centers. With her fountain pen, she draws two dashes in a notebook and scribbles the number five.

"Whatcha doing?" I ask.

"Throwing the *I Ching*. An ancient form of divination."

"Uh, come again?"

"A way to figure things out and gain insight." She pats the asphalt beside her.

I sit with my back against Odysseus's door and light a cigarette. What's Tinsley trying to gain insight about here in the parking lot? Whether or not she should do something insane and sexual again? Hopefully not here where my fellow workers can observe. I could play it cool and simply wait and see, but it annoys me that she has the ability to make me uneasy. "So, uh, what's up?"

Once again the coins clink on the pavement. "Barry told me where you work."

Right. And it's not like the factory parking lot is overflowing with psychedelically painted VW microbuses. But she still hasn't explained what she's doing here.

My fellow workers stare as they pass on the way to their cars, no doubt thinking that only a couple of weirdo hippies like us would choose to sit in a parking lot amid smatterings of broken bottles, cigarette butts, and spots of ground-in chewing gum. Do they still think I'm a spy for my father? I wonder. This is my third year at the junk-mail factory. I show up on time, do my job and anything else that's asked of me, and never leave early. If they knew anything about the counterculture, they'd understand that I'm probably the last person who'd turn on them.

Tinsley scribbles in the notebook. *Snap! Snap! Snap!* In the parking lot of the warehouse next door a couple of kids set off firecrackers left over from the Fourth of July. Four nights ago,

I took Alan up to Bayville to Adventure Park, a rinky-dink amusement center with half a dozen kiddie rides. From there we went to the crescent-shaped beach where every fifty yards bonfires burned and people were shooting off rockets and firecrackers. Alan likes to watch fireworks almost as much as he likes going on rides, but the loud bangs scare him if we get too close, so we sat on a low white concrete wall some distance away. When a cherry bomb went off nearby, he took my hand in his.

On the radio on the way home, we heard the DJ talking about Brian Jones, who'd been discovered dead in his swimming pool the day before.

"That sucks," I muttered to myself.

"Who's that?" Alan asked.

"Brian Jones? Ever heard of the Rolling Stones?"

He shook his head.

I don't know what threw me more: that Alan had no idea who Mick Jagger and crew were, or that someone as talented and famous as Brian Jones would so carelessly throw it all away when so many guys in Nam were spending each day desperately trying to stay alive.

"Think I'm strange?" Tinsley asks, bringing me back from my musings.

"Because you're sitting in a parking lot using an ancient way of figuring things out?"

"That and other things."

Is she referring to the incident at the junior high? Are we finally going to address the elephant in the parking lot? But before I can say *Yeah, that thing with your breast seemed a bit unusual,* something stops me. Instead I go with "Jim Morrison said people are strange—"

"When you're a stranger." Tinsley finishes the line.

Our eyes meet, and there's that connection again. Brautigan and Morrison—the high priests of our tribe. Either could have written the line *She does what she pleases with whomever pleases her.*

Tinsley tosses the coins again. I think about Robin. It's been eleven days since she left, the longest we've ever been apart. I've written to her every day. Sometimes twice. I've always enjoyed jotting down little snippets of poetry and whatnot, but this summer, for the first time, writing has become a salve on the stinging gash of separation. Only so far there's been no reply from my ladylove. (The change of address hasn't gone into effect yet, because yesterday the new issue of *Rolling Stone* arrived with Jim Morrison—speak of the devil—on the cover.) Is it the fault of the Royal Molasses Canada Post that no missive from Robin has yet arrived? Is Camp Juliette so deep in the sticks that the mail has to be flown in and out? I've read that in situations like that, the mail can only go out once a week.

I ache for a letter from her, reassurance that things are okay. The memory of the morning she departed replays constantly in my head, and not in a good way. The startled look on her face when I unexpectedly showed up. Her eyes filling with tears as she rolled up the window. I was so overcome with sadness at that moment that I wasn't processing much. But something about that morning has begun to prey on my thoughts. She didn't look pleased when I showed up. Didn't wave as she left. Didn't even look back.

Tinsley gathers the coins and puts them in a small drawstring sack. She plucks the cigarette from my fingers and takes a drag. "Ever been to the Planting Fields?"

"Never heard of them."

"You'll dig it." She gets to her feet and reaches down to help me up.

I hesitate before giving her my hand. "Does Barry know you're here?"

"I do as I please." She wiggles her fingers at me. "Now, come along, young man."

So **hip,**
So cool,
So **what?**

We ride in Tinsley's green Triumph Spitfire. There are some among my cohort who would balk at the materialism inherent in this current craze for British two-seater convertible sports cars. But to me the stylistic design and aerodynamic lines of Triumphs and Jaguars, Austin-Healeys and MGs, and of course the car James Bond made famous, the Aston Martin DB5 (though I've never seen one in real life), transcend materialism. They are works of art. And while Tinsley may go barefoot and dress like a hippie chick, it's pretty obvious that she's what Barry would call a postcard hippie, who's not willing to completely abandon the good life. To have a car like this, one suspects she has a PhD, as in Pop has Dough.

The Spitfire's top is down, the wind in our faces, and the new group Crosby, Stills & Nash on the tape deck. Their harmonies are mind-blowing. And guess what? They're scheduled to play next month at the music festival. Cousin Barry says that if he goes up to Zach's farm near Ottawa, they'll drive down and we'll meet there. My cousin's musical tastes lean toward blues and hard rock, so he's keen to see the Paul Butterfield Blues Band, the Who, Johnny Winter, and Hendrix (and so am I).

The late-afternoon sky is blue, and the summer air warm. We are two longhairs in a shiny green British sports car. It feels more like a movie than real life. Whenever another driver stares too long, I flash them the peace sign. Some flash one back. Some frown. A few give me the finger.

The Planting Fields are part of an old estate near Piping Rock, the golf club where Arno's parents believe he toils away the summer days as a caddy. Tinsley gets a blanket and her camera from the Spitfire's trunk. (I'm relieved that the English riding saddle remains behind—I can just imagine her wanting to play horsey in public.) We venture past a stone mansion with spouting fountains and out among the gardens and lawns.

Visitors are mostly divided into freaks and older gentlewomen. The freaks stick to the sod, a few playing guitars or throwing Frisbees. The ladies in their summer dresses stroll along the paths, admiring the horticulture.

Tinsley settles in the middle of the broad green lawn.

Having not been prepared for this adventure, all I have with me is half a J. We smoke in plain sight. If any undercover caretakers come along, we can put the joint out long before they reach us. Eating the remaining evidence is always an option.

We lie on our sides, facing each other. It may be late afternoon, but at this time of year the sun is pretty high. (As are we, especially for only half a J. I must remember to commend Arno on the quality of his weed.) Tinsley's hippie skirt settles on her curves. More buttons on her white blouse are open than closed. The green in her hazel irises comes out in the sunlight. When she sweeps her long mane off her neck, the sunlight catches the nearly microscopic blond hairs of her nape. Now that we're getting high, I'm wondering if the nervous sexual tension I'm feeling is all in my head. Is it some remnant of my pre–Semi-Miraculous Transformation self?

I flash back to the first time a girl at a party put the moves on me. We were standing in the kitchen, drinking rum and Cokes and joking around. Every once in a while when she laughed, she'd reach up and give my shoulder a playful shove. I just assumed it was what she always did. Only later did Arno irately inform me that she'd been hitting on me. It's still sometimes hard to tell the difference between someone who's interested and someone who's just the friendly, touchy-feely type.

For now, suppose I don't concern myself with why Tinsley wanted me to come here? Just because she has, or I imagine she has, an alluring, sexy vibe, does that mean I have to view it as a challenge? Instead, I find myself appreciating the ambiance of leisurely female companionship—this being something I did not have a lot of with Robin, who was always busy at school and after with the yearbook, sports, and other extracurricular activities. (No senioritis for her last spring.) Not that my heart has strayed one iota from my lady of the northern woods. My devotion to her remains as firmly resolute as Washington crossing the Delaware. But for now, lying here with a pretty girl—with nowhere pressing to go and nothing important to do—is very mellow.

❋ Long moments drift past like the clouds above. Thanks to the J, Tinsley and Lucas the Resolute settle into a fine *buzzzzzzz*. Someone nearby with a guitar picks out *"Suzzzzzzzz-anne."* In the grass, *teenzzzzzy* six-legged leafhoppers flit about. Some are all green, some green and orange with a black stripe through their *eyezzzzz*. Lucas is a blue, red, and orange two-legged hair hopper snuggling in the delicate *fuzzzzzz* on Tinsley's neck.

"That day at the junior high?" Tinsley says. "You were so funny."

"Was I?" *Wuzzzz I? Wuzzzz Buzzzzz Bunny a wabbit?*

"For a second I thought you were going to jump up and run away," Tinsley says.

Buzz Bunny's first impulse is to protest that that *wuzzzz* not the case, but why spoil this fine *buzzzzz* by arguing?

"So what *wuuzzz* that about?" Buzz asks.

"What do *you* think it was about?" Tinsley asks with a sparkle in her eye. Could merely be the reflection of the sun, but one suspects it is more than that. Though Lucas wishes it weren't. Her insistence on conversation threatens his lovely but fragile high.

A few more tokes and he would have been molten.

"It was your idea," he says. "Why don't *you* tell *me*?"

"It made you uncomfortable, didn't it?"

"Yeah, a little."

"Why?"

"Because Barry was right there?"

"So? He and I aren't exclusive. For your information, monogamy is just another stupid male paradigm foisted on women to keep us subservient. Why can't women be as free with our proclivities as men?"

"Fine with me." It dawns on him that the path of least resistance is agreement. And yet Sir Lucas the Faithful is not free, nor dost he yearn to be.

"And it *is* liberating," Tinsley goes on. "Do you know that from the age of twelve, not only was I expected to always have a boyfriend, but I was a failure if I couldn't 'keep' him? Forget about casual dating. That makes me a slut and a tramp. Just a 'thing' men can use and discard. But if a guy sleeps around, he's a stud and a playboy. Who made up these stupid rules? Men."

The male in their midst is painfully aware that a statement involving deductive reasoning has been put forth. (Or maybe it's inductive reasoning? Is there such a thing as conductive reasoning? Has anyone asked ducks how they feel about this? When asked, do they duck the question?) "So now you go around putting guys' hands on your breast?"

"If that's what I feel like doing, why not? Do you have a problem with it?"

From the mystic misty swirl inside the crystal ball comes a glimpse of the discourse ahead. Lucas has been summoned to a repartee partee. But to gain admission, it will behoove him to organize complex thoughts and multisyllabic words into compound sentences. This is not what he wishes to be doing on this lovely late afternoon, but he feels obligated to give it a try: "Suppose I'd taken your hand and put it down my pants? You'd think I was a pervert. But when you place my hand on your breast, that's just sexual liberation?"

Princess Tinsley's smile widens. While she conjures what to say next, Sir Lucas perceives a sort of liberation of his own. A sense of being able to blurt out whatever he chooses without concern for the ramifications. In contrast, when he is in the presence of fair Lady Robin, even while tripping, Sir Lucas of the Round Table(t) often feels that care must be taken concerning the proclamations that escape his lips. With Robin, there are limits to how mad or preposterous he can act and still feel "safe" to her ladyship, lest he cause her to doubt that he is indeed a suitable consort (*see* drive home from Cambridge). But with the mischievous pixie Princess Tinsley, what is there to lose? Why not let it all hang out?

But before anything is allowed to hang anywhere, a blue Frisbee lands within arm's reach. Fifty feet away, a guy with red hair waves. Tinsley hops up and whips a flawless backhand straight at him. She turns and looks down at me with a triumphant grin.

"Show-off," I say as Sir Lucas trudges off into the mystic misty swirl. The intrusion of the blue disk has broken the spell. The lark is over. Arno's grass was excellent; there just wasn't enough of it.

"Why? Because I've got a good arm . . . *for a girl?*"

Little does she know that Robin can fling a forehand that'll go half a furlong easy. Tinsley waves to the red-haired guy, who slings the Frisbee back her way. Okay, I get it. She wants to show me that she can have sex with whomever she likes and play Frisbee with whomever she wants. *She does what she pleases with whomever pleases her.* But is there something forced about it? Doth the lady protest too much?

While Tinsley exercises her freedom, I roll onto my back, wishing for no exercise more challenging than watching the hazy edges of the clouds seep into the blue above. But no dice. Invasive thoughts pierce the faded cannabis curtain. It's been eleven days and still no letter from Robin. I know that, like me, she is a practitioner of monogamy. At least serial monogamy. But what about the other aspects of women's liberation? Does she also feel restrained and suppressed by the patriarchal society we appear to live in? We've never talked about it. And speaking of patriarchs, what is the paterfamilias if not a shining example of a first-class womanizer? How can Mom stand it? Why, in this enlightened day and age, does she tolerate it?

A loud roar cuts these agitated thoughts short. High above, two fighter jets rocket across my field of vision. And thus I am reminded that we are not far from the Grumman Corporation, which makes many millions of dollars selling airborne killing machines to the government so it can incinerate, maim, and murder barefoot peasants. Such jet-propelled agents of destruction are a reminder that while Tinsley and I enjoy this beautiful, peaceful, sun-washed afternoon, eight thousand miles away,

Chris stalks an enemy through shoulder-high elephant grass that tears through uniforms and skin and causes oozing infections. We hear soft guitar music; he listens for hints of a VC ambush. I smoke grass for fun; he smokes it to dull the constant gnawing terror. I take life for granted; he has only one wish — to get through the next hour alive.

And what have I done to avoid a similar fate? I looked up Thoreau, Albert Camus, Bertrand Russell, and Thomas Aquinas in our *World Book Encyclopedia* at home, but that wasn't much help. Then I went to the library and found some books by, or about, those deep thinkers. (I probably should have tried the *Encyclopaedia Britannica* while at the library, but I've always found it hard to read.)

Anyway, those library books are currently gathering dust in my room. I keep intending to read them, but it seems that all I do when I'm at my desk is write to Robin.

Having finished Frisbeeing, Tinsley again joins me on the blanket, breathing deeply, a fine patina of sweat shiny on her forehead. She gently rakes her fingers through her long yellow hair, and as she does, her blouse opens just enough to reveal the soft inner curve of a breast. In a moment of weakness, I imagine leaning close and kissing her delicate throat, then letting my lips graze the soft skin farther down.

"What are *you* thinking?" She makes her eyes go wide and asks in a way that implies that she thinks she knows *exactly* what I'm thinking. I feel my face flush, and quickly knee-jerk an alibi.

"Uh . . . about whether the encyclopedia your parents buy you is a predictor of your future intellect. Grow up with the

Encyclopaedia Britannica and you'll be president. Get stuck with the *World Book* and you'll be mopping bathrooms."

She gives me a sideways glance. "Liar."

She's right. And why should I feel embarrassed about looking? She knows how she's dressed and what she's revealing. "Okay. I was thinking about kissing your neck and breasts."

Tinsley nods as matter-of-factly as if I'd just pointed out that it's Tuesday. "The other day my mother accused me of being a temptress. She's worried that I might be 'prone to promiscuity.' I swear, Lucas, those are the exact words the old mare used."

Once again, nervous arousal riffles through me. A little while ago, I was happy lying here, comfortable, at peace gazing at this pretty, sexy waif. (Okay, *and* enjoying the benign stirring in my loins that she evokes.) Now I feel the need once again to remind myself that my heart shall never stray from the cold Canadian woods, where Lady Robin daily fends off horny lumberjacks and hungry polar bears.

"Lucas?" Tinsley nudges me back to the Lower Forty-Eight. "Sorry?"

"What about you?"

"Uh, definitely prone to promiscuity."

"Stop it. Seriously. Tell me about your family."

Oh, no, not *that*. Dear pixie princess, must we explore territory that I don't like to venture into when I'm straight, much less while mildly high and luxuriating on a lovely early evening with a lass such as yourself?

Thankfully, Tinsley must sense my discomfort. "We don't have to talk about it if you don't want to." She claps her hands like a kindergarten teacher and asks brightly, "What shall we talk about instead?"

Thank God! *Quick, Lucas, come up with something.* "Barry said he met you at an art show. I'm not sure I ever thought of photography as art."

Tinsley makes her eyes bug out. "Seriously? You've never heard of Ansel Adams? Diane Arbus? Man Ray? Stieglitz?"

When I admit that I haven't, she launches — much to my relief — into a lecture about the history of photography as art, then admits that for her, that aspect is only a hobby. What she really wants to study is photojournalism. She's just graduated from Ethel Walker, a private boarding school in Connecticut, and was set to attend someplace called the California Institute of the Arts in the fall, but then her mother came across an article about last year's Valentine's Day dance, which most of the students and faculty attended naked. That was the end of that. Now Tinsley's trying to find a more discreet photography program, but it's too late to apply for this coming fall (tell me about it), so she's thinking about taking classes at the School of Visual Arts as a part-time student. (That won't work for me. Part-time students don't qualify for the 2-S deferment.)

But I do so enjoy hearing her go on about *her* life (if Charles thinks I live a life of privilege, what would he think of Tinsley?) instead of inspecting mine. In a way, she's not all that different from Robin. They're both passionate about causes (Robin: anti-war, Tinsley: women's lib). Both interested in careers (Robin: the environment, Tinsley: photojournalism).

Mom was a journalist before she gave it up to become a

mother. I bet there was a cause (or causes?) that she was once passionate about. (The way she advocates for Alan and tends her garden are like causes. You can see she's got that drive and focus.) Where did I hear that men are attracted to women who are like their mothers? Yikes! *Oh, man, there'll be no getting back to that fine afternoon buzz now.*

Long shadows have begun to creep across the Planting Fields' emerald lawns. We've picked up the blanket and started back to the parking lot when Tinsley says, "Tell me about your girlfriend."

"Really smart and together. Textbook example of opposites attracting."

Robin grew up with the *Encyclopaedia Britannica*. Why didn't I? Was it simply a matter of which encyclopedia salesman rang the doorbell first?

"How long have you been with her?"

"Nine months."

"Are you exclusive?"

"Yes. . . . Is that really so bad?"

"No, if that's your thing."

We've reached the lot, where the golden sunset reflects off the windshields of the parked cars. People are leaving. Both the afternoon light and the very last of that excellent high are ebbing away. The blanket goes back into the Spitfire's trunk with the saddle. I settle into the passenger seat. Beside me in the driver's seat, Tinsley doesn't put the key into the ignition. Instead she leans back against the headrest and gazes upward. Above us, the few clouds are edged with pink. Tinsley reaches over, takes my hand, and places it in her lap. *Interesting.* My jeans start to feel tight in a certain area. Temptation percolates. But so do discomfort and inner conflict. Her eyes drifting toward mine, she says, "You know what they say: Today is the first day of the rest of your life."

Hmmmm. They do say that, don't they? It's one of the mantras the counterculture has embraced. Given the location of my hand and her anti-monogamous leanings, I can only assume that she's inviting (daring?) me to join her in its practice.

Is this why she showed up at the factory today?

The siren calls, and yet something keeps me tethered to the mast. Robin would never have to know, so what could possibly be holding me back? Don't I fit the definition of alienated youth? Rejecter of the prudish and rigid mores that my parents' generation holds sacred — the paterfamilias excepted?

Or is *that* it? Is my rejection of all things paterfamilial so complete that I can't allow myself to venture where *he* would surely not hesitate to go? Even if Robin never knows, getting it on with Tinsley would be an act of betrayal. *I* would know. The guilt would be my burden to shoulder.

An unexpected sense of failure envelops me. Is it possible that I'm a phony, a pretender to those of my countercultural kind, as bogus as those plastic heads in the church basement the other night?

On July 8, 1969, Lucas Baker, self-styled rebel, socialist, and druggie, was horrified to discover that despite all his long-haired antiestablishment airs, he was, deep down, pitifully middle-class.

I remove my hand from her lap. "Tinsley, I think you're

90

incredibly attractive, and sexy and interesting, and I know this probably won't make any sense to you, but even if this is the first day of the rest of my life, it's a life in which I want to be faithful."

On the way back to the factory, we listen to more Crosby, Stills & Nash. Whenever our eyes meet, Tinsley smiles in a way that doesn't seem forced. In fact, she appears totally cool with my decision. I find myself mystified and fascinated by her. She may be a postcard hippie, but she's still not like anyone I've encountered before.

By the time we return to the parking lot and Odysseus, it's getting dark.

"Thanks for introducing me to the Planting Fields."

"You're welcome!" Tinsley replies cheerfully, and even plants a kiss on my cheek.

I climb out of the Spitfire, but before I step away, there's one last question on my mind: "The *Encyclopaedia Britannica* or the *World Book*?"

The question hangs in the warm evening air for a moment. Admittedly it's come from far out in left field.

Tinsley scowls. "Sorry?"

"Which one do you have?"

"Neither," she says.

"You have some other encyclopedia?"

"No, we don't have one."

Amazing.

WEDNESDAY, JULY 9

Days Until Camp Juliette: 16

Finally! On my desk is a letter from Robin in a white envelope with a blue stamp of a lady wearing a tiara. Like a desperate addict who's finally found his fix, I rip it open. Inside are folded sheets of lined paper torn from a spiral notebook.

6/27/69

Dear Lucas,

I suppose you can tell from the jumpiness of my handwriting that I'm writing this on the bus. Thank you for that sweet letter you gave me this morning. What a nice surprise! I've read it twice and thought a lot about us. In fact, it's all I've thought about since I got on the bus.

We're just passing Plattsburgh and I've been sitting here with this notebook on my lap for hours thinking about what I want to say. I've even cried a few times, as you can probably tell from the water spots.

Now, after all that thinking, I'm writing, but I don't know if I will ever send this to you. Maybe I'll change my mind. I think I will wait a few days before I send it. Oh, God, you probably don't care about that. You're probably wondering what I've been crying about.

Here's the reason: when it comes to you and me, I feel stuck and don't know what to do. I love you, Lucas, but there's so much about our relationship that I find disturbing. Some things have been bothering me for a while. Others didn't begin to crystallize until we went to Maine.

I have to be honest with you and with myself. I know you'd want me to. As you could probably tell, I didn't enjoy the trip very much. I liked it when we could find a quiet place to read, but I didn't like living in the microbus. I hated not being able to shower and feeling dirty all the time. (Sponge bathing in restaurant and gas station bathrooms really doesn't cut it.) I wasn't comfortable sleeping on Odysseus's thin mattress. And I hated how mean people and the police were to us simply because of our hair and clothes. Well, and because of Odysseus.

Do I sound like a bourgeois spoiled brat? I bet you think I do. And that's also something I'm worried about. I know how you despise capitalism and middle-class values. You know how much I admire your beliefs, how you work every summer in that factory when you don't have to and refuse to accept anything from your parents. But if that means you'll always want to take vacations in your microbus and wash in public bathrooms and cook meals on a camp stove, I honestly wonder if I can share that lifestyle with you.

Oh, Lucas, I'm sorry if it sounds like I'm coming down hard on you. But there's more. The drugs. You know I don't mind smoking grass once in a while. But not all the time. Until we went to Maine, I don't think I realized how much you smoked. Starting nearly every day before noon? And you must sense that I'm not comfortable with you using LSD. I was so anxious and worried during the drive home.

To be honest, Lucas, I think the phrase "not comfortable" describes how I'm feeling about us in general. There are many wonderful things about you. When we first started going together, I thought I could help you with some of the problems you were facing. Maybe I even imagined that I could change you.

But I've realized that what's happened is the opposite. You've changed me. And in ways I'm not happy about or comfortable with. (There's that word again.) Maybe what I'm trying to say is that I'm worried about where all this is leading. What's going to happen in a few months when we start college? Goddard sounds like the kind of school where everyone gets high. Do you really think you'll be able to function at a college level if you're stoned all the time? And when you come to Middlebury on the weekends, are you going to want to take LSD?

I hope it doesn't sound like I'm nagging. I'm just trying to be honest.

Robin

The spiral notebook pages end there. There's a second letter, written on unlined light-blue stationery, but before I begin reading it, I need to take a deep breath and steady the queasy foreboding that's spread through me. It feels like the floor is breaking apart beneath me. I'm not quite in free fall, but I could really use a solid handhold.

Maybe the news gets better in the next letter.

7/4/69

Dear Lucas,

Thank you for all the letters. The one about Goddard rejecting you came today (the Canadians don't celebrate the 4th) and I'm so sorry and worried about you. What are you going to do about the draft? Is there any way to get out of

95

going to Vietnam? Some way to fail the physical? Maybe Dr. Hill could write a letter?

I'm sorry I haven't written sooner. I have to be honest. It's not just being super busy with the start of camp. It's also the uncertainty I'm still feeling about us. I'm sorry to make you wait so long for a letter, but I haven't been able to figure out how I feel or what to say. It makes me feel cruel, but I know you wouldn't want me to lie and say everything is fine when it isn't.

You've been saying in your letters how much you're looking forward to driving up and seeing me in a few weeks, but are you sure you want to come all this way? Shouldn't you spend the time figuring out how to get out of the draft? I've gotten my schedule and I'll only be able to take off one day to be with you. And I'll have to be back in the bunk by ten p.m. Also, except for visiting day, they don't allow noncampers on the property. If you come up, I'll have to see you off camp property. There's hardly anything around here except woods.

Lucas, we both know how you sometimes procrastinate about important things. Please don't put off doing something about the draft. Please don't wait until it's too late.

Robin

My hands are trembling. I'm shattered. If someone suddenly appeared out of nowhere and swung a two-by-four into my face, I couldn't feel more blindsided. Chris has written about the Dear John letters some of the guys in his company have gotten. As if it isn't horrible enough to get wrenched out of your life and shipped to a hellish jungle with a thousand ways to die, guys get letters from girlfriends saying they've met someone new. One guy got a Dear John letter *from his wife* after only three weeks.

The postmark on Robin's letter is July 5. It took four days to get here. She's been gone almost two weeks, and I've written at least a dozen letters to her. In April, when her parents took her to Florida for Easter vacation, I received a long Shalimar-scented letter on lavender paper every day. Each one signed *With All My Love, Robin.*

I bring the light-blue stationery close, but there's not the slightest hint of perfume. And it's signed simply *Robin.* Sounds like she began having doubts long before she left for camp. She once told me that I had blind spots, things that I didn't see that were obvious to her. I know that's true, but in this case, is the problem that I haven't been seeing or that Robin's been hiding her feelings?

What does it matter now? My heart's deflated and my eyes are watery. Guess you don't have to be in Vietnam to receive a devastating Dear John letter. I squeeze the tears away with my thumb and forefinger. This is so unexpected, so out of the blue. I'm crushed, stunned by her ambivalence. Yes, the trip to Maine was a bummer, but I didn't think it was *that* bad. And it's not like this is the first, or even second, time Robin's voiced discomfort with my "lifestyle" and beliefs. It's not new to her. Why did she have to wait until she went away to share all these feelings? Was she afraid to tell me face-to-face? That's so unlike her.

I sit back, stare at the ceiling, feel my eyes fill with tears again. Let's be honest. She did share her feelings. The time she told me about some river in Ohio that was so polluted it had caught fire a dozen times, and I insisted that was impossible. The next day she showed me the clipping from the newspaper. For several days after that she was remote and uncommunicative. I knew she was waiting for me to apologize. Why didn't I?

And that book about the environment that she asked me to read — *Silent Spring* or something. I didn't get past the first chapter.

And the time she and I sat on the grass at the duck pond all afternoon after I dropped a pink football-shaped tab of mescaline. Everything seemed insanely funny — the way a Frisbee bumped on an air current, the way the ducks did that thing where their heads go down in the water and their feathery butts point up into the air. I laughed and laughed until my lungs hurt, not realizing what a bore I was being.

Why couldn't I have been more sensitive and aware with Robin? Why couldn't I have tried just a little harder?

A wave of fresh tears erupts. My fist slams the desktop hard enough to make everything jump and rattle. For the past nine months, Robin has been my anchor, the rock-steady rhythm section of my life. Before her, I had no idea how reassuring the attention of someone so smart and caring could be. But now that I've felt it, been swaddled in it, she can't just take it away. The tears become sobs. Shoulders trembling, I bury my face in my hands. *Get ahold of yourself, man. . . .*

Besides, there's a sliver of hope. The ground beneath me may have disintegrated, but like Wile E. Coyote in a Road Runner cartoon, I'm still suspended in that cartoon sky, churning my arms and legs. I know Robin. It was hard for her to get to the point where she could say she loved me. We started going together in October, and it wasn't until March that the words managed to squeeze themselves through her lips. But once they were stated, I knew it was for real. So if she took that long to fall in love, she's not going to fall out of love overnight, is she? Isn't saying she feels uncertain a way of asking for reassurance?

I wipe away the tears, take a steadying breath, and pick up a pen. Then change my mind and decide to use a pencil. I need to craft my response carefully.

7/9/69

Dear Robin,

It was good to finally get your letters. I was starting to worry that maybe they don't have regular mail up there in the hinterland. That they use carrier pigeons or the mail carriers travel by mooseback.

Okay, enough joking. I guess you must have known that your letters were going to shake me up big-time. And I understand now why it took you so long to send them. I understand the way you feel about the Maine trip. I guess we forget that we live in an enlightened progressive bubble on Long Island. There are a lot of jerks and squares in the world (especially Maine). Like you said, if people and the cops had been nicer to us, we would have had a better time. And I dig how you feel about living out of Odysseus. It's not for everyone. And it's not like it's something I always have to do, either. Next trip, I promise we'll figure out better places to stay. I'll make sure you get lots of opportunities to shower.

If you're thinking that's the easy stuff to fix, I agree. What's hard is trying to understand the way you're feeling. I guess the problem is that you feel like you had two bad trips in one. First was the crappy way we were treated and the second was lunatic Lucas tripping during the drive back to Long Island.

But the thing is, neither one of those bad trips was permanent. Do they really mean you have to doubt our entire relationship? We don't have to go to Maine again, and I don't have to take acid and drive again. In fact, I don't have to take acid again, period. I've tripped plenty. Maybe enough is enough, you know?

And I get the stuff about me smoking too much grass. I don't entirely disagree. I think I should cut back on all forms of inhalation (except breathing, of course). All that smoke can't be good for one's health.

Also, I appreciate your concern on the draft front. I've been talking to a draft counselor about something called a moral case for refusing to participate in war. Usually conscientious objector cases are based on religious beliefs like the Jehovah's Witnesses or Quakers because they're considered Peace Churches that have always been opposed to military service. But Charles, my draft counselor, is going to help me construct a case based on personal moral code and the just-war theories of Thomas Aquinas and secular thinkers like Camus (*The Stranger*, remember?), Thoreau, and Bertrand Russell.

I'm hoping that once I've gotten past the draft problem, we can be together next year. I could move up to Waitsfield or Warren and work at a ski area.

And as far as coming up to see you the week after next, I'm not worried about not being able to go on camp property as long as you can get off it. Even if it's only for one day, it'll be worth it. You know how much I love you, Robin. Seriously, I would come all that way even if it was just for a few hours.

So my sweet, sweet sweetheart, please don't make any drastic decisions about us and our future together. Not when we're so far apart. I remember how long it took you to get to the point where you felt what we had was real. And once you got there, you were totally committed. That's the way I still feel. I miss you like crazy. Love you like crazy. Seriously, if this is all you're worried about (is there anything you haven't brought up that I should know about?), I can fix it. Less grass smoking, no acid, and no more living out of Odysseus.

Consider it done. Love you buckets and buckets. Counting the days till we're together again.

Love,

Lucas

Finished. First time in my life I've edited and revised a personal letter and then written a final draft. My eleventh-grade English teacher, Miss Landers, would be proud. She was always telling me I didn't revise enough. (I didn't revise, period.) My hand is cramped from all that penmanship. And yet, almost immediately I feel the urge to start another letter. But I catch myself. *Be cool, man. Don't overwhelm her. Don't sound desperate even if that's the way you feel.*

The truth is, I feel shredded. Shredded, empty, and hurting. It isn't even dinnertime (not that I have an appetite), and there are hours to go until the welcoming oblivion of sleep. That mantra about today being the first day of the rest of your life may be true, but if today were to be the first day of a life without Robin, I'm not sure I'd want to live until tomorrow. I'm hoping that, sixteen days from now, I'll truck on up there and make things right. But for now, out comes my Swiss Army knife. With the Phillips head, I unscrew the bottom of my stereo and pull some reds out of my stash.

> I don't **have** a drug **problem,**
> **Except when** I don't **have drugs.**

SATURDAY, JULY 12

Days Until Camp Juliette: 13

"Don't say anything," Arno warns. His face is puffy and, except for a whitish band across his eyes, streaked the reddish-brown color of an overripe strawberry. He stinks of menthol and mothballs — the scent of Noxzema skin cream.

I can't stop staring. "What'd you do?"

"Iodine and baby oil," Milton says.

Girls use that mixture to get darkly tanned fast, but it never comes out like this. Arno's face looks like it's been napalmed.

"Fell asleep under the sunlamp. My parents were giving me grief about being so pale." He does one of his nasal imitations: "'How can you be so pale when you're outside caddying every day?' 'Some sun would be good for you.'"

"Does it hurt?" I ask.

"Only when someone asks a stupid question."

We pile into the GTO. Despite Arno's roasted epidermis, the car pulsates with excited anticipation. We are going to see Led Zeppelin, the wailingest, heaviest, nastiest band in all the land.

"Anyone want to drop?" I ask from the back seat. "Dazed and Confused" is blasting on the tape deck. After three days of nonstop despair over Robin, I yearn for psychedelic reprieve. I know I wrote that I wasn't going to trip anymore, and I intend to keep my word. But before I made *that* pledge, I'd made myself a promise to save this righteous acid for this special occasion. As of tomorrow, I'm quitting acid for good.

"Whatcha got?" Arno asks, purely from a business point of view. He's only dropped acid once. Never wanted to do it again.

"Windowpane." I hold up two paper-thin squares of gelatin for him to see in the rearview.

"Too bad it's not Owsley."

"There's other good acid besides Owsley."

"Maybe. Maybe not."

"Want a taste?" I ask Milton.

He shakes his head. He's never tripped.

"Come on, man, just this once," I urge him. "I've got enough for both of us. Tonight would be the coolest first trip ever. Led Zeppelin on acid. Something to tell your grandchildren about."

"Unless they're born without ears," Arno says. There's a rumor that LSD scrambles your chromosomes and results in abnormal babies.

Milton won't budge. "Sorry, Lucas. It's not happening."

"Oh, well. Better living through chemistry, *mis amigos*." I place the acid on my tongue and sit back.

Arno points through the windshield. The sun is low and orange in the sky. "Hey, Lucas, look. Gonna stare at it till you go blind?"

"Don't be a tool."

"Who's the tool?" Arno says. "Now instead of enjoying the concert, we're gonna have to make sure you don't climb up a tree and try to fly."

"If acid's that bad, why are you planning to sell it at the music festival?" I ask.

"Hey, I'm not telling anyone to take it," Arno says. "I'm just making it available in case they're stupid enough to want to."

"You and Dow Chemical," I taunt, then do an imitation of my own: "'Just because we make napalm, it's not our fault if the army uses it to incinerate thousands of Vietnamese women and children.'"

"Hey, what's going on with the draft, Lucas?" Arno says, deflecting. "Hear about the guy who got Four-F'ed by smearing peanut butter around his butt hole? When he bent over and spread his cheeks at the physical, the army doctor asked, 'What's that?' The guy stuck his finger back there, then put it in his mouth and said, 'Hm, tastes like peanut butter.'"

"Very funny, Arno."

Milton looks over the seat at me. "What's the latest?"

The latest is I don't want to think about the draft while I'm on the launchpad at Cape Windowpane, counting down to liftoff. The Selective Service Special Form for Conscientious Objector came in the mail yesterday. Here's how it begins:

105

1. Do you believe in a Supreme Being?   [   ] Yes   [   ] No
2. Describe the nature of your belief.
3. Explain how, when, and from whom or from what source you received the training and acquired your belief.
4. Give the name and present address of the individual upon whom you rely most for religious guidance.

There may not be any atheists in foxholes, but I'm not in a foxhole . . . yet. I spoke to Charles on the phone last night. He said not to sweat. We'll meet on Monday to discuss it.

"It's under control," I tell Milton, uncomfortably aware that it's not. "What do you hear from Rudy?"

"He's really depressed. Can't find a decent piano. When you're at his level, every day that you don't practice you lose a little bit. At this point, he thinks it'll take months to get back to where he was."

If you get back to where you were, aren't you still where you are? Or are you where you were before you got back?

I think liftoff may have begun.

The first time I tripped was November of junior year. Grass had been on the scene for a couple of years, but psychedelic drugs like mescaline, peyote, and LSD were just beginning to find purchase in the suburban New York high-school landscape. The three of us got together early on a Saturday morning at the house of a kid named Stuart. Arno, Stuart, and I dropped. Milton came along to chaperone.

Because of all the stories about people going apeshit while tripping, Stuart wouldn't let us in his house. So after we dropped, we climbed up on his roof and watched planes become huge silver hawks, and clouds turn into pink and green faces. We walked to a nearby pond and tossed rocks into the glassy water while Milton expounded on how the ever-widening ripples mirrored the ever-expanding universe. (Maybe he doesn't need acid to trip.) We wandered over to the country club to play tennis even though the nets had been taken down for the winter. Each bouncing white ball was trailed by dozens of round white afterimages.

Around four in the afternoon, we disbanded. When I got home, Mom and Musclini were waiting at the front door with stern expressions. They ordered me into the living room. Had a neighbor seen my friends and me on the tennis courts behaving strangely and called them?

My parents sat at opposite ends of the couch. I sat in a low easy chair across from them.

"We know you spent the day with Arno, Milton, and Stuart," Mom said accusingly. "We spoke to their parents."

While not tripping as intensely as I had been earlier, I was still having some bizarre hallucinations. Even though our living-room floor is made of slate, when I reached over and pressed my fingertip down, it created a depression about half an inch deep in the stone.

"You all left at the same time this morning," Mom went on. Her face had started to resemble a gargoyle's. Her skin was concrete gray, mouth beak-like. "You told us you were going to Milton's, but you didn't. Milton told his parents he was coming here."

I pressed my finger deeper into the slate and wondered how screwed I was. Acid was serious stuff. It was rumored that under its influence people had tried to chew the bark off trees, committed murder, and, God forbid, indulged in orgies.

"You went to Stuart's house, didn't you?" Musclini's hair was growing longer and whiter by the second. He'd begun sprouting a long white beard as well.

"We've told you we don't want you hanging around with him," said Mom. Were those red earrings or flames flickering from her pointed gargoyle ears?

Looking like a white-haired maharishi in a gray sweatshirt and blue dungarees, Musclini leaned forward, hands clasped, looking grim. In his eyes, I was already a failure. I'd quit tennis, refused to do household chores, taken up smoking, begun to grow my hair long, and didn't care for wheat germ.

He cleared his throat. The moment of truth had arrived: the ax was about to fall. Gravely, he asked, "Did you . . . smoke pot today?"

By now a small solar system of miniature planets and lollipops was orbiting his head. His face was barely visible beneath the long white hair and beard. Only squares over thirty called it "pot" and referred to "potheads."

"Yes," I lied.

They grounded me for a month.

• • •

108

Looming up in the cityscape, buildings inhale and exhale. Like tent caterpillars and woolly mammoths, they are carbon-based life-forms that burn fuel for energy and need water to survive. As with other living creatures, they will eventually grow infirm and fall down.

"Small houses grow into big houses, then into small buildings, and finally into big buildings." In the GTO, with the rush of the Windowpane still coming on, I expound on urban sprawl while wearing a red-and-white-striped ski hat I found on the seat next to me. It's a baby Cat in the Hat hat that hasn't yet grown all its stripe stripes.

"You're so right." Arno reaches back over the seat and pulls the hat hat off my head head.

"What'd you do that for?"

"I'm going to need it."

"You already have red stripes."

Milton laughs.

✳ "Who are the Panther Twenty-One?" Lucas the Inquisitive has paused to consider the words "Free the Panther 21" spray-painted on the stone wall beside Central Park.

"A group of Black Panthers who've been arrested on trumped-up charges of planning to blow up police stations," Milton says.

Arno hooks a finger through one of Lucas's belt loops and tugs. Buses rumble past, taxis honk, waves of headlights course through this dense, dark, humid urban fishbowl.

It's the first time Lucas of Long I Land has been to the

city since May, when Robin, her parents, and he marched in an antiwar demonstration around Greenwich Village, chanting "No more war!" and carrying signs that said HELL NO, WE WON'T GO!

Back then the war was an abstraction, a subject for passionate debate over mugs of Constant Comment and crappy-tasting carob brownies. Tonight, the war is real and immediate. It's a huge black-and-red-striped panther with long pointed white fangs stalking in the shadows.

Lucas wraps his arms around a sidewalk tree and peeks back.

Arno groans with aggravation. "Now what?"

"It's following us." Lucas feels the rough bark against his cheek, the sap inside the tree flowing like water through a hose. The Windowpane's rush continues to intensify.

"What is?" Milton asks.

"The war panther."

"How many hits of Windowpane did you say you had?" Arno asks.

"Two."

"And how many do you have now?"

"Uhhh."

"For Christ's sake." Arno pries the tree hugger away from the tree.

On a dark, winding walkway through the park, it's now Lucas with a finger through Arno's belt loop. Flying bugs rocket in kamikaze orbits around lampposts. Someone in front of them has a halo. Out of the dark, over the distant honking and rumble of engines, comes the bell-like knell of soaring guitar notes.

"B.B. King," says Milton.

The music builds, the crowd congesting on the walkway. The rush of the Windowpane has grown into an intense audio-visual swirl. Around the Wollman skating rink the horde is thick and milling, the music searing. The show itself is hidden behind tall walls. Outside those walls, huge shadowy tank-size war spiders creep behind the dark trees.

Lucas the Paleontologist wants to tell Arno and Milton about the black-and-red Vietnamese pterodactyls gliding in and out of the silver night clouds above. But the complex process of conjuring words, placing them in the correct order, and then speaking them aloud seems beyond his capability.

"I'm supposed to meet Clyde up there." Arno points at a hill-size lump of gray art-class clay and pulls on the red-and-white knit ski cap cap.

"Who?" Milton asks.

From Lucas's mouth, unbidden, comes, "Giant Clyde-eyed cyclops war panther."

Arno ignores him. "The dealer. Look for a guy with a beard and a red bandanna."

Lucas the Ignored is led up gummy steps to a doughy crag. Above them, goat-legged black-pajamaed Vietcong satyrs scamper over the clay. Across the walkway below, light foam effervesces over the tall walls around the skating rink where King B.B. rules the air.

"Here, pussy pussy," a voice in the dark growls. Someone with a beard, wearing a red bandanna like a skullcap, steps out of the shadows. It's Abe Lincoln with deadly red eyes, wearing a sleeveless denim jacket adorned with medals, chains, and patches. His bare arms are tattooed with skulls, daggers, and roses. The acrid scent of long-marinating body odor wafts into Lucas the Terrified's nostrils.

Even when one is tripping, there can be moments of clarity. Or, at least, of imagined clarity. A shudder quakes through Lucas. This is not some enterprising young college dealer picking up extra scratch. Nor some struggling musician pulling together next month's rent. This is a real, honest-to-God, smelly, tattooed, scary-looking criminal.

We're not in the suburbs anymore, amigos.

For a moment, the *tres amigos* are speechless. Then, possibly to break the ice, Milton says, "Hells Angel?"

"Pagan's, dumbass." President Lincoln turns so they can see the big white-and-blue Pagan's patch on the back of his jacket.

"Why the apostrophe?" asks Lucas.

"Ignore him; he's tripping," Arno says.

The Great Emancipator sets his hairy reddened eyeballs on Arno. "What's with your face, man?"

"Barbecue," Lucas the Wit says.

"Shut the fuck up," Arno snaps, now all tough guy in front of Bizzaro Abe, the anti-president. Then says, "Sunburn."

"Where's the bread?" The Rail-Splitter extends a hand. Long, dirty nails with black crescents. The Pagan's definitely need to bone up on punctuation and personal hygiene. Miss

112

Landers would have made mincemeat of Clyde. Nothing drove her crazier than misplaced apostrophes. Miss Landers on a chopper wearing a leather vest with paper-clip chains. Tattooed on her arms, the fourteen punctuation marks of English grammar. The patch on her back: "Hell's Grammarians."

Arno hesitates. "It's Owsley, right?"

"Crowley, yeah," says Honest Abe.

"Owsley," Arno corrects him. "The Grateful Dead's guy."

"Right." Red-eyed Clyde wriggles his dirty fingers. "So, how about it?"

"As long as it's Owsley," Arno says, stalling nervously.

"Look, you want the acid or not?" Impatient Abe snaps. The ominous tone in his voice is only outdone by the reddish menace in his eyes.

Or maybe he has pinkeye.

Arno hands over a small wad. The late great president quickly fans five Ben Franklins, then crushes them in his fist. "Be right back." He vanishes into the dark.

Even on a double dose of Windowpane, Lucas the Blitzed senses the extraordinary nature of what's just gone down. He's never even seen a hundred-dollar bill before. But it's Milton who gets to the point. "You . . . just gave . . . five *hundred* dollars . . . to . . . a stranger?"

"He came highly recommended," Arno says defensively.

"By *Good Housekeeping*?" asks Lucas.

"Shut your face!"

Loud cheers and applause erupt from the other side of the wall around the skating rink.

"B.B. must've finished his set," says Milton. "Let's go."

Still wearing the red-and-white cap, Arno doesn't move. "Can't. Gotta wait here for Clyde."

In the midst of all the noise and movement, a lull descends. Have we heard Arno correctly? Did he actually say he's *not* going to see Led Zeppelin?

"Are you serious?" asks Lucas the Dumbfounded.

"Are *you* tripping?" snaps Arno.

"We'll save you a seat," Milton says.

Keeping a tight grip on Milton's shirttail, I follow while he leads the way through the tightly pressed wriggling bodies. Sometimes a trip is a carefree frolic through soft, flowery meadows, but tonight's trip has begun to feel more like a high-wire act. Undefined menace lurks at the fringes of my peripheral vision, keeping me on edge as we are pushed forward by so many sperms trying to swim past the tall wooden walls, yearning to enter Led Ovum. Inside, the floor of Wollman Rink is an unruly sea of freaks and folding metal chairs. Milton snags three toward the back, in front of the bleachers. I'm profoundly glad to sit. Being erect while peaking on acid leaves so much unpredictable space between one's head and the ground.

All around us, people loudly chatter. The sense of anticipation is palpable. The Who and Led Zeppelin are the biggest rock acts on the planet. On the stage, roadies push equipment this way and that. The Four Tops' "Standing in the Shadows of Love" is being piped through the PA system. The audience is standing in the shadows of houselights. Waves of voices roll forward and smash against the stage in mammoth splashes of rainbow audio foam. Next to me, Milton is reading a magazine. I think it's *Life*. The page he's looking at says "One Week's Dad" and has dozens of little black-and-white pictures of fathers.

The stage goes dark, and the crowd begins to roar with excitement. Milton helps me to my feet. "Train Kept A-Rollin'" explodes out of the PA, and the crowd goes berserk. I stick my fingertips into my ears. It's the loudest music I've ever heard. The spotlights burst on and there's the band.

"There's something wrong with their heads!" I shout at Milton.

"They're wearing cowboy hats!" he shouts back.

The cheering audience is almost as loud as the music. The sound is so gargantuan, so concussive, that the Windowpane has to build a protective glass fallout shelter around my head. From the calm inside, I observe the raging audio typhoon. When preening, prancing Plant and plodding Page launch into "I Can't Quit You Baby," you can feel the air rattle. The music batters us like sheets of rain in a storm. A beach ball blows past.

Halfway through "Dazed and Confused," weird, haunting dinosaur moans fill the night. A spotlight narrows on Page, who is sawing his Les Paul in half. The crowd roars.

"He's playing with a violin bow!" Milton shouts as excitedly as if the Yankees have won the seventh game of the World Series with a Joe Pepitone walk-off home run.

But the unbearably loud din, and all these pressing bodies, is too much for my double-dosed, hyperaware senses. The glass fallout shelter shatters. Pelted by hailing music crystals, I'm forced to retreat deeper inside my skull until I'm floundering at the edge of a dark precipice. On one side, a bottomless black chasm. On the other, an onslaught of marauding horrors stampeding toward me. Time to sit, clap my hands over my ears, and try to hold it together.

Focus narrows. In the hurricane inside my head, flying mental debris, painful memories, and dark thoughts carom and ricochet. Musclini calling me a goddamn goofball. Robin freaking about the undercover-narc toll collector. Chris using a cigarette to burn black leeches off his legs. Mom pulling me toward train tracks. Tinsley pulling my hand into her blouse.

Jimmy Page's sawing guitar is grating iron against stone, then the screech of locked train wheels. John Bonham's bashing drums are pounding earthquakes to the ears. Though seated, I try to bend lower to get out of the sonic maelstrom.

But there is no shelter in Wollman Rink tonight. Nowhere to hide inside my head. A black-winged beast with the paterfamilias's head flaps its scaly wings. In one claw, it grasps tennis rackets. In the other, a yellow Wiffle bat.

"Goddamn goofball!" it caws. "Underachiever!"

From above, napalm bombs rain down from the open bays of tetradactyl B-52s. It's Robin's revenge, the poetic irony that the final acid trip of my life should be the worst. No one gets out of here alive. I bend lower until a sharp pain erupts at my waist. My bright-red appendix is the size of a sweet potato, filled with the noxious pus of regret. I'm chained by wrist and ankle to bare rock, my guts being torn open by the ravenous black-winged vulture. *Goddamn goofball! Underachiever! Loser!*

It's true! I *am* a goofball. A weak, pathetic loser. I don't deserve Robin. I don't deserve life. I deserve to be added to the kill ratio in Vietnam, a useless, expendable bit of protoplasm sacrificed to the God of Capitalist War Machines. Can I tell the draft board that the proof that there is no Supreme Being is that no loving and caring god would allow so many decent young men to die so needlessly?

But the draft board doesn't give a shit. Not as long as it needs lambs for the slaughter.

Now from out of the dark roars the worst specter of all, the glowering many-headed hydra of everyone I've disappointed — my father, mother, Robin, Miss Landers. The hydra's long sharp claws extended, keen on tearing me to —

An arm goes around me. Fingers pry my hands away from my ears. Through the enormous rupturing Zeppelin apocalypse worms a savior's voice: "It's okay, Lucas. It's just the acid. It'll pass."

Hold me, Milton. Don't let me go.

The speed of dark
In Central Park.

The houselights are on. The stage is empty, but the crowd refuses to leave. Mammoth waves of "More! More! More!" fill the air. Milton and I are on our feet. My eyes are watery and my cheeks are wet; I didn't know I'd been crying.

The band returns, plays an encore, leaves again. The crowd shouts for yet more. Space and time are still quite squishy, but having been rescued by the ever-watchful Milton, I've crawled out of the blackness and back from the terrible abyss. I never thought of this before, but there was a famous poet named Milton.

Loudspeakers tell the crowd it's time to go, but no one listens. They keep shouting "More!"

The band comes back and plays another encore.

And then another.

Finally, dazed and grinning crazily, the crowd allows itself to be coaxed toward the exits. Some, like Milton, linger a little longer, struck dumb by the spectacle. Even after being temporarily overcome by that brief, exhausting bad trip, I'm aware that this hasn't merely been a concert. It's been an extravaganza. More grandiose, sonically sumptuous, and just plain strange than anything we've ever before witnessed. (Is it possible that somewhere during "How Many More Times," Page segued briefly into the theme from *The Woody Woodpecker Show?*)

The rink is emptying, leaving behind disarray: folding chairs on their sides, flattened, turned backward; the floor awash with empty beer cans, crumpled cigarette packs, soda bottles. On the PA, someone exhorts us to quickly head to the exits.

Milton looks at his watch. "It's after one."

Realization strikes us both: Where's Arno?

In the darkness outside the rink, police with megaphones are urging everyone to leave the park. Searching for our friend, Milton and I wade through the tide of spent, trudging post-concert bodies until Milton grabs my arm and points.

Thirty feet away, in the faint illumination of a lamppost, Arno is gesticulating to a police officer. For an instant, I'm gripped with fear that he's been busted with the acid. But he's not handcuffed. The red-and-white cap pokes out of his back pocket. The police officer's arms are crossed, and there's a scowl on his face.

The cop turns away. Arno's face is contorted in iodine and baby oil sunburned outrage. He sees us approaching and complains, "Stupid cops won't do anything."

"About?" Milton asks.

"Clyde ripped me off."

It takes a moment to piece together.

"You . . . told that pig?" Milton asks in astonishment.

"Damn straight. Think I'm gonna let some scumbag get away with my five hundred bucks?"

Another officer appears on the walk. "Move along now, boys. Out of the park."

I've come down from the Windowpane enough to be geographically aware. Most of the crowd is leaving through the Grand Army Plaza exit at 60th Street. But Arno turns uptown, meaning we came in through an entrance farther up Fifth Ave. In that direction, the park path is shadowy and nearly deserted, the night air practically muted. All that remains of the concert is the ringing in my ears.

"So, I'm curious," Milton says. "What did the pig say when you told him you'd given Clyde five hundred bucks for LSD?"

"Jerk laughed at me," Arno growls bitterly. "I don't get it. Isn't it robbery? Theft under false pretenses or something?"

The hand that comes out of the dark feels disembodied when it clamps over my mouth. But another hand grabs my wrist and wrenches it behind my back with more than enough force to be convincing.

"Hey!" I let out a muffled yelp. A bolt of hot red pain shoots through my shoulder.

"Ow! Ow! Stop!" Milton howls near me. We've been jumped. I can't see the guy who's got me from behind, but the one who's grabbed Milton is big, with long stringy hair hanging over the collar of a torn denim jacket with a Pagan's patch.

"Hey! Quit it!" Another Pagan has Arno. All three of us are forced quickly down the walkway by our attackers. Amid the scrapes and slaps of rapid steps, my knees have gone rubbery. Are we being mugged? Are we about to die? The hand over my mouth is clammy and stinks of nicotine. My shoulder throbs painfully. I've never been mugged before. I've never been killed before. Blood pounds in my temples. I am scared shitless. If John Bonham himself were bashing my heart with his drum kick, he couldn't make it beat any faster.

We're herded into a small dank tunnel that's so dark I can only tell how close the walls are by the echoes. It's like being in the fallout shelter again, only here the air is rank with urine and Pagan's BO. My pulse continues to race—from fear and the haste at which we've been marched down the walkway.

"Hey! Wait! No! Let me go!" Milton's flipping out.

"Shaddup!" a voice snaps, and I hear the hard *chunk!* of hand against skull.

"You a pig?" That's Clyde's voice, high, nearly hysterical.

As my eyes gradually adjust to the blackout of the tunnel, I recognize his Lincolnesque silhouette. He's nose to nose with Arno, who's being restrained from behind by a heavy guy with greased-back hair. Under Arno's chin is the faintest glint of metal.

A knife?

Oh, God, no!

"Mffh?" Arno's answer to Clyde's question is muffled by the hand over his mouth.

"Undercover heat?" grunts the guy who's holding him.

The knife under Arno's chin becomes a sword. Clyde is a Pagan black knight in denim armor.

I'm trembling with fright for Arno. For Milton. For me. *Please, we're just three suburban kids.*

"Nffh!" Arno frantically tries to shake his head. There's the faint but irrefutable dribble of liquid splishing on the ground around his feet.

"What'd you tell that pig?" Clyde screams.

"Pfft!"

The stinky hand leaves my mouth, goes into my back pocket, and yanks out my wallet.

"Please, let me go! I need to get out of here!" Milton's begging desperately.

Smack! "Shaddup!"

"He's claustrophobic," I try to explain.

"What?"

"What'd you tell that pig?" Clyde yells at Arno again.

"Th-that y-you took my m-money. I—I thought you

121

w-weren't coming back," Arno stammers, his voice high and terrified.

"You tell him my name? You say anything about the Pagans?"

"N-n-no. I swear!"

A cigarette lighter bursts on. The flame illuminates a hairy hand holding Milton's *Life* magazine, which immediately gets flung away.

"Please," Milton whimpers. "You don't understand."

The flame illuminates draft cards, licenses, school IDs pulled from our wallets. "High-school kids?" Someone sounds surprised. A draft card is flicked away into the dark.

"This license ain't even real."

"F-for getting into bars," Milton tries to explain.

For a moment, all I hear is our heavy, scared-to-death panting. Are the Pagans trying to decide what to do next? Will a jogger discover the bodies of three young men in this tunnel tomorrow morning?

The hand holding my arm behind my back relaxes. The pain in my shoulder subsides. The distant sound of city traffic seeps faintly into the tunnel.

"Told you they was too young for undercover," one of the Pagans says.

The situation seems defused. Relief wants to creep in, but I'm not sure it's warranted.

"You stupid fuck!" Clyde punches Arno hard in the solar plexus.

"Oof!" You can hear the wind rush out of Arno's lungs. He doubles over, crumples to his knees. Our wallets slap to the ground. A hundred imaginary bats burst from of the tunnel's ceiling and flap away.

Clyde turns to me. I grimace and brace, expecting a blow. Instead, he thrusts something small and tubular into my palm. "Don't lose it, pansy."

Arno's on his hands and knees, his rasping gasps echoing off the curved tunnel walls. Milton and I are breathing hard. My queasy stomach feels like a water balloon that's been dropped from four floors up. The Windowpane has become an annoyance, making it difficult to find consistent purchase in reality. The lingering hallucinations—flapping bats overhead, tarantulas on the walls—are a distraction. Milton groans, bends over, and puts his hands on his knees. An instant later, he bolts out of the tunnel.

The splash of vomit follows.

Arno slowly gets to his feet and wipes his hands over and over on his jeans. The insides of his pants legs are stained dark. He's trembling.

Using the flame from my Zippo for light, I collect our wallets, cards, and IDs. On the cover of Milton's *Life* magazine is a slightly blurred black-and-white photo portrait of a boyish-looking soldier. The small headline reads:

THE FACES OF THE AMERICAN DEAD IN VIETNAM

In the flickering light and sputtering residue of the Windowpane, the face seems to have a rueful expression, as if it is saying, *Go back to the suburbs, children. You're out of your league here.*

Back on the walkway, Arno scrubs his hands in a drinking fountain. He's still quivering when we reach the car. We pretend not to notice the scent of urine from his jeans.

The drive home is hushed. Not even the usual distraction of radio or tape deck. In the back seat, I hold up the *Life* so the headlights from the cars behind us illuminate it. Some of the pages are torn, others curled and smudged as if the magazine's been passed from person to person for weeks. The little square pictures are not of dads but of the dead. Twelve pages of small black-and-white photos of the 242 young men who died in Vietnam during one week last month. More than thirty dead each day. I squint at the faces, dreading the thought of finding Chris's among them. But the light is too jumpy and fleeting, the pictures too small, the lingering hallucinations from the Windowpane too distracting.

Letting the magazine fall to my lap, I think about turning eighteen two months ago, then graduating from high school three weeks ago. Thanks to the Semi-Miraculous Transformation, I may have a body that places me in the category of mature young man, but I swear, ever since I graduated, there have been moments when I've felt less prepared for life than ever. Tonight was definitely one of them. Arno, Milton, and I were mere boys. Messing with a motorcycle gang? I tremble again thinking about it. Tonight was the first time in my life I truly felt the terrifying, bladder-emptying possibility of death. Those brief moments in that tunnel were both paralyzing and exhausting. Imagine being at war. Imagine having to endure that terror for months on end.

. . .

It's not until after we've dropped Milton off at his house that I remember the tiny glass vial Clyde gave me. It's about an inch long and the diameter of a pencil. I reach up and flick on the GTO's inside light. The vial is about a third filled with white powder.

Arno sees it and beams like a little kid.

SUNDAY, JULY 13

Days Until Camp Juliette: 12

3:47 a.m. The Windowpane's mostly worn off, but not enough to allow for sleep. When I got home from the concert about an hour and a half ago, Chris's latest letter was on my desk.

6/28/69

Dear Loogie,
You heard about getting into Goddard? I hope you did, man. Believe me, you DO NOT want to get sent over here, Loogs.

The whole scene over here is a total bust. No one does shit anymore. All we do is get high and listen to music and try not to die. It's a good thing they got a lot of drugs. Not just the army issued pep pills and codeine but we sure dig that shit. They got killer weed over here like you wouldn't believe. The stuff's called Thai stick and it's mind blowing. You can't take more than two or three tokes without falling flat on your face. It's got to be ten times more potent than the weed you and me used to smoke behind the shed. Man if we'd been smoking Thai stick back there I promise you wouldn't know which end of your inserter was up.

That's not all. Everywhere you go there's smack. Pure horse. Dangerous pure. Most guys smoke it in cigarettes because it don't stink like Thai stick so you can smoke it right under the NCO's nose and he won't know. But that ain't the only reason guys smoke it. The stuff's so pure that smoking is the only way you can take it without having to worry about ODing.

That is UNLESS YOU WANT TO OD. Believe me, not a day goes by that I don't think about it. 'Cause I KNOW I can't take another six months of this. We know what people back home think of this war. It's a WASTE OF LIVES. All we do is spend each day waiting to see if this will be the day they get you. Sometimes I get so tired and scared I'm ready to do anything so I won't have to be tired and scared no more.

The thing guys do when they can't take it

no more is shoot themself in the foot or butt. The second or third toe on the left foot is what I hear. You can blow that sucker right off. The butt is a tougher shot. You got to fire pretty deep to make it real but if you ain't careful you can lose a whole chunk o' butt. Then someday you'll be at the beach and people will be asking where's the other half of his ass. Pretty half assed, right?

Guess it ain't that bad if I can make jokes, right, Loogs? It's just that sometimes it IS that bad. Being all the way over here knowing no one back home gives a shit. When I first got here a lot of the guys were pissed about the protests back home. For a while I guess we believed we were stopping communism and couldn't understand why so many people back in the States were against that.

But not no more. To the gooks this war ain't about communism. If all you been doing for a thousand years is grow rice, what does it matter if your country is democratic or communist? They're fighting to protect their country from imperialist invaders. And guess what? THAT'S US.

So that's where it's at. The gooks hate us here and folks hate us back home. If that ain't the worst feeling in the world, then

128

I don't know what is. That's when you start thinking why bother with a toe or a butt cheek? Why not suck the muzzle and get it over with?

Sorry to lay that on you, man. Don't worry. I am OK most of the time. I'm glad I got you to write to because I sure can't write about it to no one else. Be good, Loogs. MAKE SURE YOU DON'T GET DRAFTED AND SENT TO THIS HELL HOLE. And write back soon. OK?

Peace, brother,

Chris

Oh, man. I can't tell him Goddard rejected me. He's already got more than enough crap to deal with.

Chris nicknamed me Loogie one afternoon when we were out behind the shed. He'd taken a big hit off a joint and started coughing his guts out. "Gotta hock this loogie, man," he wheezed, then cleared his throat and spit out a huge wad of gray-and-yellow phlegm.

I burst out laughing.

"What's so funny?" he asked.

"What you said. What was it? Hawk a loogie?"

"Hock, not hawk." He looked surprised. "You never heard that before?"

"Don't give me that. You just made it up."

"The hell I did." Chris laughed. "Man's been hocking loogies ever since . . . since . . . there was loogies to hock."

"Bull."

"Bull, my ass. What rock you been hiding under? From now on I'm calling *you* Loogie." Even though he'd just hacked his brains out, he took another deep hit off the J.

And started coughing every bit as hard as before.

"You okay?" I asked, not so much because he was coughing (he'd told me about his mild asthma), but because he was taking such deep hits. It was the kind of thing you did when you wanted to get seriously wasted, and we still had to go back inside and work.

Chris pulled a piece of paper out of his pocket. On the letterhead was the round Selective Service System emblem with the bald eagle clasping arrows in one claw and the branch of a holly bush in the other.

ORDER TO REPORT FOR
ARMED FORCES PHYSICAL EXAMINATION

You are hereby directed to present yourself for Armed Forces Physical Examination . . .

"There are ways to get out of this, man," I said. "I mean, all you have to do is go back to high school."

"That ain't the problem." Chris hadn't stopped wheezing. "They may not want me."

Maybe it was the grass, but I didn't follow. "It doesn't matter whether they want you or not. They have to take you. All you have to do is tell 'em you want to finish high school. That'll get you a Two-S status, at least until—"

Chris waved his hand at me to stop. He caught his breath. "You don't get it, man. The *army* may not want me."

That stopped me. Cold.

"It's the asthma. If I flunk the physical, my family'll think I'm a total jerk-off. My dad and uncles served in World War Two. I got cousins over in Nam. In my family, you serve your country. You do your patriotic duty."

It was a startling example of how far apart his and my worlds were. In mine, you were a loser if you let yourself get drafted. In his, you were a loser if you didn't.

"You really want to fight in that stupid war?"

He snorted derisively. "Ain't you heard that all you longhairs are traitors? This is America. 'Love it or leave it.'"

"Yeah, but how do *you* feel about it?" I asked.

"Don't matter." Chris cleared his chest and spit once more. Then he turned and went back into the factory.

It's four a.m. and I'm wiped. I could probably sleep now, but I'm looking at the faces of the dead boys in *Life* magazine again. The majority are between eighteen and twenty-one years old. Decked out in their fanciest Class A uniforms, wearing broad service caps that look too big for their heads. But not all are in uniform. Several dozen photos are lifted from high-school yearbooks. Most of these round-cheeked, clean-shaven youths look younger than me.

In Central Park tonight, my friends and I were way out of our depth. Same as the boys in these pages. A handful were seventeen when they died. Boys who, before they left for

Vietnam, couldn't possibly have grasped the mortal danger that lay ahead. Boys who died before they ever had a chance to really be alive.

All I have to do is look in the mirror to see who could be next.

Dear Chris,

Listen, man, feel free to lay whatever you want on me. That's what I'm here for. But I want to correct one thing. They won't hate you when you get back home, especially if you join the protests. To me, some of the bravest cats around are the vets against the war. To go through that horror and come back against it says a lot. You'll be a hero. We need you, man.

Stay away from the horse, okay? I don't have to tell you that heroin is killer shit. Once you start smoking it, you're just one small step from shooting up. And you and I both know that if there's lots of it around, sooner or later that's what a few guys are going to try. Hey, can you believe it? Ever think you'd hear Loogie lecture you about drugs? . . .

MONDAY, JULY 14

Days Until Camp Juliette: 11

"If you don't believe in a Supreme Being, what is the basis for your personal moral code?" In the church basement, Charles is running through the questions I can expect the draft board to ask.

"To me, if you believe in God, you're not obligated to have a moral code," I answer. "The responsibility's off your shoulders because you expect him to enforce morality for all. But if you believe there is no God, then you, the individual, are obligated to be moral, because no one else is going to do the job for you. And if no one's moral, humanity and civilization collapse. So the individual must carry the responsibility to be moral on his shoulders. That's why I can't kill another human being. It is my responsibility to live a moral life, and to adhere to it because I can't expect anyone else to do it for me."

"What if it's a question of kill or be killed?" Charles asks. His boots are up on the corner of the desk again.

"Thomas Aquinas postulated that for a war to be just, the following four conditions have to be met: The war has to have just cause. It has to be declared by a proper authority. It has to possess the right intention. And it has to have a reasonable chance of success. Vietnam fails every condition. It's a political conflict, which is not considered a just cause. It's never been officially declared a war by any authority. The reason it's officially labeled a conflict is because the United States is not in danger and therefore has no legitimate grounds for being there. The same goes for intention. Who are we to decide what form of government the Vietnamese people should have? That's their decision, not ours. And as far as having a reasonable chance of success? Even the president of the United States has basically admitted we're not going to win. Last year the best he could do was promise there would be an honorable end to the conflict, whatever that means.

"Therefore, according to my belief, to fight in Vietnam shouldn't come down to a choice between kill or be killed, because it is wrong for us to be there in the first place. But if I did find myself in a position where I was ordered to kill another human being, I wouldn't be able to. I'd refuse and suffer the consequences."

Charles flicks ash onto the floor. (Why doesn't he use an ashtray? Is this an act of rebellion? Or a statement about how he feels about the church?) His eyes lock on mine.

"I'm not bullshitting you," I tell him. "I really can't imagine killing another human being."

"Think you're the only one who feels that way?" Charles

134

swings his boots off the desk and leans closer. "Basic training's not just about getting you in shape and teaching you how to fight. It's about desensitizing you to violence and the suffering of others. The army doesn't expect you to be a killer when they draft you. They expect you to be a killer after they've trained you."

I feel myself squirm inwardly. I really thought I'd built a good argument.

"Look, it's not a bad start," Charles says. "But you're going to have to go a lot deeper on your moral responsibility if you're going to have a chance of convincing them, dig?"

Go deeper? I flash on something I heard my mother say a long time ago, back when my parents still had people over on the weekends for dinner. The grown-ups were sitting at the dining table, chatting. Mom's hair was coiffed. She was wearing red lipstick. She may even have been smoking a cigarette. "Well, to tell you the truth," she said, "I've discovered that deep down I'm really quite shallow."

The table erupted with laughter, no one laughing more gaily than Mom.

It took me hours and hours of reading and research to come up with, and memorize, the answers I've just given Charles. And now he says I have to go deeper? Depth is not my forte. I'm a practitioner of the quip. The short, pithy poem. Or the rambling love letter. Constructing long arguments based on philosophical polemics might be someone else's bag, but it's sure not mine.

"What about trying to flunk my physical?" I ask, feeling defeat creep in: Charles has already warned me that the doctors at the army induction center in Brooklyn have seen every faked physical ailment known to man. But there has to be *something* I could try. (As far as a deferment on psychological grounds, mere letters from psychiatrists may work in other places, but in Brooklyn they're useless unless accompanied by long, well-documented histories of mental illness. So no sense in asking Dr. Hill. I'm reminded of one of my favorite books, *Catch-22,* in which soldiers at war discover that anyone who asks for a psychological discharge is automatically turned down. Because not wanting to engage in bloodshed is clear proof of sanity.)

"The thinking in Washington has changed," Charles says. He's not quite as scornful tonight as he was two weeks ago. "Up till now, seventy percent of the guys getting drafted have been poor, working-class, or minority. Nixon's figured out that it's bad political mojo if they're the only ones dying in Nam. Because what does that make the college student deferment? Just another way to maintain the status quo, dig? You know that blacks and minorities die at twice the rate of whites over there?"

"Seriously? Why?" I ask.

Charles flicks his ash and gazes at a bright-yellow poster on the wall of a flower with the words WAR IS NOT HEALTHY FOR CHILDREN AND OTHER LIVING THINGS. "Why? Because whites get promoted to officer positions and blacks don't. So while you white boys are behind the lines giving orders, my black brothers are up front catching lead."

He may not be as hostile as he was two weeks ago, but he still sounds angry and resentful—with good reason.

136

"Listen, man, would you prefer I found someone else to work with?" I ask, since it feels like that's where he's going.

Charles's mouth falls partway open, and he looks at me with surprise. "No, man. I told you last time, my job is to help everyone. And as long as I'm here, that's what I'm going to do. I just think you should dig what's really going on."

A little while later, sitting in Odysseus in the church parking lot, I wonder if what's really going on is more than I can handle. If I'm going to have a chance of succeeding with the conscientious objector thing, Charles says I'll need to do more research and have deeper and better-thought-out arguments. Everything is starting to feel overwhelming. If the ground was disintegrating before, now it feels like I'm surrounded by walls pressing in.

A moment like this calls for an infusion of ganja. I close Odysseus's windows and fire up. It hasn't been easy to keep my promise to Robin about cutting back, but I'm trying. It's 9:30 p.m. and this is only my second joint of the day. I've only smoked half a dozen cigarettes, too. I pray it'll count for something.

Darkness has fallen. Lucas the Pummeled holds the sweet smoke in his lungs. It's been five days since Robin's last letter. Oh, how he wishes she'd write again. Maybe she has. It's been more than two weeks since he signed the change-of-address form. There could be a bunch of perfume-scented lavender envelopes sitting in a mailbox in Bay Shore. . . .

And while you're building castles in the sky, goofball, why not add a personal note from Nixon exempting you from the draft?

Tap tap . . . At the sound against the window, Lucas the Dreamer nearly jumps out of his seat. Heart thudding, he turns to look, expecting a cop. But it's Charles. Light-headed relief floods through Lucas's THC-infused synapses.

"Gonna bogart that joint?" Charles asks with a grin.

A moment later he folds himself into the passenger seat and looks around. "Groovy bus, Lucas."

"Thanks." Lucas hands him the joint, and Charles takes a hit that burns nearly half an inch off, then starts to cough, his long body quaking as he hacks over and over.

Lucas takes the joint back. Now that Charles is on his turf, it feels like they're equals. "Gee, Charles, I thought all you brothers knew how to smoke dope."

In the middle of his coughs, Charles starts and stares. Then he laughs. "Touché, white boy."

"Next time, try a smaller hit," Professor Lucas advises.

Charles complies. "Man, this is good stuff. No seeds popping or twigs."

"No one ever told you to pick that crap out?" Lucas asks. "Where you been, man?"

"The Congo for the last four years. And before that, home-schooled." Charles holds up the joint. "Not much opportunity for this, dig?"

"Why homeschooled?"

"Jehovah's Witness. Then four years in the jungle building schools and kingdom halls."

They each take another hit. It's good to get a buzz going. Lucas the Heretic may believe there is no God, but he sure appreciates the empty dark parking lots the Good Lord provides each evening after his work is done.

"You see my conflict, Lucas?" Charles asks.

"Sorry?"

"Helping rich white kids stay out of the draft."

Lucas is tempted to argue that he's not rich, but compared to a lot of kids, he guesses he is. Look at Chris. He once told Lucas that the four people in his house shared one bathroom. On the other hand, grass-smoking Charles with his Afro, cowboy boots, and Marlboros doesn't exactly fit the image of a Jehovah's Witness. Every now and then a couple of primly dressed ladies will knock on the front door of the house of dashed dreams, offering a publication called *The Watchtower*. "You really a Jehovah's Witness?" Lucas the Skeptical asks.

"Disassociated. What you'd call lapsed. But it got me a One-A-O deferment. I'm doing my community service at Creedmoor."

Creedmoor's a local state-run mental institution. When it was first decided that Barry needed to be institutionalized for a while, Lucas's aunt and uncle briefly considered sending him there, but the shrink was vehemently against it. Lucas got the impression it's a real hellhole.

"*One Flew Over the Cuckoo's Nest?*" Lucas asks.

"You don't want to know, my man." Charles takes another hit, leans his head back, and gazes up at the cartoon of Mr. Natural. "'The whole universe is completely insane.' Ain't it the truth." He reaches for the door handle. "Thanks for the smoke, Lucas. I'll let you get home."

He's halfway out the door when he stops and looks back, his lips grimly pursed. "Listen, my man, I know it's a bitch, but keep working the CO angle. We'll give it our best shot. If it doesn't work, you'll still have some options."

"Something besides federal prison or Canada?"

"Hey, don't knock 'em. You'll stay alive and you won't have to fight in an immoral war."

A fair point. But . . . "Any other possibilities?"

"You can always chop off a finger. But somehow you don't strike me as the type."

SUNDAY, JULY 20

Days Until Camp Juliette: 5

"They went all the way to the moon to take a nap." Arno's stubby toes press against the edge of his desk while he reclines in his chair. A narrow ribbon of bluish incense snakes from a small brown ceramic pot nearby. It's close to nine p.m. The lunar module touched down on the moon's surface about six hours ago. On TV they've been saying that the astronauts are going to take a nap and then do a bunch of things inside the LM before they venture out.

A rolled-up towel is wedged against the bottom of the bedroom door. Arno's holding a mirror in front of his face while conducting a blackhead search-and-destroy mission. The sunburn has pretty much faded. A few days ago, when his skin started peeling off in sheets, he *really* looked like a napalm victim.

I'm perched by the window, which is open just enough to keep the pinner we're smoking outside. I'm still cutting down, but it would be awkward not to smoke with my friends. Arno would want to know why, and if I told him it was for Robin's sake, he'd be sure to call me pussy whipped. Besides, we're only getting mildly fried. In a little while, when we go watch TV with Arno's parents, we can't appear too wrecked.

Tommy is on Arno's sound system. At home, I've got a record player the size of a small suitcase with a turntable and two little attached speakers. In comparison, Arno's system is otherworldly: Kenwood stereo receiver, Garrard turntable, Acoustic Research speakers the size of milk crates. Plus a ton of albums filling the bookcase, stacked against the wall, and in two big piles in his closet.

The Who is Arno's all-time favorite band. When "Pinball Wizard" comes on, he puts down the mirror and begins to air-drum along with Keith Moon. Less than a month from now, Pete Townshend and company are scheduled to come all the way from England to perform at the music festival. Other than making himself rich selling acid and being part of our last hurrah before parting ways in the fall, seeing the Who is one of the chief reasons Arno wants to go.

Milton is cross-legged on the floor, reading *Newsday*. A thin wire connects a plug in his ear to the small black transistor radio in his shirt pocket. He's the only person I know who can listen to music, read a newspaper, follow a ball game on his radio, and engage in a conversation all at once.

While Arno air-drums and Milton reads, I'm thinking about the drive up to Camp Juliette in five days. It's been eleven days since Robin's first and only letters arrived. The paterfamilias says he'll "definitely" get down to Bay Shore sometime this week to pick up whatever's been forwarded there. (I've been tempted to go myself in Odysseus, but I don't have keys for the place, so how would I get my mail? And what if I went and there were no letters?)

Oh, how I ache for her. Only sometimes at night, Tinsley gets mixed into that wistful yearning. Not that I expect to ever see the pixie princess again. It's been almost two weeks since she showed up at the factory and we went over to the Planting Fields. Haven't heard from her since. Guess I shouldn't be surprised, considering the way the afternoon ended. I tell myself it's just as well. But in Robin's absence, when the hormones start simmering, I do sometimes wonder if I was too quick to turn down Tinsley's generous offer.

Arno Moon finishes drumming with a dramatic air trashcan flourish, flips his invisible sticks away, and comes over for a hit off the skinny joint. This close, I can smell his aftershave. He exhales through the gap in the window and asks if I've heard from Robin.

"Yeah, everything's good." What a lie. I might as well be General Abrams over in Nam, claiming we're winning the war. Arno may be my closest friend, but sometimes I'm not comfortable talking to him about Robin. He's always been jealous of me for dating her. Not because she's taken up so much of the time I used to spend with him. And not because he, and many other guys, always considered her one of the most desirable females in our grade. But because she's a constant reminder that the Semi-Miraculous Transformation happened to me, not him.

143

"You are such a lucky fuck," he says for the thousandth time.

"*Was* a lucky fuck," Milton corrects him without looking up from the newspaper.

"Right." Arno starts to sing along to "Pinball Wizard," making up his own lyrics:

> *"He's a Vietnam draftee,*
> *Couldn't get a deferment,*
> *A Vietnam draftee,*
> *Gonna get his ass shot off.*
> *A Vietnam draftee,*
> *He'll soon be ducking bullets,*
> *But it's only a matter of time . . .*
> *dah dah tah dot dot dah . . .*
> *Till he comes back in a*
> *Flag-draped pine box."*

"Aluminum," Milton says, his face still in the newspaper.

"Come again?"

"The army caskets are made of aluminum. So they can be reused. Saves money. Soldiers are expensive to train, feed, house, and transport. Once you're dead, the army doesn't want to waste another cent on you."

"Uh, right." Arno gets down on his belly and starts to crawl under his bed.

"What was today's count?" I ask. Milton follows the daily casualty count as closely as he follows Roy White's batting average.

"Sixteen today. Thirty-eight yesterday." Milton looks up and our eyes meet. We are brothers in disarmament. The war has torn his family apart. It threatens to tear my family apart (not that there's much holding it together).

My simmering resentment at the injustice of it spills out. "It's un-fucking-believable. The only reason we're in this war is because we don't have the balls to admit we were wrong to get into it in the first place. And now we can't get out without admitting defeat."

"Hey, don't forget the fat cats making all the shit that war uses up," Milton reminds me. Together we list some of the items companies supply to keep the war going:

"Bombs."

"Guns."

"Bullets."

"Uniforms."

"Rations."

"Pocket-size Bibles."

"Think of it like this," Milton says. "War is the addict. Young draft-age men are the drug. The military-industrial complex makes the syringes. As long as this country keeps injecting soldiers into Vietnam, the owners and shareholders of those syringe companies get richer and richer."

Since meeting with Charles last week, I've been trying to "go deeper" into my moral argument against war. But it's hard to focus, hard to make myself work. It reminds me of what Miss Landers used to say. She was convinced I showed a talent for writing and would get aggravated when I wouldn't muster the energy to edit and revise my papers, or even correct my spelling and grammar. We had a strange love-hate relationship, surely the most intense connection I've ever had with any teacher in my life.

A sneeze explodes from under the bed. "Goddamn dust!" Only Arno's feet are visible, sticking out from under the bed. Whatever he's searching for must be pretty far back.

"Look at this." Milton gestures to a story in the newspaper about five guys on trial for burning their draft cards. "They're facing five years for burning pieces of paper." He points at a name: New York State Supreme Court justice Leopold R. Wagner. "And the SOB who's presiding over the trial? Lives a couple of blocks from here. Bastard plays chess with my father."

Something is different about Milton this summer. Last fall, only a few weeks past his sixteenth birthday, he went off to MIT an innocent genius. He's never been one to talk openly about his feelings, but I sensed he was uptight—not about how he'd do academically but about living on his own away from his family. He's come back more confident. He made it through freshman year. He's more apt to reveal his emotions now.

And yet, when he heaves the rolled-up newspaper against Arno's closet door, it catches me by surprise.

"What was that?" Arno's muffled voice asks from under the bed.

"I've had it with this civil disobedience crap," Milton seethes. "All this Gandhian drivel about winning the government over with love and patient suffering. There's still half a million American soldiers over there. They're still bombing the crap out of Cambodia and North Vietnam."

I drop the pinner outside and close the window. In one of Chris's first letters to me, he wrote about how in areas where there'd been intense bombing, he noticed that the scattered bodies left behind were sometimes naked. He was puzzled by this until his squad leader explained that a bomb's shock waves often tear the clothes off a body. In another letter, he wrote about walking through a bombed village and finding a child's foot lying on the ground. Nothing else. Just the foot. Chris has been over there for about six months. Six months to go.

If he makes it.

Arno backs out from under the bed dragging a bulging teardrop-shaped black sock. Narrow at the top, wide and round below, with a thousand little bumps like the skin of an avocado. It's show-and-tell time.

"I heard on the radio today that there may be as many as twenty-five thousand people at that festival. If that's true, in a little less than a month, Arno the Magnificent is going to perform the greatest magic trick of his life. He will turn the contents of this sock into *six . . . thousand . . . dollars.*"

He waits for us to figure it out.

"Acid," Milton guesses.

"Is right, my fine freckled friend," says Arno. "Five hundred bucks bought half a gram, which made two thousand hits, which —"

"If you sell for three dollars apiece equals six thousand dollars minus the cost of ingredients, which results in a net gain of five thousand five hundred dollars," Milton swiftly finishes the sentence.

"Is correct."

"I thought the festival is supposed to be our last big blast of the summer together," I remind him.

"It will be. I'll just be selling some acid on the side."

How is it possible that I've wound up with a best friend who's a materialistic bourgeois capitalist anachronism disguised as a longhair? No one I know wears aftershave anymore. Or tools around in a muscle car. Arno claims he doesn't wear bell-bottoms because they make his short legs look like tree stumps, but that's not the reason. He just doesn't want to be identified too strongly with the counterculture. Sometimes I think that if we weren't best friends since childhood, we wouldn't be friends now.

He opens the sock and proudly displays the multitudinous circular white tablets inside. "Took me *days* to make these suckers."

"Looks like aspirin," says Milton.

"No, they don't." Arno takes offense.

"Yeah, they do." I agree with Milton.

"The people I sell to'll know it's not aspirin," Arno says.

"How?" asks Milton.

"Because why would anyone want to sell them aspirin?" Arno asks, as if the answer is obvious.

"Uh, because he thinks they're a bunch of stupid hippies and he can easily rip them off?" I venture.

Arno's face scrunches the way it does when he knows you're

right but he can't admit it. He shoves the bulging sock back under the bed. "Let's go see what's going on with the moon landing."

"The troglodytes emerge." Mr. Exley reclines in his black leather Eames chair with his shoes off. The sour scent of feet wafts from the gold-toed black socks that stretch up over his calves. He's wearing baby-blue Bermuda shorts and a yellow paisley shirt. A half-empty martini glass rests on a small table beside him. Five days a week, Mr. Exley puts on a dark suit, white shirt, and tie and takes the train to the city. (The paterfamilias used to do that before he conned a dying friend into selling him a Laundromat chain for cheap.) At home after work each evening Arno's father sucks down two or three vodka martinis. (I can count on one hand the number of times I've seen the paterfamilias drink. And then only a beer.)

Arno's mom sits on a couch near her husband. Her dark bouffant hair is piled high on her head. Her lips, fingernails, and high heels are matching bright red. Under her blouse is a bra that comes to points like the armor of a Norse goddess. A cigarette in one hand, a small glass of sherry in the other.

The only times my mother bothers with makeup anymore are the two days a week she drives Alan to his special school in the city. She spends the day shopping and going to museums, picks up Alan after school, puts him on the train home, and then has dinner with a friend and goes to the theater. (Once Alan is on the train, he knows which station to get off at and walks home.)

149

The rest of the school week, a short bus picks Alan up at seven a.m. and doesn't return until around six p.m. On those days, Mom barely manages to get dressed.

Arno, Milton, and I settle on the floor. The Exleys' new color TV is astonishing. Walter Cronkite is wearing a gray jacket and gold-colored tie. His skin is slightly pink.

Mr. Exley sips his martini. "So, what's happenin', boys?"

"Not now, Dad," Arno grumbles. On the screen, they've cut to Mission Control. A bunch of crew-cut men sitting at long tables with little screens. Almost all of them wearing white short-sleeve shirts and skinny dark ties.

"Come on, son, it's so rare that I get to rap with your friends. What's your bag this summer, boys?"

Arno's father has a satirical way of talking to us. He pretends to speak "youth culture" language while making fun of it. I tell him that once again this summer my "bag" is operating a mail inserter. Milton's teaching himself a computer language called COBOL. Mr. Exley smiles benignly. None of us has a clue what Milton is talking about.

"So Arno's the only one who works outdoors," says Mr. Exley.

"Lay off, Dad," Arno says. "We want to watch."

"I'm hip to that, son, but I'm also trying to understand how these fine young lads can spend their summers more or less indoors and still have more color in their faces than the only one among you who's outside caddying all day. . . . At least until last week when you suddenly turned a shade of roasted tomato."

"You used to like the sun," Mrs. Exley chimes in. "When you were little, you'd turn the color of molasses every summer."

"And your arms?" asks Mr. Exley, whose favorite summer activity is reclining on a lounge beside friends' pools and turning the color of molasses.

"I wear long sleeves. Jeez, Dad, what's with the fifth degree?"

Arno's parents still treat him like a kid. It ticks Arno off, but sometimes I feel a little envious. When was the last time my parents treated me like a kid? True, I've adamantly demanded that they not. But do they always have to take me at my word?

Meanwhile, his father's prying must have gotten to Arno because he says, "Okay, if it'll make you happy, I'll get good and sunburned again tomorrow and we can make a whole bunch more trips to the dermatologist. Now can we please watch this incredibly historic event?"

At this moment, the "incredibly historic event" is a blurry image in black, white, and shades of gray. Arno frowns. "What are we looking at, anyway?"

Milton scooches close to the TV and points at a patch of black in the upper-right corner of the screen. "This is space." Then he points at a slanting stripe of bright white. "This must be the surface of the moon." Next, he points at something with a vaguely metallic glow jutting down through the white stripe. "I think this must be one of the legs of the lunar module."

The moon makes me think of the last time Robin and I made love—under an almost-full moon on a rocky beach near

Bar Harbor. She sat on my lap, facing me. It was our first time doing it outside. (Later we both discovered mosquito bites in some unlikely places.) That was almost a month ago.

Is she watching this? Do they even *have* TV in the land of permafrost and wolverines? Having heard so little from her about her life up there this summer only increases the anxiety I carry day after day since her letters of doubt and indecision arrived. *Just five days to go,* I remind myself. Then once again I will see my ladylove.

On the TV screen, a dark shadow begins to descend along the leg of the lunar module. We hear Neil Armstrong say he's near the foot of the ladder. The picture changes. Mrs. Exley gasps loudly. An astronaut in a white space suit — looking a little like the Michelin man with a big round helmet and a large rectangular pack on his back — comes into view.

Armstrong says something about the LM's footpads settling only one or two inches into the fine-grained surface of the moon. Then he steps off the ladder. "That's one small step for man . . . one . . . giant leap for mankind."

"Unbelievable," mutters Mr. Exley, sitting up straight in the Eames chair.

In amazed silence, we watch as Armstrong says that the surface of the moon is powdery and reminds him of soft charcoal ash. Then another helmeted Michelin man (Buzz Aldrin) comes down the ladder. Armstrong reads something on a plaque about coming to the moon in peace. And then America lays claim to the barren landscape by planting its flag.

In the Exleys' den, Milton rises and goes to the window.

I heave myself up and join him. We press our faces close to the glass. The moon is a waxing crescent low in the black sky.

"There are two men up there," Milton whispers so that Arno won't overhear and make the inevitable mood-crushing wisecrack. "Three days, and a quarter-million miles through the total vacuum of space. And you know what steered them there? A computer the size of a toolbox."

"Far out," I whisper back. It's *Flash Gordon* and *Buck Rogers*. *Le Voyage Dans la Lune* and *Star Trek*. Decades of science fiction becoming reality right before our eyes. For a moment this transcends all of life's headaches. The war, Robin's uncertainty, American imperialism, and all the social unrest take a back seat to this one astounding achievement.

"Hey, what are you homos doing over there?"

You can always count on Arno to ruin the moment.

The moon has disappeared below the horizon. Milton and I are standing on the sidewalk outside Arno's house. Our suburban neighborhood is dark and quiet. It's Sunday night. Tomorrow morning, yellow buses will ferry children to day camp. Wives will drive husbands to the train station (so *that's* why they call it a station wagon!) and then play tennis at the country club. The Apollo 11 astronauts will begin their journey home from the moon. Hundreds of thousands of American and Vietcong soldiers will wake to another day of death and destruction in a tiny country halfway around the world.

"Things any better for Rudy?" I ask Milton.

"A little. He's working on temporary landed immigrant

status. First step toward Canadian citizenship. Once he's got the paperwork together, he should be able to move to Toronto. At least there'll be some decent pianos."

There's something I've been thinking about. "Did he ever say why the draft board rejected his conscientious objector application?"

"Yeah." Milton's upper lip curls ruefully. "'Lack of depth in sincerity, and lack of primary motivating force in registrant's life.' Since when does not wanting to kill people not qualify as a deeply sincere primary motivating force? What bullshit."

"How'd he handle the religious-belief stuff?" I ask, since the Fischers have never struck me as a particularly religious family.

"He didn't," Milton said. "He based his argument on personal moral code and the teachings of Thomas Aquinas. Ever heard of just-war theory?"

I feel the blood drain out of my face. Have I ever heard of it? Is this some kind of cosmic joke? It's the exact same argument Charles has been encouraging me to use.

Even in the dark, Milton must see that I'm blown away. "Oh, shit," he quickly says. "Hey, just because it didn't work for Rudy doesn't mean it won't work for you."

We avert our eyes, both knowing that's 99.9 percent pure wishful bullshit. I feel like someone just punched me in the stomach.

Milton puts a hand on my shoulder. "Listen, man, if there's anything I can do . . ."

But of course there isn't.

Glad I still have a couple of reds left.

MONDAY, JULY 21

Bang! The crash upstairs makes me jump.

"What was that?" Rudy asks on the phone from Saskatchewan.

"Nothing. Someone dropped something."

Musclini is in his refuge, the attic gym. Sometimes when he finishes a set of lifts, he drops the weights to the floor. We mortals below startle. Angry Zeus hurling thunderbolts from the heavens.

I'm in Mom's bedroom. After they put the addition on the house, she decorated this room with flowery wallpaper, soft overstuffed furniture, and heavy drapes. In contrast, the walls of the paterfamilias's bedroom are off-white. A painting of a seascape hangs in a frame over the bed. There's a mirror, some teak Scandinavian furniture, and window blinds. Reminds me of a motel room. (Did he not expect to stay long?) Outside this evening, rain splashes down. Near the window in Mom's bedroom is a small writing desk with her gray Smith Corona portable, a half-finished page in it and half a dozen typewritten pages on the desktop. I remember, when I was younger, hearing rapid typing from behind a closed door, and once, an excited few days when a story of hers was published in the *Saturday Evening Post*. But it's been a long time since I've heard the clatter of those keys.

After what Milton said last night, I waited fitfully until this morning's snack break at the factory to call Charles from a pay phone. I knew he'd probably be at work at Creedmoor, but I wanted to leave him a message to call me as soon as he could. But someone at the American Friends office told he was away. I asked if I could speak to different counselor but was told that Charles is in charge of my case and I'll have to wait until he returns.

As soon as I got home from work, I called Rudy, who's just finished telling me that in his opinion most draft counselors are either idiots or scam artists. (Before fleeing to Canada, he spoke to one who offered to get him a draft deferment for five hundred bucks.)

I ask him if he thinks the personal moral code argument for CO status is still worth trying.

"In a broad-strokes way? Sure," he says. "It's being pushed by the Central Committee for Conscientious Objectors. The idea is that if we keep trying, sooner or later some draft board somewhere will accept it and set a precedent."

"So . . . no draft board's accepted it yet?" I ask.

"Not that I've heard of."

Fuck! Sure would have been nice if Charles had mentioned that three weeks ago!

"I hear you can flunk the physical by smoking cigarettes dipped in ink," Rudy says, trying to be helpful. "Cough a lot during the examination. The ink stains your lungs. Looks like tuberculosis on the X-ray."

Imagining lungs full of ink is not the most pleasant thought. "And suppose that doesn't work?"

"If I were you? I'd seriously consider prison." He tells me that draft refusers are getting sentenced to two or three years in minimum-security jails where you're not mixed in with hardcore criminals. David Harris, the husband of the folk singer Joan Baez, is in a minimum-security prison that even has tennis courts.

(*Bang!* Two small flakes of paint flutter down from the ceiling. I know Musclini's moods. When he works out this hard, he's extra pissed off about something.)

It's hard to imagine going to prison, even the minimum-security variety. Two or three years sounds like an eternity. Given the shakiness of things with Robin right now, is it realistic to think she'd be there when I got out? Once again regret and self-reproach well up. *What was I thinking last year? Why didn't I try to get my grades up for Goddard after they wait-listed me?*

Long-distance phone calls to Canada are expensive. No point in staying on the phone when all I'm doing is castigating myself. But before I hang up, I ask Rudy how it's going in Saskatchewan. He says it's lonely. There's a piano in a nearby church, but it's a piece of crap and doesn't stay in tune. He says he's felt suicidal at times; the only thing that keeps him going is the hope that life will get better. As soon as he can move, the Toronto Draft Programme's said it will place him in an apartment with other draft dodgers.

Is that my future, too? Stuck in an apartment with a bunch of draft resisters? Doing what? Jesus. Sounds depressing.

"So, what do you think you'll do?" Rudy asks.

"I don't know; all the options feel either shitty or iffy." Which pretty much describes the way I'm feeling, too.

He must hear how bummed I am. "You a musician?"

Huh? "No. Why?"

"You might consider cutting off a finger. I'll send you the information."

Would I be out of my mind to choose prison? Look on the plus side: two or three years with plenty of time to read and write, and maybe even get back into tennis.

Bang! I stare up at the ceiling. For much of my life, Musclini has been angry. In addition to the bulk-mail factory and the chain of Laundromats, he owns a small apartment building. His anger stemmed from people who broke washers and dryers or jammed the coin slots with slugs. From the apartment repairs he constantly had to pay for and tenants who were behind in their rent. Angry that sometimes he had to take them to court, and even angrier when he himself got taken to court. It was hard for me to understand why anyone would want to be involved in businesses that caused so much grief.

But next to winning tennis tournaments, the thing that

makes Musclini happiest is embarking on new business ventures that he imagines will make us "golden." With each new venture, the paterfamilias convinces himself that he knows something that will make the property or business much more profitable for him than it is for the current owner. I've never understood how, only being familiar with a property or business for a few weeks, the paterfamilias can believe that he knows more than the person who's owned the property or run the business for decades. But back in the days when he spoke to me about such things, he'd insist that all we had to do was increase capacity by 50 percent, add two stories to the property, get the current tenants out, remodel the place, and raise the rents. (It was always "we," as if in his mind I was a junior capitalist tool in training.)

Invariably, *all we had to do* turned out to be a huge headache, if not downright impossible. When he bought the bulk-mail company, he told me that all we'd have to do was add a dozen more inserters and the investment would pay for itself in five years. But it turned out that state occupancy laws prevented him from doing that. (Despite that, he must eke a small profit out of the operation or he would have gotten rid of it by now.)

The poignant irony is that while the paterfamilias imagines himself to be a corporate bigwig, for years most of the money he's made has come from the chain of Laundromats—a business he more or less stole. A friend of his from college built the Laundromat business and had a dozen of them spread out around the New York area. The man had no family, and when he got cancer, he sold the operation to the paterfamilias. More than once I've heard the paterfamilias brag that he bought the chain "for a song," as if he were some sort of entrepreneurial genius and not simply an opportunistic dick who took advantage of a dying friend.

"Tell your father to get Alan out of the tub." I've just started another letter to Robin when Mom knocks on my door. This isn't the first time I've been assigned interparental messenger duty, but this summer it's been a nearly permanent position.

Alan used to hate baths. As a kid he could go months without one and never smell too bad, except for his feet, which Mom would periodically scrub while he stood ankle-deep in the tub.

But about a year ago, around the time he turned fourteen, body odor discovered him. Now about once a week Mom bribes him with Three Musketeers bars. The funny thing is, once you get him into the bathtub, he always wants to stay. Getting him out has become the paterfamilias's job.

I climb the attic stairs. On a rainy evening like this, I'm surprised to find Musclini shirtless, his skin glimmering with sweat. Free weights and barbells are scattered about the rubber mat on the attic floor, but right now he is straining against an immobile bar in the wooden isometric rack. At five foot ten, he's more lean than brawny. He does lots of reps for strength and endurance, thus his muscles aren't he-man bulky. Better for tennis, he says.

When I was around nine or ten, I got into my first real fight and came home with a split lip and a large reddish bruise on my left temple. (The only punch I remember landing got the other kid in the ear.) Dad told me that growing up he'd been a skinny, frail kid and was beaten up regularly. It got so bad that his mother begged the school to let Dad out five minutes early each day so he'd have a head start before the bullies came after him. I was shocked to hear that. In our house, he's always been the ultimate physical enforcer. It was hard to imagine that he might have once been on the receiving end.

After the fight, I asked the paterfamilias to get me a chin-up bar because Cousin Barry had one and he was strong. Dad was thrilled. He was always trying to get me to exercise. Always encouraging me to lift weights, to do "isometric" exercises on this thing that looks like a wooden torture rack. He never came right out and said that it worried him that I was soft and weak as a kid. But so much of what he did implied it.

Now, in the attic, Musclini stops straining against the torture rack. I relay Mom's message about getting Alan out of the tub and head back downstairs to my room.

When I got home from work today, there were new items on my desk. Mom left an article reporting that enlistments fell far short of the army's goal last year (*Hell no, we won't go*). In the margin, in blue fountain-pen ink, my mother's slim script: "Won't they have to make up the shortfall by increasing the draft?"

And the paterfamilias left a Department of Motor Vehicles change-of-address form with my name and the address of the apartment in Bay Shore filled in. Paper-clipped to it is a note "From the desk of Richard Baker" ordering me to "sign immediately." I wonder what he's up to with this change-of-address stuff. No point in asking. He would have told me if he wanted me to know. I sign the DMV form in the hope that it will mean the government will have a few less tax dollars to spend on napalm.

As far as increasing the draft, it's hard to know what the government is up to. Last month Nixon declared that the United States would soon begin drawing down the number of troops in Nam, but that hasn't started yet. On the other hand, nearly two hundred thousand men have been inducted (they either enlisted or were drafted) this year, and it's only July. That's the second-highest pace of any year since the Korean War. With fewer and fewer men enlisting voluntarily, there's only one way to fill the ranks: the draft.

A shout echoes through the house, followed by Alan's cry. I'm out of my room and trotting down the hall when Musclini storms out of the bathroom, still bare-chested, his face red and glistening from his workout. Alan's in the tub bawling. Floating in the water around him are three brown turds.

It's gross, but it's Alan. Who knows why he did it. Maybe he had to go, and rather than get out of the tub and sit on the toilet wet and shivering, he figured it was easier in the tub. Or maybe he was curious to see what would happen. He's always been a barometer of the family's moods; maybe he's acting out because he can feel the mountains of tension around here.

But there's nothing malicious about what he's done. For all I know, taking a dump in the tub is the kind of thing a lot of kids try once. Including some who don't have anything wrong in the head.

But it's set Musclini off. And here he comes stomping back down the hall with the wooden paddle.

"Richard, what are you doing?" Mom shouts, following.

The only thing standing between Musclini and Alan is me, in the bathroom doorway. It's been so long since he's spanked Alan that I'm shocked he still has the paddle.

"Out of the way!" he shouts.

Faced with such patriarchal fury, the ingrained impulse has always been to cower and obey. But tonight the opposite reaction unexpectedly blossoms. Maybe it's because this is ridiculous. Alan's not a little kid anymore. Maybe it's because I can't stand by and let my brother be a punching bag. I'm bigger, taller, and weigh more than Musclini. What's he going to do if I don't get out of the doorway? Hit *me* with the paddle?

Musclini stops in the hallway, as if expecting me to clear the path. But something inside won't let me. Whatever's causing my defiance, it feels like the blood in my veins has been replaced with pure adrenaline. If I had a fuse and someone lit it, I'd probably rocket straight through the ceiling.

Breathing hard, the vessels in his reddened temple pulsing, Musclini's expression gradually morphs from fury to something akin to stupefaction. My heart is galloping, and I'm holding my breath. I've never stood up to him *physically* before. Never thought I *could* stand up to him before. But strangely, while my heart knocks anxiously and my lungs cry for air, this feels like the culmination of something that's been festering for years. It occurs to me that I might even have red-eyed Pagan's Clyde to thank; if I managed to live through what happened in Central

Park, then surely I can survive whatever my father might do, right?

Musclini tilts his head to the side, his consternation melting into something almost akin to curiosity. Is he also realizing that a balance between us has changed? That he may be the father and the boss, but his rulership by force need no longer be tolerated?

Into the space between us steps Mom, as stern as an old-fashioned schoolmarm. "Go away, Richard," she orders.

Musclini's tensed shoulders stoop. His eyes meet mine, and he nods as if saying, *Okay, you win this round.* He turns, retreats down the hall.

As Mom goes into the bathroom and opens a towel for Alan, she looks over her shoulder at me. "Thank you, Lucas."

Alan steps eagerly into the towel, and she wraps it around his shoulders and rubs reassuringly. I wander back down the hall toward my room, feeling a spectrum of emotions: relief, incredulity, pride. What just happened, wherever it came from, wasn't an act. It felt like it sprang from some conviction that's slowly been germinating inside. Something that may have begun as an abstract opposition to the oppression of the masses and a faraway war but feels like it's spread to a sense of outrage against injustice for the oppressed everywhere. Even before the floating turds, I could tell Musclini was angry about something tonight. It felt right to protect Alan. The war really has come home.

FRIDAY, JULY 25

"How long will it take to get there?" Tinsley's hand is on my thigh. I glance at Cousin Barry in the passenger seat of Odysseus. He's smoking and gazing out the window through a pair of aviator sunglasses.

"Figure nine hours," I reply. Physics alone cannot explain the degree of warmth I feel at the spot where Tinsley's hand lies. She is kneeling in the space between the front seats. She seems to enjoy tucking herself into small places like some sinuous feral creature looking for a spot where she can feel secure.

Barry looks down at her hand on my thigh. Behind the aviator glasses, his expression is unreadable. We are headed toward Ottawa.

An hour ago, on the way to Barry's house, I stopped at a gas station and picked up a case of SAE 30 motor oil. When I bought Odysseus last March, the previous owner warned me that it had a slow oil leak and needed an additional quart every couple of hundred miles. The trip from Long Island to Lake Juliette and back will be about a thousand miles, so I've stocked up.

From the gas station, I drove to Barry's. When I pulled into the driveway, he yelled down from the window of his room that he was still getting his act together. I went around to the back of the van, opened the engine compartment, and checked the dipstick. The oil level was low.

I'd just finished adding more when Tinsley came out of the house carrying a knapsack and camera bag. She was wearing round purple sunglasses and a straw hat with a wide brim. Brightly colored love beads and a leather cord with a peace pendant hung from her neck.

"We giving you a lift somewhere?" I asked, wiping my oily hands with a rag.

"Ottawa?" Her tone was teasing. She knew I'd be surprised. It's the first time I've seen her since the Planting Fields. Barry told me last week that he was coming north with me, but he didn't say anything about Tinsley coming with us. Coyly, she added, "You don't mind, do you?"

We are headed west on the Long Island Expressway with *Disraeli Gears* playing. Tinsley retreats to the mattress. There's barely enough room back there for someone to lie down beside the blank canvases, a duffel bag, a bright-yellow-and-orange butterfly kite, and two boxes of brushes and paints.

Tonight I'll drop Barry and Tinsley off in Ottawa, where Zach will pick them up and drive them the rest of the way to the farm. There's a strong back-to-the-land trend among many of our suburbanized, citified, alienated generation (though for some, the only farmland in their futures will be the rice paddies of the Mekong Delta). Tinsley says she plans to stay for about a week. Barry hasn't said how long he'll stay, but given what he's brought, it looks like he doesn't plan to come back anytime soon.

After I leave them, I'll continue north to Lake Juliette. To describe myself as looking forward to seeing Robin would be an understatement. Yesterday the mail that had been forwarded to Bay Shore finally appeared on my desk, including her second letter of the summer. It's nearly the end of July and she's been at Lake Juliette for a month. There have been many moments when I've been on the verge of calling, but long-distance phone calls are expensive, and international calls even more so. Adding to the phone bill after that call I made to Rudy in Saskatchewan would give the paterfamilias fits. (Or is that just a poor excuse for the real reason I haven't called Robin? Which is that I dread what she might say.)

On the envelope of the new letter from her, our address had been crossed out and the address for the apartment in Bay Shore handwritten in. The letter started off about camp, and the kids in her bunk, the terrible food, and her fellow counselors . . . Then this:

> Lucas, I feel bad that you've written so many letters and I've written so few. It's been so hard to get my thoughts sorted out. I do apologize for that. But now, the more I think about it,

the more I feel that when I go to Middlebury this fall I want to start over. I don't regret the things we did last spring. Well, maybe a little. But I've realized that that really isn't me. It's not who I am. Every day I wake up here and it's so beautiful. You don't have to get high. All you need to do is go outside in the fresh air. I love being outdoors. It feels so close to what is important. I feel like it could be this way at Middlebury, too.

But having said that, do you really think it will be a good idea for you to move to Waitsfield or Warren in September? You won't know anyone, and what will you do until ski season begins? You've always said the skiing is much better out west. If you want to spend a year as a ski bum, wouldn't this be the perfect time to go to someplace like Aspen or Vail? Maybe being a ski bum next year would be a good thing and give you time to figure out what you want to do with your life.

Also, is there anything new regarding the draft? Are you still pursuing the moral code conscientious objector route? How's it going? Whatever you do, please, please don't let yourself be drafted.

Finally, are you sure you want to come all the way up here just for a day? It seems so far to come, and even though it's my day off,

I recently found out that I have to be back by dinnertime because we're putting on a production of The Wizard of OZ that night and I'm in charge of costumes. So I'll only be able to see you from around eight in the morning until five. I'm not really sure what the point of it will be.

For the second time this summer, tears followed the reading (mine not hers). I've never missed anyone as much as I miss her, and yet she didn't write a word about missing me. Even worse, it's pretty obvious she doesn't think it's a good idea for me to move near Middlebury in the fall. Not only that, it sounds like she doesn't even want me to come up to visit her at camp. In her last letter, she talked about how uncomfortable she was with the way things are, and I wrote back that I could change. And I have. On any given day, I probably smoke less than half a pack, and I've cut way back on the grass, too. Haven't dropped acid since the Zeppelin concert. Big steps toward clean living. (Maybe I'll start drinking carrot juice next. Musclini would be thrilled.)

But I suspect that saying in letters that I've changed isn't enough. She needs to see the evidence herself. I plan on going nine smoke-free hours with her tomorrow. I'll have time to tell her about my plans for the future, provided of course that the future doesn't involve jungle combat. (It's Friday, and I'll be back in time to see Charles on Monday night. He's returned from his trip and has promised that we'll try to figure out the next step, one that doesn't involve a personal moral code and just-war theory.) And yes, I'll be a ski bum this winter, but I'll also be researching other possibilities, like the Peace Corps, working for civil rights, maybe applying to Goddard again. At this point, those may just be words, but if I can hold on to her long enough, she'll see that I mean them.

"Looking forward to seeing your girlfriend?" Tinsley and I are sitting on a bench outside a Thruway Hot Shoppe, watching the orange sun drop toward the rounded green caps of distant mountains. Barry is inside using the john. Tinsley is wearing her wide-brimmed straw hat and purple glasses. Drivers, truckers, and families pass on the sidewalk. Lots of double takes. Lots of stares, following the exotic scent of Tinsley's clove cigarette. She is rocking one leg over the other, the toe of her cowboy boot sticking out from under the long purple Indian-print skirt.

"Yes, very much so" is my answer. (Though I wonder what she'd think if she knew on how many lonely nights these past few weeks it's been her I've undressed in carnal fantasies?)

She exhales clove-scented smoke. Her face and clothes are tinted in orange sunlight. "What do you think of groupies, Lucas?"

"Uh, don't know." What I do know is that Tinsley seems to enjoy tossing out non sequiturs, as if ordered thoughts are yet another social construct she seeks liberation from.

"I think they're fabulous," she says. "Having sex with no strings attached. Just the way men always have."

"So, uh, gonna try it?"

She tosses her head back and laughs. "No! Rock stars are gross. My father's new *petite copine* is a booking agent, and she got me and a friend backstage passes to meet Hendrix at Madison Square Garden. We were so jazzed. But then there was this other band there. I don't know if they were an opening act or what, but they were absolutely disgusting. When you got up close to them, they reeked. And they couldn't keep their grimy hands to themselves." She flicks ash from her cigarette and shivers. "We had to leave. Never even got to meet Jimi."

Now and then Tinsley reveals a tiny glimpse into her world. The way she does it feels more natural than forced. I don't get the feeling she's trying to impress anyone. (Though how could you not be impressed? *A chance to meet Hendrix?* How unbelievable would that be?)

"Your father's *petite copine?*" I know it's French, but I don't know what it means. I took four years of the language and never got better than a C.

"His girlfriend. *Mes parents sont divorcés.*"

I used to have a friend whose parents were divorced. There were probably other kids at school with divorced parents that I didn't know about. And how many had parents like mine, who stay together but with separate bedrooms? Mom and the pater-familias might as well be divorced.

"What's that like?" I ask.

"Without him around? Better. All they did was fight. And I never saw that much of him anyway because he was always working."

"What's he do?"

"International tax law. For conglomerates that want to expand overseas. It's all about developing new markets to

171

maximize profit and minimize cyclical risk." (Does she see my eyes glaze over?) "Suppose you have a company that makes winter coats. Right now you have one selling season, the fall. But if you expand into the Southern Hemisphere, you'll have two selling seasons."

Something tells me that she could go into far more depth and detail about what her father does. And this is the same "hippie chick" who sometimes goes around with bare, filthy feet.

"Of course, *he* was the one who always took my side." Tinsley sighs. "And pretty much let me do whatever I wanted. Now that it's just my mother and me, she feels like she has to be even more of a disciplinarian than ever. I mean, this is the first summer I've lived at home probably since I was ten. And she is *so* uptight."

"She can't be *that* uptight," I point out, "if she's letting you go with Barry to Canada."

With the toe of her cowboy boot, Tinsley crushes out her cigarette. "Who said she knows?"

Three boys, maybe eleven or twelve years old, are standing nearby, staring and whispering. They're wearing matching gray summer-camp T-shirts. When I give them a curious look, two of the boys nudge the third closer.

"Are . . . are you a boy or a girl?" he asks me, then dashes away toward a yellow camp bus. The other two boys remain a safe distance off, waiting to see how I'll react. When I turn my gaze on them, one tentatively offers a peace sign. I flash one back, and they excitedly congratulate each other, as if I'm a seal at the zoo and they've gotten me to clap my flippers.

"Your mother doesn't know you're on your way to Canada?" I ask, returning to the conversation.

"Oh, she does by now. I left a note."

"What's going to happen when you get back?"

Tinsley turns her palms upward. *"Ce n'est pas important."*

A couple of guys stroll past slowly. Flattops, T-shirts with the sleeves rolled up, jeans, and high-top sneakers. They make no effort to hide their leers as they undress Tinsley with their eyes. She ignores them, but I keep my gaze steady on them.

One of them mouths, *Faggot.*

Back in Odysseus heading north, I see the first sign for Lake Placid. Suddenly I am ten years old again, and Mom is rushing around the house while I play with my green plastic army men in the den. She calls to me to put on my ski jacket while she tries to wrestle Alan into a coat. As usual, I do as I'm told. But Alan doesn't want to go anywhere and keeps trying to squirm away.

Mom gives up on the coat. Next, she can't find one of Alan's shoes. She tells me to hold Alan's sticky, nose-picky hand and keep him near the front door while she searches for the shoe.

I hold Alan's hand, but he keeps trying to yank it free. Mom's agitation makes me agitated, and I punch Alan in the arm and yell at him to stay still. Alan starts to cry.

Mom comes back without the other shoe. Alan complains that I hit him. Mom scoops him up, and out we go into the cold gray winter afternoon.

In the station wagon, Alan sits in front wearing one shoe and no coat. I'm behind him, a small suitcase on the seat beside me. Mom backs out of the driveway fast, then hits the brake so hard that my head snaps back. I think something must be wrong and start to get scared. Mom drives fast down our street and out to the main road.

We go to the train station. It's midafternoon, so I assume Dad is coming home from work early and we're there to pick him up. (This is back when he goes to the city each day and I am excited to greet him when he comes home at night. Before he uses his brilliant business acumen to acquire the chain of Laundromats. Before he becomes the paterfamilias.)

But at the train station, Mom hops out of the car and pulls open the back door. "Hurry!" She grabs the small suitcase.

To Alan, she says, "Stay here. I'll be right back."

Why are we getting out of the car? Why did Mom tell Alan to stay? Has she ever left him alone in the car before? What if he tries to drive away?

Bells have started clanging, and red lights flash. Mom squeezes my hand and pulls. She wants us to cross the tracks, but the train is coming. The loud whistle startles me. Everything is backward. The approaching train is headed toward the city, not away from it like when Dad comes home from work. Mom tugs, but I'm scared and pull back. The whistle is too loud, the train too close. The engine looks huge. The crossing gates are coming down. Mom tries again to get me to cross, but I cry out, "No!"

The gates drop and the train passes a dozen feet from us.

Close enough that I can feel the heat radiating from the engine. It's frightening. The iron wheels are nearly as tall as I am. The loud screech of the brakes hurts my ears.

The train is slowing down. Mom waves up and shouts something. We start running toward the back. By the time we reach the last car, the train has stopped. Mom leads me across the tracks behind it. The cold air stinks of diesel fumes. On the other side of the train, a conductor in a dark-blue uniform and small round cap is standing on the steps, looking down at us. I think he must have heard Mom shout. She hands him my suitcase, then quickly hugs and kisses me and tells me to do what the conductor says.

I'm going to the city alone. I don't know why I'm not more frightened. I've never gone anywhere alone except to school or a neighbor's house. Maybe I'm too young to know I should be scared. Maybe I'm not frightened because the conductor is reassuring when he tells me where to sit and not to go anywhere.

I sit by myself on a broad seat with my suitcase beside me. Some people who pass look around for an adult who should be with me. The conductor checks on me a few times, then gets off the train with me at our final stop, a huge, echoey train station filled with strange smells and surging crowds. Clutching my suitcase tightly, I wait with the conductor. Everyone is grown up, wearing coats and carrying briefcases, their hurried steps slapping on the platform. Then Dad is coming toward us. He's wearing his fedora and tan camel-hair coat. He thanks the conductor and takes me by the hand.

We climb steps and cross through the huge train station

with its crowds and noises and more strange smells. So many shoes and legs and briefcases belonging to men wearing coats and fedoras. I hold Dad's hand tight and ask where we're going. He looks surprised. Don't I remember that we're going skiing?

We leave Penn Station. The sidewalk is crowded. It's dark and see-your-breath cold. The city is all streetlights, headlights, car horns, and people in a hurry. A robin's-egg-blue Thunderbird is parked at the curb. It's the model with the round portholes in the sides of the roof. A lady with black hair and bright-red lipstick is sitting behind the wheel. Dad introduces her as Hazel. She says "Hello, Lucas" in a perfunctory manner. The car has no back seat, so the three of us squeeze into the front. Hazel smells sweet and flowery. We are going to Lake Placid.

Later that night, I sit on a bed in a room that smells like pine trees. Paintings of mountains and streams with deer and moose hang on the walls, which are paneled with glossy light-brown wood with knots and some round holes where knots must have fallen out. Dad helps me into my pajamas and then into the bed. The sheets feel stiff and scratchy, but I am soon asleep.

In the morning we have pancakes, sausage, and orange juice with Hazel. I don't remember what is said, but I do remember Dad smiling and speaking in an animated fashion that is different from the somber grumpy way he often is at home.

At the mountain, Dad rents me skis, poles, and boots, then walks me to a J-bar and tells me to ski the broad, gentle slope it feeds. Already adept at the snowplow turn, I pretend I am a white-clad soldier on mountain patrol and have fun riding the

J-bar. You are supposed to stand and let the bar make contact just below your butt and pull you up the mountain. But I am small enough to sit on the bar and ride it like a chairlift.

Around lunchtime Dad is waiting at the bottom of the lift. He is wearing his white ski jacket, but instead of stretch ski pants, he has on his gray suit pants and furry après-ski boots. We have lunch in the lodge and then he sends me out skiing again.

That night we have dinner with Hazel. Afterward, I am pooped from patrolling the mountain all day and go straight to bed.

The next morning Dad and I ski together. After lunch, we get into the Thunderbird with Hazel and start the drive home. We stop at a Hot Shoppe on the Thruway, and Dad buys me a bottle of Coca-Cola and a bag of Wise potato chips. These are treats I am normally only allowed to have on very special occasions like birthdays.

That evening we take the train from the city and a cab home from the station. Before we go into the house, Dad tells me not to say anything to Mom about Hazel. I am a dutiful and obedient son and do as I am told.

In the distance, several brightly lit booths span the dark highway. Red-and-white maple leaf flags fly above them. It's a few minutes after eleven p.m.

Barry rouses from his slumber in the seat beside me and rubs his eyes. "The border? Shit. Shit!"

I feel a tight chill. There's only one reason why he'd be so freaked. "You carrying?"

He bites a knuckle. "Zach asked me to bring a couple of lids."

Were a tachometer measuring my pulse, it'd be redlining. If we can see the border crossing ahead, then the agents in those booths can see us — or see our headlights, anyway. And right now, that's enough.

Barry has to know what a couple of ounces represents. Possession with intent to sell . . . serious jail time. "Pull over," he urges. He wants to get rid of the grass.

Too late for that. "It'll look suspicious. They'll know why."

"Shit! *Shit!*" Barry continues freaking. Tinsley squeezes into the space between the seats and gives me a wide-eyed look.

"Just be cool," I tell them. Easy to say; I'm gripping the steering wheel so tightly that my fingernails are digging into my palms.

"Fuck," Barry gripes anxiously. "Fuuuuuck!"

We can't arouse suspicion. What comes from my lips next isn't quite shouted but close. "I said cool it!"

Meanwhile, we're getting closer to the crossing and Barry's anything but cool. "I got busted last year for possession. My parents kept it quiet and made a deal with the district attorney. It's why I had to go back to Silver Hill. But I get caught again, it'll be the slammer for sure."

We do not want Cousin Barry to go to jail. We don't want Lucas or Tinsley to go there, either. At least not for drugs. I doubt you get sent to a minimum-security prison with tennis courts for possession with intent to sell.

We're nearing the booths. Barry slides out of the front seat and into the back. An unzipping sound follows.

"Don't throw it out the window!" I shout. "We're too close. They'll see."

The border agents are visible through the booth windows. Each one is wearing a dark-blue short-sleeve uniform.

"I'm putting it in your knapsack," Barry says from the back. "If they search us, you can say you didn't tell us you were carrying. They're not that hard on first offenders."

I don't know about that. I don't know about anything right now except the blood loudly pulsing in my ears. Here we come, three degenerate hippie freaks in a psychedelically painted microbus. If I were a border guard, I wouldn't be wondering *if* we were carrying drugs. I'd be wondering what kind of drugs and how much. The Canadians may be happy to accept American draft evaders, but I have a feeling they don't feel quite the same way about drug runners.

We're about twenty-five yards from the crossing. "Get in the front seat," I tell Tinsley.

We stop beside a booth, and I take my hands off the steering wheel so my white knuckles won't be visible. Despite the coursing adrenaline that makes me feel like jumping out of my own skin, I concentrate on trying to appear relaxed. A ruddy-cheeked, heavy-lidded border agent with a blond mustache glances in at us. Maybe it's my imagination, but it seems like his bushy blond eyebrows rise with extra interest when he sees that we're freaks. "Identification," he says.

We hand over our driver's licenses. He shines a flashlight on them, then on our faces. My insides whirl at hamster-wheel speed. Riding shotgun, Tinsley smoothly takes out a cigarette and lights it. Thank God she's got her act together. I can only pray that Barry doesn't suddenly burst out the side door and try to hightail it into the woods.

"What's the purpose of your visit, Lucas?" the agent asks.

"Weekend jaunt, sir."

"Oh, yeah? Where?"

"Lake Juliette, sir. My girlfriend's a counselor at a camp up there."

"Your girlfriend, eh?" The agent shines the flashlight at Tinsley.

"She's his girlfriend, sir." I jerk my thumb toward the back.

The border agent aims the beam into the back of the bus, illuminating Barry, the mattress, the canvases, and the boxes of painting supplies. "Lot of gear for a weekend visit."

"We're all painters, sir. Supposed to be some beautiful land-scape up that way."

The border agent aims the flashlight into my face, making me squint. Seconds crawl slowly past. My gut is one solid cramp from throat to butt. The blood courses in my scalp, and I feel a headache coming on.

"Don't hear the word 'sir' much from you longhairs," the agent says.

Inspiration strikes. I raise a hand to shield my eyes from the flashlight's glare. "Military family, sir. Got it drummed into me at an early age."

He lowers the flashlight a bit. "Military, eh? Not dodging the draft, now, are yah?"

"No, sir. I'm headed for college this fall. But to be honest? Were that an issue, I'd probably consider it."

I'm hoping he'll find my frank reply endearing, but he merely nods in a cursory way and shines the beam over the brightly painted psychedelia on the outside of Odysseus. "And what's your military family think of this rig, Lucas?"

"Honestly, sir? Drives 'em out of their freakin' minds, if you'll excuse my French."

The border agent studies me. His expression is unreadable. My innards clench in near spasm. I've overdone it. *Shit!* I've definitely sounded too ingratiating. Tried too hard to appear as if nothing is wrong.

The corners of his lips curl upward. He hands back the IDs. "Have a nice weekend painting."

I drive through the border feeling light-headed, my arms shaking. That was way, *way* too close.

You know you're far away from everything when not a single car passes while you stand on the side of the road watching your microbus burn.

Twenty minutes ago, Odysseus's engine started to sputter. A small red warning light in the speedometer began to glow. Tinsley was sacked out in the passenger seat. Barry was still in the back.

I thought I saw something strange in the side-view mirror. "See anything behind us?"

Barry pushed a box aside, climbed over the duffel, and looked out the back window. "Sparks."

Definitely not good. Odysseus misfired and continued to lose power. What a night. First we risked getting busted at the border. Then this. It was beginning to feel like the gods were sending a message. A second red warning light began to glow. We were in the middle of an endless Canadian nowhere. Nothing but the dark silhouette of forest on both sides of the road. In the side-view mirror, a trail of orange-red sparks had begun to swarm over the road behind us.

The headlights flickered and dimmed. Odysseus, intrepid traveler and faithful companion, was slowly failing. A short distance ahead, through the bug-spattered windshield, was a road sign: Kemptville 2.

In the seat beside me, Tinsley opened her eyes and sat up. Before she could ask what was happening, Barry yelled, "There're flames coming out!"

For the second time tonight, his voice was tight and panicky. I heard bustling and looked over my shoulder just as he was reaching for the side door.

"Don't!" I shouted.

"But . . ."

"Get your stuff together. I'll tell you when." All I needed was for him to jump out while we were moving. He'd probably break a leg, if not his skull.

Odysseus continued to slow. The fire was in the engine compartment in the rear. As long as we were moving, I hoped

182

the flames would trail behind and not spread forward into the microbus.

For all I knew, Kemptville might have been nothing more than a bar, a church, and a post office, but we needed to get as close as we could to some form of civilization before we bailed into the vast empty Canadian night.

Odysseus's headlights flickered one last time, then faded. Everything went black. It was time to abandon my beloved vessel.

Now we're standing a safe distance away, watching smoke seep out of the engine compartment. The flames have gone out. Every few moments, a small glowing red scrap falls to the road shoulder beneath the bus.

The inky world around us is so still, it feels like time has stopped.

Beside the road, in a field of tall grass and wildflowers beneath a black star-speckled dome, Tinsley and I lie on our backs under a blanket on the mattress I dragged out of Odysseus. Despite our urging that he wait until morning, Cousin Barry insisted on walking into Kemptville to see if there's a place to spend the night. I imagine that after years of hardly leaving his house, Barry's not that keen on sleeping under the stars.

I have never seen a night sky so black, or dotted with so many shimmering pinpricks. But that blackness reflects the gloom weighing on my heart. I suspect that I'm still hours from my ladylove. In the morning, even if we find some sort of public transportation to Ottawa, how will I get the rest of the way to Camp Juliette? Especially before five p.m.?

No answer is forthcoming. I guess I should wait until morning before giving up hope. Meanwhile, I have something else to mourn. It is said that you should never love anything that cannot love you back, but were Odysseus capable of emotion, I am certain the feeling would be mutual.

Unlike Arno, whose dependence on the GTO is probably a mask for feelings of inadequacy. Unlike the paterfamilias, whose pride in his MG "classic" is an advertisement for what he imagines is his maverick entrepreneurial image. My love for Odysseus was born out of its slow, rattling, oil-slurping vulnerability. The bravery with which the microbus forged ahead without power steering, without power brakes, without power, period, in a world increasingly populated by bigger, stronger, brawnier vehicles.

I knew that Odysseus's leaky four-cylinder fifty-horsepower engine was its Achilles' heel. (Oops, could Odysseus have an Achilles' heel? An Achilles' wheel? What would Miss Landers, she of the Hell's Grammarians, say about that?) I once looked into having the engine replaced, but the projected cost of parts and labor amounted to more than I'd paid for the entire microbus.

And I think of the real Odysseus, the Greek king for whom my vehicle was christened. The brave warrior who slept many nights under star-filled skies while he journeyed for ten years to reach his home. The stalwart voyager who ordered his sailors to bind him to the ship's mast so that he would not succumb to the sirens' song on his quest to reach Penelope, his wife, the woman he loved.

Earlier today I began the journey to my Penelope.

Now what?

Beside me on the mattress, the siren Tinsley sighs.

"You okay?" I ask.

"I should be asking you. I'm so sorry about your bus."

The night air is heavy with moisture. Tinsley and I pull the blanket to our chins. It stinks of smoke. I think back to the first time Robin and I shared a mattress. We'd been going together for nearly five months. She was a virgin and insisted it be at my house, not hers. I tried to be gentle, but she was tense and couldn't relax. The little mewls that left her lips were not of pleasure (sex would improve with practice). I've always felt bad that it wasn't a magical experience for her.

"Don't you love looking at the stars?" Tinsley asks. "They make everything in the universe seem closer, you know?"

"Makes everything seem really far away to me," I answer. Maybe because right now, everything important seems so far away.

Tinsley props herself on her elbow. "It's not about distance, Lucas. It's a feeling. Being part of everything. You, me, the ground, the sky." She places her hand on the blanket over my chest. "Breathe in. Feel the air enter your lungs."

I take a deep breath and feel the air. I also feel Tinsley's hand on my chest. She can't possibly be coming on to me, can she? Not here. Not now. She has to know how completely bummed I am.

And yet her face moves closer in the dark. "You were amazing tonight. I mean, at the border. I was so certain we were going to get busted. My mother would have gone batshit."

I continue to be astonished that my bluff worked. Dumb luck, I suspect.

"You had such command of the situation." She brushes some hair away from my face, her fingers grazing my cheek.

Don't, Tinsley, I hear myself think. *You've chosen the wrong guy, wrong place, wrong time.* And yet I don't stop her. Do I like her attentions more than I want to admit?

"Barry showed his true colors, didn't he?" Her voice goes hard in a way I haven't heard from her before. Has, for just an instant, a vestige of her disciplinarian mother slipped through?

I defend my cousin. "He was freaking. You know, not thinking about the implications."

"You really believe that?" Tinsley asks. Clearly she doesn't, but maybe she doesn't know my cousin as well as I imagine. Barry wasn't being rational. He was overcome with fear and panic. Another bust and they were going to lock him away. Behind that groovy exterior, the boy who was once so tough and daring has been reduced to a fragile and frightened casualty. The first couple of years after the beating he hardly left the house. Spent his days in the living room with the lights off and the curtains drawn, a shadow with cigarette smoke slowly spiraling into the air. On the rare occasion when he did go outside, it was usually to fly a kite in the street. He rarely left the block.

"When the bus caught fire. How calm you were." In the dark, Tinsley's caressing fingers rest on my face long past the

186

time required to brush a few more strands away. She leans close, blocking out the stars. The scent of patchouli is in my nostrils, an involuntary stirring in my loins. The siren calls, and I have no sailors to fix me to the mast.

But I hate the way my father cheats on my mother. . . .

Tinsley's lips, parted ever so slightly, are on mine. Why do I so passively accept them, when the lips I yearn to feel are Robin's? Am I worried about hurting Tinsley's feelings? Or is it because right now a kiss from Robin is as distant as the stars above?

Tinsley keeps the kiss short, then whispers, "That's for saving us."

She gently slithers off me, then presses herself against my side, her arm resting on my chest.

SATURDAY, JULY 26

"Zach'll be here in a couple of hours," Barry says early the next morning, stepping out of a phone booth beside a Rexall drugstore in Kemptville. Tinsley and I are sitting at a picnic table, our knapsacks, Barry's duffel bag and camping stove, the butterfly kite, and some of his art supplies on the ground beside us. Last night Barry returned in the dark to say he'd found the town but everything was closed. Half an hour ago, I bade farewell to Odysseus and wished it safe journey to that hallowed junkyard in the sky. Then, carrying what we could, we walked here. The sun is barely above the thick green tree line to the east. The gathering heat is gradually drying the dew that accumulated during the night. A harsh chorus of cicadas has started to rise. Feels like it's going to be hot today.

The *I Ching* coins clatter softly on the road map of southern Ontario that I've spread on the table. Tinsley scribbles in her notebook. Barry sits down beside her and lights a Camel.

"I'm gonna head back." I hate saying it. I want so badly to forge ahead to my ladylove, but Lake Juliette is at least eighty miles to the north and west, out many narrow roads (not all of them paved, according to the map) in the wilderness. I could try to hitch there, but I doubt I'd make it by five, the time Robin has already warned me that my visit with her will end. And even if I were to miraculously make it to the camp by dark, I'd have nowhere to crash tonight.

Meanwhile, now that my personal-moral-code conscientious objector application has no chance of succeeding, I need to get back to Long Island in time to meet with Charles on Monday and figure out what the alternatives are.

The rising chorus of cicadas fills the air. A man in overalls driving a red tractor slowly passes, pulling a wagon stacked high with bales of pale-green hay. Tinsley closes her notebook and gathers her coins. "I'm going back, too." Her eyes slide toward me. "That okay with you?"

A pair of blackbirds lands on an overhead electric line. A boxy 1950s Chevy sedan rolls past. The two gray-haired ladies inside stare at us. It can be a long, slow trip for a guy hitching alone. Most people won't pick you up. But hitching with a petite, sexy-looking blond chick? Like going from a Ford Model T to Craig Breedlove's *Spirit of America*.

But why isn't Tinsley going to the farm? Why not wait with Barry in Kemptville for Zach? Why risk the unknowns that come with trying to hitch all the way home? But then I think back to last night on the mattress, and to something I've felt ever so slightly simmering since she strolled out of Barry's house yesterday and asked if I'd mind if she came with us to Canada: a gradually growing inclination that—sometime last night or this morning—became a decision.

I glance curiously at Barry.

He picks a speck of tobacco off his lip and gazes off. "So be it."

An awkward parting. Tinsley gives Barry a hug. When I shake his hand, his eyes don't meet mine. Has he interpreted Tinsley's decision to mean she'd rather be with me than him? Are those averted eyes the gesture of someone who thinks he's been replaced? I feel bad. He's my cousin, the guy I grew up admiring. The one who has struggled so mightily with his demons for so long. Even though I had nothing to do with Tinsley's decision, I feel as guilty as if the decision had been mine.

My hand still clasping Barry's, a wave of familial affection prompts me to pull him close for a hug. "Have fun up there. Catch you on the flip side, okay?"

"The music festival," he reminds me. "Three weeks."

Right, right. "For sure, man. See you there. Peace, brother."

Full
Backtal
Nudity.

Inside the one-story U.S. Customs and Border Protection building, two uniformed agents march me into a pea-soup-green room with the shades drawn, the sunlight sending bar-like shadows across an American flag and a framed picture of Nixon.

A few moments ago, Tinsley and I were pulled out of a car at the border. The couple who'd picked us up an hour ago were hungry for conversation after a week of hiking in Gatineau Park. Now they're waiting outside while their car is searched. Meanwhile, Tinsley and I have been forcibly escorted into this building. (A female agent took Tinsley to another room.)

I am totally wigging. Nerves lit. Heart flat-out racing as if I've just sprinted two hundred yards. Bladder threatening to empty on the spot. *How could I have forgotten about Barry's two lids?*

No amount of sirring and fakery is going to save my sorry ass this time. My legs feel like rubber bands. I'm trying, and failing, to breathe normally. When an involuntarily moan escapes my lips, both agents jerk their heads up.

"Something you want to tell us?" one asks.

"No, sir." *Christ!* I might as well have just confessed.

One of the agents dumps the contents of my knapsack on a table. Three sets of eyes quickly inspect the results. Incredibly, there's nothing that looks like two lids of grass among the underwear, spare shirts, toiletries, and the blue-and-yellow license plates I took off Odysseus this morning before abandoning it.

An unintended sigh of relief forces itself out of my lungs. The agents frown. One of them unbuckles the outside pockets of the knapsack. A few eight-track cassettes, a paperback of Kerouac's *Dharma Bums,* a small robin's-egg-blue Tiffany box containing a sterling-silver love pendant with Robin's and my names inscribed.

Is it stress or relief that makes me go light-headed and bend at the waist to get the blood flowing before I keel over? When I straighten up, both agents are staring again. It's hard to imagine acting any more guilty, short of signing a written confession.

"*Sure* there isn't something you want to tell us?" asks one.

"No, sir." *Keep breathing*, I tell myself.

The agents comb through every item on the table, squeezing toothpaste out of the tube, peering at the tape in the eight-tracks. Meanwhile, all I feel is relief and an intense desire to get out of here. *Another narrow escape. Move over, Houdini. Make room for Lucasini.*

"Why were you hitchhiking?" one of them asks.

I gesture to the plates and explain that my VW microbus caught fire last night.

"You left it?"

I tell them what I paid for Odysseus and what it would have cost to install a new engine. A long moment passes while neither agent speaks. This has to be the end, right? They didn't find any drugs. There can't be any other reason for keeping me here, can there?

One of the agents starts to pull on a rubber glove. "Strip."

"What a fox! You balling her?" It's around dinnertime. A moment ago, Arno and I dropped Tinsley beside a tall black iron gate at the entrance to a winding, tree-lined driveway in Old Westbury. The house it led to wasn't visible from the road.

"No," I answer. After experiencing our first-ever body cavity searches, Tinsley and I sat on a bench outside the border patrol building while agents asked passing drivers if anyone was willing to give us a ride. (By then, the couple we'd ridden with to the border was long gone.) Tinsley's thinking of sending an account of her experience to the Ethel Walker School alumnae magazine, which is always looking for newsworthy items from graduates: *Muffy Fairchild-Worthington ('68) reports that this year's International Debutante Ball was a smashing success. Tinsley Stockton ('69) writes that she thoroughly enjoyed her first-ever body cavity search at the U.S.-Canadian border.*

We wound up snagging a ride all the way to Long Island with a salesman from the Hudson's Bay Company.

"Man, I was praying she'd invite us into the house," Arno says in the GTO. "You know she was rich?"

"That all you can think about?" I ask. It's been a long, frustrating twenty-four hours, and I am bushed.

Arno power-shifts into third. "Listen, Karl Marx, not everyone who's rich got that way by exploiting the proletariat, okay? Or by selling guns and bombs."

He's right. I shouldn't be giving him grief. Half an hour ago, he came to Little Neck to pick up Tinsley and me at the Scobee Diner, where the salesman had left us. Arno's got a good heart. He's always ready to help. When we were younger and some kids called Alan a retard, he never joined in.

I clap a hand on his shoulder. "Sorry. Thanks for coming to get us. I'm just beat."

• • •

In the house of dashed dreams, the paterfamilias's old green navy trunk is inside the front door. The TV is on in the den. Mom's in the kitchen, making salami-and-Swiss-cheese sandwiches on onion rolls. The only time she makes them is when we're going on a trip, and we haven't gone anywhere as a family in years.

"Robin called this morning. She was quite upset." Mom doesn't look up from the wooden cutting board, where half a dozen golden-brown deli onion rolls lie split open, both sides smeared with French's yellow mustard.

"What's going on?" I ask.

Thunk . . . thunk. The knife blade slices through salami and strikes the wood.

"Mom?"

"Alan's going to camp." She places three disks of salami on each roll. I feel my mouth fall open. Mom's never let Alan go away anywhere alone before. Not even for a sleepover.

"For how long?"

She won't look at me. "Until the end of August."

"Why?"

"We can't let him sit in front of the television for the whole summer, can we?"

I don't get it. "There's no day camp around here for kids like him?"

Thunk . . . thunk. The knife blade hits the cutting board. Finally Mom says, "It's best this way."

•   •   •

The house has three phones: one in the paterfamilias's bedroom, one in Mom's, and this wall phone in the kitchen. I dial zero and ask for the long-distance operator. At Camp Juliette, the person who answers says that Robin is busy with last-minute alterations to the costumes for *The Wizard of Oz*. Is this an emergency? I say that it's an urgent family matter.

I'm told to hold on. While I wait, Mom asks what happened. I tell her about Odysseus.

"What about Barry?" she asks.

I tell her.

"And his friend?"

I assume she knows about Tinsley because she speaks to her sister, my aunt Jane, practically every day. "She hitched back with me."

Mom's forehead bunches. She must be wondering why a young woman would go with Barry most of the way to Zach's farm in Canada, then decide to turn around and hitch all the way back with me. (I'm wondering about that, too. And part of me can't help thinking that maybe it wasn't so much that Tinsley wanted to be with me as that she was having second thoughts about taking off without permission. There's also the possibility that she really does go by the *I Ching*, though I'm not sure that jibes with the sort of personality who could probably explain in great detail why creating corporate conglomerates maximizes profit and minimizes cyclical risk.)

After getting only four or five hours of sleep on the mattress in the field last night, we could hardly keep our eyes open on the way home. But the Hudson's Bay salesman wanted to talk about

American politics, and especially what happened last week on Martha's Vineyard, when Senator Ted Kennedy (brother of JFK and Robert—both assassinated) drove off a bridge, and the woman (not his wife) in the car with him drowned.

"Want to know why Kennedy waited ten hours to tell the police?" the salesman said. "Because he and his cronies were busy crafting a story to cover it up."

(They should have consulted the paterfamilias. He's an expert in that area.)

It's taking forever for them to get Robin. I will definitely catch hell when the phone bill comes with the charges for this call and the one to Rudy in Saskatchewan.

Finally she gets on, sounding breathless, and asks where I am and if I'm okay. The kitchen phone has a long cord, and I stretch it through the doorway and out into the hall. The theme song from *The Dating Game* trickles out of the den.

When I tell Robin where I am, she starts to cry. (Is she sorry that I didn't make it? Or is she simply crying with relief after spending the day wondering if I'd died in a traffic accident?) I wait until she collects herself and then tell her about the demise of Odysseus and how I couldn't call sooner because I was hitching back home.

(But I could have—from the phone booth outside the Rexall in Kemptville, from the Thruway Hot Shoppe when the salesman from the Hudson's Bay Company stopped for gas, from a pay phone at the Scobee Diner, where Tinsley and I grabbed a bite while we waited for Arno to pick us up. All I'd needed to do was ask a cashier to change ten dollars into nickels and dimes. So why didn't I? Was it because Tinsley was there?)

Robin can't stay on the phone; she has to get back to *Oz*. She doesn't ask if I'll try to come north again to see her. She's in the camp office, where others can hear. Feeling a sense of urgency, I pour out a rushed synopsis of what I'd hoped to say face-to-face: I really love her. Never felt like this with anyone before. I've changed, cut back on smoking. I was driving up there to show her. She'll see when she gets home from camp. I just need the chance. That's all I'm asking.

Her reply is a loud sniff. In the background, a voice says, "Honey, they need you in the rec hall."

"I'll write to you," Robin says, and hangs up.

A terrible sense of apprehension coils itself around me and squeezes. Once again I think back to the day Robin departed for Canada. How she didn't seem pleased that I'd unexpectedly shown up to bid her adieu. How when I whispered I loved her, she didn't mouth the same (so her father wouldn't hear). How she didn't wave or even look back as they drove away. In every letter I've written, I've said I love her. She hasn't written it in any of the three letters she's sent. Even in the crowded camp office just now, when I said it, she could have said something like, "Me, too."

I feel drained. It's not only due to lack of sleep and residual stress from losing Odysseus and being searched at the border. The dread I feel regarding Robin weighs heavily.

Back in the kitchen, Mom is wrapping the sandwiches in

tinfoil. They're sending Alan away? It's the clearest sign yet that life in the house of dashed dreams has entered crisis mode, that it's gotten to a point where they don't want Alan to witness whatever's going on. Despite the fog of fatigue, I think back to a time when there was hope that with special schooling and tutoring, Alan would someday get up to speed. Back before Dad's faithlessness became a fact of family life. Back when Mom used to love to take us to Jones Beach. When she was sometimes lighthearted and capable of unexpected laughter. When, even on the days she drove Alan to and from the city, she managed to put dinner on the table.

"How is she?" Mom asks.

I've never spoken to her about my relationship with Robin. When I tell her that Robin's okay, she nods doubtfully, the way people do when they know they're not getting the whole story.

"Does she know you've been rejected by Goddard?" she asks.

"Yeah, she knows."

"And," Mom says next, "what about the draft?"

"Under control," I assure her. That couldn't be less true, but between Alan and Dad, she has enough grief. Besides, after the phone call with Robin, I'm not sure I give much of a damn. That letter she said she's going to write sounds ominous. Feels like I've been found guilty; the only question now is what the sentence will be.

This would be the moment when the door from the garage opens and the paterfamilias enters, wearing a white Lacoste tennis shirt and cream-colored tennis shorts. His face and arms are tanned except for the ring of pale skin around his right wrist where he always wears a sweatband.

He contemplates the prodigal son and her tormented ladyship. His expression doesn't change. He could be looking at cardboard cutouts. I realize it's been a long time since I've seen my parents in a room together. Unless you live in a castle, it takes effort to accomplish that.

"What happened?" the paterfamilias asks.

Guess he noticed that I'm home a day early and Odysseus isn't. I deliver my report regarding the demise of *der Wagen*.

"You're going to need a way to get to work." He looks at Mom. For an instant, I wonder if he's going to suggest that I use her station wagon. But Mom's eyes narrow in warning.

"He can use the MG," she says.

Not likely. I've hardly ever been allowed to drive the paterfamilias's cherished golden chariot. Heaven forbid I should put a scratch in those lustrous eleven coats of Rolls-Royce Willow Gold.

The color seems to drain from Musclini's face before racing back to a deeper reddish hue. I expect him to veto the idea and instead suggest that I drive his business car, a green Mercury Cougar, while he drives the MG. But, amazingly, he agrees. "To the factory and back. That's all. And be careful."

Things in the house of dashed dreams have indeed taken a strange turn.

And speaking of strange turns: "You're sending Alan away?" I direct the question at the paterfamilias.

His eyes dart at Mom. "It's your mother's decision."

199

"He's your son, too," I point out.

Musclini straightens up and puffs out his chest. He dips his forehead forward like a bull preparing to charge. "It's what's been decided," he says in a raised and deepened voice—a warning shot across the bow.

But it's just bark. Feels like we're back in the bathroom doorway again. "You said Mom made the decision. What about you? Do *you* think it's a good idea?"

You can feel the tension in the air. You can feel Mom and the paterfamilias forcing themselves not to look at each other. The paterfamilias maintains his confrontational posture. "I . . . agreed with her."

The kitchen grows hushed. The theme song from *Get Smart* seeps out of the den. The strain is unrelenting. The paterfamilias's shoulders gradually stoop. It's the way he's looked the few times I've seen him lose a tennis match. He leaves the kitchen.

Mom glances at me with a quizzical expression.

"What?" I ask.

She smiles weakly. "I believe you're growing up."

I yawn and drag myself out of the kitchen and down the hall. Once again I've stood up to the paterfamilias. But where I might have imagined feeling proud, instead I feel insecure and wary, as if, by inserting myself into the muffled hostilities between my parents, I've thrown off the precarious balance we've lived with for so long. Now what? What happens next?

Thankfully, I'm too tired to dwell on it. The long journey, the ominous conversation with Robin, the news about Alan, the confrontation with Musclini — all compound my weariness. In my room, my mattress on the floor is in the same tousled, unmade state as when I left. Suddenly I'm so wiped I can't be bothered to undress, other than to drop into the chair and start to tug off a boot.

That's when my eyes travel to my desk, where a white envelope lies. The return address states:

SELECTIVE SERVICE

OFFICIAL BUSINESS

IF NOT DELIVERED WITHIN FIVE DAYS
RETURN TO:

Selective Service
Local Board No. 3
Great Neck, NY 11021

I don't have to open it to know what it says.

MONDAY, JULY 28

Days Until Armed Forces Induction Physical: 32

"You shittin' me with this toy car, man?" Charles is bent over in the passenger seat of the MG. His knees are squeezed up to his chin, and his Afro is squashed against the fabric of the convertible roof.

I pass him a joint. "Think of it as a white man's pimpmobile."

"A white midget, maybe. So what happened to that groovy van?"

I deliver Odysseus's obituary.

"Bummer." Charles's knees are pressed so close to his face that he's having trouble getting the joint to his lips. The British clearly don't consider anyone over six feet two inches when they design sports cars. In the dimness, small drops of sweat glisten on Charles's forehead. Yesterday and today have been scorchers, and it's supposed to get worse before it gets better. I wonder if that's why the paterfamilias didn't insist that I drive his Mercury this week. He must have heard a weather forecast and decided he'd rather be in his business car with its AC. "Your old man really drive around in this thing?"

"Mostly to and from tennis on the weekends."

Charles wipes his forehead with his sleeve. "What'd you say his business was?"

"Different stuff." I find myself reluctant to tell him that my father owns two relatively small companies as well as some real estate. Nor do I want to mention that the paterfamilias has achieved the ultimate goal of capitalistic suburban life: not having to commute to the city. He's reached that venerated state of "making his own hours," which basically means taking time to play as much tennis (and chase as much tail?) as he wants. Coincidentally, one of the main tenets of the cultural revolution is also breaking out of the nine-to-five "rat race." The paterfamilias once told me he thought of himself as an "iconoclast." (According to the dictionary, "a person who attacks cherished beliefs or institutions.") I guess that's true in some ways, but it's definitely not in others. He's still pursuing the almighty dollar, still paying his workers less than they deserve, and no doubt charging higher rents than he needs to.

Charles exhales a cloud of smoke. Back in the church base-ment a little while ago, I showed him the order to report for the armed forces physical examination that had come in the mail, and told him why I was giving up on the personal-moral-code CO. He admitted that the argument's success rate has been negligible so far but added that, according to the Chinese philosopher Lao-tzu, "The journey of a thousand miles begins with a single step." I said I could dig that, but Lao-tzu probably wasn't facing one-in-five odds of getting his ass shot off.

"Try not to take this the wrong way, Lucas," Charles now says in the smoke-filled MG, "but you have got to be the stupidest white person I've ever met. You know how many brothers would kill to have your life? And you've done everything you could to throw it away."

It's hard to argue. My physical examination at the army induction center in Fort Hamilton, Brooklyn, is scheduled for August 29 at seven a.m.—one month from tomorrow. I can't stop thinking about those 242 dead men-children in *Life* magazine. About a photo I saw of the interior of an air force transport plane filled with row after row of flag-draped reusable aluminum caskets. What are my choices now? Canada? Prison? Fingerectomy? Maybe I could hide in the fallout shelter until the end of the war. A subterranean Anne Frank.

I was so distracted by my looming army physical that I couldn't focus at work today. My inserter jammed so many times that the foreman, Mr. DiPasquale, asked if I was okay. At lunch I raced over to the library to read up on David Harris, the husband of Joan Baez, who chose prison rather than fight in Vietnam. Turns out that Rudy didn't have the facts quite right. Harris is currently in the San Francisco County Jail. He's *supposed* to be sent to a minimum-security prison camp in Texas, where inmates live in barracks (so it's like the army, only you're not required to kill anyone), but that's not guaranteed. Draft resisters can be sent to either medium- or minimum-security prisons depending on where the federal prison system has vacancies. So I *could* get sent to a place where I might have a hard-core criminal for a roommate. Given the possibility of two or three years in a cell sixteen hours a day with someone like Red-Eyed Clyde of Pagan's fame, I'd seriously have to consider life with one less finger.

But tonight there's new hope for avoiding the draft. Last week Charles wasn't around because he was out in San Francisco, where he spent an afternoon talking to other draft counselors at the Berkeley chapter of the National Mobilization Committee to End the War in Vietnam (aka "the Mobe"). Recently the army doctors out there have started giving anyone who asked 1-Y draft status, which means the military won't call you into service unless America itself is attacked.

"All we gotta do is set you up with a phony address in the Bay Area, make it seem like you're actually living there. You cool with that?" Charles said back in the church office.

Cool with it? I was blinking back tears of relief and gratitude. Fake an address? Hey, I'm a pro. It's no different than pretending to live in Bay Shore, only, according to Charles, I won't have to sign any change-of-address forms. He warned me not to tell anyone about the scheme because if all the other "rich white kids" find out about it, they'll all start trying to shift their physicals to San Francisco, and that'll be the end of it. As soon as the Berkeley chapter of the Mobe creates the fake address, I'll fly out there for my physical, get my 1-Y, and be a free man.

"Were you out there on vacation?" I ask.

Charles gives me a disdainful look. "Could you please try to be a little less bourgeois, white boy? I know it's hard, but don't make me regret telling you about San Francisco."

"Sorry." *You can take the white boy of out of suburbs, but . . .*

"It was an exploratory expedition. Spent most of my time in Oakland, with the Panthers."

I stare through the smoke at him. The charges against the Panther 21 in New York may be trumped-up bullshit, but the last I heard, the organization was still a self-proclaimed violent revolutionary group. Members have been convicted of murder, as well as of engaging in gun battles with the police.

"Easy does it, my man." Charles puts his hand on my arm when he sees the surprise on my face. "Yeah, they can be violent, but only when violence is used against them. The reason they organized in the first place is because the Oakland pigs are the most racist and brutal police force in the country. How else were they supposed to protect themselves? Maybe you haven't noticed, but we live in a racist society, dig? The Panthers make an important point. Why should brothers be fighting for the freedom of the South Vietnamese when what we should really be fighting for is our freedom here?"

He lets go of my arm. "Last week opened my eyes. Things have changed. The Panthers are into social programs now. Feed the children. Kids who've had breakfast do better in school. Makes sense, right? It's hard to focus on learning when you're hungry and not sure where your next meal'll come from."

Even in my barely functional family, I've never, ever had to worry about not having enough to eat. Never even *considered* the possibility of police brutality. There are no black kids at my high school, no black families in my all-white community or at the country club. It seems incredible that for so much of my life I didn't even *think* about how anyone else (except for farmers) lived. Rich white boy, indeed.

Arno's one-joint-rebreathe-the-smoke experiment may not have worked in the fallout shelter, but here in the cramped and enclosed confines of the MG, the result appears to be more fruitful. Charles and Lucas the Honky Cracker finish the joint and space out in the fumy humid haze. Hard to imagine two people more similar and dissimilar. "Know what, Charles?" Lucas says.

"What's that, my man?"

"You may be a dissociated Jehovah's Witness —"

"Dis*a*ssociated," Charles corrects him. "If I was *dissociated*, we'd be having this rap at Creedmoor."

"Uh, yeah, right. Anyway, like I was saying, I think you've still got religion, man."

"Oh, yeah?" Charles chuckles. "What makes you say that?"

"Because tonight, in that office, you saved my ass. And you didn't have to, man. Maybe you didn't even *want* to. Maybe I don't deserve it. But you did it because you knew it was the right thing to do."

Charles looks off into the dark and then back. "Remember, it's not a done deal yet. But we'll see what we can do. And if that's your way of saying thank you, white boy, then you're welcome."

"That is definitely my way of saying thank you. I mean it, man, from the bottom of my bourgeois white heart."

Charles laughs. He says he'll be in touch with the fake-address details soon, and unfolds himself from the MG. Lucas watches him stroll off into the dark. There goes someone who is sacrificing for the greater good. Someone who spends his days ministering to nutcases over at Creedmoor and his nights voluntarily advising rich white boys on how to avoid the draft.

What are you doing for the greater good? the bourgeois white boy asks himself.

No answer is forthcoming. Lucas starts the MG and steers out of the church lot. Stops at a traffic light. Feels himself smile. The albatross is taking flight. Lucas Lindbergh imagines the MG sprouting wings. In his mind, the traffic light turns green and he accelerates through the gears, hits takeoff velocity, the *Spirit of Long Island* lifts—

"Sweet ride, babe." A voice comes from his left.

Lucas slowly turns his head. It's a guy in a Stingray in the lane beside him. Stingray Man is grinning, but when he sees that Lucas isn't a babe, his jaw drops. His face hardens. The light turns green, and it's the Stingray that hits takeoff velocity, leaving rubber.

One small gaffe for Stingray Man, one annoying reminder for Lucas that we are what we drive.

Brought back to earth by the stink of the Stingray's burned rubber, I put the MG into gear and ease through the intersection. Even though it's practically sweltering out and the MG doesn't have air-conditioning, I drive with the top up, not wanting to be seen. That's why the guy in the Stingray thought I was a chick. It's night and all he saw was a classic car and long hair.

But this minor incident pushes me over an invisible line. Each time I settle into the MG's red leather seat, I find myself surrounded by a hornet's nest of memories. The hours of drudgery spent washing, simonizing, and waxing, not to mention scrubbing road tar and dirt off the wire wheels with brushes soaked in a noxious cleaner called Gunk. And seeing the blond woman in the passenger seat when Robin and I drove to Maine. I hated driving into the factory parking lot this morning, where my coworkers stared. *Rich white boy, indeed!* I hate feeling beholden to the paterfamilias for lending me this symbol of financial excess and infidelity.

I'm going to have to do something.

TUESDAY, JULY 29

Days Until Armed Forces Induction Physical: 31

"What do you think you can afford?" Lou Wilkinson dabs his flushed red face with a stained, yellowed handkerchief. The showroom at Wilkinson Motorsports is dimly lit, filled with uncomfortably warm, stagnant air and dusty European motorcycles like BMWs, Triumphs, Nortons, and Ducatis.

What guy hasn't dreamed of having a motorcycle? Ever since Dylan wore that Triumph T-shirt on the cover of *Highway 61 Revisited*, it's been on my mind. Could anything be cooler? Besides, with everyone going off to college in a month, it's not like I need a vehicle I can give my friends rides in.

I tell Lou what I can spend. It's not nearly enough for a Triumph, but he does have a used BSA B40, a British cycle with a 343 cc engine, that will fit my budget. He proudly tells me that BSA stands for Birmingham Small Arms, a company that makes everything from motorcycles and bicycles to machine guns and armored cars and has been in business for more than a hundred years. (I feel momentary discomfort about purchasing a cycle made by a company that profits from the business of war, but I'm not aware of the U.K. being involved in Vietnam.)

I've never ridden a cycle before, so we take the BSA out to the parking lot, where Lou shows me how to kick-start and shift gears. Thanks to Odysseus and the MG, I'm familiar with the coordination of clutch and gearshift. Lou encourages me to take a spin around the parking lot. I like the throaty rumble of the BSA's exhaust.

Doing laps in the parking lot, I imagine hightailing it up to Canada. Ever since that phone call with Robin, I've dwelled in a state of nonstop anxiety awaiting the letter she's promised. There are moments now when I regret not continuing north by any means possible the day after Odysseus perished. Even if I'd arrived at Camp Juliette a day or two late, even if I couldn't actually spend time with Robin, it would have been a huge gesture of my feelings for her. Lucas Hoffman at the end of *The Graduate*, hammering my fists against the church window and shouting, "Robin! *Robin!*"

What if the dreaded letter contains the worst news imaginable? *(Dear John — I mean, Lucas — I'm sorry to do this in a letter, but...)* Then there'll be one more option besides Canada, prison, or chopping off a finger — I could throw some clothes in my knapsack, jump on this cycle, and light out for the great unknown, a fugitive from "justice" (as if there's *justice* in killing innocent civilians), the powerful claws of the draft system left grasping at my dust.

•   •   •

Alan's gone to camp. The house of dashed dreams is eerily still without the sound of the TV. The shag carpet in the den is matted and slightly threadbare in the place where he usually sits. Another thin white air-mail envelope from Chris *(Thank God! He's still alive!)* is on my desk, my address crossed out and the Bay Shore one written in. But before I read the letter, I chew two Tums to settle an anxious stomach, then open the window and spend a few quality moments with Mr. Water Pipe. I really have been cutting back on my consumption of grass, but given the anxiety of having another letter from Chris to read, plus everything else that feels like it's going off the rails in my life, a modest self-medicating buzz should be permissible.

7/12/69

Loogie,

I'm so tired of trying to make it through each day alive. It's hell over here. WE ARE NEVER GONNA WIN THIS WAR. Everyone knows it. Everyone's just trying to stay alive until they can get out.

To make it worse I got the worst case of jungle rot. Everyone's got it on their hands and feet. Your toes itch like crazy and the skin between them melts down to the red and oozes all the time. Now I got it in my crotch too. They tell us to practice good foot hygiene with air drying and powder. Whatever fucktard military desk jockey came up with that crap

212

never spent a week tromping through rice paddies with the temperature at 120 degrees and 95% humidity. I can't even remember the last time my feet were dry. Powder? The second you shake it out of the bottle, it turns into white mud.

And how am I supposed to air dry my crotch? WALK AROUND THE BASE BAREASS NAKED?

But that's typical of what's wrong with everything here. You got the brass hats sitting in air-conditioned offices in Washington that don't know shit about what it's like here. Probably they don't want to know.

You know all that stuff you used to say about military contracts going to the lowest bidder and American companies getting rich while they sell the army crap gear? You were so right, Loogs. The gooks have Russian AK-47s — a hundred times better weapon than our M-16s that jam all the time and need constant cleaning. The other day a squad got wiped out near here and when the rescue teams brought back the bodies and gear guess what? HALF THE RIFLES WERE JAMMED!

When our weapons aren't jamming, we get blown up by land mines and fall into punji stick booby traps that are so sharp they go right through the bottom of your boot.

Know what a punji pit is? The VC dig holes about 4 or 5 feet deep with punji sticks sticking up from the bottom. They cover the top of the hole with tree branches and grass. You can't see them on night patrol. Guys fall in and get impaled. And the VC cover the sticks with animal shit so the wounds get good and infected.

So many guys refuse to go on night patrol now that if they court-martialed all of us there'd be NO ONE LEFT TO FIGHT THIS STUPID WAR. A LT got fragged the other night for ordering his men to go out to the perimeter. I felt bad about that. The guy was a dick for sure, but I heard he had a wife and kids back home.

It's so friggin hard to live like this. If it wasn't for Thai stick and horse I would seriously think of offing myself. A guy in the next company did it. Hung himself from a lychee tree so everyone saw him hanging there in the morning.

Can't say I blame him.

What's the latest with your draft status? DON'T EVER LET YOURSELF GET SENT OVER HERE, MY FRIEND.

Peace,
Chris

Dear Chris,

*Every time I get one of your letters I'm just glad you're
alive (even though I know it sucks over there big-time).
Man, the stories you tell tear me up inside. So that squad
that got wiped out was being attacked and in the middle
of it their guns stopped working? It's unbelievable! I
mean, it's bad enough that the government has decided
it's all right if you die as long as ten VC also croak, but
the same government giving you crap weapons to fight
with? That is some seriously fucked-up shit.*

    *I hope the talk about offing yourself isn't serious,
man. I know it totally sucks over there, but it's not
forever. Every day you stay alive you're one day closer
to coming back. And careful with the horse, okay?
Remember what I said. You don't want to get to the
point where you're injecting. Promise me you won't do
that. . . .*

In the wee sleepless hours, my anxious thoughts once again drift
to Robin. Did she really not have time to see me the morning
she left for Lake Juliette? Or did she simply not want to? Is it
possible that a friend of hers saw me with Tinsley at the Planting Fields and wrote to her about it? Doubtful. The Planting
Fields freaks aren't her friends' types.

    The apprehension of waiting for her letter is unceasingly
wearying. Should I call her again tomorrow? No. Acting desperate won't help at this point. I wish I could sleep. Wish I could do
anything but lie here in the dark, thinking.

But when Mary Five-Fingers comes a-calling, it's Tinsley I
fantasize about.

Alone in his room
With music low.
Sneak a toke
Out the window.
Get off, jerk off, stare off,
Wonder what brand of shit
Will hit the fan next.

FRIDAY, AUGUST 1

Days Until Armed Forces Induction Physical: 28

7/26/69

Dear Lucas,

There's something I haven't told you, but now I have to. There's someone else. His name is Samuel and I've known him for a long time. He's from Montreal and used to go to the boys' camp across the lake. Now he's a counselor like me. Until this year, it's always been an innocent summer thing between us. But this summer it's changed and gotten more serious. I'm not sure why, or what it means for the future. Next month he's going to the University of British Columbia in Vancouver.

I know you must be angry, but I want you to know that when you and I started going out last fall, I felt like I was going to be with you from then on. Being with Samuel never entered my thoughts. I had so much hope for you and me, that's all I thought about.

But now I know that I wasn't seeing things clearly. I didn't think the drugs and your lack of direction were that important. Like I've said before, I thought I could help you with those issues.

But it didn't work out that way. You didn't want help. You didn't want to, or maybe couldn't, change. In a way, I respect that about you, Lucas. But as you know, even before I left for camp this summer I'd begun to have second thoughts. There are so many things I love about you. You're kind and funny, serious about your beliefs, and smarter than you give yourself credit for. I think a lot of your issues, including the low self-esteem you sometimes feel, are a result of you blaming yourself for things that have happened in your family that aren't your fault.

I hope that someday soon you'll figure things out and give yourself the credit you deserve. I hope you're doing something about not getting drafted. Seriously, Lucas, don't put it off. Do something while there's time.

That's really all I wanted to say. I know it must come as an awful shock. I'm truly sorry about that, but it's taken some time for me to get a handle on how I'm feeling. Even now I'm not completely sure. It's hard to imagine that this thing with Samuel will last when he'll be so far away next year. I'm trying not to think too much about the future.

And as I said, in many ways I do still love you.

Robin

Mom stands in the doorway of my room, arms crossed, staring at the fist-size dent in the wall with a small hole at its center. She heard the muffled thump and came to investigate. The knuckles of my right hand throb.

Robin's isn't the only letter I found on my desk this afternoon. The other was from Rudy, with the information on "the proper way" to cut off a finger. I'm not sure why I read it after reading Robin's letter. Was I in shock? Denial? Simply unable to immediately digest Robin's devastating news? *(Robin with another guy? Someone she's known for a long time? Someone she knew she'd be seeing this summer? Was she thinking about him when she said there wouldn't be time to see me the morning she left for camp?)*

Rudy's letter has come with a smudged and wrinkled piece of mimeographed paper that I assume I'm supposed to pass along to the next desperate draft resister who's considering self-mutilation.

Unless you happen to be in possession of a miniature guillotine, a proper finger-lopping requires three participants. (Don't bother asking a doctor for help. There's something called the Hippocratic oath.) Participant number one supplies the doomed digit, laying his hand palm side up on a wooden cutting board that's been thoroughly doused with alcohol. Participant number two positions the sterilized, super-sharpened knife over the joint between the intermediate and proximal phalanges of participant number one's ring finger. Participant number three holds the brick, rock, or other suitably heavy object that he will slam down on the knife's spine.

Have plenty of antiseptic on hand. An elastic tourniquet to slow the bleeding is optional. (Apparently no one's ever bled out after losing a finger.)

Idly, I stood in front of the wall, my first clenched and drawn back, blocking thoughts of Robin from my head, imagining instead asking Milton and Arno to assist (the only question was who would pass out first), and wondering how much pain I could stand.

But the momentous impact of Robin's letter began to sink in. I started to think of how I wished I could be angry at her. How much I wanted to be angry at her. But I couldn't muster the oomph. It was my own goddamn fault. Why hadn't I taken her hints—about drugs and school—more seriously? Why couldn't I have tried a little harder to be the person she wanted me to be?

It wouldn't have taken much of an effort.

I'd blown it. Lost the best girl I ever had. The only one I'd ever loved. I wondered if I should write back. Could I beg her to give me one last chance? She did write that in a lot of ways she still loved me.

And she didn't say she loved Samuel.

But she's so levelheaded and thoughtful. So circumspect

and deliberate. She had to know the effect the letter would have, which means she wouldn't have sent it unless she was sure. Besides, upon careful review, one could see where to read between the lines: *There's something I haven't told you, but now I have to.*

Why now? Take a wild guess.

It's always been an innocent summer thing between us. But this summer it's changed and gotten more serious.

She's with him, soul *and* body.

That's when my fist made blunt contact with the bedroom wall.

It hurts like hell. Note to self: when chopping off finger, take plenty of painkillers first.

Standing in the doorway, Mom looks from the dent in the wall to me. "Are you okay?" she asks.

I nod, even though we both know I'm not.

Late at night, Icarusfish flails through liquid space toward the blurry yellow sun cemented in the sky blue ahead. His eyes sting and his lungs are starting to burn. Can Icarusfish get there before he runs out of air? He no longer recalls why, exactly, he wants to get there. Was it to prove that he wouldn't melt? To see if he would?

But this body is not built for underwater travel. Its spastic, gangly unstreamlined arms and legs hinder forward progress. What he needs is a tail.

A pale dolphin torpedoes into the water, leaving a trail of shimmering mercury bubbles. The dolphin becomes a squid with long golden tentacles. The tentacles become billowing yellow hair. The dolphin/squid becomes a mermaid with pink nipples and dark pubic hair.

Icarusfish kicks to the surface and gasps for breath. In his lungs, a zillion tiny red roses open to accept the fresh chlorine-scented night air. Icarusfish's vision is a wavy rainbow kaleidoscope blur.

Cousin Itt from *The Addams Family* surfaces nearby. Golden hair clings to his head, covering his face. Cousin Itt parts the hair and becomes Mermaid Tinsley. Tears drip down her face and off her chin.

"Your hairline is crying," Icarusfish tells her.

Treading water requires effort, coordination, and concentration. The jointed appendages attached to Icarusfish's body fail to work in the specific disjointed unison necessary to keep his head above water. Icarusfish feels his chin, then lips, start to slide under.

"Here." Tinsley pushes a pink raft to him. Lucas holds on while she tows him to the side of the pool, where he grabs the fat chrome ladder and climbs out. Tinsley follows. From the ends of her hair, sparkling streams run down her sides and back. The ridge of vertebrae along her spine is reptilian. Will she evolve into a bird? Will her skinny, jointed appendages grow feathers? Will she become a seagull tossing *I Ching* coins with an orange claw?

Tinsley wraps herself in a big white towel and becomes Tinsley Polar Bear on a chaise lounge. Lucas stands wet and naked before her. Tiny droplets cling to the dark hairs around his nipples. Farther down in a dark shrub of pubic hair, his shriveled penis is hardly visible. "Pathetic penis," Lucas complains, and he starts to shiver.

"You're cold." Tinsley hands me a thick square of white terry cloth that unfolds into a towel. The post-swim chill has clipped my fins and returned me to the mortal coil (though hopefully not for long). I pull the towel around my shoulders and settle onto the lounge next to hers.

Beneath the shimmering surface of the pool, the sky-blue walls billow. Rays of pool light separate into incandescent jiggling jellyfish. Tinsley dries her hands, places two cigarettes in her lips, lights both, and hands one to me. Multiple glowing-red afterimages follow. The red tracer tip pulsates when I inhale. The Federal Trade Commission orders the zillions of tiny red roses in my lungs to fold closed until further notice.

This acid is amazing. As pure and unadulterated as any I have ever experienced. It came from the small glass vial Red-Eyed Clyde placed in my hand after the Led Zep concert. Yesterday, when Arno gave me the vial, it appeared empty except for the faintest dusting inside. Arno told me to wet the base of a paper match, make one small swipe along the inside of the vial, then eat the moistened paper.

An hour ago, when Tinsley and I took the acid, we couldn't even see the chemical clinging to the wet match. But Arno had warned that if there was enough to see, it was far too much to take.

On the lounges beside the pool, Tinsley and I are pupae

in white cocoons, smoking glowing red-tipped tracerettes. For the first time in astronomic history, waves of green, yellow, and purple northern lights wash across the dark night sky above Long Island. The gurgling pool filters are witches' bubbling cauldrons. The outdoor lights are swirling pastel funnels. The lounges are life rafts on a boundless sea of phantasmagoria.

When I reach over to take Tinsley's hand, she squeezes and then lets go. I'm hip to that. At a trip's apex, touching is dangerous. A hand becomes a spider and crawls up an arm. Fingers blend together and become inseparable. It was Tinsley who suggested skinny-dipping. Thoughts of sex have periodically skipped through my acid-infused synapses, but it's out of the question right now. We can't even hold hands without it getting mucho weird.

Far above the Arctic Circle, lonely Robin shivers in an icy igloo. Samuel of the North in his caribou parka and polar bear chaps has been gone for weeks, plodding among icebergs, clubbing baby seals to death. Lucas the Narwhal swims under the ice pack beneath Robin's igloo, wishing his unicorn tusk could break through to save her from her frigid solitary Canadian existence, but the permafrost around her heart is too thick.

On the lounge beside me, a tear slides out of Tinsley's eye. A real tear, not pool water. "I'm okay," she says.

I appreciate that she knows to reassure me. That she's handling whatever is causing the tears. She's a good tripping partner. It's like getting on a tennis court with someone you've never played with before and discovering that you're well matched.

Somewhere in a family photo album is a picture of a tow-headed toddler in a diaper, holding a child-size tennis racket under one arm and a tennis ball in his pudgy little hand. Thus from infancy is young Lucas groomed. Year-round lessons, a few weeks of tennis camp every summer. Musclini drags him out of bed at seven on weekend mornings to hit tennis balls. This, young Lucas will eventually realize, serves a dual purpose: practice for him and extra warm-up time for his father so that he'll have an advantage over whomever he is scheduled to do battle with at eight.

Mom is the reader in the family, but over the years, the books on the shelves in the den give way to ever-multiplying tennis trophies. Dad reads, too, but only about strategy and winning. (At the country club, his name is annually inscribed in gold letters on the champions plaques—singles, doubles, mixed doubles. Young Lucas is often introduced as Richard Baker's son.)

Lucas is eleven when Mom is assigned to drive him to regional tennis tournaments. Dad's goal is for his son to earn a tennis ranking in the twelve-and-under category. (Lucas can recall winning only one match—against a kid who clearly hated being there even more than Lucas did.)

Actually, Lucas likes tennis. It's fun to play with his friends. Fun to race after a ball and make a good return. Fun to come to the net for a winning put-away. At the country club, he plays with Arno and pre–Rat Fink Johnny. They're on the courts for hours, rallying, trying out trick shots, and sometimes doing wacky stuff like seeing who can smack the ball the highest and farthest. They make up games like double-court doubles, where there are four on a side and you can hit the ball anywhere as long as it's in one of the two courts. Many a summer evening, they play until it's too dark to see, then lie down and stare up into the starry heavens, the residual heat from the sun-blasted courts warming their backs.

But Lucas hates the tournaments his father sends him to, which always feel weighty and crucial. Where the only thing that matters is winning. The more pressure to win, the more he chokes during important points. Then he gets down on himself and chokes even more until he's trapped in a downward spiral and can barely get a ball over the net.

The only way to save face is to convince himself that he doesn't care. He forgets the score, lets his mind drift instead of concentrating on the game, serves into the wrong box, tries ridiculous trick shots. Anything to demonstrate to himself and the world that winning isn't important.

At home, the paterfamilias gives him books about strategy, about how to develop a winner's mind-set. Lucas skims them, but they don't help. They're all about winning, and he is not a winner.

SATURDAY, AUGUST 2

Days Until Armed Forces Induction Physical: 27

> Yesterday was the last day
> Of the best of my life.

With dawn and the first faint hint of gray light, Tinsley leads me to the pool house, which has a small kitchen, bar, fireplace, and couches. Half a dozen long thin poles that vaguely resemble golf clubs, only with leather handles and wooden hammer ends, are piled into a corner, along with several pairs of high black leather boots with spurs. Near a back door are a number of tennis rackets, cans of balls, and tennis shoes with ochre stains around the edges.

Tinsley and I drop our towels, my formerly pathetic penis now prone for promiscuity, and descend onto a shag rug.

Sex is unhurried, every delicious sensation intensified, explosions of Day-Glo colors on the insides of eyelids. Tinsley takes charge. There is surprising strength in those slender legs and arms. When I put my lips on her and her legs go taut against my ears, the muscles of her thighs are as hard as flesh can be.

This is how Tinsley's mother discovers us. Mrs. Stockton stands in the doorway of the pool house with her arms crossed tightly, as if to keep herself from flying apart. The clenched tightness of her face is bereft of surprise, instead filled with glowering anger. Something tells me this isn't the first time she's walked in on her daughter in flagrante delicto.

"Get dressed," she snaps harshly, then backs out of the doorway.

Tinsley and I wordlessly pull on our clothes. Emptied of arousal, my brain feels sluggish, muddled, and filled with regret.

What have I just done? What am I even doing here?

It isn't revenge for whatever Robin's doing with Samuel. (I've never seen much point to that.) Did I run to Tinsley last night for comfort? If so, I've badly miscalculated. Now that I'm down from the acid and drained of lust, a gritty discomfort fills the void. Tinsley seems hardly aware of me.

"You okay?" I ask.

"Bitch," she growls.

The end of a trip is never pretty. The world takes on a yellow cast. Skin feels waxy, clothes grimy and smoky. I feel hollowed out and haggard, filled only with the woe of losing Robin. Now it's my turn to yearn for a long hot shower, a boatload of soap and shampoo—and the strongest, most reality-dulling downers available.

Outside the pool house, I see what wasn't visible in the dark last night—the red clay tennis court behind a tall green hedge. The garden cupola surrounded by wildflowers. The morning air is cool and fresh. Three matching light-brown long-haired dogs of some breed I've never seen before bound over the lawn after being inside all night. Tinsley's mother stands by the French doors of the large beige-brick chateau on the other side of the pool. Without saying goodbye to me, Tinsley stomps toward her. Meanwhile, Mrs. Stockton's eyes meet mine and she points at a slate path around the side of the manse. "You can go that way."

The path leads to the fountain at the head of the driveway. That's when I remember that we came here last night in Tinsley's Spitfire.

Looks like I'm walking home.

> Is it better to have
> Had your wish
> Or to only have
> Wished you'd had?

The long winding driveway is lined with evenly spaced trees and immaculate white fencing. To the right and left spread spacious green lawns with a smattering of barrels and low jumps that I imagine are the practice tools of a serious equestrian. (The morning Tinsley and I sat on the bench outside the U.S. Customs and Border Protection building, waiting for them to find us a ride back to Long Island, she told me that until this year, she'd spent her summers at a riding academy in Bern, Switzerland. This explained the saddle in the Spitfire's trunk and the strength in her thighs. And those golf club–like poles in the pool house must be polo mallets, left behind, I suspect, by her father.)

I let myself out the tall metal gate. After being up all night on acid, I feel like my brain is mired in sludge and running at about 50 percent. But that doesn't prevent more regret over Robin from oozing in. Strangely, this morning one thing seems to have come into sharper focus—I can't give up on her. I just can't. It's so weird because last night I recalled how easy it had been for me to give up on the tennis court. How I could tell myself that it didn't matter, that I didn't care. But I can't do that with Robin. What I did this morning with Tinsley doesn't matter. What's going on between Robin and Samuel doesn't matter. I must try to get her back.

From Tinsley's, I find my way to the service road of the Expressway. There's no sidewalk, so I stay close to the curb, where my boot heels scrape along the road grit, cigarette butts, and other detritus. The same rubbish I used to ride past when I was younger and ferrying jars of coins to banks for the paterfamilias. Most of the cars give some berth when they pass, but now and then a car or truck barrels past within a few feet and the trailing wind whips my hair around. Someone shouts, "Get a haircut!" Someone else throws an empty RC Cola can that misses me and lands in the weeds beside the road.

A white Jaguar XK-E passes.

• • •

The first time the paterfamilias goes to see the junk-mail factory, he brings me along. It's the beginning of sophomore year, and I guess he wants to introduce me to the fascinating world of business. He should be taking Arno; I could care less. The only reason I go is because it's easier than not going.

The factory smells of ink and is filled with workers feeding stacks of mail inserts into clicking, wheezing inserter machines. The owner is an older and grayer version of the paterfamilias, tanned, nattily dressed, trim and athletic looking. His office is neat and orderly except for a large corkboard covered with snapshots of him, his friends, and lots of dead fish. The owner points to the framed photo on his desk of his gleaming white fishing cruiser. He tells us that every summer he fishes off Montauk Point at the eastern end of Long Island. Every winter he hires a captain to take the boat down to an island in the Bahamas called Bimini. A couple of times a month, he flies down with his friends and fishes there. These stories are the owner's way of making sure we know he's made a lot of money by paying his employees less than they deserve.

While he talks, the owner keeps looking out the window at a dark maroon Jaguar XK-E parked outside. It sparkles in the fall sunlight. The owner says it's brand-new. That is another way of saying he has a lot of scratch, in case we didn't get the message the first time.

The owner places some ledgers on the desk so the paterfamilias can inspect them. The paterfamilias skims thoughtfully through the pages. In a low, confidential tone, the owner says that the company is a gold mine, easy to run and practically prints money. He says he'd always hoped his sons would take over the business, but one son is a big-shot lawyer in New York and the other is a big-shot producer out in Hollywood and neither wants anything to do with junk mail. The owner pretends to be sad about that, but you can tell he's proud that his sons are big shots.

Then the owner looks at me, with my longish hair and work shirt, bell-bottoms, and boots. He's probably thinking that there's no way in hell I'll ever become a big shot. To him, I probably look more like the kind of losers he takes advantage of in his factory.

The paterfamilias asks the owner if he'd mind if "his people" look through the books. That is my father's way of letting the owner know he's a pretty heavy dude himself, even though no such "people" exist. The owner says that's fine, but that if the paterfamilias is serious, he shouldn't dawdle, because "other parties" are interested.

In the car going home, I wonder what that meeting was really about. My father's father — I guess that would make him my grandfather, but I never knew him — abandoned his family when Dad was four. My father grew up poor during the Depression. He worked his way through college, living and serving as the janitor in a boardinghouse, where he made twenty-five cents an hour. Is that why he's become a bloodsucking capitalist blowhard? It wasn't even like he and the owner of the junk-mail business were trying to outdo each other. It was more like they shared a willingness to swallow each other's baloney. The paterfamilias and his make-believe "people." The owner and his make-believe "other parties."

Is this the life the paterfamilias wants for me? To be able to show off? To be able to acquire more material possessions than the next guy and let everyone know it? (Welcome to Capitalist Bullshit 101.)

It takes me more than an hour to walk home from Tinsley's. As I trudge up the driveway, the garage door opens and there's the paterfamilias in his fresh white tennis clothes, on his way to the club for his first match of the day. He tosses his tennis bag into the MG, then turns and sees me. Guess it's obvious I'm coming back from a long night out. I nod as I go by. He nods in return. Ships passing in bright daylight.

SUNDAY, AUGUST 3

Days Until Armed Forces Induction Physical: 26

8/3/69

Dear Robin,

This is probably the sixth time I've started this letter. Each
time I get about this far and don't like what I've written and
tear it up. But this time I've gotten this far and haven't torn
it up. Look, I've gotten a little farther. And now even farther.
Hey, look, it's a paragraph.

Okay, enough of that. But I really have tried a bunch
of times to write to you. Yeah, as you expected, I was totally
blown away by your letter about Samuel. But you may be
surprised to learn that I'm not angry. Not at you, at least.
If there's anyone I'm angry at, it's me. I see now that I put
you in some really uncomfortable situations. It wasn't my
intention. But like you've always said, I've got those blind
spots. I could have, should have, been a lot more sensitive to
your needs. I can't begin to tell you how sorry I am about that.

By the way, was Samuel ever in one of those blind spots? Did you drop hints about him that I didn't pick up on? I can't remember any, but if I could, I guess they wouldn't be blind spots, right?

Here's the thing. I really, really, really love you. More than I thought I could love anyone. I love you so much that I can't give up and walk away from what we have together. I'm still hoping that somewhere deep down you feel the same.

I know I've made mistakes. And I know you dropped hints that I didn't take seriously. I guess I didn't realize how serious you were. Now I'm hoping that your letter about Samuel was actually your way of letting me know how serious you are about what has to change for us to continue together. If that's what it was, let me tell you, it worked. I'm ready to change. I'm ready to do whatever I have to do to keep your love. Some of my options are kind of limited at the moment (it's not like I'm going to find a college close to Middlebury that will accept me), but I do have some promising alternatives. Hopefully I'll be able to take the army induction physical in San Francisco and get a 1-Y deferment. (I know you're in Canada, so it's not like anyone up there would care, but please don't tell anyone about that, okay?)

Once I've gotten my 1-Y, I still plan to move to Vermont. Maybe after a year working up there, I'll have a better idea of what I might want to study in college, or maybe I'll go into the Peace Corps. By the way, I've cut way down on the grass and cigarettes.

Sweetheart, I know things didn't go well on that trip

to Maine, and I'm really sorry about that. But please don't forget all the good times we've had, because we've had a ton more of them than bad times. The ski trips we took last winter. Tobogganing in the park. Building snowmen. Hot chocolate with marshmallows. Reading e. e. cummings. Popsicle stick sailboats on rainy days. The prom. The beach on senior cut day. I could go on and on. Seriously, we both know there's been much much more good than bad. Let's give it another chance, okay? What we've built together is far too important to let crumble. Believe me, I'm ready to do what needs to be done.

Love you forever,

Lucas

MONDAY, AUGUST 4

Lou Wilkinson has taken a shine to me. The fact that I showed up in the paterfamilias's British-made MG appears to mean that we are kindred spirits who appreciate the finer, and quirkier, aspects of British automotive engineering. Hungry for any kind of distraction from the empty gloom of a Robinless existence, I fall into a routine with him. Each afternoon after work, I sit in Lou's hot, stuffy showroom office for five or ten minutes while he bitches about the cheap "Jap" Honda and Yamaha cycles flooding the market. Motorcycles that "lack pedigree and gravitas." Then he lets me take the BSA out to the lot for a practice session.

Entering the showroom this afternoon, I pass a familiar-looking, heavyset man in a blue blazer on his way out. We share a brief nod. Where have I seen him before?

Lou is polishing the silver fender of a cycle with drooping handlebars. "Beauty, isn't she?" he says. "A forty-eight Vincent

Black Shadow. One of the fastest bikes ever built. Just came in this morning. You don't see many in this condition."

I point back to the showroom entrance. "Was he interested?"

"Mr. Brown? Oh, yes. Quite the collector of fine British motoring. Comes by now and then when I've got something interesting. Hopefully he'll snap this up before someone else does. I believe he was a colonel in the war, stationed in London. Something to do with military intelligence." Lou pauses, then drops his voice. "Always considered that a bit of an oxymoron."

I've heard that one before but smile obsequiously. Maybe Mr. Brown looked familiar because I've seen him here?

"Actually, I believe he's still involved in the service somehow," Lou goes on. "Came back to the States and got into real estate. Electrical engineering, if I'm not mistaken. Made a fortune wiring those cookie-cutter houses that popped up all over Long Island after the war." Lou puts his hand on my shoulder. "Well, now, lad. Shall we complete our transaction?"

In the showroom office, the stale scent of grease and tire rubber hangs in the air. Late-afternoon sunlight filters through the filmy plate-glass windows. While Lou fills out the paperwork, I smoke a cigarette and think about writing another letter to Robin. But what else is there to say? The thing is, I have this yearning to write . . . something. Maybe I'll send Chris a letter telling him what's going on with Robin. Or what about a diary? (Locked and hidden from my parents, of course.)

The paperwork is complete. I pay for the cycle with the last few hundred bucks in my savings account. Lou explains that it will take three or four days to get the insurance and registration.

After that I can take possession of the BSA. He dabs his face with that yellowed handkerchief and asks if I have any friends "who are like me" and appreciate cycles built with old-world craftsmanship and tradition. I get the feeling he hopes that the counterculture will flock to European motorcycles the way we've flocked to VW microbuses, Volvos, and Saabs.

Later, Tinsley picks me up to see *Easy Rider*. A couple of nights ago, while we waited to get off on the leftover acid from Arno's vial, she told me that as a result of going (however briefly) with Barry and me to Canada without permission, she'd been grounded. But what the rich call grounded must be different from what the rest of us think it is, because here we are going to the movies. (Could it be *literally* grounded, as in "You're not allowed to use the family airplane"?)

Before going in, we get high behind the theater. (I'm not the wasteful type. In order to cut back on smoking weed, I first need to use up my current stash. Besides, this is the first time I've turned on in a while. It's true that Tinsley and I *did* trip a couple of days ago, but no ganja was consumed.)

Having burned through a fatty, we enter the theater in an improper state of mind. Tinsley places on my lap the flowery shawl I'd assumed she brought in case the air-conditioning is too cold. Next thing I know, she takes my hand and slides it under the fringed leather bag on her lap. Once my hand is properly positioned there, she slides her hand under the flowery shawl.

Princess Tinsley of Lapland and her risk taking. Maybe she

needs it. I'm not sure I do, but why spoil her fun? Thus, the movie isn't the only thing we find stimulating. (Have the folks sitting behind us noticed our quickened breaths?)

As best as Lucas the Distracted is able to follow, the movie is about two longhairs who use the profits from a drug deal to buy motorcycles and ride across the country looking for truth and meaning. Along the way, they encounter the sorts of bigotry and hostility that long-haired freaks often encounter. Only because it's a movie, theirs is more extreme and violent (though, come to think of it, considering what happened to Cousin Barry, maybe not).

The two actors ride choppers with extended front forks and lots of shiny chrome. One has ape bars. These are the kinds of cycles that Lucas associates with motorcycle gangs like the Pagans and Hells Angels, not with peace-loving longhairs. He feels bad for Lou Wilkinson. *Easy Rider* is the number one movie across the country this week. Any freaks who see it are bound to think that custom-made choppers are the way to go, not clunky old British bikes with pedigree and gravitas.

After the movie, Tinsley drives to the junior high and leads Lucas to an isolated spot in the woods. Along the way, another doobie gets reduced to ash. The golden-haired woodland sprite finds a spot suitable to her whims and spreads the blanket. She doesn't ask if this is what Elf Lucas wants; she just assumes. Well, she's right. It's not like they were merely holding hands during the movie. Elf Lucas feels ready to go. (Besides, it would defy belief to think that up near the polar ice cap, Lady Robin's only been rubbing noses with Samuel the Skuzzbucket this summer.)

Tinsley and I start to make love. But despite our being primed for action, it feels strange that we're doing this. Last time, we were tripping—two ids, stripped down to instinct, impulse, and lust. But now my brain is going AWOL. It's watching the days peel off the calendar month of August, each day counting down to the Dreaded Induction Physical. Next, it's in an army examination room in San Francisco, anxiously waiting to see if the doctor really will give me a 1-Y deferment. And now it's with Robin, doing the *New York Times* crossword in the high-school library.

Oh, what I'd give for it to be Robin on this blanket, not even having sex, just knowing she wanted to be here with me.

Alas, my brain isn't the only part of my body that's not cooperating. Short of a surprise visit from a bear or a forest ranger (neither likely on Long Island), there's nothing like a systems failure to bring you down. I'm finding it hard (well, maybe "difficult" would better describe it) to comprehend. I mean, I know there's a first time for everything, but at the lusty age of eighteen?

Despite Tinsley's best efforts, it's just not happening. Finally, we inch apart and readjust our clothes. Tinsley plucks two Benson & Hedges from a red metal tin, lights both, and hands one to me. I pull my legs up, rest my chin on my knees, and wish

I were anywhere but here. Not only not in these woods, feeling humiliated, but here in this lost, bereft, fretful place in my life.

Sitting cross-legged, Tinsley gazes up at the dark trees. Crickets chirp. From somewhere nearby comes the hoot of an owl.

"What are you thinking?" she asks softly.

"What makes you think I'm thinking anything?" I appreciate her concern but can't say I feel like talking right now.

"You're always thinking, Lucas. Even when you pretend not to be."

"What are *you* thinking?" I ask petulantly. *Can we please not focus on me?*

"I asked first."

"So? I'm asking second." It comes out harsher than I meant.

"Don't be like this, Lucas. It's not my fault. It's not your fault."

She's right. If it were just my dick, it might be acceptable (on a one-time-only basis). But it's not just that. It feels like my *entire fucking life* isn't working. And I can't pretend not to know why. *Whatever a man sows, this he will also reap.*

So if this really is the first day of the rest of my life, does anyone mind if I get off at the next stop?

"I'm sorry. I'm just . . . It's hard to explain."

"Did something happen with your girlfriend?"

I feel an involuntary grimace and take a drag of the Benson & Hedges. A dog barks somewhere in the distance. "Is it *that* obvious?"

"It is to me."

So I tell her about Robin and Samuel. Remarkably, Tinsley doesn't take offense at learning that the person who just failed to have sex with her couldn't consummate because he was thinking about his (former?) girlfriend.

"It wasn't because you weren't able to visit her, was it?" Tinsley asks.

I shake my head. Once again I can't help thinking back to the morning Robin left for camp. Did she already know she was going to break up with me? Was she looking forward to seeing Samuel? *Seriously, Lucas, does it matter now?*

It's late. We pull into my driveway. The Spitfire's top is down. The stars are out. Here and there among the houses on my block, a single bedroom light glows behind a curtain.

"Have you heard from Barry?" Tinsley asks.

"Not recently." The pointed angst and frustration I was feeling in the woods have diminished, thanks in no small part to Tinsley's frank and mellow attitude.

"Think he likes it up there?" she asks.

"Guess I'll find out next week."

"At the festival?"

"Uh-huh."

"I heard on the radio that they're expecting something like forty thousand people. It's going to be such a blast." She sounds wistful.

"Maybe you can still get tickets." It's within driving distance, if grounded does indeed mean no trips on the family airplane. (Wait, they can't *really* have an airplane, can they?)

Tinsley sighs. "I think I've kind of pushed my mother to the limit this summer."

The Spitfire's engine is running, so this isn't meant to be a long goodbye. I lean over and give her a quick kiss. "Thanks for the movie. Sorry the rest of the night didn't work out."

Tinsley reaches up and strokes my hair the way a mother might. "I wouldn't worry, Lucas. Something tells me it's not a permanent condition."

I can't help smiling. "You know, in some ways you're a pretty amazing person."

"Just in *some* ways?" she teases.

A moment later, I'm watching the Spitfire's taillights grow small and dim in the dark. Tinsley insists that she doesn't want to be tied down, but sometimes I wonder if she really means it. It does feel like we have a real connection. I briefly flirt with the notion of pursuing her in a more meaningful way, but the kind of deep yearning I feel for Robin isn't there with Tinsley. She's smart, perceptive, and exotic, but also, something tells me, capable of being dangerously fickle and capricious. It's moments like this when I miss Robin — with her even keel and thoughtfulness — the most.

I noiselessly let myself into the house, take off my boots, and tiptoe down the hall past Mom's bedroom. For the first time in years, I hear typing from inside.

TUESDAY, AUGUST 5

"Come, come!" Milton's father herds us into the kitchen. It's Milton's birthday, and Arno, Tinsley, and I have come over to help him celebrate. Not that I'm in a celebratory mood, but I'm game for anything that distracts from the thought of what Robin's up to with the moose herder.

Milton's parents have accents. They were both born in Austria. A lot of families in our neighborhood have put additions on their houses since moving here in the late 1940s and early 1950s. My parents added the attic gym, third and fourth bedrooms, playroom, and fallout shelter. Arno's parents expanded their kitchen and garage. But Milton's house is still mint 1948. So are Milton's parents. Mr. Fischer is an electronics engineer and amateur inventor whose glasses have thick black frames, whose shirts have short sleeves, and whose pants have cuffs. His mom is a physics professor at Adelphi and wears pointy horn-rim glasses and pleated dresses with petticoats rustling underneath.

On the Fischers' kitchen counter is a boxy chrome appliance with a door and two dials. Milton's told us that his father works for a company that is developing a new kind of oven. Mr. Fischer wants us to watch while he puts a stick of butter on a glass dish inside and turns a dial. The machine hums loudly for a minute. Milton's father opens the door and takes the dish out. In it is a yellow puddle.

"Every time we have a visitor, I lose another butter stick," Mrs. Fischer laments.

"So . . . it's a butter melter?" Arno asks, puzzled.

"No, no. It cooks!" Mr. Fischer cries excitedly. "Without heat! We call it the Radarange."

"How?" I ask.

"With microwaves," Mr. Fischer explains. "Set at a frequency to agitate the water molecules. They vibrate, creating their own heat." He hands me the glass dish. "Feel."

The glass is cool. I dip my pinkie into the melted butter. It's hot. It doesn't make sense.

"Groovy, Mr. Fischer." Arno pats the top of the Radarange. "What's one of these babies go for?"

"Four hundred ninety-five dollars."

Silence. I paid $300 for Odysseus. Arno said his father forked over $350 for their new color TV. Why pay nearly $500 for something slightly larger than a bread box that heats stuff? Why not just use an oven?

Mrs. Fischer claps her hands. "Everyone into the dining room."

The heavy wooden dining table is set with dessert plates and glasses. In its center is a pitcher of milk and a pot of coffee. The white cloth napkins are trimmed with lace.

"How quaint!" Tinsley gushes, primly placing a napkin on her lap.

Milton is struggling not to stare at her. When we arrived, she gave him a full-frontal hug and gaily wished him happy birthday. Then she held him at arm's length. "Oh, you're so cute!" Rarely have I seen Milton look so flushed and dazed.

Tinsley's dressed for the occasion in a pink, yellow, and orange flower-pattern minidress that barely covers her buttocks. She's wearing high white go-go boots and those round purple glasses. As usual, her neckline is revealing, and you'd have to be severely farsighted not to notice the absence of a certain support garment.

The Fischers are models of old-world hospitality. Of course, they've known Arno and me for years, and Mrs. Fischer is used to longhairs from teaching at Adelphi. Mr. Fischer is more or less oblivious to anything that doesn't involve blueprints and calipers. Most people in our neighborhood use their garages for cars, but the Fischers' is a workshop of table saws and lathes. Mr. Fischer's hobby is inventing things. His specialty is handles and grips. He created something called the Finger-Lock knife handle that you can actually find on some knives in stores. (Maybe he can recommend a good one for digital amputation.)

He also invented the Fischer Grip for glue guns and electric drills.

Mr. Fischer turns down the lights. From the kitchen, Mrs. Fischer begins to sing "Happy Birthday" and we all join in when she emerges with a chocolate cake with seventeen candles. Sometimes I forget how young Milton is.

She sets the cake down in front of her son. "Make a wish."

The birthday candles bring out the freckles on Milton's face. His lips are pressed tightly together and his eyebrows slant inward and down. "I wish Rudy was here. I wish something could be done to stop this stupid war. I wish someone could bring back all the human beings, not only American soldiers, who've died needlessly. I wish someone would take all the politicians and corporate bigwigs and generals and line them up and—"

"Please, dear," Mrs. Fischer interrupts softly. "Just blow out the candles."

"Sure we're allowed to build a fire?" Milton's looking around nervously in the dark. We're on the beach in Bayville. In the moonlight, small waves lap against the shore. I reassure him that they have bonfires up and down the beach and shoot off a ton of fireworks on the Fourth of July.

The beach is a mixture of pebbles and sand. Tinsley's sitting next to Milton with her arm around his shoulders, being affectionate and extra sweet. She's treating him like a long-lost little brother. Nobody asked her to take on that role, but Milton's dazzled, so it's a nice birthday present.

Arno and I are on our knees, scooping out a depression for the fire. We learned to make fires the year pre–Rat Fink Johnny convinced us to join the Boy Scouts. Arno and I reluctantly agreed, even though we thought that earning merit badges was stupid and that the Scout master was a jerk because he always insisted our uniforms be neatly pressed, our ties knotted properly, and our shoes polished.

He knew we didn't like him and was keen to find an excuse to boot us out of the troop. He finally got it on an overnight campout after Arno and I told some eager new Scouts that earning the Hole Digging merit badge by shoveling the five required holes in under two hours was way faster and easier than the First Aid or Personal Fitness badges, which could take months to earn. As specified in the *Boy Scout Handbook,* the five holes were: narrow and deep, wide and shallow, a circle, a square, and the famously challenging S shape. At first, the newbies went full bore with their foldable army spades, but by the third hole, they were bushed. No one managed to dig all five holes in the allotted time.

One of them must have said something to the Scout master. A few days later, Arno and I got the boot. (There's no such thing as a Hole Digging merit badge.)

Rat Fink Johnny went on to become an Eagle Scout, of course. (His parents bought the *Encyclopaedia Britannica.*)

Using driftwood and a whole lot of liquid fire starter, we get a pretty good blaze going.

"Burn, baby! Burn." Milton mutters the mantra from the Watts Riots of a few years ago, when a large swath of the Watts neighborhood in Los Angeles was burned to the ground in a protest against police racism and brutality.

"Oh, come on, Milty-Wilty," Tinsley coos, squeezing his shoulder. "Don't be a downer."

From a cooler, Arno produces Dixie cups and a bottle of champagne he liberated from the home refrigerator. He toasts. "Happy birthday, Milton. Just think. A year from now, you'll be able to drink legally."

We sip champagne and roast marshmallows. Arno's brought a portable radio, and he and Tinsley sing along to "Alice's Restaurant." Being at the beach at night reminds me again of that last time Robin and I made love, up in Maine. The throbbing gash she's left in my heart is bright red. I can't stop blaming myself.

When the champagne bottle is empty, Arno lights a joint. The disc jockey on the radio is talking about the Woodstock Music and Art Fair, which won't be held in Woodstock or Wallkill but at White Lake, in the town of Bethel, New York. He names all the bands scheduled to be there, including the Who, which the DJ says is the hottest band on the scene right now.

"Damn right!" Arno says gleefully.

"You know Dylan's gonna be there," Milton says. "He lives up there." Dylan is Milton's and my absolute favorite songwriter. We both bought *Blonde on Blonde* the day it came out. I played my copy so many times it wore out and had to be replaced. Dylan hasn't appeared in concert since his motorcycle accident three years ago. At first there were rumors that he was crippled, brain damaged, even dead. Then reports began to filter out that he was alive but in seclusion (and other rumors that the "accident" was a ruse to cover up a mental breakdown). Regardless of all that, to see him at the festival after all this time won't just be a blast; it will be historic.

Even though the festival is just ten days away, I've been too distracted to give it much thought, other than to occasionally get excited about the unparalleled lineup of bands that are scheduled to play. But sitting here around the fire with my two closest friends, I'm reminded that the original plan was for the three of us to celebrate the end of summer before going our separate ways.

"Suppose you leave the acid home?" I ask Arno. "We could have such a bitchin' time hanging out and grooving on the music without you running around trying to unload two thousand hits. Then you can take all that acid to Bucknell and be the biggest dealer on campus. You're worried about making friends? You'll have more friends than you'll know what to do with."

Arno looks like he's actually considering it.

Tinsley sighs a bit dramatically. Despite what she said the other night about pushing her mother too far, I sense that she's fishing for an invitation.

"You can still get tickets." Arno gestures to the radio. "He said there's a number to call."

"Murray Hill seven, oh, seven, oh-oh," Milton recites.

The rest of us stare at him. We've just polished off a bottle of champagne and have nearly finished the joint. I don't remember the DJ saying anything about a phone number.

When a burst of firecrackers comes from down the beach, followed by laughter and voices, we all turn to look. It's hard to see in the dark, but it sounds like a bunch of guys.

Snap! Crack! More firecrackers flash and spark, followed by loud talk and laughter. Now we can see their silhouettes. *Crash!* A bottle smashes against a rock.

"Maybe we should go," Milton says.

"Why? We have as much right to be here as they do," Arno says.

But when the group down the beach grows quiet, I feel my chest compress. Something tells me they've noticed our fire.

Footsteps start to crunch on the pebbles and rocks. They're coming.

"We better split." Milton rises to his feet.

"Slowly." Arno starts to get up. Tinsley and I do the same. Whatever buzz we'd gotten from the champagne and the J instantly evaporates, replaced by the sober chill of fear. Still, Arno takes his time with the radio and cooler. He wants to send the message that we're not scared and that it's just a coincidence that we're leaving as they approach.

The crunching footsteps grow louder and faster. "Hey!" one of the guys shouts. "Where you think you're goin'?" There are six of them. They're around our age—or maybe a little older—wearing T-shirts, jeans, and work boots, their hair greased back and spit curled.

The GTO is parked on the street about thirty yards away. We might be able to reach it before they reach us, but I doubt there'll be enough time to get in, start up, and escape.

One of the unburned pieces of driftwood we collected for the fire is roughly the length and thickness of a baseball bat. I pick it up.

"What're you doing?" Arno whispers.

"Get in the car and go," I tell him in a low voice.

"Are you crazy?"

"Just go! Come back and get me later." Heart galloping, I turn to face the approaching horde, my body feeling like a thousand volts of electric current are flooding through it. I don't know what's impelled me to make a stand, but I'm thinking of Robin and how I've failed her. How I've failed myself. How pissed off I am at me. How tired I am of living in a world where the powerful impose their wills on the meek.

Arno goes about twenty feet more, then stops. I mouth the words *Keep going!* at him. Tinsley and Milton continue toward the car.

The hoods stop a dozen feet away from me. The leader is the smallest, but muscles bulge under his tight T-shirt. "Where you runnin' off to, hippie?"

"We aren't running anywhere," I tell him, gripping the stick tightly but keeping it at my side.

"Looked like running to me," the leader says. "You afraid of something?"

"Whoa, check out the hot chick." One of them nods at Tinsley, standing beside the GTO in her short dress and white go-go boots. Milton's with her. Arno's still about halfway between me and the car.

"That is some choice hippie piece of ass," says another.

"I get it." The lead hood leers. "You don't want to share."

Shit! Why didn't Arno and the others go when they had the chance?

The gang steps closer. Even with this stick, six-to-one odds really stink. Then again, if I get the crap kicked out of me, I might not have to go all the way to San Francisco for my deferment. Surely the army doctors in Brooklyn will be compelled to flunk me if I show up in a body cast. But then I think of what happened to Barry. Nothing about this is funny.

"We don't want any trouble," I tell them.

"Too late, hippie boy," the leader says. "You ain't from here. You come to our beach, leave your fire burning. Leave your bottles and cups. What do you think we are, garbagemen?"

Arno takes a few steps closer. "We'll clean it up."

"Oh, yeah? Maybe I don't want hippie garbage like you pickin' up hippie garbage like that." The leader turns to his pals, grins proudly at his clever turn of phrase. A regular lowbrow Oscar Wilde. Then he steps nearer. "What are you, hippie boy, six two?"

"About that." My heart drums. I squeeze the stick hard.

"Go one eighty? One ninety?"

"About that." I'm trembling. If they come any closer, I'll get into batting stance. Hopefully, when they see I'm serious, they'll have second thoughts.

Lamebrain cracks his knuckles. "So you got five inches and twenty or thirty pounds on me. What do you say you drop the stick and we settle this mano a mano?"

"Lucas!" Arno calls anxiously from behind.

My breaths are coming short and fast; my heart is a jack-hammer. "I don't think so." I raise the stick. "What do you say you guys just go away?"

Lamebrain laughs scornfully. "Believe me, *Luke-ass,* that ain't in the cards."

The goons begin to spread out. A couple of them reach down and pick up rocks.

Bang! With a flash, a firecracker pops behind me. The bad guys jump. "Mother of Mary," one says with a gasp, and points behind me, where Milton's standing with something dark in his hand.

"He's got a gun!" someone says.

I don't know where Milton got the firecracker, but he set it off and is now holding up something small and dark that he knows can be mistaken for a gun in the night. Pure genius.

"Don't do nothin' stupid, okay?" Lamebrain takes a step back. The others drop their rocks.

These bozos are buying it! I almost burst out laughing.

The hoods start quickly away, sand and pebbles crunching under their boots, looking back over their shoulders to make sure Milton isn't following. My knees go weak, and I have to lean on the stick, using it as a crutch while I catch my breath. When the hoods are mere silhouettes down the beach, I turn to congratulate Milton on his brilliance.

But Arno speaks first: "A gun? What the fuck, Milton?"

"It's not a gun, stupid," I start to explain. "It was a —"

Milton lifts the dark thing in his trembling hand. *No, it can't be. . . .* But it is: a black pistol with an unusual-looking brown wooden grip.

"Your father's?" I ask.

He nods. Now I recall that after the birthday cake, when we told Milton we were taking him out to continue the celebration, he'd asked for a minute, then disappeared into the back of the house.

"Peaceful demonstrations aren't going to change anything," Milton says in the back seat of the GTO. The Stones' "Street Fighting Man" is on the radio. A few minutes ago, when Arno started to drive home, no one said a word. I guess we were all in our own worlds and thoughts. I keep replaying in my head what just happened at the beach. Not the gun part, but the part where I almost got into a fight. I haven't stopped alternating between relief and incredulity.

What was I thinking? I could have gotten the shit kicked clear out of me. But what choice did I have? The idea of those guys getting their hands on Tinsley. And what they might have done to Arno and Milton . . .

"The Panthers know it," Milton goes on. "Malcolm X knew it. Nonviolence is *exactly* what the Man wants. As long as we're being peaceful, he doesn't have to do doodley-squat. You think the colonists would have gotten their independence if they'd staged sit-ins at Lexington and Concord? The British would have laughed their limey asses off."

"But sit-ins and marches have worked," argues Tinsley, who's sitting beside him. "Look at civil rights."

"Yeah, right. King endorsed nonviolence and look what it got him," Milton counters. "I'm telling you guys, it's time to bring the war home."

"Are *you* willing to die?" Tinsley asks him.

Milton gazes out the window into the dark. "It won't come to that. We just have to show them we're willing to fight."

At Tinsley's gate, I get out of the car with her. "Thanks for making Milton feel special tonight."

"Thanks for being our knight in shining armor," she says.

We're standing in the headlights of the GTO. I sense she's waiting for something, but what? A good-night kiss? With Arno and Milton watching in the car, it feels a little awkward.

She steps close and whispers. "We can use the pool house. I'll drive you home later."

After I couldn't get it up the other night, you'd think I'd be eager for a second chance, but it's the opposite. I'm spent and drained by what happened at the beach. I'm actually glad I'm feeling this way. Ever since the other night, there's been this nagging thing in my head. It almost feels like my body was trying to send a message that fooling around with Tinsley isn't going to help increase whatever meager chance I have of winning Robin back. I should have figured that out a long time ago. Look at my father's "relationship" with my mother. You can't have it both ways.

"Thanks, but . . . I should really go."

Tinsley studies my face. "The girlfriend?"

Astonishing . . . and somewhat disheartening. "It's really that easy to read me?"

"Sometimes." But her voice and expression are flat, without emotion. She turns away and lets herself through the gate. Something tells me I won't be seeing her again anytime soon.

"She's really nice," Milton says dreamily as we drive away. He sounds like he's twelve.

"For a cock tease," Arno grumbles.

We drop Milton at his house but don't go directly home. Arno wants to cruise and smoke. It's late and dark. Not many cars on the road. Suburbia has shut down for the night.

"What would've happened if Milton hadn't pulled that stunt with the gun?" Arno asks.

"Guess there would've been a fight."

He glances at me. "Have you lost your mind?"

"Was there another option I wasn't aware of?" I ask.

Arno doesn't answer, but something about the force with which he flicks his butt out the window tells me that he's pissed off. "Looked like Tinsley was waiting for something when we dropped her off," he says.

"Nothing important."

"Didn't look that way to me."

"Leave it alone, man. It's been a bizarre night. Let's go home."

"You're such an asshole," he grumbles. "*And* a lucky fuck."

"Jesus, Arno, what are you so angry about? You worried that Tinsley thinks you're a wuss because you didn't do anything at the beach?"

"If only she knew what a wuss *you* once were," he mutters peevishly.

"Robin did."

"Nah. Back then she didn't know you existed. Tinsley know about her?"

"What difference does it make?"

"But Robin doesn't know about Tinsley, right?"

I stare out into the night as we pass dark house after dark house. God, how I wish sometimes that Arno would get a life of his own so he didn't have to be so wrapped up in mine.

"Well?" he noodges.

"Arno, I don't know what crawled up your rectum and died tonight, but either drop it or pull over and let me out."

He responds by speeding up. "What happens at the end of the summer when Robin comes home?"

"What happens *next week* when the three of us go up to the festival and instead of hanging out, you have to spend every waking moment trying to unload that huge stash of acid?"

"There's no way I'm gonna be able to sell all that shit at Bucknell." He's practically yelling now. "I don't even know if there are two thousand kids in the whole student body."

"Well, why the hell do you have to do crap like that anyway?" It's my turn to practically yell. I'm not sure where it's coming from. Pent-up tension? Aggravation? Frustration that Arno values the almighty dollar as much as, if not more than, our friendship? "It's not like you need the money. The only reason you sell drugs is because you think it makes you look cool. Want to be cool, Arno? Stop wearing aftershave, start wearing bell-bottoms, and trade this stupid car in for a Volvo!"

The radio's on low, playing Dylan's "Visions of Johanna." We cruise in near silence. It's not the first time we've yelled at each other. Probably won't be the last. But I've hurt his feelings.

"Sorry, man, I shouldn't have said that. I just don't know why you can't leave my life alone. Want to know what's really going on? Robin dumped me."

Arno shrugs dismissively. "So? You've still got Tinsley."

"No, Arno, I don't still have Tinsley. It's not the same. I realize this may come as a shock to you, but human beings aren't interchangeable."

Arno turns up his nose and does one of his mincing nasal imitations: "'I realize this may come as a shock to you, but human beings aren't interchangeable.'"

He's right. It sounded pompous. I sigh. "And if you want to know the *whole* truth, I couldn't get it up with Tinsley the other night. Couldn't stop thinking about Robin. And how the draft's got me dead in its sights. And how my family's falling apart, and how, if by some miracle I don't get drafted, I'm looking at the end of the summer when you guys go away to college and I'm stuck here with nothing to do and no future in sight."

There. I've laid it out for him plain as day so he can see that maybe I'm not quite the luckiest fuck ever. Arno drives quietly, one hand on the wheel. Someone else would appreciate the honesty, but what does he do? Says, "For your information, limp-dick, some girls *like* aftershave."

That's it. "Pull over, asshole."

"What?"

"You heard me. I'm gonna walk the rest of the way."

"Suit yourself."

He hits the brakes and screeches to the curb. I get out, am about to slam the door, then think of something and stick my head back in. "What about the gun? We can't just let him walk around with it."

"Maybe he should give it to you. Probably help where you're going." Arno pops the clutch, and the GTO's tires scream loud enough to wake the dead as he leaves forty feet of rubber.

WEDNESDAY, AUGUST 6

Days Until Armed Forces Induction Physical: 23

"I understand completely. He shouldn't have done that. I'm sure if you sit him down and speak very seriously . . . Yes . . . Yes . . . No, he will cooperate. Alan just needs to see that you're very, very serious."

Mom has stretched the long white telephone cord taut, all the way to the sliding glass doors that face the backyard. With one hand she holds the phone to her ear and listens. The other hand is clasped tightly over her mouth as if she is trying to keep from screaming.

"Yes, I do understand. I cannot begin to tell you how sorry I am. . . . Yes, I realize it's beyond the scope of your responsibilities. If you'll give him . . . Of course I'll speak to him. . . . Yes, yes, I'll tell him that. Those very words. . . . Oh, thank you. I can't tell you how grateful I am. . . . Yes, yes, thank you. Really, thank you so much."

She crosses back. The receiver goes on the hook. I've just gotten home from work. Once again, the emptiness of the house of dashed dreams is magnified by the lack of TV background noise. Before Alan left for camp, I didn't know if I'd miss him, but I do. A lot. He's the glue that's held this family together. Our concern for his well-being was the only thing left that we had in common. Without him, there's nothing to keep us from splintering into small pieces.

Mom's wearing a pale-blue housedress. Her face and arms seem thinner than I remember. Her eyes are red rimmed, and she looks drained, white as milk, beyond weary. She tells me that Alan left the camp without permission, setting off a search that included the state police until he was found walking along the road five miles away. When they asked why he'd left, he said he wanted to watch TV.

"Got a cigarette?" Mom asks. This from the mother who leaves newspaper articles on my desk about why I should quit.

When I give her a Marlboro, she clasps my wrist and frowns disapprovingly at my gnawed fingernails. "When did you start doing this again?"

"About the time you started smoking again."

She smirks, then starts toward the patio behind the kitchen. When I begin to follow, she holds up her hand. I watch her go out and stand in the sunlight with her back to me, her arms crossed. She brings the cigarette to her lips and exhales a plume of smoke into the air.

Why does this make me think of Robin? Unless it's because everything makes me think of her. It's like looking at the world through Robin-colored glasses: "Suite: Judy Blue Eyes" comes on the radio, and tears force their way into my eyes. I think of

Odysseus and there she is, sitting beside me. Or I notice my copy of *The Stranger* on the bookshelf and recall that magical day last fall when we sat in the school courtyard and talked for an entire period.

And sometimes the tears seem to come for no reason at all.

Once again I feel the urge to write. Another letter to Robin, even if I don't send it? A poem? All I know is that more and more, writing feels like an antidote for the emptiness.

On my desk is an application for a library card from the Bay Shore Public Library with a paper-clipped note: "Fill out immediately." There's also a new driver's license with my address now listed at Penataquit Avenue, Bay Shore, New York. A note from the paterfamilias clipped to the license says I should throw out my old license and replace it with this new one.

The familiar twinge of defiance rears its head. *Why should I?* For so long I did what I was told. Then I swung 180 degrees and stopped. Is it psychic weariness that now lets the pendulum swing back toward the path of least resistance? It just feels like there are so many bigger issues to confront than whatever stupid scam the paterfamilias is involved in. Who has the energy for mindless rebellion? I take out my wallet and replace my old license with this new one.

Then I pick up a pencil and begin to write.

Lucas was twelve when his father began to enter them
in father-and-son tennis tournaments. With his father
on the court beside him, Lucas felt intimidated by the

pressure to win. Every time he swung at a ball, he felt his father's demanding gaze. Lucas always choked, and he and his father always lost. And it was always Lucas's fault. Sometimes they would drive all the way home from a tournament without speaking. Sometimes Lucas's father would talk about the match and what they could have done to play better. His father said that if they kept playing, eventually Lucas would get "tournament tough." But with each tournament, Lucas would still choke. He started pretending he didn't care if they won or not. Finally the day came when Lucas's father lost his temper and yelled that he wished to God that Lucas wouldn't be such a goddamn goofball.

Lucas's father wanted Lucas to be just like him. Not a goofball. Lucas's father owned some businesses and made his own hours so that he could take time off to play tennis tournaments all over the Northeast. He won lots of tournaments and collected trophies. In their den at home, the trophies multiplied like rabbits. When Lucas was young, he wondered what those little golden men were doing at night. Were they sneaking out to meet women's tennis trophies? Did women's tennis trophies get sent to stay with relatives far away when their little golden tummies began to expand?

Like most kids, deep down Lucas wanted his father's approval. So when he was a sophomore in high school, he went out for the tennis team. The coach paired him with Johnny, who was Lucas's friend and someone he often played tennis with in the summer. Lucas and Johnny played third doubles, the lowest position.

Johnny was a good athlete and after a few weeks, the coach moved him up to second doubles. Lucas's new partner was an obnoxious kid who wasn't very good. But that didn't stop the kid from criticizing Lucas every time he missed a shot.

Things were changing for Lucas. That fall he had started growing his hair long and smoking grass. He was getting tired of always doing what his father wanted. He hated his obnoxious tennis partner on the school team and didn't like having to go to practices every day. Finally, he quit.

Johnny kept playing tennis. By junior year he was the best on the team. By then Lucas and Johnny were in completely different crowds. Johnny's crowd was all straight-A, top students who wouldn't touch grass in a million years.

The summer between junior and senior years, Lucas's father's regular doubles partner tore his Achilles tendon and had to have surgery. The recovery was expected to take a year. Lucas's father asked Lucas how he'd feel if Johnny was his partner for the annual country club doubles tournament.

It was a weird moment. Lucas knew it probably made sense for his father to team up with Johnny because they'd be the strongest doubles team in the tournament. But still . . . Lucas couldn't help feeling like he'd been replaced.

Lucas's father and Johnny won the club doubles championship. Only it didn't end there. That summer and fall, they went on to play other tournaments. They won a bunch of them and were ranked number two in the East.

The next summer, Lucas's father's former doubles partner had recovered from Achilles' tendon surgery and was ready to play again. But Johnny was younger, faster, and a better player. Lucas's father decided to keep Johnny as his doubles partner. They won the club championship again and traveled all over the Northeast playing other tournaments.

Lucas worked in his father's factory and pretended not to care.

By the time I finish the story, it's almost ten p.m. I missed dinner and didn't notice. This is the longest piece of prose I've ever written voluntarily. After rereading it, I think maybe it's a little too maudlin. Nonetheless, I'm proud of it. It may not have much of a setting, but I think it has well-defined characters, a conflict, plot, and theme. My first short story!

I put it in an envelope and address it to Miss Landers, care of the high school.

> Every writer you've ever heard of
> Was at one time a writer
> You'd never heard of.

THURSDAY, AUGUST 7

Days Until Armed Forces Induction Physical: 22

"We'll go underground."

It's 4:30 a.m. and Milton stinks of gasoline. Sirens wail in the distance. A few minutes ago, I was awakened by a *plink, plink, plink* against my bedroom window. It sounded like small hail. In the middle of summer. I dragged myself out of bed and pulled back the shade. Milton's face was pressed close to the glass, which he was tapping with a fingernail.

There's nothing like the odor of gasoline to clear out the cobwebs. Milton is pacing around my room. I can count on one hand the number of times I've seen him this wound up. (Most have been this summer.) But what he's just told me is mind-boggling: ten minutes ago he threw a Molotov cocktail at the home of New York State Supreme Court justice Leopold R. Wagner.

If it weren't for the sirens, I'd think either I heard him incorrectly or he and I have a different understanding of what a

Molotov cocktail is. To me, it's a bottle filled with gasoline and a rag sticking out of the neck. You light the rag and throw the bottle at the target. The bottle breaks and the gasoline ignites in a violent explosion. The target goes up in flames.

The sirens appear to confirm that that is what Milton thinks a Molotov cocktail is, too. A few days ago, the gun, and now *this*? Has his mind been taken over by malignant spirits? The SDS? Che Guevara?

"Did anyone get hurt?" I ask.

He shakes his head. "It hit the front walk." He lifts his sleeve close to his face, sniffs, and wrinkles his nose.

It's understandable if I can't quite believe this, right? If Milton gets caught, he's not getting up in the morning and going back to learning COBOL. He's probably not going back to MIT in the fall.

If I go to prison, we could be cell mates.

"Why?" I ask.

"Yesterday that douchebag put five draft-card burners in prison *because they burned pieces of paper.*"

I raise my hands, gesturing for him to lower his voice.

"They got two and a half years in jail for what?" Milton goes on. "Disagreeing with a government that's responsible for the deaths of nearly a thousand American soldiers every month? And nearly four thousand Vietnamese soldiers and civilians? It's a violation of their human rights. It's a violation of their freedom of speech. *They burned pieces of paper,* Lucas."

It's coming back to me. "That's the judge your father plays chess with?"

"Probably not anymore," Milton says ruefully. He resumes pacing, then absently picks up the album cover of *Fresh Cream*, looks at it, puts it back down.

"Why go underground?" I ask.

"Someone saw me." Milton explains that the first two times he threw the Molotov cocktail, it landed on the Wagners' lawn and went out. Twice he had to retrieve it, relight it, and try again. "Damn thing wouldn't break. I won't use a Welch's jelly jar next time — that's for sure."

"*Next time*, Milton?"

He lifts his hands and drops them in a gesture of frustration.

"Who saw you?" I ask.

"Guy who lives next door. The jar finally blows up and the next thing I know, someone's calling my name. 'Milton? Milton Fischer, is that you?' I look over and there's this guy in pajamas standing on his front lawn."

Can you picture it? Joe Schmo gets up for a four a.m. snack. He's poking around in the refrigerator when he hears something outside. Looks out the window, and there's this kid from the neighborhood throwing a Molotov cocktail at the house next door.

Milton slumps into the desk chair, wringing his hands. "My grandparents were forced to flee Austria. Rudy had to leave this country. I'm not running. It's time to stay and fight, Lucas. A true patriot must defend his country against his government."

Sounds like revolution is in the air. Only . . . "What does going underground even mean?"

"You go to a cemetery and find someone who died before

they were ten years old—someone who wouldn't have been old enough to work so they wouldn't have needed a Social Security card. You use their name to apply for one. Once you've got that, you get another ID, like a library card or something. You use those IDs to get a driver's license. Presto, you have a new identity." Weird—it sounds like what my father's doing with me. Only he's using my name. "And then?"

Milton's eyes slide away. His forehead bunches. He props his elbows on his knees and leans forward. "There have to be others. Draft resisters. Antiwar advocates. The SDS. We join them and fight to end this stupid war."

In another part of the house, a phone rings. It's 4:40 a.m. Not hard to guess who's calling.

"It's your parents, man."

Milton straightens up. His eyes dart left and right, and he presses his hands down on the arms of the chair like he's about to spring up and make a break for it.

"Milton, they've already lost Rudy."

He slumps back into the chair and bites his lip. His parents would be devastated. "Then we'll go to Canada. Join Rudy. My parents'll know we're together."

He may be a genius, but right now he's not thinking straight. "That's the first place the cops would look for you. With Rudy. Canada may not allow the extradition of draft dodgers, but I have a feeling it's not the same for arsonists."

Milton makes a fist and bangs it against the desktop. "Shit. *Shit!*"

There's a soft tap on my door.

"Come in, Mom."

The door opens. Mom's wrapped in a blue robe, blinking the sleep out of her eyes. Her hair is flat on one side. She sniffs. "Gasoline?"

"Milton's parents want him home?" I think it best to move the conversation along.

She nods. "What's going on?"

"Nothing, Mom."

"Oh, of course," Mom says with a drollness I've forgotten she was capable of. "It's the middle of the night and your friend is here reeking of gasoline. What could possibly make me think something was going on?"

In the predawn darkness, the air is heavy with moisture. Houses are shadowy silhouettes. I've pulled on pants and a shirt to escort Milton home. A week ago, if someone had asked me if he would ever carry a gun or throw a Molotov cocktail at a house, I would have said never, not in a million years.

"Listen, man," I tell him. "What happened to Rudy is beyond shitty. You have every right to be pissed, but right now you have to fix what happened tonight. Then go back to MIT and keep doing whatever you're doing. You've got more promise than Arno and me combined and multiplied. So don't blow it, okay? There are plenty of other people around to protest the war and all the other crap that's wrong with this country. But they don't have one-tenth your brains. Let them be the ones who go underground while you go on to a lifetime of accomplishment."

Milton's quiet for a moment. Then says, "You didn't just make that up."

"I might've started thinking about it back in my room," I admit. "How'd you know?"

"'A lifetime of accomplishment?' Get real."

"I was trying to make a point," I say defensively.

"I know. And it shows talent. Ever consider going into speechwriting?"

"Seriously, Milton."

"Okay, okay. I heard you."

Somewhere in the dark, a bird begins to chirp. It's getting close to dawn. The lights are on in Milton's house. The front door opens before we reach it. Mrs. Fischer's eyes are glistening. Mr. Fischer looks grim. They put their arms around their son and lead him inside. They don't ask what happened.

They already know.

Mom's sitting at the kitchen table with a cup of coffee. Once she's up, she's up. "Tell me."

When I do, she looks stricken. "Oh, dear God. His poor parents." She shudders. "All of you, with the bodies of men and the brains of infants."

Guess that about sums it up. She sips her coffee. We sit in silence. She hasn't asked about my draft situation lately, but she must be wondering. I tell her I've airmailed a letter to the Berkeley chapter of the Mobe. Inside is another letter addressed to the Great Neck draft board requesting permission to take my induction physical in San Francisco. Someone at the Mobe will post the letter so that it will look like I mailed it from California. As soon as they receive a reply from the Great Neck board, the Mobe will let me know and I'll fly out there for the physical.

"It's going to be expensive," I warn her. "Think Dad'll spring for it?"

I'm mostly joking, but Mom takes it seriously. "Of course he will. He loves you."

Ire spikes inside me. "Why —?" I start too loudly and catch myself. "Why do you always defend him, Mom?"

The kitchen grows still. In the first faint hint of dawn, the backyard has turned gray. Mom starts to lift her cup, then sets it down. She reaches for my hand and again studies my bitten fingernails. "Lucas, don't let"—she pauses, as if choosing her words carefully—"whatever happens between him and me affect your relationship."

"*What* relationship?"

She lets go of my hand. The crows'-feet around her eyes deepen. "You know, young man, you haven't exactly been the easiest son."

"And he's been an easy father?"

Her gaze goes down to the table. "It's been difficult for him."

I assume she's talking about Alan. And me. And Dad growing up poor without a father of his own. But it pisses me off. "It hasn't been easy for you, either, but I don't see *you* sneaking around on *him*." I press my hands down on the table, push myself up, and head back to my room.

FRIDAY, AUGUST 8

Days Until Armed Forces Induction Physical: 21

SUSPECT SURRENDERS IN LOCAL FIREBOMBING

"Feeble Attempt," Says Police Official

Milton Fischer, 17, was charged after surrendering himself . . .

At home after work, I call Lou at Wilkinson Motorsports and learn that the registration and insurance have come in. Arno will give me a ride over in a bit, but first we sit in the GTO, a copy of *Newsday* spread open between us. Like so many times before, we've wordlessly agreed to call a truce to the argument we had a few nights ago. (If you've ever wondered if it's possible for two teenage boys to act like an old married couple, I offer Arno and me as evidence.)

In the newspaper's black-and-white front-page photo, someone with a jacket pulled over his head to hide his face is bent forward, his hands behind his back, no doubt locked there by handcuffs, while a detective escorts him.

The story jumps to an inside page and a picture of cops and firemen standing amid a tangle of hoses in the street in front of a vaguely familiar-looking house.

"He never could throw straight." Arno lights a half-smoked joint and starts to back out of the driveway.

It isn't hard to find the house. A police car is parked at the curb. Halfway up the front walk is a blackened spot edged by singed grass and a partially immolated azalea.

"The burning bush." Arno keeps the roach low between his legs when we pass the cop car. "How could he think that dumbass move was going to make a difference? How can anyone that smart be so stupid?" He hands me the roach, yellowish brown and less than half an inch long. Pinching the back edge between my fingertips, I inhale hard, then dab the burning ember with spit and eat the warm remains. Saturated with THC, it should add to the mild buzz.

"He knows he screwed up. We talked about it."

"When?"

"He came over after he did it. Said he wanted me to go underground with him."

"What about me?" Arno asks with a hurt pout.

"Why would you go underground, Arno?"

"I don't know. To be with you guys. You'd leave me?"

How can anyone so gruff be so sensitive?

"You're going to Bucknell in a few weeks," I remind him.

"You still could've asked," Arno says with a sniff as we turn a corner. "So, what did the genius say?"

"Maybe it'll help add to the message that a lot of people are seriously against what's going on. And possibly, instead of thinking it was stupid, some people'll wonder why a kid smart enough to go to MIT at sixteen would do something like that."

"Or they'll think he's a fruitcake," Arno says. "And after the gun thing the other night? I wouldn't argue." He drives out of our neighborhood. The radio's playing the Doors' twelve-minute Oedipal dirge "The End," a song that lends itself to contemplation.

"It ever occur to you that maybe we're to blame?" I ask. "It's not like MIT's a hotbed of radicals. We're the ones who turned him on to music and drugs. And from there, it's not a big jump to the antiwar thing. Maybe we should've left him alone. Let him be an engineering nerd like his dad."

Arno lights a cigarette. "I take it back. *You're* the fruitcake."

"At least he believes in something. What do *you* believe in?"

"Turn on, tune in, drop out, man." Arno facetiously repeats the mantra of the LSD guru Timothy Leary. And by extension everyone like me who'd rather make love, not war.

"Seriously, Arno, besides making money, what do you believe in?"

"I'm against the war," he says defensively.

"Join the crowd. But have you *done* anything about it?"

"What have *you* done?" Arno shoots back. "Other than go

on a couple of protest marches with your hot girlfriend and her parents."

On the radio, Jim Morrison has gotten to the part where the narrator tells his father he wants to kill him and tells his mother he wants to *AAAAAAAAARGH* her. People always stop to listen to that. What have I done about the war? To be honest, other than try to save my own ass from going, not much more than Arno's done. But maybe I could do more. Over the past month, I've learned a lot. If I can find a way to stay out of the war, maybe I could become a draft counselor like Charles. That's the thing about not getting high as much as I used to. I suddenly have a lot more time on my hands. (Yeah, yeah. I know I just polished off the roach, but that's not a *real* high—just a little buzz.)

"When did you get a motorcycle license?" Arno asks in the lot behind Wilkinson Motorsports. Lou gave me the registration and insurance papers, and I just put the tag on the BSA. The cycle is now officially mine. Before entering traffic for the first time, I want to take a few more practice laps.

I buckle the helmet strap. "I have a permit."

"How's that work with motorcycles?"

"You're supposed to be supervised by someone with a motor-cycle license. They're supposed to be within a quarter mile."

"Know anyone with a motorcycle license?"

"Know anyone with an LSD license? Got a permit to sell two thousand hits at the music festival?"

"That's different."

"Right. I get stopped without a motorcycle license, the worst I'll get is a ticket. You get picked up with that much acid, you're guaranteed fifteen years in the slammer."

"Not gonna happen. I'm only gonna sell to freaks."

"Ever hear of undercover narcs?"

"Think I can't tell the difference?"

"Arno, what do you think 'undercover' *means*? The whole *point* is to not be able to tell the difference."

"Bite me, Lucas."

I ride around the parking lot in a wide circle. Why do I keep picking fights with him? Is it because I'm ticked off about the royal mess I've made of my life and have no one else to vent at? Is it because we've been friends for so long that I know he's the one person I can dump on without fear of rejection? Each time I pass him in the lot, he dishes it right back at me.

"Rebel without a cause."

"Junior Hells Angel."

"Mouse on the motorcycle."

He's going to Bucknell in less than a month. *What will I do without him?*

At home, I park the BSA in the garage behind the MG. It's not like my parents can miss it.

Neither of them says a word.

SATURDAY, AUGUST 9

Days Until Armed Forces Induction Physical: 20

"You get picked up without a motorcycle license, the bike gets impounded, you get a ticket, and your regular driver's license can be suspended."

"You asked a cop?"

Arno and I are headed for Milton's. The GTO reeks of something sickeningly sweet and vaguely reminiscent of Good & Plenty candy.

"What's that smell?" I ask, rolling down the window to get some air.

"What smell? I don't smell anything."

"New aftershave?" I guess.

"Maybe."

A minute later, we stop at Milton's. When he comes out of his house with his hair shorn close to his skull and the scraggly mustache gone, he looks more like a sophomore in high school than someone entering his second year of college. He gets into the back seat and sniffs. "What's that smell?"

"His new aftershave," I tell him.

"What'd you do, Arno, take a bath in it?" Milton rolls down the windows in the back.

"Fuck you very much. And while you're at it, you can both drop dead," Arno growls, and starts to drive.

"Wearing that stuff, I'm surprised you haven't," Milton shoots back.

I look over the seat. "So, what happened?"

Milton reaches into his pocket and turns down the volume on his transistor radio. "Court date's in a few weeks."

Maybe it's my imagination, but he seems pretty relaxed for someone who's been charged with attempted arson. Arno turns onto the Expressway service road and accelerates. The GTO's throaty dual exhausts rumble (the mating call of the muscle car). Because the windows are open, I have to hold my hair back so it doesn't whip into my eyes. Milton taps me on the shoulder and hands me a rubber band.

It's around nine o'clock, but there is still a trace of light in the sky. It's Saturday night. I feel a searing ache in my heart, wondering what Robin and the baby-seal killer are up to.

Arno adjusts the rearview mirror so he can see Milton and yells over the wind rushing through the car. "You'll never be a lawyer now!"

"I don't want to be a lawyer," Milton says.

"Or a doctor or a politician."

"Not those, either."

"Well, it's gonna make things hard, no matter what you want to do."

"The oracle hath spoken," Milton jeers.

"At least you got rid of that smudge of dirt over your upper lip."

"Thanks, zitface."

"You get a lawyer?" I ask.

Milton darts his eyes at the back of Arno's head. There's something he doesn't want him to hear. He'll tell me later.

At Nathan's, we get hot dogs, Cokes, and fat, greasy crinkle-cut French fries. (Robin never liked this place. She thought it was too dirty and noisy.) When Arno goes to the bathroom, I lean across the table to Milton. "What's the story?"

"The old-Austrian-boys' network," Milton quips. "My parents had Judge Wagner over for linzer torte and a chat. Everything's been ironed out. The understanding is, I pay for the damage, and the charges get knocked down to malicious mischief. And because I'm seventeen, I qualify for youthful offender status. Two or three years' probation, and as long as I don't mess up, the record gets expunged."

"And no more guns and Molotov cocktails, right?"

Milton's eyes shift left and right, then he leans closer and whispers, "We blow up the Great Neck draft board and call it a day, okay?"

What! He can't be—

Milton leans back and grins. "Wish you could see your face."

Arno returns to the table. "What're you homos whispering about now?"

"What'll happen next week when you get busted with all

282

that acid," I reply. I've finally figured out what's bothering about Arno and his bulging sock of LSD. It's not only tha he doesn't need the money. It's not just that his real motive for being a dealer—so people will admire him and think he's badass—is flawed. It's that, after my recent run-ins with border agents, and with all the other hassles in my life, the last thing I feel like doing next weekend is being in Arno's car or at the festival feeling paranoid about getting busted. It's another one of those reality-check moments. Back in high school, I'm not sure I actually ever believed we *could* get busted. *Well, guess what, Toto? We're not in high school anymore.*

"You're still coming, right?" Arno asks Milton.

Milton lowers his eyes. It dawns on me that a three-day drug-infused art and music festival might not be the best choice for someone who's been warned to stay out of trouble. "I can't."

"Aw, man." I'm completely bummed. "You sure?"

"I can't risk it," Milton says. "Especially with Mr. Drug Kingpin over here."

So much for our last big hurrah of the summer. Arno crosses his arms and grouses, "That's right—blame it on me."

"He has a point," I argue.

"So you're saying that if I didn't bring the acid, you'd go?" Arno asks Milton.

Milton hesitates, then shakes his head.

"I rest my case," Arno says to me. Then to Milton: "So we can have your tickets?"

"I'd like to sell them," Milton says.

Arno gives me a look and mouths, *Tinsley.*

I'm about to break the news to him that she's been grounded by her mother and that I haven't spoken to her since Milton's birthday. But then, from close by, comes "Mom, is that a boy or a girl?"

Jesus Christ, not this again.

Sitting next to us is a woman with dyed-blond hair, wearing a too-tight T-shirt and short shorts. She and her two blond kids are staring. The boy who asked the question looks like he's nine or ten.

The woman starts to rise. "Come on, kids, we're moving away from this hippie trash." The kids obediently pick up their trays and follow.

"Girl," I call out after them.

The boy looks back and frowns.

"It's the ponytail." Arno runs a hand over his own hair, which partly covers his ears and in the back ends thickly at his shirt collar. "Mine's more acceptably long. But you've crossed the line."

I wave him off. "Frequently wrong. Never in doubt."

Milton laughs so abruptly that he coughs out a half-chewed French fry. The radio earpiece falls into his soda. He fishes it out and sticks it back in his ear.

Arno can't let go. "Cut it a little shorter. It can still be long. Just not so long that it attracts attention everywhere you go."

"What about when everyone else's hair is as long as mine?" I ask.

"Never."

"The oracle hath spoken yet again." Milton sniggers.

Nothing eggs Arno on more than when we don't take him seriously. "When are you gonna figure out that this long-haired hippie-dippie shit is just a fad? Remember when it was spit curls and duck's asses? Tapered pants and engineer boots? Now we laugh at those guys."

"This is different."

Arno rolls his eyes. "Oh, really? All these barefoot flower people eating brown rice and alfalfa sprouts? You don't think they're gonna get tired of being dirty and hungry? And free love? Enjoy the crabs and clap, man. This whole back-to-the-land thing? Isn't that why we had the industrial revolution? So we don't all have to be farmers anymore?"

He is so good at getting under my skin. "You don't get it, Arno," I tell him. "You're never gonna get it."

Arno sits back and smugly crosses his arms. "We'll see who doesn't get it."

Dessert at Carvel. Robin would always get vanilla swirl with sprinkles in a cup, never a cone. She didn't like it dripping down her hand on warm nights.

I'm bummed about Milton not going to the festival, but it should still be an outrageous weekend of music and fun, plus an opportunity to catch up with Cousin Barry. (I can always hang out with him and Zach while Arno's off peddling his wares.)

We're paying for our cones when from the parking lot in the back comes the loud revving of a car engine followed by the squeal of tires.

We join a crowd watching a Corvair do donuts, the acrid

285

smoke of burning rubber in our noses. Clouds of white billow from the wheel wells while the car spins in a tight circle. This teenage ritual sacrifice of tires dates back to the aforementioned days of spit curls and engineer boots. Is Arno right? Will people someday look upon long hair, bell-bottoms, and peace symbols with the same amused disdain that we feel watching these nut-jobs shred tread and transmissions?

The Corvair gives way to a souped-up Nash Rambler that draws chuckles from the crowd. By now there must be forty people watching.

And one of them is Tinsley, about thirty feet to my right. She's turning her head away when I spot her, which makes me think that she saw me first. A guy with longish hair, bushy side-burns, and a thick black mustache is standing close behind her. He's wearing jeans and a leather vest with no shirt underneath. His chest is covered with curly dark hair.

His hands are on her shoulders.

SUNDAY, AUGUST 10

Days Until Armed Forces Induction Physical: 19

"How would you feel if your mom and I got divorced?"

When I roared into the garage on the BSA a few minutes ago, the paterfamilias came out of the house. He'd been gone all weekend without explanation. I guess with Alan at camp, he doesn't feel the need for pretenses anymore. I was sure he was going to give me grief about having a motorcycle. Instead, he suggested a stroll.

So he wants to get divorced. What am I supposed to say? *Gee, Dad, sounds fantastic. Really happy for you. Come to think of it, except for the fact that you show up here to sleep and change clothes, it kind of feels like you're already divorced. But all the same, thanks for asking.*

"Why?" It's a stupid question, but I want to hear him answer it.

"It's hard to explain," he says.

"Give it a try." The words probably surprise me as much as they surprise him. Have I ever given the paterfamilias an order before? I expect him to react, but he doesn't. Then it hits me: Is it possible that, thanks to the Great Bathtub Turd Incident, he's realized that I no longer need to bow before his bluster?

He stares off. Still not much eye contact. Whenever our eyes met in the past, it always felt like he was looking inside me for all that should have been there but wasn't: The desire to win. The desire to become a capitalist tool. The desire to be golden. Now I just can't look at him, period.

He rubs the back of his neck. "There's nothing left. You had to know that. The separate bedrooms. The silence. There are things a man needs, Lucas. I'm not just talking about sex. I'm talking about love and affection. . . ." He trails off, but he's said enough to leave me feeling profoundly ill at ease.

It's January 1967. I am fifteen and have begun to grow my hair long. At home, I am accused of being fresh, sullen, and uncooperative. With Presidents' Week vacation approaching next month, Dad announces that he and I need to spend some special time together. I think not, but he proposes that we go to Aspen, the mecca of American skiing.

Mom has to stay home with Alan, who won't ski anymore. He used to, but he refused to go to ski school and thus never learned to turn. At the top of a slope, he'd aim his skis downhill and go straight to the bottom, where he'd drop to his butt and drag to a stop.

None of us saw what happened on that icy day at Bromley

the year Alan turned nine. But it wasn't hard to imagine him flying down the hill and plunking down in his customary drag-butt manner. With scant friction on the hard-packed slippery snow, he slid farther and faster than usual and smashed into the ticket checker's booth. One front tooth was knocked out cleanly. The other had to be removed by a dentist in Manchester that afternoon. Alan hasn't been on skis—and has been wearing a bite-plate with two false front teeth—ever since.

In Aspen, Dad signs us up for a private lesson. We've never skied in powder and want to learn. Our Austrian ski instructor keeps saying "Rhino." "Rhino, we ski face of Bell Mountain." "Rhino, you follow me."

Dad and I are mystified. Does the instructor think Rhino is Dad's first name? Did someone tell him that's how all Americans begin each sentence?

This goes on all morning until we realize that Rhino means "right now."

Rhino becomes our private joke. "Rhino, I go to the bathroom." "Rhino, I order dessert." Dad and I don't talk about life back home, about me quitting tennis, not doing my chores, or doing badly at school. We just ski. It's actually fun. Fun with Dad. A unique concept.

One day, while we're eating lunch at the Sundeck at the top of Aspen Mountain, Dad starts chatting with an attractive woman. She laughingly says that she thought Dad and I were brothers. Dad shows his teeth a lot and converses animatedly with her. I am old enough now to recognize the heightened level of charm he saves for social occasions and flirtations with attractive women. But, hey, it's vacation. We're just having fun.

That evening Dad and I have dinner at the Copper Kettle, his favorite Aspen restaurant. It feels special. The food is delicious. Afterward, I'm bushed from skiing all day and ready to hit the sack, but Dad wants to go hear music. This is odd. He never listens to music at home. But, hey, it's vacation.

We walk along the sidewalk, snow falling out of the dark sky and the scent of wood smoke in the air. This is really cool. We're going to listen to music together. Another first. He takes me to a crowded place where people sit at long tables drinking mugs of beer while an oompah band plays. Not exactly the tunes I had in mind, but I'm ready to go with the flow.

Especially since it's beer that's flowing. When Dad orders a pitcher and pours us each a mug, I can't believe it. Not only does he hardly ever drink at home, but I'm fifteen. There is no possible way that this can be legal. Thus, it is beyond cool. Together in Aspen, on our own and far away from the rest of the world, Dad and I are father-and-son party animals. It feels like I'm with a whole new person. Someone who for once isn't being judgmental or critical. Someone who just wants to have fun . . . with me.

I finish my beer and Dad pours me another. At this point in my life, I've hardly had any drinking experience. After two mugs at an altitude of eight thousand feet, I'm three sheets to the wind and feeling no pain.

I don't remember exactly when the woman from lunch joins us. All I know is that her name is Sharon, and once again Dad is chatting her up unctuously. He pours me a third mug of beer, lets me finish it, then puts me in a cab and gives the driver a hotel room key and fifty bucks to make sure I get there safely.

Not a whole new person after all.

On the sidewalk near our house, the paterfamilias has just said something about having never felt this deeply in love before. How Antonia is the true soul mate he never dreamed he'd find. I guess all those other women — the Hazels, the Sharons, plus the ones I never met but sensed were the reason for his "late nights at the office" (when he worked for himself and could make his own schedule) and "business trips" (when his businesses were nearby) — weren't his soul mates. They were simply the women an iconoclast like him gets to cheat on Mom with.

He's never spoken to me this honestly, this frankly before. I guess this, too, is part of the post–high school landscape. I gaze across the street at our neighbors' well-kept houses and neatly trimmed lawns. The only sounds are cicadas and the distant hum of a lawn mower. Despite my antiestablishment leanings, this summer I've come to realize that this has been a good place, maybe even a great place, to grow up. In a roomy home, in a safe neighborhood with lots of space to play and a private country club. Children never go hungry here. They have their own bedrooms. Not only was Chris expected to drop out and go to work when he turned sixteen, but until he went into the army, he had to share a bedroom with a younger brother. And how many millions of kids would think *he* had it pretty good compared to them?

So, let's face it, folks, I've had it good. Only, Rhino I can't look at the person who made it all possible. That Presidents' Week trip to Aspen two years ago was the last time any of us traveled anywhere together. How convenient that on the top of Aspen Mountain we should run into an attractive woman who happened to be skiing alone. How strange that the paterfamilias should suddenly decide he wanted to go listen to music. How remarkable that we should run into the same woman (alone again) at the beer hall after the paterfamilias had gotten me plastered.

And that was supposed to be our special time together? Pardon my French, but give me a fucking break.

"Is Antonia the one you went to the classic-car rally with?" I ask.

The paterfamilias does a double take, then stares at me with wide-eyed stupefaction. I explain that I saw her in the MG with him when Robin and I drove out east to catch the ferry to New London on our way to Maine.

He looks down at the sidewalk and says "We're deeply in love" for the second time.

A cramping sensation seizes my guts. How is a son supposed to react when a father tells him he's deeply in love with a woman who's not his mother?

"She lives in New Jersey," he volunteers. "So I'd probably move out there. She's got young boys who could use a father."

To get to the very closest parts of New Jersey takes at least an hour—more in any kind of traffic. Depending on where in New Jersey Antonia lives, the drive could take a lot longer. If he moves there, am I supposed to visit?

"What about Mom and Alan?" I ask.

"I'd make sure they're okay," he says. "They seem to do fine without me."

What, exactly, does *that* mean? Alan may not be a kid anymore, but he's still the paterfamilias's child, still living at home, going to his special school. But he won't be going to special schools forever. What then? What happens to people like my brother? Are they sent away someplace? Mom would never allow that. So then . . . will he always live with her at home? And if something happens to Mom, then with me? It's hard to imagine true-love Antonia taking on that responsibility when she has children of her own. So that means the paterfamilias would leave Alan in our hands. Emotionally, I guess he did that years ago. But at least he stuck around to be here in an emergency.

Now he'd really be gone.

From Mom.

From Alan.

From me.

For good.

This is the guy Mom says loves me?

So here we are on the sidewalk on a summer afternoon, talking about a future in which he walks away from his family to take over a new one. One where he feels appreciated by the new love of his life and needed by her children. All he has to do is divorce Mom and he'll be golden.

It reminds me of the last time he asked for my blessing to do something that was important to him. When he asked if I'd mind if Rat Fink Johnny became his doubles partner. What did he expect me to say? At that point, I hadn't picked up a racket in nearly a year. He knew I hated playing competitively. The only reason he asked was because he felt guilty and wanted me to absolve him of that burden.

It's the same thing now, isn't it?

He wants me to say something like *I understand, Dad. Don't worry about shirking your responsibilities to your family. Go to Antonia. After all, she's the soul mate you never thought you'd find.*

That's not what I say. What comes through my lips is "Do whatever the fuck you want."

I'd rather have a bottle in front of me
Than a frontal lobotomy.

It's truly mind-blowing how many small brown glass bottles are in the medicine cabinet in Arno's parents' bathroom. A regular pharmacological cornucopia. A few moments ago, I was in Arno's room listening to *Blind Faith* and helping him paint one side of each of his homemade acid tablets a festive violet color. Acid usually has a name (Orange Sunshine, Blue Cheer, Purple Haze), and Arno's come up with Violet Rush. The Woodstock music and arts festival is less than a week away, and he doesn't want potential customers thinking he's trying to burn them with tabs that look more like aspirin than acid.

After giving the paterfamilias my answer to his question, I started walking and ended up at Arno's house. I just couldn't be in my house after that. Arno was happy to have someone help him paint each of his two thousand tabs with a mixture of blue and red food coloring.

I was headed for the kitchen to get something to drink when I remembered the built-in bar in the den where Mr. Exley makes his vodka martinis. I poured myself a nice big glass of orange juice and added some vodka. Or maybe I poured a nice big glass of vodka and added some orange juice. Anyway, I was headed back to Arno's room but wound up in his parents' bathroom instead.

It smells nice and perfumy in here. And there are all these little brown bottles filled with pills.

Wonder what would happen if I took two of each?

> One for the money,
> Two for the show.
> Swallow with vodka,
> And away we'll go.

✳ It's getting dark. Arno grips Lucas the Unstable's arm, walking his friend along the foggy sidewalk. Lucas stumbles, the toe of his boot catching on the rough concrete. Feels like he's wearing ankle weights. It's bad luck to step on the cracks, but Arno keeps tugging.

This summer the *Invasion of the Tent Caterpillars* has been worse than ever. In the trees lining the sidewalk their silky nests have grown large, filled with plump, creepy-looking caterpillars. Any leaves that haven't been gnawed away completely are riddled with holes. (*Defoliation.* Instead of napalm, why doesn't the military drop tent caterpillars on Vietnamese jungles?) When Lucas was younger, he used to pretend that the caterpillars and their nests were actually colonies of alien invaders from outer space. The paterfamilias encouraged him to prune the tented branches, douse them in gasoline, and burn them at the curb. Lighting fires was always fun, but the odor of burning alien larvae was sour and yucky.

Maybe Lucas should ask Milton if they could put a nest in the Radarange and see what happens. How cool would it be if the caterpillars blew up? Then Lucas has an idea! He points at the nests and says to Arno, "We should get Mr. Fischer to build a Radarange laser gun with one of his special grips. Then we could blast those suckers right out of the branches."

"Sure," Arno grunts.

Lucas the Exterminator wants to slow down and study these wormy invaders from Planet Tent in the Larval Galaxy, but Arno the Annoying is still tugging at him.

"Lay off!" Lucas's attempt to wrest his arm from Arno's grasp feels sluggish and weak.

Arno yanks him along.

It occurs to Lucas that they must be going somewhere. "Where are we going?"

"Your house."

"What? I don't wanna—" Lucas tries to dig his heels in and nearly topples over.

"No stopping." Arno tightens his grip and holds him up.

A little while ago, Arno noticed that Lucas's tablet-painting skills had become noticeably diminished. Most of the violet dye was winding up on Lucas's fingers and on the newspaper. Arno asked what was going on. Lucas must have told him, but he's too wrecked to remember for sure.

Through the mist, two people come hurrying along the sidewalk toward them. Lucas forces his eyes to focus. "You called my *parents?*" He tries to stop again.

"Come *on*, jerk." Arno yanks him hard.

"Why are you so angry?"

"What? Jesus Christ, Lucas, when are you gonna grow up and stop feeling sorry for yourself?"

"Wha . . . what's *that* mean?"

"You're such a fuckin' idiot."

Faces portraits of concern, Mom and Dad meet them. Lucas is handed over. Why exactly *did* he take two of every pill in Arno's parents' medicine cabinet? The thought of killing himself never entered his mind. Nor did any concern about overdosing.

Blind spots.

Mom slides her arm around Lucas's waist. It's a typical summer evening in suburbia. Across the street, Mr. Patrick moves his sprinkler to a patch of front lawn where the grass has turned brown. The Lewandowskys' station wagon passes filled with kids. The Bakers hustle their totally spaced-out son home.

In the kitchen, Mom's on the phone. The paterfamilias

paces, pretending to care. They don't get angry at Lucas any-more. They've moved on to resignation. At the kitchen table, Lucas's chin keeps dipping. He keeps jerking his head up. Sure seems cloudy in here. On the phone, Mom's telling someone that she doesn't know what Lucas has taken, but for some reason both of his hands have turned violet. "Not violent. Vio*let*." She hangs up and calls Arno. Now it appears that she's writing down the names of the medicines in the Exleys' medicine cabinet.

She's on the phone again, telling whomever she's talking to what Lucas ingested. "Never mind his hands. They were fooling around with food coloring."

Lucas's head feels heavy. His chin dips. *Oh, dear, is that his drool on the table?*

Mom hangs up and tells the paterfamilias that too much time has passed to have Lucas's stomach pumped. That's good news. Lucas knew a girl at school who had to have her stomach pumped. She said they don't put the tube down your throat because it makes you gag. Instead, they put it through your *nose*. It reminded Lucas of how the Egyptians got the brains out of mummies by sticking a hook up the nose and pulling the brain out through the nostrils.

(Did the guy who decided the stomach pump tube should go through the nose think it was a no-brainer? *Life without a brain might be an improvement.*)

Mom has Lucas's left arm and the paterfamilias has his right. *Hey, look! They're doing something as a family again!* Lucas's stomach is bloated and sloshing with orange juice. His brain feels bloated and sloshing, too. It appears that whoever Mom spoke to told her that to prevent brain damage, Lucas should drink lots of orange juice and stay awake and moving. (There's something ironic about the prescribing of orange juice, but it's difficult to get a handle on at the moment.)

Flanked by his parents, Lucas slowly trudges, his arms and legs having turned to lead. The route takes them from the living room past the dining room and through the den, where the rows of little golden tennis trophy men glower from the shelves. A Roman tribunal giving Lucas the thumbs-down.

Feed him to the lions!

(Considering what Lucas has ingested today, if they do, there'll be some seriously blitzed kings of the jungle.)

His parents start the loop again. It's a path they've all taken before. As an infant, Alan never crawled. Instead, he skimmed across the floor on his butt. Later, in their search for answers and cures, the Bakers found a doctor who postulated that by not crawling Alan might have missed a critical stage of development. The next day, four sets of red rubber knee pads appeared. That evening the family strapped on the pads and crawled along this very same route.

They crawled each evening for a week. *Just another one of those fun Baker family activities!* Then Mom and Dad started alternating evenings. Then they both stopped. Did they have unrealistic hopes for quick results? Maybe they got tired of being on their hands and knees. Like so many other household chores, the nightly crawl with Alan was left to Lucas. To keep his brother interested, Lucas made up games. Carrying toy guns, he and Alan crept around furniture, shooting at bad guys. They crawled into the kitchen and barked until Mom put bowls of water on the floor to lap from. Alan eventually lost interest. After that, no amount of cajoling or bribery with candy or comic books worked. He went back to staring at the television.

Now it's Lucas's turn. As they escort him through the pharmaceutical haze, his chin keeps dipping and he keeps jerking it up. The frustrated look on Mom's face reminds him of when he'd bring home those elementary-school report cards peppered with Ns (Needs Improvement) and the occasional U (Unsatisfactory).

Lucas's feet drag. He's so weary. His field of vision narrows. Is it getting late? Or are the effects of the drugs he ingested still intensifying? Can't they just let him lie down and sleep?

What difference will a few million less brain cells make?

WEDNESDAY, AUGUST 13

Days Until Armed Forces Induction Physical: 16

"We have to go tonight. Tell Tinsley."

Arno's parked at the curb when I get home from work. His parents have just told him that he can't go to the festival. All day the radio's been reporting that traffic to Bethel, New York, has been backed up for dozens of miles. A week ago, they were estimating that the crowd might reach forty thousand. Now they're saying it could be more than double that. The police are warning people not to go. But Arno's got two thousand hits of Violet Rush to unload, so he's going no matter what his parents or the police say.

"What about the traffic?" I ask.

"Sammy Steckler used to go to camp near White Lake," Arno says. "He gave me directions for the back way in."

I'm still disappointed that Milton won't be there, but right now this festival is what I'm living for. For three entire days, I won't have to think about army induction physicals, or Robin, or

Chris, or my parents getting divorced. For seventy-two blessed hours, the center of the universe will be Crosby, Stills & Nash, the Who, Hendrix, the Jefferson Airplane, and maybe even Dylan himself.

For the past week, the music festival has been the only thing longhairs have talked about. All you have to say is "You going?" You don't even have to say where. The day after I saw her in the Carvel parking lot, Tinsley called and said she'd changed her mind and wanted to go (but not with Mr. Leather Vest Bare Chest; she confided that he was a possessive chauvinist pig) and asked if I knew anyone with extra tickets. She was thrilled when I told her she could buy Milton's from him. Like Arno, she'll be sneaking out of her house tonight. I never thought of this before, but the bigger the abode, the easier it probably is to duck out unnoticed.

And she isn't the least bit fazed that Barry and I are planning to rendezvous. She'll be going to the festival with one former paramour. So what if she sees another while she's there?

I tell Arno that I'll convey his message to her. I suspect there are a couple of reasons why he's keen for her to go. He probably thinks that having a pretty, sexy hippie chick around will help create the impression that he's some sort of big-time dealer. And, as a bonus, maybe he'll get into her bell-bottoms.

Arno heads to his house. I park the BSA in the garage. As with my purchase of the motorcycle, there's been no fallout from my spontaneous ingestion of random pills in the Exleys' bathroom the other night. I was prostrate on the living-room couch the next morning when the paterfamilias woke me for

302

work. My skull felt filled with slowly drying mud. But I got on the BSA and managed to get to the factory without falling off. I'd never tried coffee before, but that seemed like a good day to start.

Now I let myself into the house and see Mom in the backyard on her knees with her pruning shears and trowel, weeding a flower bed. She always gardens in khaki slacks, a blue chambray shirt, and a straw hat, and uses a pair of the red knee pads we got for Alan's failed crawling project.

I've come home late the past few nights. As a result, I haven't seen much of her since we trudged laps through the house in my pharmacologically induced stupor. When she sees me approaching, she settles back on her haunches. "I think you should start seeing Dr. Hill again."

So much for thinking there'd be no fallout from my adventure in indiscriminate pill popping. Or is her suggestion due to my lack of direction?

Or is it because of the situation with the paterfamilias? Why have we spent so many years tiptoeing around Dad and his affairs? Why haven't we ever spoken about them before last week? Did we each think that if it remained undeclared, we were protecting the other? That we could pretend things were okay?

Well, not anymore. "Dad told me he's thinking about a divorce."

Mom cocks her head curiously. She switches from her haunches to her butt, sitting cross-legged on the grass. It's an invitation for me to do the same.

I settle down. "I mean, now that I think about it, it's kind of weird that I took it so hard. It's not like I haven't known forever that he was messing around."

"You mean you *assumed* that because we had separate bedrooms?" Mom asks.

"No. I mean I *knew*. I even met some of them."

Her eyes widen, then narrow with consternation. "Really? How?" She pulls off her gardening gloves. "Cigarette?"

We light up and I tell her what I remember about the trip to Lake Placid with Hazel. About Sharon in Aspen. About seeing Antonia with Dad in the MG a month ago. And about the other times I suspected he wasn't working late, or was off on a trip that wasn't exactly business.

Mom closes her eyes and presses her fingers against her temple. "I'm sorry he put you in that position. That he made you go through that. It's . . . It's narcissistic behavior, Lucas. He's incapable of understanding the effect he has on others."

She reaches for my hand as if to give comfort. It reminds me of how, when I was younger, I felt so close to her. She was the one I tearfully ran to with a skinned knee or a bruised ego. She was the one I could always count on for tenderness and understanding. Then something changed and I pulled away. That's what teenagers do, right? They need to prove they can stand on their own. But now I'm feeling something I never expected—how much I've missed having her to confide in. "Like I said, Mom, you'd think that after all that, the divorce thing wouldn't come as a shock."

Mom smokes like a lady, holding the cigarette daintily

between index and middle fingers, turning her head away and blowing the smoke in a puckered stream. "Unless you simply assumed that life would always go on the way it has."

"Did you?" I ask.

She gazes off. "I'm not sure what I've assumed. I've just tried to live day to day and focus on you and Alan."

"Why didn't you ever call Dad out on it?"

"Oh, I did, darling. Many times. But by then we had you and Alan, and given Alan's needs, it didn't seem plausible for us to separate. So we had the extra bedrooms added and more or less agreed to lead independent lives under the same roof."

"But what kind of life was that for you?"

Mom picks some dirt off her khakis. "I had you and Alan to raise. And I have my friends, and the theater. My books, my gardens."

But the separate bedrooms. We may be speaking more openly than we have in years, maybe ever, but I'm a long way away from bringing up the topic of a love life. I mean, she's *my mom,* for God's sake. But she and Dad have slept apart for years. Though . . . *leading independent lives?* Is it possible that Mom had someone on the side? I mean, she never left the slightest clue. But could you blame her if she *had* had someone?

"What about now?" I ask. "If you get divorced?"

"I'll be able to stay here with Alan. . . . And you, too, if it comes to that. Have you decided what you'll do this fall?"

"I guess it depends on what happens with the induction physical out in San Francisco."

Mom takes a deep drag of her cigarette. "Still no word?"

305

I shake my head. I'd been hoping to hear from the Mobe before my friends and I headed upstate to the festival. I guess if we get there and I find it's weighing on me, I can always hit Arno up for one of his Violet Rushes.

I'm a little surprised, but also thankful, that Mom doesn't ask me if I have a backup strategy for the draft. Chances are she'd be somewhat less than thrilled with Plan B:

> `This little piggy went to market.`
> `This little piggy stayed home.`
> `This little piggy got chopped off....`

Mom presses her cigarette out in the grass and then drops the butt in the wooden basket half-filled with dandelions and crabgrass. I try to picture what her life will be like without Dad — and without me, for that matter. Just her and Alan.

"You've started writing again?" I ask.

She looks up. "You heard the typing?"

I nod. "Do you ever regret giving it up?"

"You mean when I was a journalist? No. I wanted to have a family."

"And now?"

Mom draws herself up. "We make choices. Some we can undo; some we can't. You find a way to cope."

Something about her answer makes me feel like it's a question she's asked herself many times before. For a few moments we sit together in the warm sunlight beside her bed of flowers. Maybe getting divorced won't be such a bad thing. She could stay here with Alan, have her gardens, maybe have some kind of a social life as well. Live in the house without having to see Dad or suffer his oppressive presence. As a kid, you can't imagine how your parents' getting divorced could be a good thing. But I'm not a kid anymore, am I?

In my room, the latest batch of mail is on my desk. My heart skips at the possibility of a letter from Robin. It's been ten days since I last wrote, saying how much I still love her, vowing to change, and reminding her of the many more good times than bad we've had. Since then I've repeatedly imagined the letter she might write in return, the one in which she describes coming to her senses and realizing what a ridiculous mistake her dalliance with Samuel has been. The one in which she vows true love forever and asks if I can ever forgive her for briefly straying with the moose rustler. (You bet I can.)

But the only letter on my desk is from Chris.

7/24/69

Loogie,
I don't think I'm gonna make it. My hands are all swollen and infected from jungle rot. I can't even grip my K-bar without it sliding loose from pus and blood. I'm worn down to the point where I can't hardly get up in the morning. And why should I? I ain't doing no good here. None of us are. We are all just waiting to die.
    There are things I ain't told you before, Loogs, because they're too horrible but I want

307

you to know because someone back home needs to. It's the odors, man. Even the TV and newspaper reporters don't write about it. They know about it because sometimes they're with us in the middle of the action. Maybe their bosses take it out.

When you get to a village that's been bombed or burned, you smell it. When you get to the scene of a firefight that happened three days ago, you smell it. It's the odor of burned human flesh and the odor of rotten flesh, Loogs. Once you've smelled it, you never forget.

You see corpses torn to pieces. You find pieces of bodies. Burned bodies. Half eaten bodies. It's hot and wet and us and the VC can't always get to the bodies before the bugs and animals do. If a body's left in the sun, by the second day it stinks horrible. Guys puke left and right.

All the time now I feel like I'm cracking up. Minute by minute torture, waiting to die. When you're awake it's terror and when you sleep it's nightmares. I wake up every morning in a pool of sweat. I'm always shaking. Five more months of this? I can't take five more days.

Promise you won't say nothing to my parents.

Swear it, Loogs. Think of this as my dying wish. It won't make no difference. We are in the A Shau Valley now. Know that Doors song where he says no one gets out of here alive? This is the place. We are so deep in the jungle and away from the supply chain that I wonder if you will ever get this letter.

I am waiting for the right time. Maybe the next firefight. There are ways to do it in battle so you look like a hero. I want my family to be proud of me. So I'll get some kind of posthumous medal they can hang on the wall.

I wish I'd listened to you, man. Now it's too late. I can't take this no more.

Your friend,
Chris

Jesus. Jesus. JESUS!

My hands tremble as I set the letter down. What should I do? What the *fuck* should I do? Tell his parents? What would they be able to do? And based on what he said about his family and their attitude toward war, wouldn't I be betraying him? He mailed this letter almost three weeks ago. What if—aw, Christ, my stomach wants to heave. *What if he's already done it?* If I tell his parents about the letter, they'll know he didn't die a hero.

Okay, okay, wait. Can I call the army directly?

And say what?

Hi. There's a friend of mine way out in the jungle. Three weeks ago, he sent me a letter saying he wanted to kill himself.

If Chris was really going to do it, wouldn't he have done it by now?

It's nearly seven o'clock. I'm supposed to go with Arno and Tinsley to the festival in a few hours. But I can't. Not knowing this.

Fuck!

The Dodsons' is one of a dozen small brick houses nestled close together along a block lined with parked cars. In the fading evening light, a balding man is pushing a hand mower in neat lines across the small front lawn. He has a potbelly and is wearing a sleeveless T-shirt with patches of graying hair poking out along the neckline. A shrine to the Madonna stands beside the porch steps. An American flag hangs from the eave.

"Mr. Dodson?" I hold my breath. Does Chris's father look like a man whose son has recently died? It's not the kind of thing I have any experience judging. I glance at the front of the house, not exactly sure what I'm looking for other than some sort of indication one way or the other.

Chris's father stops pushing the mower. His eyes go to the motorcycle helmet under my arm. "Yeah?"

"My name's Lucas. I'm a friend of Chris's."

"Oh, yeah?" His narrowing eyes and pronounced scowl plainly state that until this moment he didn't know Chris had any long-haired motorcycle-riding degenerate hippie friends.

"From work. I, um, well, ever since he went over to Vietnam, we've been exchanging letters. Only, it's been a while since I've heard from him."

Mr. Dodson turns his head so he's looking at me mostly with his right eye. "You know Chris from that junk-mail place?" he asks skeptically.

"That's right."

Mr. Dodson's eyes dart around as if he's nervous one of his neighbors will see him talking to me. "You wanna come in?" he asks.

"Uh . . . okay, thanks."

On the small front porch, Mr. Dodson takes off his shoes and leaves them by the door, so I do the same with my boots. The doors and windows are open, and an attic exhaust fan whirs loudly overhead. The house is dark inside and filled with the mixed aromas of stale cigarettes and a recently finished meal. The sound of running water and the clinks and clanks of dishes and pots being washed come from the kitchen.

"Mother, we got company," Mr. Dodson calls.

A short woman comes out of the kitchen. She's wearing an apron and drying her hands with a dish towel. She's probably around my mother's age, definitely not old enough to be Mr. Dodson's mother. I assume she's his wife (though I've never heard of married people addressing each other that way before). Her face is flushed from the heat. She frowns when she sees me.

"He says he's a friend of Chris's from the junk-mail place," Mr. Dodson says with a hint of doubt in his voice.

Mrs. Dodson blinks. Her eyebrows rise. In a lifelong smoker's raspy voice she says, "The owner's son?"

"Yes, ma'am."

Now it's Mr. Dodson's turn to frown.

"Please, have a seat," Mrs. Dodson says.

"Thanks." There's a small couch with a plastic cover that squeaks when I sit. A fairly large Jesus on a cross hangs over the fireplace. In the center of the mantel stands a ceramic statue of the Madonna and three framed photos. One frame has a faded black-and-white photo of a soldier and a couple of medals inside. (It could be Mr. Dodson; I'd need to take a closer look.) The other photos are in color, of young soldiers in full dress uniform. Their white army service caps sit high on their heads. My thoughts go straight back to the pictures in *Life* magazine. One of the soldiers on the mantel is Chris, looking too young to be in such a getup. The other photo's of someone else. At either end of the mantel, a white candle burns. I feel my breath catch. *Oh, shit! Are they memorial candles?*

"Can I get you something?" Mrs. Dodson asks. "We just finished dinner, but . . . a piece of pie?"

I haven't had dinner, but right now I have no appetite. Mrs. Dodson isn't acting like someone who's in mourning. So that's a good sign, right? "Something to drink would be great, thanks."

"Maybe some iced tea, Mother," Mr. Dodson says, sitting in a plastic-covered chair across from me. Mrs. Dodson goes back into the kitchen. Mr. Dodson leans toward me and in a low voice says, "She only puts these on in the summer. Sweat and dirt, you know?"

312

I nod.

"So, the owner's son, huh? How long you say you known Chris?" He's using the present tense—but is it because Chris is alive or because they haven't yet heard otherwise?

"About three years." And I have to ask: "Have you heard from him lately? How's he doing?"

"We just spoke to him this morning," Mrs. Dodson says cheerfully, coming in with a tray. She pours iced tea into a glass with a gold rim and pink roses painted on it, and hands it to me. "It was night there. He's behind the lines at a base near Long Binh."

When a laugh of relief bursts involuntarily out of my chest, I realize how tense I must have been. The muscles in my neck and shoulders start to relax. Meanwhile, both Dodsons scowl. But Chris is alive and—"Wait. You said *behind* the lines? He got transferred?"

Mr. Dodson's scowl deepens. "It's called reassignment. When you enlist, those recruiters, they want to know what jobs you've had. In case you're already trained to do something they need. The only job Chris's ever had was at that junk-mail place. So he wrote down that he had experience with the mail. He got reassigned to the military postal service. My soldier son is a mail clerk."

Mr. Dodson doesn't seem pleased about that. It's hard to understand how any father could want his son to be on the front lines.

"He sounded very happy," says Mrs. Dodson, glancing at her husband. Mr. Dodson gives her a hard look in return.

313

The front door bangs, and a guy wearing high-tops, basket-ball shorts, and a jersey takes the stairs two steps at a time without even looking at us. It must be Chris's brother, the one he had to share a room with until he went to Nam.

"I'm glad he's okay." I take a long, cool sip. It's real tea, not a mix.

"So, uh, what can we do for you, uh . . . ?" Mr. Dodson asks.

"Lucas. Nothing . . . I was . . . just getting worried."

"That's why you came all the way over here? To find out if Chris is okay?" Mr. Dodson sits back in the chair and presses his fingertips together thoughtfully. "No offense or nothing, but you ain't got a phone?"

"Eddie," Mrs. Dodson says sharply. Then to me: "It's very nice of you to be concerned. I remember Chris telling me about you. He likes you very much."

I'm not sure a hush falling over a room has ever been more palpable. Mr. Dodson glowers. Things may be getting awkward. Mrs. Dodson goes back to the kitchen, leaving her husband and me alone.

Mr. Dodson takes a long silent sip of tea, then hunches for-ward and runs a fingertip over the condensation on the glass. Finally, he looks up at me. "Your father serve, Lucas?"

"He commanded an LST in the Pacific during World War Two."

"What about his father?"

"We don't know much about his father."

"Your mother's father?"

"Also in the navy. But between the wars. He was a ship's cook."

"So, what do they think about you bein' against this war?"

No need to ask him how he knows this. In his mind I probably look like a poster boy for the antiwar movement. "My mother's father's passed away. My father's against the war and against me fighting in it."

"And why's that?"

I give him the same reasons I would have given the draft board had I applied for conscientious objector status: there's no reason to believe that the United States is in any danger of being attacked and therefore we cannot claim to be defending our country. Nor is there evidence that the Vietnamese people themselves want us in their country. Meanwhile, every day hundreds on both sides of the conflict die.

He takes another sip. From upstairs comes the sound of a shower. Mrs. Dodson peeks in from the kitchen. How strange is this? Sitting in a house I've never been to before with people I've only just met, and already we're debating the war?

"How'd you say you an' Chris got to be friends?" Mr. Dodson asks.

"We both ran insertion machines."

Chris's father has one of those faces that reveals almost everything he's thinking before he says it. Right now, he's asking himself why the son of the owner would do the same crap job his son did. But then his face darkens and he nods at the mantel. "Chris tell you about his cousin? My nephew Peter? He was killed last month near Tam Ky in the Quang Tin province. A fine young soldier."

"I'm sorry to hear that, sir. I'm sorry to hear that anyone's died in this war. I really am."

Mr. Dodson puts down his glass and rubs his hands together. "If that's true, how come you kids spit on soldiers when they come back?"

"I can only speak for myself, but I would never do that. As far as I'm concerned, it's not the soldiers who are at fault. It's the government that's sending them over there."

The way Mr. Dodson winces, you'd think he'd just been slapped. "Know what they say about kids like you? If you don't like it here, leave."

Looking apprehensive, Mrs. Dodson comes to the kitchen doorway but no closer. I get to my feet. "I do like it here, sir. In a lot of ways it's probably better than anyplace else. But that doesn't mean I'm required to believe in my country right or wrong. If we've made a mistake, then we should admit it. And stop sending young men like your son and nephew over there to die."

Mr. Dodson also gets to his feet but doesn't choose to argue. Instead, he gazes at the photos on the mantel again. I also look, and see that he is indeed the soldier in the older black-and-white photo, the one with the medals. The eyes, the shape of the jaw, the cleft chin.

Mrs. Dodson steps cautiously out of the kitchen. I thank her for the iced tea, tell them both that I'm glad Chris is okay, and that I'm sorry about their nephew.

Mrs. Dodson thanks me for coming. Mr. Dodson silently shows me to the door, where we stop for a moment. "A lot of good men have died over there," he says. "If I was you, I'd be careful about telling their parents and friends that they died for nothing."

He doesn't offer his hand.

Back at the curb I straddle the BSA and strap on my helmet. Like Chris said that day behind the shed last summer, he never had a choice.

THURSDAY, AUGUST 14

Days Until Armed Forces Induction Physical: 15

"Going somewhere, boys?" In the Exleys' backyard, I'm blinded by the glare of a flashlight. It's a little after midnight, and Arno has just passed a knapsack, a canteen of water, and a sleeping bag out his bedroom window to me.

A hand reaches out of the glare and yanks Arno's knapsack out of my hands.

"Dad!" Arno starts to protest from the window, but it's too late. Mr. Exley pulls out the bulging tear-shaped sock. "Whatever could this be?"

The Exleys had been suspicious for a while. The iodine-and-baby-oil sunlamp scalding only increased their misgivings. They called Piping Rock and learned that Arno had caddied there only once. So where was the money for maintaining the GTO, for the expensive stereo equipment, and for all the albums coming from? They could have confronted him then, but Mr. Exley wanted to understand exactly what his son was up to. They searched Arno's room and found the pill press, but weren't clear on what it was for.

They are now.

SATURDAY, AUGUST 16

Days Until Armed Forces Induction Physical: 13

Light rain falls in the gray predawn light. It's a little after five a.m. on Saturday. I've left the BSA down the road and walked the last fifty yards to Tinsley's. The tall iron gate across the driveway is always locked, but there's a spot at the corner of the property where the fence meets a brick wall. Tinsley's told me about the old wooden ladder hidden there behind some shrubs.

When Arno was busted by his father just after midnight on Thursday, things got completely screwed up. By the time I got home and called Tinsley to warn her that we weren't coming, she'd already snuck out of her house. Her mom answered the phone and I immediately hung up, but that was enough to make Mrs. Stockton suspicious. She went to investigate and discovered that Tinsley was gone.

A little while later, when Arno and I didn't show up at the planned rendezvous point, Tinsley tried to sneak *back* into her house. Her mother caught her and basically put her under house arrest.

For the past two days, I've waited for word from her about when she thought she could sneak out again. She finally called last night, proposing I come get her at dawn. As I lean the ladder against the brick wall and start to climb over, I wonder what awaits us. During the past two days, the news about the festival has gotten crazier and crazier. The New York Thruway has been shut down. (We'll avoid it by going up Route 17 through New Jersey.) There's word that the national guard may be brought in. The governor of New York has declared a state of emergency. It sounds like the coolest thing ever.

The toes of my boots grow dark in the rain-soaked grass as I carry the ladder across the lawn and around to Tinsley's side of the manse. Beneath her bedroom window, I open the ladder and climb up as far as I can. From inside, the shade is swept aside and the sash goes up. Rapunzel grins mischievously and pushes a small knapsack out. It tumbles over the eave and into my arms. A moment later, she's inching, crab-style, over slippery slate shingles.

I guide her boots to the top of the ladder and help her down. The scent of patchouli is in the damp air. On the lawn, she throws her arms around my neck and hugs me excitedly.

The BSA's seat is long enough for two. Behind it, I've lashed my knapsack and sleeping bag to a small luggage rack. Tinsley wears her knapsack on her back. I give her a spare helmet and a red bandanna with which to periodically reach around and wipe the raindrops off my goggles.

With Tinsley's arms tight around my waist, we light out through the rain and mist. The trip takes us over the Throgs Neck Bridge, across the Bronx, over the George Washington Bridge, and into New Jersey—the very route that may someday separate Alan and me from the paterfamilias. The rain is sometimes heavy, sometimes light. It soaks through our jackets and pants legs. Many of the cars going in our direction are filled with longhairs. When we pass a slow-moving psychedelically painted microbus, I feel a wistful pang for Odysseus and Robin.

Here and there, straggly-haired freaks stand on the road shoulder with their thumbs out. No one bothers with handwritten signs. There's only one place anyone's hitching to this morning.

On Route 17 the traffic grows progressively heavier until, near Monticello, it slows to a crawl. An hour ago, we were part of a pilgrimage. Now it's a long-haired, tie-dyed crusade.

Ahead, the exit we want is blocked by fifty-gallon oil drums. Two state troopers in yellow slickers are waving at cars to continue north. The oil drums may block cars from the exit, but there's plenty of room for a motorcycle to slip through. With a rush of adrenaline, I twist the throttle, feel the cycle accelerate and Tinsley's arms grow extra tight around my waist. We veer out of the traffic and zip between two oil drums and down the misty two-lane road beyond. It feels like a scene out of *Easy Rider*.

The wet pavement is lined by trees, farms, and fields of corn under low-hanging patches of fog. We begin to pass cars abandoned haphazardly along the roads' shoulders and hundreds of freaks walking toward the festival, many of them in rain-darkened clothes, their hair wet and matted.

The road itself becomes so clogged with people and abandoned cars that it's impassable, even on a motorcycle. I have to pull off and ride slowly along the edges of grassy yards and fields, weaving in and out of the endless column of trudging bodies.

Heading up a slight rise, we join a large crowd tromping over a portion of shiny new chain-link fence that's been trampled into the wet grass. No one's taking tickets: everyone is free to enter. Moments later, while trying to get around a wide muddy puddle, I feel the cycle slide out from under us. Tinsley and I find ourselves sitting on the muddy grass, the BSA on its side at our feet, the rear wheel slowly turning. A bearded, barefoot freak with a red bandanna wrapped around his forehead plods through the mud and holds out a large green gallon jug of wine. "You look like you could use this."

We've arrived.

An ocean of freaks—by far the most enormous crowd I've ever seen—is spread over the broad face of a gradually sloping hill. Not one football field's worth, but a dozen or more. Thousands and thousands of cultural heretics and flower children standing, sitting, lying on the ground. Tinsley and I share a wide-eyed look. Who could have imagined anything like *this*?

At the bottom of the slope, hundreds of yards away, an outdoor stage sits among tall yellow scaffold towers. From where we stand, on a dirt road at the fringe of the crowd, the people on the stage are the size of ants. It's before noon and the day's lineup of acts hasn't begun. Off to the distant right and left are fields filled with tents and microbuses, cars and psychedelically painted school buses. Leaving the BSA on the dirt road, Tinsley and I make our way through the crowd—many seated or lying on blankets or sleeping bags—trying to get closer to the stage.

In a spot where there's hardly enough bare ground for a blanket, we spread my unzipped sleeping bag, nod hello to the folks around us, and settle down. Space is tight. Edges of sleeping bags and blankets touch, but each blanket or sleeping bag is its own island. Those on the move respect one another's space, trying their best to walk along the edges and bits of grass between blankets. There's an endless chant of *excuse me*s from the barefoot wayfarers who pass.

The rain has stopped. Before the music begins, an emcee delivers announcements through public address speakers on the scaffolding: "There are a lot of things going on with all these elements conspiring, like the sticky mud wiggling between our toes and the drippy rain rolling down our necks, but it's all part of the high."

And: "This is the first free city of the Aquarian age."

And: "Richard Norris, please go to the pink-and-white medical tent immediately."

When the emcee tells us that there are half a million people here, I can't help thinking that, short of some miraculous coincidence, the chances of finding Barry are nil. He told me he'd be flying a kite, but even if there were a breeze, there's no space for him to launch one. Then the emcee warns us that the brown tabs of acid circulating through the crowd are bad. Tinsley and I share another look. In our experience, public address systems have been the voice of authority used in school for morning announcements, to say the Pledge of Allegiance, or to call kids down to the office. Now the voice of authority is advising that if we are determined to try the brown acid, we should use caution and start with half a tab.

Despite the damp and muddy conditions, people are in good spirits, talking, laughing, sharing smokes. There's a sense of camaraderie amid the awe-inspiring realization that there are *so many of us*. We may all be strangers, but we have much in common. Our hair, our clothes, our drugs, our music. Our general sense of alienation. Our mistrust of the government. Our opposition to the war.

Tinsley shoots pictures of the shaggy-haired guy on a blanket next to us wearing a blue-and-red-striped necktie as a headband. Many of our fathers wear similar ties, but around his head like that, it's a symbol of rebellion and rejection of uptight middle-class existence. The guy hands us the joint he's been smoking and says to pass it along. We grab handfuls of Cocoa Puffs from a meandering box and wash them down with water from a glass jug that soon follows. Despite the ache I feel for Robin, I know that she would never have felt comfortable here.

The grass results in the munchies. The guy with the necktie headband shares a peanut-butter-and-jelly sandwich with us. He's from Ohio, got here on Tuesday, and volunteered to help build the concession booths that look like medieval tents up the hill behind us. If we need more food, that's where we should go. He tells us that some hippies are giving away food but to be careful. Some have cooked corn they picked from a neighboring field, not realizing that it was feed meant for livestock and guaranteed to give humans a bad case of the runs.

Over the PA comes the news that a baby has been born. Not far from us, a naked woman stands up and begins shouting unintelligibly, gesturing in some strange, frantic form of cheerleading. Two other women cover her with a blanket and get her to sit down.

"Brown acid," says the guy with the red-and-blue tie around his head.

Down on the stage, a band called Quill starts to play. We try to listen, but the band is not well known, and this far back in the crowd, many people continue to talk and mill about. The band may be difficult to hear, but there's no shortage of entertainment. Mostly crowd watching.

Tinsley and I are engrossed in the spectacle. The masses of gaudily dressed, braless, drug-using longhairs; the music; the sensation of being in the midst of something huge and unlike anything we've experienced before. A tall stringy-haired vagabond wearing a colorfully knit poncho and using a tree branch as a walking stick weaves haphazardly through the crowd. His eyes fix on Tinsley and he makes a beeline for her, then leans close, his face only inches from hers. "Want to ball, baby?"

"No, thank you," Tinsley replies.

He wanders away.

The sun comes out. Country Joe McDonald does an

acoustic set, leading us in the Fish cheer: "Give me an *F.* Give me a *U.* Give me a *C.* Give me a *K.* What's that spell?"

"*FUCK!*" roar half a million freaks.

"What's that spell?"

"*FUCK!*"

"What's that spell?"

"*FUCK!*"

He plays the "I-Feel-Like-I'm-Fixin'-to-Die-Rag," the anti–Vietnam War anthem for our generation. The largest chorus in the history of the world sings along.

Clouds drift in overhead and a light rain begins to fall. Tinsley covers her head with her damp denim jacket. We're both hungry, so I tramp through the crowd toward the concession stands. The lines for food stretch for a hundred yards. The wait is long but not intolerable thanks to the numerous meandering joints that come my way.

By the time Lucas the Ravenous gets his hot dogs, he is both ripped and has been ripped off. They're charging a dollar for a hot dog that would cost twenty-five cents anywhere else. Maybe Arno's right about the fleeting nature of the hippie spirit.

When Lucas somewhat miraculously finds his way back with five precious wieners, Tinsley is on her feet and there's a guy beside her wearing an olive-colored safari jacket. They're facing the stage, so Lucas first sees him from behind. He's tall, with wavy black hair that falls over his collar. Cameras with long lenses hang from straps over his shoulders.

A moment later, Tinsley introduces Lucas the Surprised (though should he really be?) to Bernard, who is handsome and faintly rugged-looking, with a prominent nose and long sideburns. Bernard offers his hand and says hello with a heavy French accent. Lucas guesses that he is in his late twenties.

"Bernard's a photographer with *Le Monde*." Tinsley's eyes are bright with excitement as she pronounces the name of the French newspaper with an accent of her own.

"Uh, groovy," says Lucas *sans* enthusiasm.

Tinsley turns to Bernard and speaks in what sounds like nearly flawless French. *Le photographe* replies in kind. Through the cannabis haze comes the sudden realization to Lucas the Startled that his time with Tinsley is up. She's moving on. No need to toss the *I Ching* here. Bernard offers his *main* to Lucas and says, "A pleasure to meet you," then heads off.

"He's coming back later," Tinsley announces, not looking at Lucas. "We're going to shoot pictures together."

They settle uncomfortably back onto the sleeping bag to consume the franks, a strained silence between them. Ever since he ceased pleasing she-for-whom-pleasure-shall-not-cease, Lucas the Vanquished has been vaguely aware that he has no claim on her. But he did expect that they'd see this adventure through together, especially now that it will be impossible to find Barry in a crowd this size (assuming he wasn't among the hundreds of thousands the police turned away).

Quel drag.

A band called Santana puts on a rousing performance. The sun starts to poke through the clouds, and it grows hot and humid enough for a lot of guys in the crowd, and even some women, to take off their shirts. Many get to their feet and bop to the Latin-infused rock, including Tinsley and Lucas. Thanks to the awesome music and the unending parade of joints, Lucas's hurt feelings are slowly assuaged.

No sooner does Santana's set end than Bernard returns, and he and Tinsley go off to take pictures. Lucas remains behind listening to the Incredible String Band, a quirky British folk group whose music seems better suited to a coffeehouse than a huge outdoor festival. Tinsley's left her knapsack, so maybe she'll change her mind about Bernard like she did with Mr. Leather Vest Hairy Chest. Indeed, as dark falls, she returns alone with a paper plate of brown rice and a real treasure: a can of SpaghettiOs. Lucas pries it open with his Swiss Army knife, and they feast on cold canned pasta and rice for dinner. Not bad when you're high and famished.

SUNDAY, AUGUST 17

Days Until Armed Forces Induction Physical: 12

Sometime after midnight, after a soggy set by the Grateful Dead, the rain ceases and the show takes off. Creedence Clearwater, followed by Janis Joplin, followed by Sly and the Family Stone, who put on an insane performance that wakes anyone who's sacked out and has us all on our feet, dancing and cheering.

It's still dark when the Who launches into *Tommy*, but dawn is nearing. While the band explodes onstage in the dark glen at the bottom of the slope, morning light begins to illuminate the distant surrounding hills. Bare-chested Daltrey—wearing an open jacket with long wild white fringe—and Townshend in a white jumpsuit are manic rock-and-roll acrobats while Moon is his normal berserk self on the drums. How I wish Arno were here to watch his favorite band thunder into the dawn.

The Who is followed by a raucous Jefferson Airplane set. By the time Grace Slick and band finish their encore, a little after nine thirty a.m., Tinsley and I have been awake for nearly thirty hours. Using my knapsack as a pillow, I curl up on the sleeping bag, cover my face with my jacket, and fall asleep.

When I wake around lunchtime, Tinsley and her knapsack are gone.

In the drizzly distance, a bearded figure carrying a long stick propped against his shoulder is weaving around vehicles and tents in the muddy grass field behind the stage. I've been waiting for nearly an hour by the big pink-and-white-striped medical tent. People come, or are brought, into the tent with all sorts of injuries, but mostly cut feet. Later they leave with one foot bandaged, the other still bare.

An hour ago, I handed a note to a big guy wearing a cowboy hat at the makeshift wooden wall by the stage entrance: "Barry, meet Cousin Lucas at the medical tent. Urgent." The guy said he'd get the note to Chip, whoever that is.

Before that I'd spent several hours huddled under a hay wagon with a bunch of others, trying to stay dry while rain and windstorms barreled through.

About twenty minutes ago, someone read my message over the PA system. I figured I'd wait an hour or two just in case Barry had made it to the festival. The bearded figure is getting closer. The stick he's carrying juts half a dozen feet into the air. Dangling from the end is something yellow and orange.

"Get 'em off me! Get 'em off me!" A bare-chested freak wearing only cutoffs thrashes wildly as at least four guys and a girl try to maneuver him toward the medical tent. At first I think he's yelling at the people holding him, but every time he yanks a hand free he starts to swat at his own body. "Spiders! Get 'em off me!" He thinks he's covered with spiders.

Barry tromps up looking like a bearded overgrown Middle Earth hobbit. He's wearing a Peruvian poncho and pink granny glasses. His wet, straggly hair hangs down to his shoulders. Having been abandoned by Tinsley, I'm extra glad to have found him, but before we greet each other, we watch a waif who can't be more than sixteen, wearing a loose tie-dyed dress, many strands of love beads, and a fringed jacket, come out of the medical tent and stand before the flipping-out guy while the others struggle to restrain him. Now he's screaming, "Don't come near me! Don't come near me!"

"What's your name?" the girl calmly asks half a dozen times before he's able to focus and answer: "Steve."

"You're going to be okay, Steve," the girl says. "You've taken LSD and you're having a bad reaction. You understand what I'm saying, Steve?"

Remarkably, Steve, who is probably close to six feet tall, stops thrashing. The hippie girl, who is as lithe as Tinsley, though a few inches taller, steps closer and gently strokes his arm. "I don't think these people should hold you like this, Steve. Would you like them to let go?"

His eyes fixed on her, Steve nods. The others release their grip. Steve and the hippie girl sit on the muddy grass. Not only has she gotten him to simmer down, but it's as if she's cast a spell. "I want you to drink some tea. Okay, Steve? It will help you feel better."

Steve accepts the tea and sips. His friends sit with him. Like a mystical healer who is finished exorcising evil spirits, the waif rises and glides back into the tent.

"Far out," Barry says softly. We hug.

"Glad you made it, man." I gesture at the enormous crowd. "Can you believe this?"

"Crazy, right?" Barry grins gleefully. "When'd you get here?"

"Yesterday around noon."

"Grooving on the scene?"

"When it's not pouring."

"Where're your friends?" he asks as we start away from the medical tent and through the intermittent rain. I tell him Milton and Arno couldn't make it and that I came with Tinsley, but she met another guy and split. Barry pats me sympathetically on the shoulder. Guess we're part of an exclusive club.

We tromp toward some woods, passing groups huddled under sheets of clear plastic, trying to stay dry. A couple of soaked, completely mud-covered girls and guys race past us, whooping and yelling. Others lie nearly hidden inside squishy-wet sleeping bags.

Among dripping trees we find Zach and his girlfriend, Eva, under a dark-green tarp strung between some branches. Barry tells me the three of them have been camping here for more than a week. Sleeping bags are rolled up. The camping stove I borrowed for Maine is set on a rock, heating a pot of tea. Boxes of brown rice, cans of beans, and bags of bread are packed into a wooden milk crate. Canteens hang from branches.

They're camped at the edge of a clearing where four

psychedelically painted school buses are parked in a circle like covered wagons. It's a whole different scene back here. The hippies who've come to the festival in these buses appear to be here not as much for the music as to get together with others of their kind. When the rain lets up, some start playing guitars and recorders and thumping on congas. The air smells of body odor and wood smoke. A guy with a beard and long blond braids, wearing only a breechcloth, stirs a large metal pot over a fire with a broom handle. Everyone is barefoot and skinny, their long hair scraggly, what scant clothes they wear mud-stained and tattered.

Watching them, I feel like I've come upon a lost primitive tribe. Arno's words from Nathan's come back: *All these barefoot flower people eating brown rice and alfalfa sprouts? You don't think they're gonna get tired of being dirty and hungry? And free love? Enjoy the crabs and clap, man. This whole back-to-the-land thing? Isn't that why we had the industrial revolution? So we don't all have to be farmers anymore?*

He forgot the drugs. Some of the hippies are nodding off, zonked out, swaying to the music. A couple of skinny dogs sniff around. Packs of dirty, naked towheaded kids run this way and that, playing with sticks. One guy keeps trying to get them to take hits off a bong. A kid who can't be older than nine takes a hit, exhales smoke, then runs off to rejoin his friends. Near us, a long-haired guy holds a joint to the lips of the woman sitting next to him while she breastfeeds a baby.

· · ·

Turn on,
Tune in,
Drop out,
Get drafted,
Die young.

"They spread-eagled me on the ground, wrists and ankles tied to stakes. Put a nest of biting ants on my chest. Stuck slivers of bamboo under my fingernails. Fuckin' animals, man. I'm screaming in pain and they're laughing."

It's raining, and under the tarp we're being regaled by a strange guy wearing a torn, stained green army shirt. He sits cross-legged, talks nonstop, lighting the next cigarette off the last. His name is Karl and he says he was a prisoner of war in Vietnam.

"They gave us this watery soup with pieces of shit in it. You either ate it or starved to death. My best buddy? He got ahold of some lye and swallowed it. Can't imagine a worse way to go, right? But he'd had it. Enough was enough. They'd hung him upside down and whipped him with bamboo sticks until he was bleeding head to toe." Karl's been here five minutes and hasn't stopped talking or blinked once: speed freak.

It's early evening. Still light out. From the distance come the sounds of drumming and a crowd chanting. Eva nudges Zach and they cut out. Karl keeps right on rapping. His cheeks are sunken, cheekbones protruding. When I look closely, I realize that his long brown hair is a wig. His bony fingers tremble each time he brings a cigarette to his lips.

Karl is appalling and fascinating, pitiful and damaged. You can't watch and you can't not watch. But mostly you feel like you have to listen. He and five other soldiers were captured and held in a jungle camp. The Americans attacked and the Vietcong abandoned the camp, quickly executing the prisoners before they left. Karl played dead, lying among the corpses of his fellow soldiers, covered in their blood.

No one I grew up with—and except for Chris, no one I've ever met—has had to face anything close to that.

"I came home and people spat on me and called me a baby killer. How's that for thanks?"

You sense he's told these stories a thousand times, trapped in some loop of constantly reliving the horror. A terrible sense of guilt grips me. I recall those stamp-size photographs of the 242 dead men-children in that *Life* magazine. Since the beginning of the war, more than thirty thousand American soldiers have died over there. And then there are the wounded. We've all seen the photos of GIs with one or both legs amputated at the knee. GIs with their heads bandaged, torsos wrapped in bloodied gauze, a buddy holding the plastic bag of saline solution being IVed into a forearm. But this evening I'm seeing the psychic damage . . . close up for the first time. Karl may have his limbs, but what's left of his mind?

Chris has written about guys going crazy, guys hanging themselves. But like so many things, the atrocity of war isn't truly real until you see it for yourself. Charles said the odds of being killed or injured were one in five, but what about the invisible wounds? How many guys come back whole yet forever broken?

Karl's unending horror loop continues: "They tied my wrists behind my back to my ankles and left me lying on the ground for days. Burned me with cigarettes." He pulls up his sleeve to show us the burn scars—round pink craters in the skin of his gaunt wrist. But there are also dark scabby marks inside his forearm.

"What's with the wig?" I ask Barry later. We're alone. Karl had been in the middle of his rap a few minutes ago, then suddenly stood up and wandered away.

"Wants to fit in. Probably just got out of the army and hasn't had time to grow it."

The rain collects in the branches and drips with loud plops onto the tarp over our heads. We talk about what's been going on back on Long Island, about me working on a way to stay out of the army, about Alan going to camp. Barry and I have never shared deep confidences about our families beyond the routine, but here in the woods, in this damp, strange atmosphere that feels so disconnected from everyday life, I tell him that my father asked me how I'd feel if he divorced my mother.

Hippies and freaks tromp past, hair plastered to their heads, clothes soaked. A baby cries somewhere in the clammy mist. Barry takes a drag off a Camel. "About time."

"What makes you say that?"

"He's been messing around forever. You think your mom never told my mom?"

"And your mom told you?" I ask, surprised.

"Come on, man, all you had to do was be in a room with them to see how much they can't stand each other. I mean, separate bedrooms? If it wasn't for Alan, he would have been out of there years ago. Couldn't you see that?"

337

What I saw was Mom's stoic silence and Musclini's anger. Was I wrong about where that anger came from? Was it not from the frustrations of business as much as the crappy state of their marriage?

"You know where it all started, right?" Barry asks.

I frown uncertainly.

"Your mom taking the baby out in the cold?"

Brett was born in December. One school of thought suggested keeping babies inside for the first six weeks. Others maintained that as long as the infant was properly clothed, taking him outside was fine. On a cold and sunny day in January, Mom bundled Brett up and took him out in the carriage. A week later, he died of pneumonia.

Taking him outside might not have had anything to do with it, but they'll never know.

"Guess your old man's finally got the money to move out," Barry says.

"What are you talking about?"

"That school Alan goes to? It's like a college tuition. And your father's been paying it since, what? Since Alan was four? And your mom's Park Avenue shrink? Two times a week? How much do you think *that* costs?"

Alan is fourteen. The paterfamilias has been paying for that school for ten years. But Mom has a shrink? I knew she'd gone to see someone at some point. I didn't think she was still . . .

Barry must see the surprise in my eyes. "Man, you don't know anything, do you? All these years that your mom's been taking Alan to the city twice a week? What do you think she does all day while she waits for him?"

I thought she shopped and went to galleries and museums.

Do I have blind spots? Or am I completely blind? All these years, all the paterfamilias's schemes. Was that what being golden meant to him? Being able to make enough money to buy his freedom? Was the frustration of having to wait until he had enough money the source of his anger? But if all he'd wanted to do was get out, then why didn't he? It's not like he has expensive tastes. How much could it cost to play tennis, exercise, and buy natural peanut butter?

So why didn't he cut out years ago?

And it hits me. Maybe because that's what his father did to him?

So he stayed . . . because he felt obligated to pay for Alan's school and Mom's shrink (not to mention my tennis lessons and giving us a comfortable home), even though he probably felt that he wasn't responsible for the crappy way things turned out.

Holy shit. Is that why, even when she knew about his cheating, Mom continued to defend him? Because despite all the wrong things he did, he also did *the one right thing* that she, Alan, and I needed more than anything else?

Raindrops plop onto the tarp over us. The sound of a guitar drifts over from one of the hippie school buses. I feel Barry's eyes.

"Man, I don't know what you were just thinking," he says with a grin, "but I do believe I watched a mind get completely blown right before my very eyes."

That you did, dear cousin. That you did.

339

MONDAY, AUGUST 18

Days Until Armed Forces Induction Physical: 11

"License and registration."

In a service station in Wayne, I can see two miniatures of myself in the reflective shades of a New Jersey state trooper.

"All I'm doing is fixing a flat tire." I'm amazed by the audacity of my answer, but since I don't have a motorcycle license, what's there to lose? I suspect hunger, weariness, and aggravation also contribute to my confrontational response.

The trooper's jaw tightens. I know he came in here looking for me. This is the second gas station I've been to since the BSA's rear tire went flat. At the first, they took one look at my long hair and jeans stained with dried reddish mud and told me to get lost. I pushed the cycle across Route 17 to this station, where they're not only friendlier but lent me some tools to take the tire off so they can patch the inner tube. (I didn't have enough money left for the labor *and* a patch job.) There's no doubt in my mind that the guys at the first gas station told this trooper that some long-haired hippie from the festival was here. There must be cops all over the Northeast hunting us like migratory fowl.

Last night, when the rain let up and the music started again, I left Barry in the woods with my knapsack and sleeping bag and caught an outstanding set by Ten Years After. Later, when I headed back into the trees in the dark, it took a long time to find the clearing and the hippie school buses. When I finally did, Barry was gone and there were two couples under the tarp. The wooden crate of food, the camp stove, my gear, and Barry's sleeping bag were still there. The yellow-and-orange butterfly kite on the pole was leaning against a tree trunk.

It started to rain again. Expecting Barry to return, I asked the couples if I could lie down while I waited.

When I woke this morning, Barry hadn't come back. There was no sign of Zach and Eva, either. The others under the tarp were still asleep. The rain had stopped and music was playing. I wandered back down to the concert, now a muddy wasteland of soggy paper plates; empty cans and bottles; abandoned, soaked sleeping bags and clothes; and plastic sheets, some with freaks sleeping under or on them. The relatively small crowd—compared to the days before—that remained was watching Sha Na Na. A girl wrapped in a mud-spattered blanket told me that Hendrix would play next. I knew he was the closing act. Had Dylan ever shown up? I asked, thinking that he might have played while I'd slept last night. She shook her head.

"What's in the knapsack?" the trooper asks now.

I suspect that I'm under no legal obligation to show him, but I dump the contents on the garage floor anyway. With the shiny tip of his black trooper shoe, he nudges the dirty underwear and socks, a crumpled jacket. Meanwhile, I squat and finish fitting the patched inner tube inside the BSA's rear tire. My hands are nearly black with road grit and chain grease. Stomach growling hungrily, I'm dirty, sweaty, and profoundly tired.

Without another word, the trooper leaves. A jagged-edged sense of reprieve spreads through me, along with a reminder that, the festival over, I've returned to the real world, where drugs are illegal, I'm a member of a despised minority, and no one over thirty can be trusted. I need to get home and see if there's news from San Francisco about my physical.

And, maybe, a reply from Robin to my last letter.

But I know that, after what Barry laid on me last night, I won't ever be able to look at my tiny sliver of the universe in quite the same way again.

"Where's Tinsley?" Arno asks. It's late afternoon and he, Milton, and I are in the GTO. The BSA's rear tire went flat again on the Cross Bronx Expressway near the old school for the deaf that looms up from the marshes like something out of *The Addams Family*. There were no gas stations around there, only a diner. I called Arno and then settled down to enjoy the most delicious cheeseburger and fries I think I ever ate.

When Arno and Milton got to the diner, they looked at me like I'd just returned from the moon. Turns out that the festival dominated the national news over the weekend. Did I know that New York State had declared the festival a disaster area, and several newspapers suggested it be quarantined as a public health hazard? Or that by the end, a local police chief was quoted as saying the attendees were the most courteous, considerate, and well-behaved group of kids he'd ever encountered? Or that the commander of the state troopers said he was shocked that a crowd that size could go three days with insufficient food and water, and yet not a single act of violence or theft was reported?

Maybe if I weren't quite so wiped out, I'd find that interesting. I tell them that Dylan never showed and Tinsley went off with Bernard, but that she was pretty decent about how she did it, and maybe it was just as well, because I managed to find Barry. Then I ask Arno what happened to his acid.

"Two thousand hits down the drain. The sewer system's full of tripping turds."

"They punish you?"

"You don't think that's punishment enough? I had a chance to get rich, man."

"Uh, probably not. People were sharing what they had. Anyone selling acid was asking a buck a tab."

"It wasn't Owsley."

"They didn't care. To them, acid was acid. Except the brown acid. They made an announcement that it was bad stuff."

"Announcement?" Milton perks up. "How?"

"On the PA."

"What about sex?" Arno asks.

"No announcements about that on the PA."

"You're a riot, Lucas."

"Someone had a baby." I yawn, barely able to keep my eyes open. Probably got less than a dozen hours of sleep since Friday at 4:30 a.m., when I left my house to get Tinsley. Wonder where she is now.

"Was everyone doing it?" Arno asks.

"Sure, Arno, all over the place. You couldn't take a step without stumbling over some balling couple."

"Really?'

"No. It was a music festival, not a giant orgy. If people were doing it, it wasn't where everyone could see."

"You said people were getting high where everyone could see," Milton points out.

I yawn again. "I think there's a slight difference." Using my knapsack as a pillow, I lie down on the GTO's back seat. Eyes close and refuse to open.

At home, my weary spirits sink when I sort through the latest pile of mail and find there's still no reply from Robin. But there *is* a letter from the National Mobilization Committee to End the War in Vietnam. *Thank God!* I rip open the envelope. Inside is another envelope, this one from the Great Neck draft board addressed to me care of a San Francisco address. Holding my breath, I tear that letter open.

Dear Mr. Baker:
We have received your request to have your induction physical moved to San Francisco. Before your request can be considered,

we require additional information regarding your change of residence. This must include the following:

1. A photocopy of either:
    A valid driver's license from the state of residence.
    or
    The signature page of a valid lease. (You must include the name, address and phone number of the landlord.)

2. An original of one of the following:
    A phone bill with your name and address.
    or
    A utility bill with your name and address.

My innards seize up. I have none of the above. Thanks to the paterfamilias, my legal address is in Bay Shore.

I am completely, inalterably fucked.

"Charles isn't here anymore," someone named Mary Ellen tells me over the phone. She's a draft counselor at the American Friends office. "I've taken over his cases."

"Know where he went?"

"No. He just stopped coming in one day. We called Creedmoor and he hadn't shown up there, either. We found some Black Panther literature in his desk, but that's all."

I'll bet anything that he's in Oakland helping to feed hungry children before school.

I catch Mary Ellen up on my case and tell her I've got

eleven days until my induction physical. What does she think of smoking cigarettes dipped in ink?

"Forget it," she says. "The army doctors are wise to that one. The last guy who tried it was sent to a military hospital for three days. When they x-rayed him again, the spots had disappeared and he was inducted."

Shit! "So what's my best shot for failing the physical?"

She tells me to hold while she consults the other counselors. I wait, my insides in turmoil, my thoughts going back to Karl, the Vietnam vet. How many more are there like him? There is no fucking way I'm going over there. None.

Mary Ellen gets back on the phone and asks how tall I am and what I weigh.

I tell her, then wait while she does the calculations: "Lose forty pounds between now and your physical. You'll be exempted as severely underweight."

Four pounds a day.

Okay, Lucas, it's time to suck it up and start starving.

THURSDAY, AUGUST 21

Days Until Armed Forces Induction Physical: 8
Days of Starvation: 3

It's a hot, breezy August day. Gusts blow small clouds of fine particles off the mound beside the open grave. This is the first funeral Lucas has ever attended. He is not stoned; he is in disbelief. Or what did Charles call it? Dissociation? And like so many other things he's heard about and thought he could imagine, it's something that must be experienced to truly comprehend. The stunning sadness. The wretched emptiness and loss. The simultaneous disbelief and inescapable reality. He is here, but he can't be here.

Several dozen people have gathered around the grave, Tinsley among them. Lucas is surprised when he sees her but guesses that he shouldn't be. It's the first time since the music festival, which the press is now calling Woodstock and treating like a momentous history-changing cultural event.

Particles blow into Lucas's eyes. People sob. Tinsley's short diaphanous dress flutters around her thighs. The ends of her long blond hair dance in the breeze. She lifts her gaze to meet his and then looks away.

One day about a year ago, when I hadn't seen him for a long stretch, Barry turned up unannounced at our front door with Zach and a skinny girl who looked oddly familiar. I was shocked by my cousin's appearance. He'd lost weight, and his skin had a grayish cast. All three of them were disheveled, their clothes looking like they'd been slept in. They were chain-smoking and jittery.

With a grin that looked more like a grimace, Barry said, "Hey, man, spare some bread?"

When I gave him the ten dollars in my wallet, he showed it to Zach, who made a face. The girl tapped her foot impatiently and gazed off, dragging hard on her cigarette. Her brown hair hung limp and unkempt. Her cheeks were hollow. Our eyes met for an instant.

"Adriana?" I said.

Adriana Fox may have been two grades ahead of me, but she was someone every guy in school was aware of. Pretty, sexy, haughty, loud, she hung out with the jocks and was at the red-hot center of the social solar system. She'd probably weighed twenty pounds more back then, but not an ounce had been superfluous. Now she was a walking skeleton.

"Do I know you?" she asked.

"You were two years ahead of me."

She looked away as if she didn't want to be reminded of the person she'd once been. Meanwhile, Barry's forced attempt at cheerfulness had devolved into groveling. "You couldn't spare some more money? Maybe a twenty?"

It had to kill him to beg. He'd always been the cooler, stronger, more dominant one. But by then I'd completed junior year, a grade further than he'd managed to go. I was at the tail end of the Semi-Miraculous Transformation — taller, probably stronger, surely in a better place mentally.

I went to my room and came back with a twenty. It was a given that the money was for drugs, but I was naive. The suburban scene was dominated by grass, hash, acid, sometimes pills. Now and then someone might score some opium or speed, but there was never enough around to imagine that anyone could get hooked on either.

And heroin? Forget it. That was strictly a ghetto drug.

Last night I managed to track down Adriana Fox and get Zach's number in Canada. On the phone he sounded distraught as he told me that on Sunday night at the festival, after I left the woods to see Ten Years After, Karl came back, and he and Barry went off together. It started to rain again and Eva was cold. She and Zach talked their way into one of the hippie school buses to crash. That's why they weren't under the tarp when I came back. They spent most of Monday searching for Barry, and when they couldn't find him, they left a message for him with the festival organizers that they'd gone back to the farm in Ontario.

Late in the day, my aunt got a call from a hospital in Monticello, New York. Two men had brought Barry into the emergency room and left before anyone could question them. An hour later, Barry was dead of a heroin overdose.

"I'm so fuckin' sorry, man." Zach sounded close to tears. "We didn't know what happened to him. We figured he and Karl must've taken off or something. And we had to get back to the farm."

"Was he doing heroin up there?" I asked.

"Here? No, never. Not in a million years. I swear on my mother's grave, Lucas. We were done with that shit. I mean, grass? Sure. But no more smack. Man, I'm telling you, I was totally blown away when I heard it was smack. But you saw how it was at the festival. All the dope that was around. And all that craziness. Best I can figure is it was just once for old times' sake. It's fucked up, man, but it's the only thing that makes sense."

We hung up. Zach's surprise when I asked if Barry'd been doing heroin at the farm sounded genuine. Besides, I'd seen my cousin when he was doing heavy drugs, and he didn't act or look anything like the Barry I'd hung with at the festival. In a way it makes his story even sadder. He'd climbed out of the darkness. Finally gotten out of the house. Started creating art. And then . . . one small but horribly lethal mistake.

The casket is lowered into the open grave, part of a family plot I didn't know about. How can one person know so little about his own family? Is it because such things aren't spoken about until there's a reason? But there was a reason. In the ground a few inches from my shoes is a small footstone:

BRETT CARSON BAKER
DEC. 12, 1953 — JAN. 25, 1954

The funeral ends. Friends help Aunt Jane and Uncle Phillip to a car. Soon the only ones left are my family and some funeral workers in overalls waiting nearby. I catch the paterfamilias's eye and look down at Brett's footstone. The paterfamilias winces. He doesn't want to deal with this right now. He's been dealing with it for nearly sixteen years.

He puts an arm around my brother's shoulders and leads him toward the car. Yesterday, I volunteered to drive up to the camp and get Alan, but the paterfamilias said he wanted to do it.

The hot, dry wind whisks more dust off the pile of dirt. My stomach growls angrily. I feel sluggish, light-headed, and mildly nauseated from hunger. It's a hell of a lot harder to starve myself than I had imagined. (Forget the finger; maybe I should just chop off the whole fucking arm. That'll help me lose weight.)

Mom steps beside me, looks down at the footstone.

"Why don't we ever talk about him?" I ask.

"What's there to say, Lucas?" She lifts her chin and has the impassive look of someone who for a long time has been trying to get past tears.

"Barry told me that you took him out in the cold. But that doesn't mean it had anything to do with him getting sick, right?"

Mom slides her arm through mine as if she needs to keep me close. "But it might have."

Her words hang in the hot summer air.

"We'll never know," she adds.

It was almost sixteen years ago. She's still going to that shrink in the city. What a thing to have to live with.

I wipe my face with a bandanna, feeling the windblown grit that's collected on my forehead. Stomach growls again. It's been three days of sheer agony. I don't know how I'm going to get through another week of this.

I'm ready to go home. There's too much sadness here. Barry, Brett. But Mom holds my arm tight. "If it hadn't been for you and Alan, I don't know how I would have survived." It feels like she's relieved to be able to tell me. As if she's been waiting a long time.

"Mom, can I ask you a question?"

"I wish you would."

"Do you . . . think this has something to do with the way Dad's been all this time?"

She squeezes my arm and looks down at the footstone again. "I think he tried to accept what happened. I think he really tried not to blame me. But he wasn't able to do it. I tried so many times to get him to talk. If not to me, then to a thera-pist. He went a few times, and then . . ." She shakes her head and trails off.

"And then you had Alan."

Shovels scrape and clatter as the cemetery men start to scoop the remaining dirt back into Barry's grave. Mom sniffs, wipes a tear away. I can't recall ever seeing her cry before. Her grip on my arm stays tight, but her voice quavers. "We'll never know who Brett was, or what he might have become. It's so easy to project on him all the hopes and dreams you have for a child. To imagine he would have been everything you could have wished for. I think that's what your father's done. He's never been able to let go of what might have been. Brett, not Alan. He can't help himself."

And Antonia has two young sons who need a father. Somewhere in Dad's head, does he think it's a do-over?

The cemetery men shovel with short, efficient strokes. Each scoop of dirt that lands with a soft thump on Barry's casket is another reminder of how real, how horribly irreversible, what's happened is. Mom wipes away another tear. I slide my arm out of hers and put it around her shoulders. "I love you, Mom."

"Thank you, Lucas. And, of course, I love you."

We walk back to the car, where the paterfamilias and Alan are waiting. I get in the back with Alan. No one speaks during the drive to Barry's house. No one spoke during the drive to the cemetery, either.

I bet Brett would have been a brilliant student. A terrific tennis player, too.

People gather at my aunt and uncle's house. Sitting in one of the rusty chairs on the small back patio, I smoke the umpteenth cigarette of the day. My throat is raw and my chest feels full of sludge, but smoking helps dull the gnawing craving for food.

In the yellow ashtray on the filmy-glass table, the remains

of unfiltered cigarette butts still float in their brownish broth. The breeze blows long thin needles out of the trees and onto the ground. The backyard is small, no more than a few dozen feet on each side. When Barry and I were younger and did on occasion play together, it was either basketball in the driveway or football or baseball on the street.

The patio door opens, and Tinsley comes out. The scent of patchouli whisks past when she sits. I offer her a Marlboro, but she taps a cigarette from a blue pack of Gauloises. I cup my hands to protect the flame while she lights her cigarette, then catch a whiff of strong, pungent smoke.

"I'm so sorry, Lucas. It's . . . so hard to believe."

Even at the age of eighteen, I'm beginning to see how we meander along a winding path filled with blind corners and switchbacks, at times thinking we're dealing with some pretty heavy shit (broken hearts / draft / college / future?). Then the phone rings or there's a knock on the door. And it's instant implosion. The path vanishes into a vacuum that nothing can fill. Part of you is snatched away. Suddenly, nothing you thought of as heavy shit before even comes close.

Tinsley exhales. Like Barry's life, smoke races away on the breeze. It doesn't seem possible that someone you've grown up with, someone you've known for so long, someone you spent so much time comparing yourself to, can suddenly not be there.

The wind rattles the tree branches. More long brown pine needles sprinkle down. Tinsley says, "I'm going to Paris."

"With Bernard?" I ask.

"*Bien sûr*. But also to study. Have you heard of Henri Cartier-Bresson? They say he's the father of photojournalism."

"Sounds very cool, but what about your mom?"

"I think it's a blessing in disguise for her. I'll be out of the house and she can tell her friends that I'm studying abroad. It's so"—she strikes a pose and bats her eyes—"so *terribly* chic."

Inhale, exhale. My throat feels like sandpaper. My stomach growls and cries. Tinsley's long yellow hair lifts on the breeze and settles.

"You're not angry, are you?" she asks.

That Barry is dead? That my family is falling apart? That it's been three weeks since I last heard from Robin? That Chris and thousands of men-children like him might, could, will die? That to avoid the same fate, I will have to endure the minute-by-minute torture of starvation for seven more days?

But I know that what she means is, am I mad at her for going off with Bernard at Woodstock. "No. You came back with the rice and that can of SpaghettiOs. And you stayed for Saturday night when you didn't have to."

"It wouldn't have been right otherwise."

"You mean it wasn't the *I Ching* that told you to come back?"

Tinsley smiles archly. It's been almost a month since the night we lay under the stars on that smoky mattress in a field near Kemptville, Ontario, and she said looking at the stars made the universe seem closer. Things do seem closer now. Unfortunately, those things include death, war, bereavement.

"How's your girlfriend?" she asks.

"Not good."

"Not because of me, I hope?"

"No. Because of me."

Tinsley takes another drag off her cigarette and plunks the butt into the brown broth. It hisses. She rises from the chair and gives me a peck on the cheek. "I hope you fix it, if that's what you want."

"Thanks. Good luck in France."

"*Merci beaucoup.*"

Canned laughter seeps out of the den. At Barry's house, Alan got bored and wanted to watch TV, but the living room was full of mourners, so Mom asked me to bring him home. She said she and the paterfamilias would get a ride back later.

On the way home, I asked Alan how camp was. He said he was the best rower.

"In a rowboat?" I asked.

He nodded.

"So you liked it?"

"Uh-huh."

"Would you go back next summer?"

"Uh-huh."

"Even without TV?"

He said he'd think about it.

Standing at the living-room window at home, I gaze out at the street. The late-afternoon light floods in, illuminating the slowly floating bits of fiber and dust in the motionless air. Every now and then, a particle catches the light and refracts it in a tiny burst of rainbow spectrum, then vanishes forever.

The bathroom scale reads 162. I need to get down to 135. After three days of famine, my clothes feel loose and I'm pulling my belt to the last notch. Even with the countless cigarettes and glasses of water, I don't know how much longer I can bear this agony.

I didn't have the energy to go anywhere last night, so I asked Milton and Arno to come over. We sat on the back patio and I laid it out for them: if I can't keep starving myself, or if it gets close to the physical and I haven't lost enough weight, I'm going to need their help. I'm not going to prison or Canada.

Milton said he'd had a feeling I might call upon him; Rudy had told him about what we'd discussed.

"I'll do whatever you need me to," he said.

Arno squirmed and scratched his chin nervously. "Man, you can't just help people cut off parts of their bodies, can you? It's got to be illegal."

"Arno, you were planning on selling two thousand hits of acid at the festival."

"That's different."

"How?" I ask.

"I don't know. It just is."

"Chicken?" Milton taunted.

"Shove it, idiot-stick."

"Great story to tell your new friends at Bucknell," I suggested.

Arno lifted his eyebrows. He appeared to mull it over, then leaned forward. "What're you going to do with it?"

"My finger?"

"Yeah." Suddenly his eyes were bright.

"You *cannot* be serious," Milton muttered.

"What would you do?" I asked Arno. "Dry it out and wear it on a cord around your neck?"

"No, flea-brain. I'd put it in a jar with alcohol. Keep it on my desk. I mean, tell me that wouldn't be the coolest thing ever."

Was he serious? I didn't know what to say. I looked at them both, and it was the craziest thing, but inside me so much emotion suddenly welled up that I had to blink back tears. Milton with his gun and Molotov cocktail, his head practically shaved for court. Arno with his GTO and two thousand hits of acid, his Good & Plenty aftershave still stinking up the place. Maybe we didn't get to have our last hurrah at Woodstock, but what a summer it had been regardless. Only in a week or so, Arno was going to Bucknell, and Milton was going back to MIT, and I was going . . . Well, I was going to miss them so damn bad that I was almost tempted to cut off a finger right then and there and give them each a piece of it to remember me by.

In the den, Alan's back in his old spot in front of the boob tube. Any moment now, Mom and the paterfamilias will return. The paterfamilias will probably have to hang around the house. It would be unseemly to go off and play tennis on the day his nephew is put in the ground. Maybe he'll go up to his gym in the attic and work out. The amount of stress around here will once again rise to palpable levels. But at least now I've gotten a glimpse of why.

Still, the hunger, the misery of losing Barry, the anxiety of my looming induction physical—it's almost too much to bear. In the past when I've felt like this, there's always been a way out. But that's changed since the music festival. I keep thinking about those hippies. The *real* hippies, living in school buses, eating gruel, and being high all the time. What gets me is the sense that that's the way they always live. Not just for a few days at a festival. I feel about as far from those feral beings as I am from the generals who are sending young men to die in Vietnam.

The laugh track from the den ebbs and flows. I ache—for Cousin Barry; for my aunt and uncle; for Brett, the brother I've never known; for Robin; for a cheeseburger. Getting intimate with Mr. Water Pipe would be the perfect escape. Maybe take a few reds to get numb. I can barely remember the last time I went this long without getting wrecked. But every time the impulse strikes, so do the words *When are you gonna grow up and stop feeling sorry for yourself?*

Fuckin' Arno.

The mailman is coming up the walk, his bulky gray canvas satchel slung over his shoulder. Last night—even though I promised myself I wouldn't write to Robin again until she answered my last letter—I broke down and wrote to her about Barry and how devastated his death has left me. About how tenuous and precious life really is. I wrote about Karl, and how (without going into the gory details) one way or the other I'll be staying out of the army. About how, less than two months ago, I was almost annoyed that after graduating high school, life suddenly felt so serious, but now I realize that life *feels* serious because it *is* serious.

Envelopes and magazines slide through the front-door mail slot. Bending to pick them up, I wish for a letter from Robin, but at this point any mail for me would go to the address in Bay Shore. A white envelope pokes out from under a *House & Garden* magazine. The return address says:

Selective Service
Local Board No. 2
Bay Shore, NY 11706

It's addressed to Mr. Richard Baker. That's strange. Why would the Bay Shore draft board write to my father? I hold the envelope up to the sunlight, which outlines a card inside. It's the same exact size and shape as a draft card. It doesn't make sense. I tear the envelope open and find a pale-yellow draft card with my name and selective service number. It is dated August 18, 1969, and signed by the executive secretary, Norman C. Brown.

It states that I, Lucas Baker, have been classified 1-Y.

It doesn't make sense. How is this possible? I study the card closely, flip it over, flip it back, searching for anything that might reveal it to be a fake. But it's real.

It's fucking real.

The slices of Wonder Bread tear when I spread Dad's glutinous natural peanut butter on them. I ravenously stuff hunks of the white-and-brown conglomeration into my mouth and wash it down with milk, barely pausing to chew.

I'm 1-Y!

How is this possible?

I go into the garage, my cheeks bulging with Wonder Bread and peanut butter. When I came home with Alan before, the MG wasn't in its usual spot. Something about that felt odd, but there were too many other things to focus on. Now I see that not only is the sports car gone, so are the snow tires and the detachable plastic side windows that go on it in cold weather. And so is the brass knock-off hammer for loosening the wire wheel hubs.

Through the open garage door, I see a car stop at the foot of the driveway. Mom and the paterfamilias get out. Mom nods at me and goes up the walk to the front door. The paterfamilias comes up the driveway, then stops. We both stare at the dark oil-stained patch of concrete where the MG used to sit.

Memory fragments filter through my mind: *Norman C. Brown . . . the heavyset man in the blue blazer . . . "Quite the collector of fine British motoring." The metal badge on the grille of the red Jaguar that said Bay Shore Sports Car Club. "She's a beauty, just as you promised."*

I hold up the yellow draft card for the paterfamilias to see. "You are not to say anything to anyone," he sternly commands. "Not your friends, not a draft counselor. No one. Understand?"

Don't say anything to your mother about Hazel.

Don't tell anyone at the bank where the coins really come from.

I'd appreciate it if you didn't mention Sharon.

It's another one of his scams. Only this one's entirely for my benefit. The change-of-address form, the library card, the DMV form—it was all so that I would fall under the jurisdiction of the Bay Shore draft board, so that Mr. Brown could arrange to have me classified as 1-Y: only required to serve during a national emergency. Dad traded his precious MG for my sorry ass.

It's amazing! It's un-fucking-believable!

It feels like a harbinger for how it will be from now on. How I'll never look at Dad the old way again. I've blamed him for so much. But what if sometimes there is no one to blame, because no one is at fault? Sometimes things happen that will never truly be resolved or settled, and the best you can do is just get on with it and make your own peace.

He starts toward the door that leads to the house. There's a war on the other side of the planet that I have no say in. There's one much closer that I do.

"Dad?"

He stops, probably as unaccustomed to hearing that word come through my lips as I am to saying it.

"Thank you. I mean it. Really."

He quietly appraises me. It's a familiar gesture. For an instant I'm reminded of being twelve and a goddamn goofball because I've just blown a crucial point in a father-and-son doubles match.

But then he says, "You can quit starving yourself. You won't need to worry about that physical now."

I blink. He's done despicable things, but he also taught me

to ski. Taught me to play tennis. Provided for his family. Built a fallout shelter when he thought it was crucial. Gave me a job. Probably taught me the meaning of work. *Saved my butt just when it looked like my ass was grass.*

There's another picture in a photo album somewhere of him and me dressed in matching dungarees and gray sweatshirts. I must be five years old. We're sitting on the front step, and his hand is on my shoulder. He's smiling, but I have a bigger smile.

"Have you decided what you're going to do?" I ask. I can't bring myself to say "about Antonia," but he knows what I'm talking about.

He shakes his head.

"Well, whatever you decide . . ." I begin. "I want you to know that it'll be okay with me."

His forehead creases. He pulls his lips in. His eyes become glittery.

He goes inside.

SATURDAY, AUGUST 23

8/18/69

Dear Lucas,

Thank you for your letter. Thank you for being so understanding and not being angry. I've always known that you're an amazing person. Once again you've proved it.

In a way, you've made things harder for me. It would have been easier if you had gotten mad about Samuel. Instead you reminded me of all the good times we had last year. And of course you were right. We did have lots more good than bad.

I'm so confused. I was unsure before, and I'm even more unsure now. Maybe you're right about me using Samuel as a way to let you know how serious I am about getting you to change. I don't know. I hate the idea of using anyone, so it could be true and I just don't want to admit it.

Things feel so uncertain. I'm sure part of it has to do with going to Middlebury next month. And maybe it's also the way things are in our country right now. Everything feels so up in the air. It's not only the way people are so violently divided about this terrible war. You must have heard about that cult killing in California? And all the children who are starving to death in Biafra? And that woman dying in Senator Kennedy's car? Doesn't it feel like we're becoming unhinged?

I wish I knew what to say about us. I wish I understood what I'm feeling. I hate being this way. I hate to keep you in suspense. You don't deserve that. I do love you, Lucas. But as I said before, I can't go back to the way things were last spring. And I'm scared that if we get together again, that's what will happen. I didn't intend to become that person last time. So what's to make me think it won't happen again?

xoxoxo Robin

My heart swells. Robin's letter is written on the lavender stationery she last used over Easter vacation, when her missives arrived every day, saturated with Shalimar and professions of love. I bring this one close to my nose. No perfume, but that's okay. Tears seep through my squeezed-closed eyes as I laugh, and sob, and laugh.

MARCH 1970

Dear Chris,

Did Mr. DiPasquale say anything about you taking off early on Mondays and Wednesdays for school this summer? My father said he'd talk to him about it. I guess it has to be night school, right? After what you've been through, it would be totally weird to go back to high school with a bunch of kids.

Man, I still can't believe that working in the factory may have been what saved your butt. Not that you learned anything about how the postal system actually works, but that's the army, right? And speaking of which, can you believe that story about all those officers trying to cover up that massacre near My Lai? I sure hope you never saw anything like that over there.

I know what you mean when you say life before the army feels like ancient history. Or maybe what's ancient are the

dopes we were back then. Almost every night after dinner,
most of the guys I know go to bars or stay at their places and
get ripped. I'm starting to think that it was a good thing that
we got most of that lunacy out of our systems when we did.
Not that we don't enjoy a beer and a toke now and then. I
mean, let's be real.

Anyway, since you asked what I've been up to here in the
Green Mountains . . . the ski season is starting to wind down.
It's mostly spring skiing now. Since we work at the shop until
10:30 every morning and have to be back by 2:30 or 3, we
ski midday, sometimes in shorts and even T-shirts. With the
sun's rays reflecting off the snow, you can actually get a pretty
serious sunburn if you're not careful.

Most of the guys in the shop don't give a crap about the
business and just put in their time so they can ski every day,
but I've been learning stuff. I don't dig the sales part. It's
typical capitalist bullshit. Dave, the owner, wants us to sell
whatever gear gives him the biggest profit margin. But the
technical side of the business is pretty interesting. There's a
ton of stuff you need to know about how the different brands
of skis, bindings, and boots work together. Binding placement.
Adjustments and blah blah. Dave took me aside the other day
and said if I was serious about it, he'd send me to some tech
clinics next fall.

That's a possibility, but the other thing is, from his
days in ad sales at Time magazine, my father knows some
people at Ziff Davis, the company that owns Ski magazine.
They have some trade journals about the ski business, and

he's going to find out if maybe they'd give me a job. I've been doing a lot of writing. Short stories and things like that. Might try sending a few to literary magazines. In the meantime, how amazing would it be if I could get a job writing about skiing?

Guess I'll have to see where things are with Robin next year. Most of her friends at Middlebury think it's pretty groovy that she's got a ski bum boyfriend. But a couple of weeks ago she asked me if I planned to work in a ski shop for the rest of my life. So of course I said yes just to give her grief. But between you and me, I doubt it. Working in a shop and having to deal with deranged customers is a drag. I can't imagine making a career of it. And like I said, writing about skiing would be a dream.

For now I'm planning on hanging around here until Robin's semester ends. Then we'll spend June and July in Boston. Robin's roommate's family owns a restaurant where we can work part-time. The rest of the time, we'll be working for the Student Mobilization Committee to End the War. Then in August Robin wants us to go to Europe for two weeks. I thought we could hitchhike around and camp out, but she insists that we get Europasses, travel by train, and stay in hostels. Did I hear you mutter "henpecked"? Who, me?

So that's it for now, my friend. We'll be home for a week before we go to Boston, and I'll give you a shout. And as I said before, it's fantastic to have you back in one piece on this side of the planet. I'm glad you want to get your high-school

diploma. You've got too much on the ball to spend the rest of
your life operating a junk-mail inserter.

Peace, brother,

Lucas

As great as it is to have Chris home, there are still hundreds
of thousands of kids like him over there killing and dying. Last
November, a couple of months before Chris finished his tour,
Robin and I marched in Washington, D.C., in a giant protest
against the war. And just days after that, the world saw the
photos of all the Vietnamese women and children who were
massacred by U.S. soldiers near My Lai a couple years ago. Who
knows how many other atrocities like that haven't yet been
revealed? We have to stop this war. Now.

MAY 1970

"Nervous?" Robin asks as we pass an orchard of trees covered with white blossoms. We're driving home from Vermont in her VW Beetle (she learned to drive a stick last fall when she got this Bug). A few hours ago, she took her last final of the spring semester.

"Yeah." I haven't been home since October. Will it feel strange reentering the house of dashed dreams? Seeing the folks again? Will it be just as tense as when I left? But I am looking forward to seeing Alan, Arno, and Milton. Arno and I exchanged a few letters over the winter. Sounds like he managed to make friends at Bucknell without needing to sell acid or display someone's finger in a jar on his desk. And I spoke pretty regularly on the phone with Milton; he and some pals at MIT built something called a blue box that allows them to make long-distance phone calls for free.

Around Robin's neck is the sterling-silver love pendant from Tiffany's that I'd planned to give her last summer at Lake

Juliette. When I reach over and tuck a few errant strands of her hair behind her ear, she turns and briefly smiles. She says Samuel's out of the picture, and given how solid things between us have been for the past eight months, there's no reason to doubt her. And I told her about Tinsley. It seemed like the right thing to do. I didn't want to live with the idea of being like my father and keeping something like that a secret. I guess there are two ways to look at the examples our parents set. You can learn from them what to do, or you can learn what not to do.

Anyway, Robin was cool about Tinsley. In a weird way I think it was good that Robin had her fling with Samuel. Somehow it feels like it's made what we have stronger.

"Has your dad said anything more about Antonia?" she asks.

"I know he's been playing a lot of tennis tournaments in New Jersey, but he's still living at home most of the time. Alan's got three more years of school. Maybe he's decided to stick around till then." As long as Dad continues to do right by Mom and Alan, who am I to say what else he should do?

And even though I've moved away, I know I've got to stay involved in my brother's life, too. Alan and I talk on the phone now and then, mostly about what amusement rides he's gone on and the shows he's watched. The funny thing is, the kid who never wanted to talk in person turns into a chatterbox on the phone. Go figure.

Robin's hands are in the precise ten-and-two position on the steering wheel. It's strange to think that less than a year ago, my hands were on Odysseus's steering wheel while I tripped my brains out on Orange Sunshine and drove us from Cambridge

371

to Long Island. It feels bizarre to think that tripping freak was me. Hard to imagine these days that I'd ever impulsively drop acid, then get in a car and drive down a busy highway for hours. Or be so reckless that I'd risk being drafted instead of putting in the work to apply to college. Sometimes it feels like those are the memories of someone else. It makes me wonder why it is that even when we're not sure of ourselves or what we're doing, we can still insist on being so firm in our beliefs. Is it because it's too frightening to admit that we may never know anything for certain?

"You think it's possible that no matter who we think we are at any given time in our lives, ultimately we never stop changing?" I ask.

Robin shoots me a quizzical glance. "Where did that come from?"

"Just wondering."

She looks back at the highway. "I guess. Maybe it's a good thing. It could be kind of boring to be the same person your whole life."

In twenty years, we can ask Arno. If there's one person who'll never change . . .

We enter a long blind curve in the shadow of a hill that blocks the afternoon sun. Robin's shoulders are hunched while she concentrates on steering. We'll spend a week on Long Island and then head to Boston, but the trip to Europe in August is on hold. There's too much that needs to be done here. Instead of trying to end the war, Nixon's expanded it into Cambodia. Two weeks ago, National Guard troops at Kent State University in Ohio actually shot and killed four college students who were protesting. The Student Mobilization Committee is calling for a referendum next November asking Massachusetts voters to support an immediate end of the war. They'll need a minimum of forty-eight thousand registered voters to sign petitions to get the referendum on the ballot, but the SMC leaders want to get at least a hundred thousand signatures, and hopefully more, to make a point. So that's what we'll be doing this summer.

We come out of the curve, back into the sunlight and onto a long straightaway that leads toward some distant low green mountains. Off to the right is a sun-washed red barn, and beyond it broad fields with long, straight rows of brown dirt topped with thin green sprouts. It's the beginning of another summer. How many times last summer did I escape disaster by the skin of my teeth, whether it was from Vietnam, border guards, gangs of hoods, OD'ing on pills, or nearly losing Robin?

(Arno's right. I really have been a lucky fuck. Not only because of the Semi-Miraculous Transformation, but for reasons even the *I Ching* probably can't explain.)

Barry's death is still a throbbing ache, but other events from last summer seem like distant memories — some of them funny, some frightening, some sad, and some astonishing. It's crazy how much has changed. Can today truly be the first day of the rest of your life? Yeah, I think I'm probably living proof that it can. Maybe that's what life is — a whole series of first days.

Just as long as we never forget how incredibly lucky we are to be alive.

AUTHOR'S NOTE

A few people have asked why I waited so long to tell this story. A big part of the reason was that I didn't want this book to be published while my mother and father, and aunt and uncle, were able to read it. They'd all been through enough in their lives and didn't need to be reminded.

While many of the episodes in the book are based on personal experience, there are some that came to me second-hand. The scene in the tunnel with the Pagan's motorcycle gang after the Led Zeppelin concert (and what a concert it was!), the Molotov cocktail incident, and the run-in with the hoods on the beach are three such "borrowed" incidents.

The same is true of the characters. Some are conglomerations of people I knew at the time. For instance, the young woman who introduced me to the Planting Fields, and with whom I went to Woodstock on my motorcycle, was not the one I hitched home with after leaving my partly burned microbus in Canada. Likewise, the friend who bought the half a gram of pure acid was not the one who complained to the police when he thought he'd been ripped off by a fake dealer. From surfing I've learned that close to a storm, waves tend to be many and disorganized, but as they travel away from the storm center, they meld—thanks to the physical law of conservation of energy—into one another and become organized sets of fewer waves. A similar process happened as I wrote this book. Where two characters could be blended into one, they naturally did so, thus conserving the amount of energy it required to keep the character in the reader's consciousness.

In addition, even those characters who maintained their singular identities have had some details of their lives changed to better fit the story and narrative. After Woodstock, my cousin died from a heroin overdose in Vancouver, not Monticello. The businesses my father was involved with were not the ones described in the book, although I did indeed work in a bulk-mail facility. Also, I graduated from high school in 1968, not 1969, and while the danger of being drafted loomed ever-present in my life, my own circumstances never became quite as dire as those of my alter ego, Lucas.

And as far as the Semi-Miraculous Transformation? As anyone who knows me can attest, it may have happened to Lucas, but it sure didn't happen to me.

The author, early August 1969
Photo by Anita Green

ACKNOWLEDGMENTS

My deepest gratitude and thanks to:

My editor, Kaylan Adair, without whose long, detailed, and insightful editorial letters and comments, this book simply would not exist. Also to Betsy Uhrig and Hannah Mahoney, for their diligent and detailed copyediting; Jackie Shepherd for her wonderful cover; and Nathan Pyritz for his help, and patience, with the interior design. And to all of Candlewick Press for being a place where such books are nurtured and supported.

My agent, Stephen Barbara, for his unwavering support and attention, and for bringing me to Candlewick in the first place.

My elementary- and high-school buddies Jed, Joel, David, Ken, George, Jon, and Tom, for answering my queries about the past, sharing their memories, and correcting mine. Also to Anita and Rick (wherever you are), for sharing so much of that summer.